Zeta Rodgers Needs to Relax

Elanna Moon

AMBERJACK
PUBLISHING

CHICAGO

Published by Amberjack Publishing
An imprint of Chicago Review Press Incorporated
814 North Franklin Street
Chicago, Illinois 60610
ISBN 978-1-948705-84-4

Library of Congress Control Number: 2024944119

Cover design: Jonathan Hahn
Cover illustration and hand lettering: Sarah Gavagan
Typesetting: Jonathan Hahn

Printed in the United States of America

1

"Thanks for driving. I haven't been out in forever," Zeta sighed, a small smile turning up the corner of her mouth. She stretched slowly, lifting herself on her tippy-toes for just a moment before settling back, checking with herself.

No dizziness, no lightheadedness. Fine, she was fine.

"Are you sure you're OK?" Pixie, medium height, bronze skin, and a bright green wig on for the night, was in full alt anime Black girl mode. The *Sailor Moon* T-shirt and tight miniskirt hugging her curves complemented her full face of makeup. She held her door open, ready to climb back into the car and take off, cancel all their plans, and call in for pizza. "If you're still not feeling well, we can just bail and have the guys come over to your place. Or my place. Or we could go over there, if you really want to get out of the house."

Zeta's look was much more low key. Black skater dress that was loose around her hips and belly, her curls half pulled up into little buns with a lot left flowing down around her shoulders and framing her round golden-brown face, and just lip gloss and lotion. She hoped she looked at least presentable. She closed her own door. "Don't worry. It was just a summer cold. I'm fine now." It wasn't a lie; she did have a cold, caught after a short beach trip with her aunt. "Too much in and out of that air," Aunt Josie said the day after she returned home when Zeta checked in with a little sniffle. A little fever, a little sinus pressure, and she was in bed. Only she wasn't, because she had to work, so really she was at her computer wrapped in a blanket working on a financial planning mobile app for a small company. A little lightheaded while she typed away, building up code, but she didn't faint, even when she couldn't stop coughing for five minutes straight. So partial credit for resting. She flashed a wide smile and hoped Pixie didn't call her bluff. She wanted to see the guys. "Come on, everyone's waiting!"

Zeta stepped away from the car toward the bar entrance, ending the discussion. They were going, she was going. The cooled-down-enough-to-be-comfortable August night air kissing her skin, the sound of the crowd inside reaching her through the glass. Zeta was thankful that the rain, which had stopped during the drive to the bar, had given them a break from the August heat. She stopped for a moment, checking herself over in the weak reflection on the door. She smoothed her dress over her round hips and belly before rubbing her face. She was excited. She hadn't seen everyone since before she went on vacation with her aunt. It had been weeks since she'd come out—after her time off, she'd needed to work. But that was over now. She was free.

Zeta squinted at what should be golden-brown skin. *Do I look pale?* She wondered briefly before dismissing the idea. *I look fine. Stop worrying or you'll worry everyone else.* The door made a horrible mirror. Still, she dug out lip gloss from her floppy, gray canvas bag, applied some more to her lips, and smiled again. Compared to Pixie's vibrant, green-haired beauty no one would notice her, but that was alright. She came out to see her friends, and those were the only people she cared about.

The air changed from warm to hot as soon as they entered, the room filled if not over capacity then near to it with a group of loud and joyful partygoers. The main hall of the bar looked just as tacky as she remembered it, with island-inspired decorations that mingled with neon beer signs. Behind the wooden bar, the bartenders worked double time to keep up with the loud crowd, which to Zeta's eyes seemed like a group of office workers. Lots of ties, rolled up sleeves, and smart heels. *Must be a team building thing*, she thought, frowning at the memories they brought up. Not the main reason she'd left in-person work and went freelance, but avoiding those interactions was certainly a plus.

Pixie hooked her arm and led her to the private party room in the back and the atmosphere changed immediately. There were rolled sleeves here too but more T-shirts and sneakers, slides and shorts. The laughter was unrestrained, and her friends sat with arms and legs thrown over each other even with the extra space the private room afforded them. Actual air circulated. It didn't smell like roses, but at least she could breathe.

The dimly lit party room was the size of a large living room with a '70s-style conversation pit in the center, square sectional couch in ugly burnt orange included. A few other couches and some small tables lined the walls, and a tiny bar that seemed to only be slinging bottles was at the right side of the door.

"Hey, Pixie!" Brand called from across the room. His dark, rounded eyes sparkled from his tawny face, knee-length shorts and a plain orange T-shirt hanging over his lanky frame. "You brought Zeta! Cody! Zeta came!"

"Zeta, you're here!" Cody said popping up from a table, his gray eyes light above red cheeks and under a mess of brown hair. His lumberjack body in his ratty flannel, unbuttoned over a faded T-shirt and cutoff jeans, took up more space than everyone else.

Zeta held up her hands, even though she couldn't hold back her cheesy grin, imploring everyone to calm down as Cody crossed the room with arms out, moving in for his customary hug. She obliged, letting him wrap her in a bear hug despite the heat. All the attention embarrassed her, but she couldn't deny that the over-the-top excitement did make her feel loved. "Happy . . . Lammas?" she guessed, squeezing him back for a second before pushing him gently away. She knew a pagan celebration was Cody's reason for calling for a get-together but still wasn't quite sure she'd remembered the right one.

Cody grinned. "A week off but yes!"

"Come on! Have a drink with us!" Brand half commanded, wrapping her in another quick hug.

"Sure, just a beer is fine. Whatever they've got," Zeta said brightly. *I missed this.*

Brand led the group to the conversation pit, the whole reason they *always* rented that room, and why the party had to be a week late. The pit was the key. Brand dropped to the couch, Pixie next to him, and Cody held Zeta's hand as she slid into the seat, lowering herself on the ledge and then into the seat, legs crossed like a guru. Like a king in his castle, Brand called for a beer and one was handed to him. He popped the top off and passed it over to Zeta with a flourish and a bow.

She laughed and lifted the beer, tilting her head in a soft mimic. "Thank you, my good sir."

"Yes, yes," Pixie spoke as she scanned the room, "everyone's happy to see our darling Zeta. Did anyone invite—"

"He's not here," Cody confirmed casually, like the news was nothing. "He's with his new girl."

Pixie whipped around to Cody. "He's got a new girlfriend?"

Zeta rolled her eyes, took a swallow of her beer, and grimaced at the taste.

"Yeah," Brand started. "What was her name? Started with an *A* . . ."

"Is it Amber? That fucking bitch," Pixie cursed.

"No, that wasn't it. I remember!" Brand said. "Her name is absolutely none of your fucking business."

"Because you're totally over him," Zeta supplied, without looking up. She was frowning, but her focus was on reading the beer label. "What is this?"

Brand nodded in agreement and ignored her question.

"I just want closure," Pixie whined.

"Closure is when you decide to stop letting toxic people back into your life," Zeta advised, still focused on the label, trying to work up enough spit to wash away the bitter taste. "This beer is nasty, why did you give me this?"

"Everyone can't be as uncomplicated as you," Pixie snapped back.

"It just takes practice," Zeta said, looking for somewhere or someone to ditch the beer with. "You too can achieve these heights. I believe in you."

"Keep drinking. It gets better after a few sips," Brand encouraged.

She handed the bottle back to him. "I actually don't think that's true though, so I will not. Is the bar selling anything else, or do I have to go back out?"

Pixie made a disgusted sound and, with a pout, settled back on the couch. "Take this seriously, please!"

"We are all taking this very seriously, but it's time to move on," Cody said. "That relationship has more than run its course."

Zeta laughed and jabbed her finger into her friend's side. "And you are just wasting your time pining for him when you could be out there meeting someone who you could actually have a future with. Turn that frown upside down, get out there, and find a new person to get under!"

"What if *he's* my person though?" Pixie whined back, sullen.

"If he were, he'd still be here. Besides, you were too good for him. You're amazing and he's just some guy," Zeta said.

"I know, I know! This is sad; I'm being pitiful." Pixie took a deep breath, balled her fists up, and put on a tough face. "OK! This is done! No more moping!" She took the beer that Zeta was still trying to get rid of and swallowed deeply. As her face twisted, she gagged, "What is this?"

"I told you!" Zeta exclaimed, throwing her hands into the air. "It's disgusting."

Brand raised his own hands in mock surrender. "Alright, alright! I get it, it's gross. It was tonight's two-buck special."

"Yeah, well, I think we know why. Told you it wouldn't work," Cody said. "Tastes like ass. I'll get you guys some drinks. What do you want? You can have anything as long as it's rum and Coke."

"You guys are so cheap," Zeta complained. "Anyway, how have you been? It's been a while."

"Yeah, it has. How was the beach that you didn't take us to?" Brand asked.

They fell into easy chatter about vacation and work, catching up. Zeta settled into the same comfortable rhythm she remembered, sharing in the gossip: Who left the city, who broke up, who was getting married. New jobs, new babies, and a few *have you heard froms*. They were getting older, their twenties leaving or left, more moving away and *whatever happened to so-and-sos* than she liked, but a lot of people she cared about were still there. Other friends came to say hi; partygoers invited to their little celebration wove in and out of the conversation.

The night wore on. More friends and acquaintances arrived, replacing ones that left, those who needed to get home for kids, or work even though it was Saturday. Zeta smiled and laughed, but she began to feel the change in the room. The air felt hotter, heavier. The edges of her vision were fuzzy, Vaseline smeared on glass, and turning made the world sway. A shift that turned her mind slippery. It was always like this before it all got bad. Zeta ran through the possible reasons. Was the air too dry? Had she had too much to drink? Or was it just way too many people? She couldn't pinpoint it—she hadn't been paying all that much attention to herself or else she would have caught it sooner. She was stalling. She didn't want to leave, didn't want to make people worry, but she had to.

Whatever the reason, she had to get out of there or else she was going to black out.

"Guys, I think I'm going to go get some air for a few minutes," she said as she stood.

She watched as her friends' expressions changed, all the playfulness gone, their eyes serious and locked on her. They had all been talking to other people, but now, all three of her closest friends were turned to her. The people they'd been in conversation with were instantly forgotten and now stared in confusion.

"You OK?" Brand asked, taking her hand, ready to physically support her.

"I'm fine, just need some air. I'll come back," she replied, squeezing his fingers gently before stepping away from the couch. "I'm just going to sit out on the deck."

Pixie stood. "I'll come with you."

Zeta shook her head, holding up her hand. "No, stay. Really, I just need a couple of minutes and I'll be back. Promise. You don't have to sit with me."

They didn't look convinced, but she smiled and they let her move. Cody reached for her at the steps to help her up, and she waved him off. "Come on, it's three steps. Calm down. I'm fine!" She flashed him a smile and started off before he could argue, hiding her wobble. She confidently walked up the three steps out of the pit, through the crowd, and out the door, making her way down the hall. She walked through the winding hallways until she finally reached the end. At the deck door, she slipped outside to find it empty and damp.

She took a deep breath of the fresh night air, cool after the hot press of the bar. She leaned against the railing, slowly breathing the rain-scented air, eyes closed. When she opened them, the lights of the city twinkled in the valley below the stony mountains, green dappled by day but now dark against the starry sky. The bar was inside city limits but on the outskirts enough that the heavens could be seen. Zeta wasn't sure if it was the air or the picturesque night, but she was already beginning to feel better. *Overheating*, she mused, diagnosing the issue. "Ten minutes, no more," she hummed, hands on the railing, damp wood wetting her palms, holding her in her body. She stared at the city, blinking slowly in time with her breathing, letting the scene go from dreamy to sharp.

"Ten minutes," she repeated as she let go of the railing, ignoring that it had already been ten minutes. She wasn't ready to go back but couldn't admit even to herself that she needed more time. Zeta walked steadily to the table, the chairs put up from the night before and left up due to the rain. She pulled one from the tabletop, turning it over, splashing water over the wood below.

She tested the seat with her hand: dry enough. Sitting down, she pulled her legs under herself and rummaged in her purse. Wallet, tissues, three types of lip gloss, phone, hard candies, a key ring full of keys, half of them no longer in use, and her Switch. The thing she was actually looking for. She took it out of the case, woke it from sleep, and sighed, comforted by the familiarity of Nintendo. *Cozy Grove* would do. The task list was short and finite; she wouldn't get sucked into an endless to-do. Perfect for taking a short break and then back to the bar. Like a grown-up. Find the packages, bake some food, take care of some weeds. She fell into a familiar cycle, relaxed.

Just ten minutes, she thought. *Besides, someone will come get me eventually. I'm surprised they let me come out here alone at all.* She leaned back just a little to see the deck door. There was no shadow on the other side of the frosted glass, so Pixie or Brand or Cody wasn't just hanging out waiting for her on the other side. They had all been a little overprotective after her big breakup. She hadn't really been out since then—she had to work too much—and when she did go out it was different. They felt bad, like they should have protected her more, but she was an adult and made her own choices. Zeta didn't blame them for their attentiveness, even loved her friends more for it, but she was tired of being handled with kid gloves.

Before it had just been consideration for where they hung out and what activities they picked, making sure he wouldn't be there. Just normal care from friends, but it went on for months: *Are you sure you're sure* and *No, let's all go.* Maybe they were getting over it; maybe they saw that, yes, she was really OK. She'd taken some time; she'd dealt with her feelings.

Like an adult.

She was doing better. She was fine. Zeta found the letter in the game. "Just ten minutes," she sighed. They were all moving past it. She was fine.

"I know what you're up to, and the answer is no," Ash mumbled into his soda, shoulders hunched up about his ears. His frown was so deep it was beginning to hurt his face. Even with his poor posture it was clear that he was tall. White with short, blond hair and blue eyes, he was handsome—but his frown turned his face cold and hard.

"What was that?" Randall laughed, turning his attention back to his mopey friend. He was shorter by a few inches but still tall. His dark, close-cut beard didn't hide his grin. The man was clearly enjoying himself. His cheeks already held a soft, red glow.

Ash, on the other hand, was not drinking and had long ago lost the battle to hide his desire to leave.

The bar wasn't the problem, not really. He didn't decline when Randall told him the destination. It made sense that his friend wanted to spend time with him before he left. It was what his friend *wasn't* saying, the real reason that he had called him up and dragged him to this tacky bar to attend his office party like a last-minute plus-one.

Randall was making a last-ditch effort at matchmaking. Ash should have caught on when Randall questioned his attire—a pair of slacks and a button down with the sleeves rolled up, usually just fine for a few drinks. But when Ash saw his old friend casually scanning the crowd, he knew this was a setup.

Ash wasn't sure which woman in the crowd it was. There were a few he thought Randall would think were appropriate, his type— tall, slim, girl next door. He had a flight to catch in the morning and no time or energy to entertain whatever baby of a relationship Randall hoped to foster between him and his top pick.

Ash liked to date. That wasn't the problem, either. The problem was he wasn't looking for a relationship. Not right now, not when he had so much coming up professionally. It wasn't his first time on an international deal, but it was the first time that he would be taking the lead. After he'd finished with his work in Scotland, his father would be handing over the reins in the home office. He hadn't said anything yet, but Ash was sure it was going to happen. He needed to be prepared to act aggressively, make his mark, let everyone know that he was qualified, not just lucky. He would shut down the slew of minor divisions that were draining them. Cut the waste, move into a brighter future. But before all that, he needed to get home, double-check his luggage, make sure the house sitter had the correct list of duties, and try to get enough sleep so he didn't pass out in the airport. There was no time for a relationship, no time to start something. It wouldn't be fair to her, whoever she was. He had to focus.

"I've got an early morning. Like," Ash pulled his phone from his pocket, "six-hours-from-now early."

"You can sleep on the flight. It's nine hours long! A full night of rest. Don't be a killjoy." Randall pounded him on the back, and Ash's frown pushed impossibly deeper. Randall pretended not to notice, leaning back on the bar, eyes still on the crowd.

Ash slumped against it, a mockery of his friend's casual posture. He wasn't going to hide his annoyance from Randall. "I know I agreed to this but—"

"But you're staying. Since I won't be here when you get back, we've gotta drink to your good fortune and promotion now! You're finally getting what you want."

"Yeah, finally," Ash said, too softly to be heard over the sounds of the lively bar. It's what he wanted. He'd set up the new branch with their new partners, prove that he could run things smoothly with no oversight by the old man, who'd hand over the keys to the kingdom when Ash set down on American soil again. In six months, Cross Construction would be his, and he wouldn't have to answer to anyone.

Then he could breathe, relax. Do everything else he wanted.

Randall laughed, "Still, I'll believe it when I see it. He's been on the verge for ten years."

Ash couldn't disagree. If it weren't for his mother, he was sure that his father would have married his job. Ash might as well have been married to the job too, but it was worth it. It's what he'd worked his whole life for. It's what he had always been meant to do. His dad built the company, Ash would take over, keep it going, and then his kids after him. It was their legacy. "Mom's been bugging him about retiring."

Randall took a drink from his own bottle. "All you do is work these days. Bet you're thinking about work right now."

Wrong, Ash thought. *I'm thinking about sleep.* "No, I'm just not in the mood. I have a long flight; you know, you've been there."

"Sure, which is why I wanted to take you out tonight. You can nurse your hangover on the plane in the morning."

"I'm not going to have a hangover," he said, lifting his soda.

"Come on, let loose a little." His friend turned away and faced the party that was going on behind them, conveniently blocking the exit. "It's time you found something besides work to occupy yourself."

Ash turned, whip fast. "No."

"When's the last time you had a date? Lots of single women here tonight." Randall slid away from the bar, smooth as the condensation down the side of Ash's glass. He wasted no time, didn't even try to hide that he had it all planned as he found his way into the crowd of his coworkers, fitting seamlessly into the group. Ash couldn't remember what the company party was about. It had been background noise, unimportant and quickly forgotten.

Ash shook his head, sat on the bar stool, and watched, the soda flat in his mouth.

I want to go home. I have a reason to go home, he thought. *I need to sleep.* He was tired, but it wasn't just sleep. He was tired of the process. The *So what do you do, what are you into* casual dates to the *So what are we* to the *I guess we're a couple.* A few months of a relationship that never went anywhere, and then a breakup. He hated the cycle of it that always ended the same way. It was him, he was sure, and maybe his job was the only long-term relationship he could make work. But it didn't matter because it was starting again.

He was attractive and well off. Ash was a catch even with his divorce. Randall had been telling him that for years, and yet, since his divorce five years before, none of his relationships had lasted more than a few months. But everything happened in its time, and when it was time, he would go about finding his partner in an organized manner. That's not to say Ash didn't date. He did when the loneliness began to creep in, but there was an unspoken time limit on his relationships. And when they ended—gently, quietly, and without a fuss from either side—he was never surprised.

Randall returned with a coworker, his real reason for springing the after-hours social on Ash last minute. Staring down Randall's very obvious intentions, he had no idea how or why he fell for *Come out, I need an excuse to leave early.*

The woman was beautiful, with olive skin and long, flowing hair. She was made up with smoky eyes and dark lips. Her cream-colored blouse was open, showing a healthy line of cleavage, and her black skirt hugged the curve of her hips. She was stunning, but looking into her eyes, he saw that they were too bright, a little unfocused. She was drunk. He wanted to get out of there and go to bed. Alone.

But there was Randall, and now his friend, waiting for him to say something, do something.

"This is my buddy, Ash. He's shy," Randall explained.

Not shy, Ash thought, pulling his lips into a smile. "Hi, and you are?" he asked, holding out his hand to take hers. *Is that right, do you shake hands with women in bars? Or am I supposed to hug them? No, that's too much. This is why I date online.*

The woman looked at it strangely for a moment and then with a light giggle took his offered hand delicately. "Regina." Her smile sparkled in the neon lights.

He swallowed his sigh, straightened his back, felt his forced smile drop. She'd expected the hug and he'd already run out patience. Regina blinked, puzzled for a moment, and then smiled again, dazzling. He picked up his soda. Everyone knew what parts they were supposed to play. "So, what do you do?" he asked, sounding bored but, he hoped, at least not mean. He knew how mean he could seem when he was only disengaged, and the woman didn't deserve that.

"I'm a sales rep for a beauty brand," she replied. Vague.

"That sounds nice." He tried to make it sound neutral, not a blow off. But he didn't know what else to say and couldn't quite muster up the energy to figure it out.

"What do you do?" She put her hand on his arm, just above his elbow. She slid closer, squeezed his arm gently. Friendly.

"I'm in management. Nothing exciting." More vague.

Her smile changed, less teeth, more full lips, a tilt of her head as she leaned in closer, close enough so he could smell her shampoo, floral and sweet, over the sweat and beer of the bar. "That sounds exciting to me."

Ash forced another smile, cold but there. She didn't seem to notice. "It's not. It's mostly meetings and paperwork."

"Randall told us that you were going on a trip tomorrow for work. That sounds exciting." Regina's voice had a slight purr to it.

He cut his eyes to his friend who smirked in return. Of course he had said something. *And he left it open so their imaginations could fill in all the juicy details.* Another silent sigh. He needed to get out of there.

"Actually, speaking of, I've got to check on some things. I'll be back in a moment." Ash pulled his phone out as he spoke, backing away. He shrugged, smiling, good natured. *Sorry, business calls,* he hoped he was saying with the silent communication. Behind the woman, out of her line of sight, Randall held his hands in front of him in a silent *Come on, really?* Then the woman was turning away from him, back to Randall.

Ash looked down at his phone as he walked out of the crowded bar and into the first hall, searching for a bathroom. He heard laughter rolling from behind the doors and looked up to see other, smaller groups. He kept walking, turning down another hall, surprised that the dive bar had so many backrooms. It didn't look so large from the outside. For a second he'd worried that he'd stepped into some endless alt reality, the actual Backrooms. But then there was a door.

A frosted glass door that led straight outside. A deck.

Cool air met him, the smell of rain still lingering. He took a deep breath as he made his way to the railing. He looked at the city below, all lights in the dark, and wondered how long he could stall out there. It was near identical to the view outside of his office window—the angles were different, but it was all the same pieces. There was a calming familiarity in it, a reminder of his obligations. He should go back in, smile more, be nice. She seemed like a nice woman, and there was no reason to be rude. He wouldn't take her home; he would excuse himself politely and be on his flight in the morning.

He could just leave. He wanted to, but he couldn't quite commit to letting his friend down after he had brought him out. Randall was worried about him. He knew it even if he didn't say so. He was worried that Ash was becoming a shut-in, that he'd had his heart broken once and was locking himself away to keep it from happening again. But it wasn't that at all. Ash wasn't in the mood; the time wasn't right. But he did appreciate the care. Besides, Randall was a little bit right. If he wasn't careful he'd end up worse than his dad. No significant relationships but work and work-adjacent ones. And thinking about it, standing on the deck, wasn't that what his marriage had been anyway? Hope, Ash's ex-wife, was the daughter of one of his father's business partners. *Maybe my life is already set*, he sighed, and then stopped. *No, it's just . . . not time.* Forcing his lips to halt in their path to a frown, Ash turned to the door, preparing himself to return, and saw a woman.

Her head was down, focused on something in her hand. A game system, he realized. *Who plays video games at a bar?* The question held him. *Does she work here? Is she on her break?* Her hair was up in two buns on either side of her head with some of it out in the back, and he couldn't quite see her face. She wore a black dress with her legs crossed under her, body hunched over. There was a suggestion of a rounded, welcoming figure.

She didn't seem to notice him, and he didn't want to frighten her. Ash cleared his throat.

She looked up, the light from the screen in her hands illuminating her. Her eyes were dark, softly questioning under lifted brows. He had thought she was younger when he saw her at first, but now he could see that she was youthful but grown, and he couldn't look away. He knew he must seem weird, was probably making it all weird, but he couldn't stop staring. Ash's face was hot, his ears were burning. Her face was rounded and looked like it would sit perfectly in his hands—he wanted to hold it in his hands. Her skin looked smooth, soft, unmarked. Her lips sparkled in the light, parted softly as her head tilted, a question, unasked but he wanted to answer it, whatever it was. Wanted to hear her speak. Needed to hear her speak.

Ash raised his hand in greeting, not sure of what else to do. "Hi," he offered and immediately ran out of words to say.

2

Zeta heard the door open but didn't look up. *Just Pixie coming to check*, she thought, pressing up on the control pad to move her scout to the next fishing spot. Did she need fish? No, just *ten minutes*. But Pixie didn't say anything, and the footsteps walking across the wood didn't sound right. The deep sigh was definitely not Pixie.

She took a peek expecting it to be Brand or Cody ready with a disapproving glare, but it wasn't. A man leaned against the railing. Tall with short hair, blond from what she could see in the light from the bar. He looked fit; the shadows cut across a trim frame in a pair of slacks and a button-down shirt, the sleeves rolled to his elbows. *He must be with that group from when we walked in*, she thought, turning back to her game. *Hope he's not bringing friends.*

He cleared his throat.

She looked up again to find that he had turned toward her. In the light spilling across the deck from the door, she could make out some of his features. Straight nose, strong jawline. He stood stiffly, deer in headlights. Clearly he had thought he was alone. He raised his hand. "Hi."

"Hi," she replied slowly.

All the tension went out of him at once, turned into a spill of words, nervous, jittery. "Sorry to bother you! You must have come out here to be alone. That's why I came out here, but it's OK! I mean, I'm sorry I'm bothering you!"

"It's fine." She smiled, the corners of her mouth pushing at her cheeks on impulse. He just had the kind of look that warranted a smile, like a puppy or a cute cookie display, and she couldn't stop her lips from complying.

"Are you playing a game?" He crossed the deck to her, shortening the distance between them but stopping before he entered her personal space. A gentleman in his awkwardness.

"Yeah," she answered slowly. *Weird*, she thought. He looked like he would start shaking from nerves at any moment, but closer now she could tell that he had no reason to be nervous. *Pixie would say he looked like a bishonen anime boy, or he would if his hair was longer.* And then she was imagining him with longer hair, a few too many buttons open on his shirt. Zeta chased the thoughts away.

"Can I, um, sit out here with you?"

"I'm not the ruler of the deck. The deck is a free land." She looked back at the game in her hands, anime boy creeping into her thoughts. Zeta pushed back on the excitement of the mystery man. He was just a person getting some air. Just like her. Still . . . an electric tingle ran through her as he pulled his own chair from the table and sat it next to her. Far enough to be respectable but close enough that she could smell his body wash. Something subtle and natural like sage and . . . good.

The desire to lean on his shoulder and breathe him in was strong. *God, don't be a weirdo*, she scolded herself.

"Know any good games for this thing?" he asked suddenly, pulling out his phone and showing her the device like he was new to the cellular age.

"When you asked me if you could sit out here with me, were you really asking if we could talk?" she asked slowly around her own disbelief that the tall, good-looking man possibly wanted to talk. To her.

"No," he said, the word coming out in a rush of breath.

Zeta's heart, which she hadn't even realized she'd let float on a hope, dropped.

"Well, maybe? That's not really the response I was expecting," he continued, eyes diverted and—she couldn't be sure, but it looked like he was . . . blushing?

"What response were you expecting?" she said slowly, more confused now than she was before.

"I thought you would just say no? And I could springboard from that . . . somehow? I don't really have a plan here." Flustered but earnest.

"Well, life is full of surprises because I do have an answer!" Still surprised, still sure that he was bored and not *flirting*, Zeta wrapped herself in the comfort of expert knowledge. "You can try out *Pretty Pretty Magical Dragon Farm*. That's kind of fun. Very easy and low key. Although you should avoid it if you're the kind of person that is easily swayed by microtransactions. *Alone in the Multiverse* is really fun if you like puzzle RPGs. It's like ten bucks but a better idea if you do have a problem with microtransactions."

He nodded with the intensity of someone in a high-stakes meeting, eyes on the phone in his hand, but when he looked back up, his smile was gentle, and this time Zeta couldn't ignore the soft pawing at her belly of her own attraction. Delighted but on edge for claws.

"OK, what else? And also, what's an RPG? And a microtransaction?"

"Microtransaction?" The question caught her off guard. Who didn't know what a microtransaction was? This presumably adult man who had been clearly grown in lab because he was both attractive and respectful and appeared to have never played a video game in the modern era. "Small purchases that help you get through the game faster. Sometimes you need them for special things but really they're, like, a scam. Just a way to keep you spending money. RPG means role-playing game. You know, brave hero, killer storyline."

"I actually don't know. I don't really play games."

Oh, here's the pickup line. Half of her rolled her eyes, knew this had to end soon, but the other side leaned closer, vibrated with anticipation. She shouldn't want to hear it; she didn't know this man, and the come-on would be heavy handed and obvious. But, "No games at all?"

"Well, I've played games, but they were like Monopoly and Scrabble, board games, I guess? I never really played video games. A bunch of my friends were into a football one in college, does that help?"

"Why the sudden interest? Strike out at the bar?" She regretted it as soon as it left her mouth. There was too much bite in it, more than she meant. Zeta didn't think it was going to go anywhere, but she still wanted to enjoy it, talking to a cute guy that that was fresh and mysterious, just a little longer.

"No. At least I don't think so?" He stopped, and even in the little light that was coming from the door she could see the blush change his color all the way to his ears. "Can we pretend I'm cooler than this?" he chuckled before continuing. "I just needed some fresh air, and I'm not ready to go back in yet. You?"

"No, I didn't strike out, but the night is young," she replied without thinking, picking up the obvious punch line, making banter before she could catch herself.

His mouth dropped and he tried to say something, the words stumbled over each other. She laughed. They were both fumbling, his embarrassment canceling out her own. "It was a joke! I'm not that cool either!"

He grinned. "You seem pretty cool though."

Zeta rolled her eyes, made a disgusted sound in her throat. "Oh my god, can we stop saying cool?"

He leaned back in his chair and laughed enough to release the nervous energy he was clearly carrying. "I'm Ash," he said.

Zeta stuck her hand out. "Zeta, it's nice to meet you."

Ash stared at her offered palm for a long moment. Long enough that Zeta's ears started to burn with her own embarrassment. Her fingers began to curl, her hand dropping, when he finally grabbed it.

His hand wrapped around hers, swallowing it. "It's nice to meet you, Zeta."

Warmth ran from Zeta's palm all through her body, and for a moment there were no thoughts, just the vibrating heat of her attraction to him. He said her name like it was a gift, and she couldn't think of anything to say—and didn't realize that she was staring until he released her.

"So, so what are you doing here tonight?" she asked, face hot, trying to bring things back to casual from what felt suddenly way outside of that.

"I came out with my friend. He's got a work thing." He pulled back, and Zeta told herself that she wasn't disappointed.

"Aww, you ditched your date," she joked. "Why'd he bring you? Are you his getaway driver, excuse to leave early?"

Ash gave a small smile, amused at least. "No, I wish! I've got, um, work tomorrow."

"Sucks, you gotta work on a Sunday. What do you do?"

He relaxed into his chair, letting his long legs stretch out. "I work on the admin side of a construction firm."

"Don't take this the wrong way," Zeta said, relaxing, mimicking his mood unconsciously, "But that sounds really boring, so I'm not going to ask anymore questions about it."

Ash laughed. "That's fair. What do you do? Is it more exciting?"

She almost laughed but he wouldn't have understood, and she didn't want to get into why that was funny. Her? An exciting job? No. "Absolutely not. I'm a freelance programmer."

"That sounds exciting," he said.

"Hardly. I prefer to get it done and over with so I can spend time with my true love."

"Is it the video games?"

"It is, yes," she laughed.

"So the . . . is that a Switch? Is that your date tonight?"

"I thought you didn't know anything about this stuff."

"I have seen commercials. Been to a couple of stores. I've seen it around."

"Honestly surprised you have a TV at this point."

His laugh was rich, matched the even timbre of his voice. "It's like one of those big tube sets that sits on the floor though. It doesn't work with these newfangled devices."

Zeta guffawed. She liked his sense of humor, liked the way he sounded and smelled and looked and knew it would suck when she had to go back to the gang, but it was better that way. Zeta thought for a moment that maybe . . . but no. She didn't know him, and what if *a thing* happened? No. It wasn't a good idea. But for right now he was funny and nice, and she was enjoying herself. "Wait, it's not really, right?"

"No, it's not really. Is the Switch really your date?"

"Oh! No! I came with my friends too. I just needed some air. Actually, it's kind of weird that they haven't sent a search party. Hold on."

"Take your time," he responded.

Zeta dug in her bag again, searching for the phone by touch. It had nestled into the bottom of her bag. The notification light was blinking when she pulled it out.

Guess you were too busy to notice the door opening. Pixie's text was followed by an eggplant emoji.

"Oh my god," Zeta said under her breath.

"Everything OK?" Ash asked, and when she looked up his eyes were large and questioning, like a puppy.

Her mouth suddenly had too much salvia. She swallowed. "Yeah, it's fine. My friend is just being goofy, whatever." *I'm not going to respond.* But she replied anyway, **Just talking!** She looked at the time; it had gotten late. *I should say good night, let him get back, but . . .*

"So what are you interested in? Maybe we can find something you *want* to play instead of just what the weird deck girl suggested. Guitars? I don't know, I'm thinking music guy?"

That rich laugh tumbled from hm again. "I do like music, but I can't actually play a single instrument."

"Really? I thought for sure you could play a mean 'Wonderwall.' OK, I'm not very good at this, so tell me. Gimme your phone."

He handed her the device without question, her fingers brushing his, the warmth tingling along her skin. She looked at the screen to avoid his eyes. It was a close-up, artistic shot of a plant with green leaves spotted with white.

"What I'm into?" he hummed. "Plants. I read and watch movies. Normal stuff."

"You garden?" Zeta felt her nose wrinkle, forced it smooth so he wouldn't get the wrong idea and see it as disdain instead of surprise.

He didn't seem to notice at all, replying with a shy smile. "No, more like house plants. Mostly."

"Oh, neat." Zeta typed some keywords into the app bar and started scrolling. "What's the last movie you watched?"

"*High Life*, the one with Robert Pattinson in it. What about you?"

"Don't judge me. It was *Avengers: Endgame*. I hadn't seen it yet, and it feels like something I had to for society reasons." She turned the screen toward him, handed the phone back.

"No one will know if you skip a Disney film." Again his fingers touched hers. She wasn't sure, but she thought he was watching her, reading her reactions. It set off butterflies in her stomach. Reminded her that she shouldn't keep going.

"Disney will know," she deadpanned.

They both laughed a nervous, *this is alright*, shy, tension-breaking kind of laugh. The conversation flowed from the complaints of how every movie these days was a "cinematic universe" to what their favorite Disney film actually was. Zeta's was *Wreck-It Ralph*—"A movie with every single reference to a video game you could make?

Come on, easy answer."—and Ash landed on the forgotten *Treasure Island*, with a shrug and no explanation.

"What is this?" he asked when he finally looked at what she had downloaded for him.

"A game about growing plants, *Eden Apartment*. Since you're totally new, I thought it might suit you better. I didn't peg you as a cozy gamer though."

"What did you peg me as then?"

Uwu. Heat crept up her neck and she shivered at the connection; the words weren't quite right, but it was close enough. Were they flirting? She couldn't tell. It didn't feel like a come on, whatever they were doing, but it didn't *not* feel like it. It didn't have that hookup-focused line that she was used to. He wasn't trying to sell himself or impress her. They were just *talking*.

Discussion of the last time they'd each gone to a movie in a theater bled into how they had spent their summer. She confided that she was getting over a cold after a beach trip. He admitted he hadn't managed to take a vacation lately but he did see his parents recently.

"Close family?" she asked, because it seemed like the most natural thing to ask.

"Close enough. You spend a lot of time with your friends?"

Zeta could feel the tension, the not-wanting-to-get-into-it, and was happy to move past it because she didn't want to get into her own history either. Wanted this easy, nice thing to stay that way. "I try. Gets lonely otherwise. The city's really big, but it's lonely, you know? Especially when you work from home. You?"

"I work too much," he laughed.

"That's not a surprise, Mr. Work-on-Sunday. What is a surprise is that you're still out here talking to me."

"This is better than sitting in a crowded bar sipping soda all night."

She wrinkled her nose, letting it happen this time. "I should have had a soda. The house beer is horrible. What *is* that stuff?"

"I have no idea and I'm not going to find out now. Are you thirsty? I can go get you something. Or at least I think I can. That place is a maze," he said, frowning at the door.

"Maybe that's why your friend left you all alone back here. Because they're lost." Zeta giggled. "This place is weird though. They've got more private party rooms than I've ever seen. But if you're the DD don't you need to report back to duty?"

"He can call an Uber," Ash shrugged.

"Not worried about your friend making it home?"

His expression shifted, more thoughtful, with a slight frown and Zeta's back tensed. He didn't like the question. Too much like an accusation? Too personal? She felt the tremor in the bubble they'd made, the structure ready to pop, and it pushed her back into the real world.

"I'm not the only friend he has here tonight. I'm sure he'll be alright. On the other hand, he's the only person I know here so really I'm the one in danger," he explained, smiling warmly again, playfully.

Zeta shifted, relaxed, settled, rested her elbow on her thigh, her cheek in her palm. "What danger are you in out here on the deck?"

He shrugged, matching her pose playfully, but it brought him closer, closing the distance between them. "I don't know yet."

She almost snapped to her feet, embarrassed at his closeness, at the jittery wave of energy it sent through her belly to her throat. Remembered herself just in time to keep from causing a disaster. No telling how her body would react to a jolt like that. *This is dangerous*, she thought but asked, "Do you not drink?"

"I do, I'm just not tonight. Work tomorrow, and I always over-sleep when I drink."

"Don't want the boss to be mad," she sang. "That's why I free-lance."

"It doesn't bother me so much; I'm an early riser. Is that why you freelance? Later hours?"

Zeta paused, almost laughed and told him the truth, that she couldn't handle the stress of working outside of her house. He was so easy to talk to, and she was getting too comfortable, the dangerous moment quickly fading from memory. It didn't feel like flirting, but it felt like something. She smiled and nodded, "Yeah, so I can stay up late."

"Playing video games of course," he laughed. "What else do you do in your free time? Or are you, like, headsets and in a league where you play an orc mage or something?"

"Oh, you lied to me; you said you didn't know anything about video games. And no, I don't play those kinds of games or anything online. I prefer a standalone, contained experience."

"I *do* watch TV, I read. I know about things," he said lightly. "And I wouldn't lie to you."

"You just met me," she half scolded, half reminded him. Reminding herself that she was getting too comfortable, that she should leave. "What do you read anyway?" She sighed, giving up on leaving. The vibrating, warm part of her wouldn't allow it. It would all have to end but not right now. Right now, she was just a girl in a bar talking to a boy, and that was enough. She could have that.

"Fiction, mostly. I'm trying to catch up on classics."

"Classics, like *Moby Dick*?"

"More like *The Time Machine*."

"I have seen that movie. It was pretty forgettable. How was the book?"

"It is . . ." He shifted in his chair and heat rolled off of him, crossing the distance that was smaller than Zeta remembered from five minutes before to dance along her skin. "Pretty unforgettable."

Ash was looking at her again, doing more than just seeing her, and that was too much. Zeta stood, quickly. She swayed at the sudden movement and blinked the sudden dark spots in her vision away.

Gently, he placed his fingers on the back of her hand, drawing her attention, holding her still. She looked down at them, long with perfectly clipped nails, and then to his face. She felt her lips part but there was nothing on her tongue. Her mind was blank, melted by his touch.

Wide eyed, he snatched his fingers away with the sudden realization of what he'd done, what he was doing, just as she had lost the ability to form any thoughts at all. "Sorry! Do you have to go? I didn't mean— It's just really nice talking to you." His face held a frown, and she couldn't tell if it was embarrassment or annoyance, but she decided she liked it. His cheeks were red, and he was flustered, and it was adorable and arresting.

"No." Without the touch of his hand, her brain came back online. "I've been sitting, and I need to stretch my legs." *Just ten minutes*, she promised, and then she would go. She wasn't trying to torpedo their back-and-forth, at least not in a mean never-talk-to-me-again way, but she needed to end things. Needed to go back to where people knew her. She'd already nearly made a mistake in getting up too fast. But she didn't want to ruin things. Maybe she could let things taper gently, carry on into something she could manage and control, a small, more rational voice suggested. They could trade numbers, text for a few weeks, see how it went, go on a real date, but every other part of her wanted more *right now*.

The smile spread on his face, long and slow. Goofy, silly, and just far too *honest*. And Zeta wasn't sure what to make of that at all. She walked to the railing of the deck to get away from his goofy smile and handsome, way too handsome, face.

"Glad it stopped raining," she said, taking in a deep breath, clearing her head, finding her center again.

"Me too. It turned out to be a really great night," Ash replied. He walked over, settling against the railing, facing her with his back to the view.

Does he mean . . . no. It is a nice night, stay cool. I can make some space so that maybe this can . . . be something. But Zeta's heart was pounding all the way into her ears, and the smell of his soap and skin had replaced the breeze. She could feel him like a storm all through her body.

"Do you live in the city or out in the suburbs?" he asked.

"The city. I think over there?" she said, pointing toward the east.

Ash looked over his shoulder, followed her finger's direction. "Hmm, yes, I'm very familiar with that particular neighborhood," he said teasingly. "They've got great streetlights."

Her reply came out on the tail of her chuckle. "What about you? City or the 'burbs?"

"The city. I live there." Ash turned and pointed toward the center of the city.

"Fancy! So, like, no pets and ten roommates to afford it?"

"I don't have any pets. Have been thinking about a dog, not sold on the idea." He turned back, focused on her.

"Then why not a cat? All the cuddles, none of the walking." *This is good; I can ease down from here, and if it's something it can be something next week. There's no need to rush.* Good, rational thought.

"I have too many plants. It's dangerous. Some of them are toxic."

"Plants before pets?"

"Yeah, but not before people." Was he closer? She couldn't tell, but that sage scent, the air felt sharp between them. His lips weren't quite frowning, his brows not quite furrowed, and his eyes were focused below her face.

He touched her hand. Slipped his long fingers into her palm, held it delicately, loosely. "The view is really beautiful here."

But you're not even looking, she almost said. But he was looking, intently. The same way he had been looking at her. She kept her hand in his, his fingers closed around it, warm, comfortable, and Zeta did not move.

"Am I making you uncomfortable?" he asked slowly, looking at her face again.

Troubled, she thought. *He looks worried.* She shook her head. "No. I'm sorry, I'm a little—"

"Can I kiss you?" All in a rush, the four words almost tripped over each other to get out of his mouth, like he'd been dying to ask, like he'd die if he didn't ask.

They hadn't talked about anything real. He was just a guy on a deck with not terrible taste in movies and a pretty face. She'd let it go on too long, and now, she couldn't. It was too dangerous. The question stopped whatever retort would have come to Zeta's tongue. Her heart was racing, her face was hot, too hot. She wanted to say yes—that vibrating, soft animal of desire in her howled to say yes—but she couldn't. "What?"

"I'm sorry, I know, it's sudden. I'm not very good at this, but you're beautiful, and I want to be clear, I'd really, really like to kiss you," he explained, all awkward nervous laughter, words toppling over each other, eager.

"Oh. No. You can't. That's not . . ." She needed air, she needed to collect herself, find better words to explain. But he was holding her hand.

Ash laughed, released her, and the world went cold. He brushed his hand over his head and looked away. "Sorry, I must have misread things."

No, I made the mistake, my fault, I shouldn't have let . . . Everything was spinning. She had to answer. "No! It's not that. I do want you to kiss me!"

He looked at her, frown on his face, head tilted to the side like a puppy. "Now I'm confused."

"Just . . . give me a minute." Zeta closed her eyes, taking a series of slow deep breaths before speaking again. "I've got this condition where if my heart speeds up too much I'll faint. I have to avoid stress and strenuous activity," she explained, too frazzled to think of anything but the truth.

"You have a heart condition?" he asked.

"No, my heart is fine. My brain overreacts and shuts everything down. Kind of like those goats, only not, because that's this muscle disorder and mine is a brain thing, and you know what? That's not important." She was babbling. She had to stop it, gain some sort of control. She could not handle this.

"So, you can't kiss me?" he asked, his frown deepening.

"No, I can. I just," her phone buzzed. There was too much going on. She pulled it out of her purse without thinking. "I bet Pixie would take you home, so your night isn't a total loss."

"Pixie?" he asked more confused.

She read the message quickly. "Yeah, she's my friend. She's trying to get over this guy. She's way prettier than me, and you're so handsome, so I'm sure you can hook up with her, no problem." *That was a weird thing to say*, she thought, but couldn't stop herself. The world was starting to spin faster.

"Are you trying to pass me off on your friend? Do you not like me at all?"

"No! She's just better for you. Here, this is her." She showed him a photo they had taken together. Pixie smiled up at the camera, deep violet wig and a cute yellow sundress on while Zeta sat next to her in plain, black yoga pants and a pink tank top, her hair in loose, fluffy curls around her head. They were in Zeta's apartment, right before she left for the beach.

"Is that you with her?" he asked, taking her phone from her fingers.

"Yeah, I guess it's kind of dark out here, so you can't really see me."

"I saw you just fine; your game lit up your face. Just so I'm clear here, you have a health condition you need to be mindful of but you can in fact kiss me and you also think I'm handsome?"

"Yes. I mean, yes." Her face was hot. Mortified at everything. There was no chance this man should ever want to talk to her. She was strange and awkward, and he was still talking in almost exactly the same tone as if none of this were happening. Amused, easy, and she was dying.

"Now provided that goes well, the kissing I mean, and you'd want to, could we go further than that? Could we sleep together?" His tone was light, but there was a serious undercurrent. It wasn't a hypothetical; he was asking to know the answer.

"Yes, of course I can. There's nothing wrong with my—" she

blurted out, stopping herself before she could finish the sentence, realizing that she had just met him. That she didn't know him. What she was about to say. "Oh my god, I'm so embarrassed. I should go. It was so nice meeting you, really. I'm—I'm going to go." She needed to leave before she crashed to the ground in embarrassment. "You have my phone. Can I? I'm sorry about all of . . . this."

"Alright," he said calmly, as if Zeta hadn't said anything more than good night. He lifted her phone, and the shutter sounded.

Ash handed it back to her, his smiling face on the screen. Blue eyes, blond hair, strong chin, straight nose, white teeth. He looked like a statue. If his hair had been longer, she would have thought he was an angel. "So that's me. Now, can I kiss you?"

Even after she'd panicked, even after he saw her in clear daylight, he still wanted to kiss her. Wanted her—and she wanted him, couldn't ignore that she wanted him. No waiting, no figuring things out. Just wanted.

All Zeta could do was nod.

3

That worked? The impossibility that simply *asking* to kiss her worked, that she didn't run away when he asked if they could sleep together, a desire that he certainly had but in no way meant to voice out loud. But Zeta said . . . yes. Well not yes but maybe. She was open. She was interested.

Interested in kissing him.

This was not his first time, but it felt like a brand new experience. His heart pounded so hard he was sure she could hear it, and he thought his hands were shaking. Zeta stared at him, her eyes large and dark, her still sparkling lips parted, and he wanted to dive into her.

But he couldn't. Not yet. Ash's head spun, but some part of his mind held on to what she'd told him, put the pieces together. Understood how he had to go about this, how he had to kiss *her*.

Ash touched her face, Zeta's skin soft and hot under his fingers, tilting her head up as he bent to meet her lips. Carefully, he pressed his against hers, and she met his pressure with her own softness. The sweet taste of her lip gloss lingered as he pulled back. "Are you OK?" he asked unsure if the question was directed at Zeta or himself.

"Yes, why?" she stuttered. There was some comfort in her awkwardness. She'd been so quick all night, and it was nice to know that he could catch her off guard, surprise her, but he had no idea how long he could keep his cool. The desire—the need—to kiss her had overwhelmed him. He forgot about Randall, his trip, everything. He just wanted more time with Zeta.

That's why he didn't tell her that he was leaving the country in the morning. He didn't want her to think that it couldn't be something. He didn't want their conversation to become about his job or his downtown apartment. He didn't want her to look at him like the woman from earlier whose name or face he couldn't even remember.

Ash didn't think that Zeta would change like that, but he couldn't let himself risk it. Couldn't give her a reason to walk away from him.

"Because your face is hot and," he shifted his fingers to her neck where her pulse beat a rhythm against her throat, "your heart is beating really fast." *So is mine*, he added to himself.

Zeta touched her chest. "I'm OK, it's not bad. I just need to get used to what's happening."

"Good. Why don't we sit down? I'm very tall." Ash took her hand, butterflies bursting into flight in his belly as her fingers curled around his. He sat and guided Zeta to him. "I can't kiss you over there," he explained.

Zeta held still, looked down at him. "Are you sure?"

"Why wouldn't I be sure? Come here." He held his arms open, and she maneuvered into them, settling the comfortable, warm weight of her body against his. She seemed to be unsure, tense. "Relax," he said softly. "I won't drop you."

"It's not that. I'm not exactly small," she laughed.

"I noticed." He pulled her closer, rested his nose in the curve of her neck, breathed in the clean scent of her soap, the candy sweetness of whatever was in her hair, and laid a kiss on the exposed skin, pulling a shiver and squeak from her. He wanted to hear that sound again.

"Let me kiss you some more." Ash heard the desire in his own voice, hoped Zeta heard the space he left for her to say no, even though he had his arms wrapped around her, her body tucked against his so that he could feel the soft press of it all along his chest. He wanted to reassure her that he heard her, that he wouldn't rush her. He wanted to pull all the little sounds of pleasure and delight from her lips. Wanted to feel her body lean into his, uninhibited, fold against him like he was her favorite chair. He wanted to please her. Anything else was secondary, unimportant. His pleasure was only in finding hers.

Her eyes, her cute little ears, and her body—god, her body was designed to be held. She's so beautiful, he thought, breathing in the scent of her, waiting for her to give her permission, to let him press forward. He stroked her thigh, and she put her hand on his chest. The touch twisted around his core, slithered into his belly and set fire to him.

"If you're going to kiss me, it's OK to just kiss me," she said, laughter under her words, nervous or amused he couldn't tell.

"We don't have to do anything. Tell me if I'm going too far." He looked her in the eye, tried to let her know he meant it. They could stop, but he didn't want to stop. Hoped she didn't want to stop.

Zeta sighed, frowned at him, and his heart dropped into his stomach. Ash moved to release her, to help her up, and she shifted in his arms.

She leaned forward, pressed her lips to his, taking him by surprise. Zeta kissed sweetly, slowly, but sure in a way that his kiss hadn't been. Her arms slipped around his neck, and he brought his arms tighter around her, pulling her closer. Ash, emboldened, slipped his tongue between her lips, tasting the soft, welcoming space of her mouth, swallowing the sound of surprise from her throat. She settled against him, body bending toward him, and he moved to accommodate all of her, his hands tentatively learning the landscape of her body.

His fingers stroked her back as he ended the kiss, letting them breathe before bending back toward her, his mouth on hers, her lips returning his touch immediately, as hungry as he was. Ash felt himself harden with want. He shifted, hoping to hide it, and slipped one hand around her waist to steady her, keep her from moving too much so he didn't lose control of his own urges. His free hand found her breast, made a distraction of it to hide his own arousal. Zeta gasped into his mouth but didn't pull away; she let his fingers stroke and explore, pressed herself into his touch.

Zeta made a soft whining sound. "I'm sorry," she said pulling back, mouth still so close he could feel her words on his lips. "Wait, I need to breathe."

"Don't apologize," he mumbled, and he lowered his head, kissing her neck, tasting her skin, hoped his touch wasn't as clumsy as he felt. *How long has it been?* Certainly not as long as Randall would make it out to be but longer than he remembered. Randall dragged him out to meet somebody often, but for the first time he was thankful for it. Zeta wasn't what he expected to find, but she was what he wanted. And now she was a warm, malleable weight in his arms. He forced himself to keep his touch slow as he pressed firm kisses into the heat of her throat. *Take your time, don't scare her*, he thought. But his body wanted something else, his hardness pressing tight against the fabric of his pants, begging to sink into something softer, wetter.

"Are you alright?" he asked, voice heavy and needy. "Can I keep going?"

Zeta nodded, and Ash drew his thumb over the budding peak of her nipple, slowly teasing it taunt. She moaned softly, her hips rocking gently, just the right pressure to make him shudder with pleasure.

"Sure you don't want to take a break, adjust yourself?" she teased, laughing as she repeated the movement, Ash's body reacting on its own.

"I'm sure," he said. He captured her earlobe in his teeth gently, drawing a surprised gasp from her before she could tease him more.

He released it and covered her lips with his own again, kissing her deeply, slowly. *When was the last time I kissed someone like this?* he thought absently, the question background, forgotten a moment later. The kiss tapered off, broke apart.

Zeta looked up at him, dreamy, kiss drunk, and he could only imagine he looked the same. The gloss on her lips was gone, sucked and nibbled away by his own mouth, but her lips weren't any less alluring. "Are you done kissing me?" she asked, voice edging on a whine. Cute, playful.

I don't think I'll ever be done kissing you, he thought but said, "No, can I take you home now?"

She smiled slow and sweet, and he didn't think he'd make it that far, not when she was looking at him like that, but then she pulled away. Stood slowly, stretched. "Sure," she said, turning back to him, "you can take me home. Do you mind coming to my place?"

He smiled, "No, I don't mind at all."

"Cool, thanks. I know you've got to work in the morning, but I don't have a car. It's late as hell to order a Lyft. They'll probably jack the price way up." She laughed.

I didn't tell her. I need to explain things, Ash remembered suddenly. *I should stop this. I shouldn't do this*, he thought, but Zeta chuckled at her phone and everything else slipped away. Plans, work, his flight, all of it gone with the sound of that laugh.

"You coming?" she asked, putting her phone away and holding out her hand. He took it, nodding like fool at his good fortune, taking her lead. As she zipped him through the maze of the private rooms, he wondered how he had gotten so confused to begin with. They were back in the main bar a moment later and out the door. He didn't even stop to see if Randall was there, didn't care to tell him he had gone. Zeta was holding his hand, and all he could see was her full figure in front of him, skirt swaying with every step. Outside she looked back at him, "Which one's you?"

"I'm over here." Ash motioned in the direction of his car. He felt giddy, light headed, like he had been drinking. But the only thing besides soda that had touched his lips was Zeta. He felt his sloppy smile, but he couldn't help himself and she didn't seem to mind. He led her to his car, a plain four-door Hyundai, and opened the passenger side.

"Why do you have to go into work on Sunday, anyway?" Zeta asked as he slid into the driver's seat.

He froze. He hadn't thought this far, didn't think she'd ask again. He didn't want to talk about work, didn't want to talk about his leaving. "The office is behind on paperwork," he shrugged, hoping it was casual and enough to end it, move on to something else. Not a complete lie; they *were* behind on paperwork in some department, probably. The guilt of it turned his stomach, but he would explain. Before he left.

"I'm sure that overtime will help pay that downtown rent," she said as she put her address into the GPS.

"I thought we weren't going to talk about my job. It's boring, remember?" *Talk about anything else*, he begged silently.

"Hmm, you're right," she snorted. "So radio roulette it is! Pick a number between one and twenty-five."

Ash relaxed, "Is this a game? What are we doing? Twelve."

"I'm going to hit scan, we're going to listen to whatever the twelfth station is for at least twelve minutes."

It turned out to be a sports radio show they took turns taking jabs at and laughing until the mandatory twelve minutes were up, and by then, they were nearly at her door. There wasn't enough time for another round. Zeta turned the music on low and pulled out her phone.

"Give me a minute, OK?" she asked sweetly, tapping the screen.

"Sure," he nodded, smiling. He'd give her whatever she wanted. Tinny music came from the device as she swiped her fingers over the screen. He snuck peeks at her as he drove, caught her nose wrinkling, lips frowning slightly. Adorable, whatever she was doing.

She looked up as they arrived and directed him on where to park. Three minutes later she led him into her home.

Ash walked into Zeta's first floor apartment, the bottom half of a duplex, and looked around. It was clean in the way that people who don't like to clean kept their space, picked up and imperfect. Garbage can full of takeout containers, a few dishes in the sink. Lived in.

A neat, little kitchen was the first thing he saw. A little table covered with a fan of mail, a couple clothing catalogs, and a shell picture frame of her and an older woman at the beach in loose dresses and big hats. The little living room to the left of the kitchen had a sofa bed, all pulled out, covered with blankets, the silver rectangle of a laptop thrown on top of them. Dark gray blackout curtains hung over the large front window to the side of the couch. In front of the sofa was a TV sitting on a stand, and she walked toward it, Switch in hand, to settle it on a dock that waited to the side. A stack of game cases sat next to it.

The walls had photographs on them, pushpin-hung Polaroids, but he couldn't tell who or what was in them, not from where he stood.

"You can come in. You don't have to stand in the doorway." Her laugh came out nervous, unsure, and he wanted to make her sure.

"I'm sorry, I'm awkward. I don't usually do things like this." He couldn't stop himself; the truth jumped from his lips into the air. He wanted to bury his face in his arms, hide his embarrassment, but he was standing in her apartment.

"Me either! We can be weird together. Do you want something to drink?"

As soon as she asked, he realized his throat was dry. How long had they been talking? "Yes," he said stepping inside, closing the door gently. In the opposite direction of the living room was a short hall. A bathroom, door hanging open, light off. Another open door, and at the top of the hall, a closed one. Two bedrooms. *Does she have a roommate?*

She swept past him. "Take your shoes off," she said quietly, and then he noticed hers by the door and did the same. "Ugh, OK.

I've got, like, half a mouthful of juice and some milk. I'm sorry, I've been sick. I guess I need to go shopping." The same cute little laugh. He wanted to swallow it.

"I'll just have some water," he smiled, He walked into the kitchen, watched her stand on her toes to reach for a glass from the cabinet. Her movements were measured, careful, and her body in the light of the kitchen was all round curves and smooth hills. "Why are we whispering? Is it your roommate?" he asked to distract himself, calm down.

"I don't have a roommate. But the guy upstairs is an ass. Complains about noise all the time—not that I'm noisy! He's just a jerk. But I don't want to give him a reason to bother me tomorrow."

I do, Ash thought, taking the glass from her. He felt his face turn hot and turned away to find something, anything, to distract him. "I didn't know there were still places that were developing photos."

"What?" she asked, getting her own glass, and he pointed at the wall in her living room. "Oh, no! Well, maybe, I don't know. I have those printed at CVS."

"So you're into photography? You didn't mention it." He walked across the room to the wall, looking closer at all of the images. An assortment of different people, some making repeat appearances. He did recognize Pixie after a moment, different hair color in almost every photo. One white and one Asian man appeared a lot, and the older woman, maybe the same as the one in the photo on the table, showed up more than once, but mostly it was a sea of one-time faces. Restaurants, amusement parks, living rooms other than hers. A photo album on the wall. A puzzle that he was missing a piece for and he wanted to find it, understand what all those pictures meant.

"I'm into keeping my memories," she said, joining him.

Her tone had changed. He didn't know her well enough to know if it was sad or thoughtful, but he wanted her to laugh again. "You didn't take a picture of me. Does that mean you don't want to remember me?" he joked.

Zeta was silent, and when he turned to look at her she was looking at her wall, but her gaze was far away, thoughtful, and he realized how heavy the question was. How much he wanted the answer to lean one way because she was interesting and adorable. He wanted to kiss her again.

"Kinda of depends on how the night goes," she said.

"Are you sure you're OK with this?" The words came out all in a rush, but he needed to be sure, wanted her to be sure. Didn't know what would happen later, but right now, he just wanted her to want him. "I can go home right now."

She raised an eyebrow, "Yeah, I'm OK. I'm not drunk if that's what you're worried about."

"No, I just want to be sure. You look really cute with your hair like that, in this outfit," he said turning his whole body toward her.

She rolled her eyes. "You've never seen me in anything else, but thanks."

"That's not true. You showed me that picture with your friend. And there's the one on your table at the beach. So with confidence I can say that you look very good right now."

Zeta's lips stretched into a smile. "Thank you. Your hair looks cute too," she giggled

I should tell her I'm leaving tomorrow. Tell her that I want to call her, talk to her more. But she was laughing, and her smile was so beautiful.

Ash didn't really think, couldn't think. Her face was in his hands and his mouth over hers. Her laughter turned into a questioning hum, but she leaned into the kiss. She sighed in pleasure, and Ash forgot about everything else.

4

Ash's kiss hit Zeta like an eruption, all shock and confusion and then the slow, relentless roll of liquid fire through her body as he pulled her tightly to him. She knew she should tell him to slow it down, but she really, really didn't want to.

"Is that your bed?"

She felt his words on her lips; he was so close, his voice so low, almost a growl. It made her forget feeling nervous about having someone inside her less-than-spotless apartment. Almost made her forget that she had to talk to him, explain things more. Because he wasn't a boyfriend or even a friend—he was a stranger. But she could feel him pressing against her body. It would be OK; she just needed to explain. She put some distance between them, let the air clear of the tickling feeling of his words on her mouth, the fog of pleasure over her brain. Shook her head half in response, half to reclaim her ability to think. "No, I have a bedroom. I'm a real adult."

Zeta meant to make him laugh, slow things down. The rules of their engagement were already piling up in her head.

"Take me to it. Tell me what I need to know about you."

Ash's voice had changed, lost its awkwardness. Become firm, sure of itself. The sound of it sent another tremor through her, but really it was what he had said. He had asked her. Remembered that he needed to take care instead of pushing to see how far he could get. Zeta knew there was another side of him after his first kisses on the deck. For a moment she thought that it had all been some kind of con, that the puppy she met first had all been an act. But no, she could still see it in him, the soft begging in his eyes, the way the tips of his fingers settled on her arm.

"You have to go slow. I can't go up and down very fast. Sorry this isn't going to be some wild night. Feel free to bail!" She laughed, finding all the awkwardness he had shed.

"Is that all?" She could hear the smile in his voice, the hint of the man she had met on the deck. And now that she'd said it, it didn't seem so much to ask. He closed the distance between them, his fingers sliding along her arms around to her back.

"I need to breathe. If I get too hot, I'll . . ." Zeta let the sentence trail. His hands were tracing a pattern on her back. Like a spell.

"Got it. So. Take me to your bedroom. Please." His voice was low, pleading, and his body echoed it.

Her bedroom door stood open. She crossed the room, turned on the standing lamp, and felt her face heat with embarrassment. The dresser next to the door was covered in figurines from her favorite games. They felt silly, childish, now that there was a stranger looking at them. The drawers hung open, spilling her clothes over their edges from when she'd been searching for something to throw on for the night. The bed on the opposite wall from the door, under the window was a mess of blankets and stuffed animals, some of which spilled onto the floor with the clothes. She looked like a slob.

Ash's eyes darted around the room, and he plucked up an *Animal Crossing* figurine, turning it over carefully in his fingers before setting it down.

"Sorry about the mess, I wasn't expecting company," she said guiltily, as if that explained what was obviously her general state of being.

Ash hummed thoughtfully and then unbuttoned his shirt. He crossed the room and pulled Zeta into his embrace, locking her into his kiss.

He pulled away, looking down at Zeta. *That must be what "smoldering" looks like*, she thought, suddenly understanding every romance novel she'd ever read. She squirmed out of his arms, and he let her go with a low whine that made her shiver and wish she didn't need to breathe. That she didn't need to get herself under control. The flood of desire between her thighs tried to convince her otherwise, but he was a stranger. She couldn't and shouldn't rely on him to look out for her. She turned around, peeled off her socks, and tossed them into the dirty clothes because it was a normal thing to do, a way to bring her back in the real world. When she looked again, she knew it didn't work. Ash had taken off the shirt, undone his belt, and now stood bare chested in front of her, the lines of muscles clear on his torso. His chest was covered with fine, almost invisible hairs that got darker as they went downward. A trail of gold. Zeta wanted to follow it with her fingers, slip them under the band of his underwear and find out if there was more treasure to behold. Her face went hot.

"Whoa," she breathed as he reached for her.

Ash gathered up her dress in his fists, lifting it over her head and leaving her in her underwear. She expected him to pull her back into a kiss, get her into the bed as fast as possible, but he just stared.

Zeta stood shyly, self-conscious, moving her arms to cover her belly, face hot. The unicorn panties that had seemed so cute hours ago suddenly felt childish instead of whimsical. "I really didn't plan for—"

"Wow," Ash said slowly, drawing the word out, his voice barely a whisper. Zeta's face bloomed hot as his eyes, deep and blue, focused on her body. The dress had been loose and hung from her breasts. Without it the full expanse of her curves was on display. Not just the round handfuls of her breasts but the pouch of her belly, the dimple across the center where she bent at. It didn't quite hide the meeting of her thick thighs, no space between them. She thought that he was going to reach for her breast, but his fingers landed on her belly, hot tips following the dimple. The smile on Ash's face, soft and joyous, made Zeta's heart skip a beat.

She took off her own bra to be done with it. Ash sucked in his breath.

He wrapped his arms around her, placing his hands on her bare back, traveling up her spine so that her bare body touched his, his firm torso to her giving one, his eagerness pressed into her belly. Hot like a stove, slow warming heat, hotter with each second, winding up to unbearable, to engulfing. But not yet. She ran her hands along his chest, followed the golden path of hair with her fingers. Skin to skin, heat to heat. He smelled of the night air still, sweat and sage. She trailed her tongue against the bare skin of his chest, her fingers teasing his still-trapped cock.

He groaned, pleased. "No more teasing." He bent, brought his face level with hers. His voice was a deep whisper across her cheek to the cusp of her ear. A sure, quiet strength, no question, an order she was eager to follow.

"Are you sure?" she asked, slipping her fingers past his waistband to wrap around him.

A growl and his mouth was on hers, pushing her lips open, tongues meeting. She wasn't sure how she reached the bed, didn't remember moving or how he'd lost his pants, but her head was on the pillow and Ash was looming over her, fully naked and erect.

"You're so cute." His words made her blush more than the touch of his mouth on her throat and then lower, to her breasts, a wet trail of kisses. He teased her nipple with his tongue, and Zeta felt the touch low in her stomach, between her legs. He took one in his mouth, making her gasp and squirm with want, while he toyed with the other between his fingers. She brushed her own fingers over the nape of his neck, stroking him gently in her pleasure as he moved his mouth, his fingers over the peaks of her breasts.

"Not too much," she said, half distracted by his touch because it was dragging her to the edge, threatening to tip her over. "I don't want to finish too soon, I want . . ."

His fingers slid over her belly and moved her underwear to the side. Already wet, the cold air was a shock quickly replaced by the shock of his fingers exploring the folds of her. "Too soon?" he hummed into her ear. "Then we'll just go again."

He dipped into her opening before smoothing her own wetness over the hard bead of her clit. She wrapped her arms around his shoulders, buried her face in his chest, dug her fingers into his shoulders as his touch sent tickling, electric pulses through her entire body. In the heady excitement of his touch, all thoughts of being careful, that they had just met and he didn't really know her, fled from her. He moved over her like he'd met her body a thousand times before, made her feel desired, familiar in his arms. She wanted to feel him buried in her. The only thing that stuck in her mind was keeping it down so the neighbor didn't complain, didn't interrupt with a loud bang on the ceiling, a knock on the door. She took small, halting breaths between each stroke of his fingers, in time with them, swallowing louder cries as best she could. Her head was beginning to spin—she wasn't breathing, couldn't breathe because it was all so good.

"Wait, wait, wait!" Zeta said, shifting her hands down to his chest.

"Too fast?" he said, smiling with a sigh.

"I'm sorry," she replied, frowning, expecting him to laugh, to tease, to try to convince her otherwise.

"Don't apologize." The eyes that stared back at her were hungry with need. Zeta thought for a moment to just tell him to go ahead, fuck her, because how long could he possibly wait? And she didn't want him to change; she didn't want to hear *Come on, just let me do it.* She had never seen that look on anyone and didn't want it ruined. She opened her mouth to say as much, but then his lips were on her jaw, her neck, and then her mouth. Barley touching, his movements slow and sensual against her. "Tell me when, tell me what to do. Tell me what you want. Guide me."

A gift of obedience. It was all just too perfect. "Ash," her voice was a low purr, sexy even to herself. "Why are you being so good?"

"Why wouldn't I be? Why wouldn't anyone be good to you?" He matched her lusty tone with his own, deeper, his lips at her ear, the sound followed by the sensation of his tongue against the outside shell of it, then the gentle pressure of his teeth pulling a shiver from her. A question that sounded like a statement. *I'll be good to you; everyone should be good to you.* And Zeta fell into the fantasy of him because he was warm and her skin smelled like his. His heart beat in time with hers through the press of her lips on his throat.

His touch danced up her body and his palm cupped her breast, thumb teasing the nipple until it stood dark and hard against it. Then his mouth covered it, heat burning away her thoughts. The tickling electricity he drew from her pulsed just at the edge of climax but never quite there, and she was settling into it, learning to breathe between his kisses, discovering the rhythm in his movements. Zeta found herself doing as he asked, guiding him. "Touch me here," she breathed, placing his fingers on the line between her thigh and her hip where the band of her panties sat, and he responded with his lips and tongue, pulling the fabric away. Bit her thigh gently, sending shivers all through her.

"Can I?" he asked, moving to stare down at her. His eyes were wide and pleading. "Zeta," he said her name like a spell, "will you let me have you now?"

Under the furnace heat of his body Zeta was impossibly wet, somehow completely wound up and totally relaxed. Entirely ready. She nodded.

He grinned wide, excited. "Where do you keep your condoms?"

Zeta sat up suddenly. "Shit!" she half shouted, too loud, and then the dizziness came. She gripped her head and mumbled it again. "Shit."

He pulled himself up from between her legs and met Zeta at her side. His hand was hot on her back. "Are you alright?" Concern, not disappointment.

"I'm fine, I just sat up too fast. And I don't have any condoms," she explained. She couldn't meet his eyes; it was all too embarrassing. She should have thought about it. They could have stopped on the way. It's not like she didn't know what the plan was.

"I think I have one in my wallet, but we don't have to. I mean, we can finish in other ways," he offered.

"No! I really want you to fuck me!" she responded before she could think. She slapped her hands over her mouth. "I can't believe I just said that!"

Ash just laughed, moved her hands, and kissed her. "I really want to fuck you too," he said back, playfully. He hopped up from the bed to fish his pants off the floor. Ash pulled out his wallet while she sank back into the pillows and tried to calm down.

Zeta closed her eyes, took a deep breath, and forced herself to relax. The mattress shifted under Ash's weight, his hand touched her face, and she leaned into it as his thumb traced her lips. She licked it, tasting a hint of herself still on his skin. She met his eyes, and he smiled at her, content and easy already, and she thought if she said no, if she pushed him away, he would listen. *If anything happens, it'll be OK*, she thought, and it warmed her, settled her as he settled himself over her, his cock pressing between her legs, against her cunt.

"Is it still OK?" Ash asked, tense above her, ready for it to not be, to stop.

Zeta smiled, wrapped her arms around his shoulders. "Yes."

He sighed as her body accepted his. Already soaking, her body gave no resistance as he moved into her. He sucked his breath in, and a shiver ran through his body, eyes closed. When he looked at her again, his eyes were wide and bright before he kissed her, his breaths short and gasping a moment later in her ear as he composed himself.

How cute, she thought stroking his hair again, running fingers over his shoulders, muscle flexing smoothly under his skin as he settled into her.

Ash thrust and Zeta bit her lip to keep from crying out again. His movements sent small shocks of pleasure through her. Tiny earthquakes that were slowly shaking her all apart. It was more intense than when it had been his fingers, maybe because he'd kept her on the edge so long. She didn't know, didn't care. Her body was trembling, needy under his, and he responded, hungry, relentless.

"Good," he murmured as he thrust into her. "You're so cute. Cutest girl I've ever seen. You're beautiful. God, you're beautiful."

Zeta tightened her arms around him, inviting him to come closer to her, and he shifted, bringing his mouth to hers, kissing her before she pressed her face into his neck, sucking in his night scent. She sighed into his ear, and he held her tighter, his breath coming in gasps between the wet touch of his mouth on her skin, the press of his tongue on hers.

"Are you alright? I want to . . ." His words trailed off as she kissed his face, and his hips moved faster against her. He mumbled her name between praise, but she couldn't follow the words.

The world was swallowed by the press of his heat, a flow of lava and earth, and she was gladly melting under the pressure of his body until she was nothing but a bundle of nerves and then she erupted, sending tremors and waves all through her. Ash followed her a moment later, his breaths gasps, still planted deep inside of her before stilling and breathing hard against her.

"You OK?" His voice seemed heavier as he brushed his lips over her forehead, her eyelids. "Give me just a minute."

Sleepy. She wasn't sure if she meant him or herself. Zeta's body was limp in his arms. She wanted to stay wrapped in his heat. "I usually ask for ten."

"If you insist," he hummed, shifting to break their connection and lie down next to her. "I want to talk to you about something. But in a minute."

"Alright, inna minute," Zeta said, cuddling into his chest, his arm wrapped around her, hand on her hip. A buzzing sound, so faint, she thought she dreamed it. "I think a phone's ringing."

"It's Randall," Ash said. "He can wait ten minutes."

It was late. Zeta was fading, too comfortable in his embrace. Ten minutes or more passed, she wasn't sure, half dozing. He finally moved standing.

"Shit," he said.

She opened her eyes, the sleepiness rolling off, sitting up. "What?"

Zeta was answered by only Ash's back for a long moment before he turned, a frown on his face, the used condom in his fingers. "It broke."

"Oh," she said, wide eyed and slow. It took her a moment to put the pieces together. The condom had broken, she wasn't on birth control, and she went cold. *Shit.* Deep breath, no reason to panic, there were things to be done, it wasn't like she was the only person in the world to have a slip up. She stamped down the reaction before it had a chance to begin. "OK. OK. So."

"I'm really sorry. I don't have anything, I just got tested last month for my trip. So, you don't have to worry about that. Are you on the pill or anything?"

She shook her head. "Your trip?"

"Oh. Fuck. I'm really sorry about this." His phone rang again from the floor.

"You should get that. They've called twice now, and it's very late." *His trip?*

"A moment, I have to . . ." he was looking around. Zeta handed him the tissues from her nightstand, and he pulled the failure of the condom off. His phone rang again.

"Please answer that. It's OK, I'll just get the morning-after pill tomorrow. Don't worry about it."

"Right, OK, hold on." He fished out the phone, stared at it dumbly for a minute like it was a foreign object. "Five calls," he mumbled. The ringing stopped, started again. He answered it. "Hello?"

He didn't speak more than to agree as he pulled on his pants. "I'll call you back in about five minutes. I'm on my way." He ended the call, his face cold and hard. A stranger.

"Is everything OK?" she asked slowly, knowing that it was not.

"It's fine," he said, retrieving his shirt and pulling it on. He paused as he buttoned it, looking at her. Her guts twisted. Something had changed. "I'm sorry, I have to go. I have a flight in a few hours. I was going to tell you. I have to . . ." He was mentally already gone though he was still standing there in her bedroom.

"OK. Well, this was fun," she said, taking the hint. She forced a smile to her face, wished he hadn't been so sweet. *No reason to get sad; you knew what this was. It's fine, it's fine.*

"How much is it? The pill or whatever?" he asked, still looking around on her floor for something.

"I don't know. Hold on, I'll Google it," she offered, feeling more and more surreal, out of step with everything.

"Here, let me know if you need more," he said, pulling out a couple of bills and stuffing them in her hands. "Goodbye, Zeta, I'm sorry I have to leave so suddenly. My trip," he said distractedly, turning toward the door.

"Hey Ash?" she called.

He stopped and looked back, his form taking up her bedroom door.

"Have a safe flight and enjoy the games."

He blinked, his hard mask faltering for a moment. "I will."

He looked as if he wanted to say something more, but instead he nodded and turned. She waited until she heard the door close before standing and locking up behind him. She took a shower, washing the traces of him from her skin, and then retrieved her phone from her purse. She'd forgotten it in everything.

She realized then, too late, that they'd never even exchanged numbers.

I'm safe, he left, she texted Pixie.

Are you going to see him again? Her response came quick.

No, he's going on a trip.

That's what they all say.

She chuckled before wrinkling her nose up. *No need to bring up the condom*, she thought as she made her way back to her bed. She fished the bills he had handed her out of her blanket where she'd dropped them, intending to stash them on her dresser before putting them in her wallet and paused.

What she had expected to be a few twenties turned out to be a few hundreds, all rolled up. Five of them, ten times more than she thought she needed.

She shook her head, chasing away any lingering emotions about the man. "Whatever, if he wants to waste his money, let him."

She stuffed the money in her nightstand and turned off her lamp. *Too cute for sure*, she thought, dismissing the whole encounter. She considered calling a ride and running out to the nearest all-night pharmacy but decided against it. There wouldn't be many drivers out at three in the morning, and the surcharge would probably make the ride more than the pill. Plus it was the middle of the night, and she was all alone. No, she'd wait until morning. It was only a few hours away, and it would be easier and safer all around.

"Problem for Future Zeta," she mumbled, flipping her pillows over so she wouldn't smell Ash on them. She fell asleep quickly, deeper than she had in months. She woke for a moment, thinking she heard a storm, before sinking back under.

5

There was something wrong.

Zeta couldn't quite place it. Something in the apartment had shifted. She shook off her sleep, looked around her room for something to be different, something changed, but everything was exactly as it had always been. Late morning sun filtered through the small gaps in her curtains. She threw them open, revealing the high fence that separated her little yard from the rest of the world. It wasn't much of a view, but she didn't have to keep her shades closed all the time either. Zeta lay back down in the sun, trying to force herself more awake, to figure out what was so *off*. She checked in with her body. She could definitely still feel his touch between her legs, but otherwise she was loose, fine.

"God, I wish he hadn't been so nice," she sighed. She had to pee. Had to get back to her regularly scheduled life. She sat up, stretched, committed to actually getting out of bed this time, sure that it was just lingering feelings from the night before. "Maybe

Pixie is right, maybe I do need a new boyfriend. It was nice up until the end. Ugh, I have to go out today," she mumbled to herself.

She yawned and then she knew.

A smell. Something smelled *wrong*. She sniffed the air. "Salt?" she asked the empty room. She stood up, crossed her room, and opened her door to look out into her dim hall and dark bathroom. Her foot sank into the carpet, a puddle welling around it.

She snatched it back so fast she almost lost her balance but caught the door. The smell hit her then. Salt for sure, salt water. A flood had come to her apartment, and she lived nowhere near the ocean. "What the hell?" she asked the still-dripping ceiling as she crossed the hall to the bathroom, the floor a pool. Her heart was beating faster, head swimming.

"It's OK," she said to herself. "Calm down, a broken pipe, it's fine." She used the bathroom, took the couple of seated minutes to calm herself, thanked her good fortune that the toilet paper had been spared, and three minutes later wished that good fortune hadn't been wasted on something so replaceable.

Her living room was destroyed.

Whatever had gone wrong had happened there too, and in the kitchen. Water had poured down through the cabinets onto the stove. Over her couch, her TV. She checked the blankets and found that somehow it had missed her laptop. Her pictures would need to be reprinted. Some still hung, others rested on the swamp of the floor. *It's OK, replaceable. They're backed up in the cloud, no worries.* But seeing them destroyed still stabbed at her guts. The smell was worse out here, not just salt but something dead. She swallowed bile, swayed on her feet.

You're OK, she thought, picking up the computer before the water soaked its way to it through the blankets and mattress. Her footsteps made squelching sounds on the floor as she walked back to her bedroom. She deposited her laptop on her bed to keep it safe.

She closed her eyes, took a deep breath before walking back into the hall. She turned to look into the room she was dreading the most. Zeta reminded herself that it would be fine, there was nothing that couldn't be fixed. It would be alright.

Zeta opened the door to her office and found it underwater.

The ceiling had fallen in and crashed down on her computer. Wood and plaster covered her desk. One monitor was on the floor, the other on its face still on the desk. The computer itself still stood but was directly under the hole that used to be a ceiling. All her posters, gathered from game stores throughout the years when the announcements were over, were destroyed by the water still trapped in the frames. Her bookcase full of classic games, no longer played but saved from childhood, might have been safe, but she wasn't sure. She couldn't focus on anything enough to figure it out.

Her head was pounding with her heart. She wanted to scream, she wanted to cry. Zeta did neither and instead breathed shallowly through her mouth and tried to focus. She couldn't faint. She'd drown in the inch of water that covered her carpet.

The room was wrong. There was too much glass.

And dots of color.

"Fish," she said slowly. They were dead, but they must have been the neighbor's pets. She didn't know anything about him, just that he disliked noise. The whole thing was impossibly random, and she'd laugh if the smell wasn't so awful. If she wasn't right on the edge of toppling over from the shock. She looked up at the hole. The apartment above was dark. "So where is he?" she said, backing out of the room and closing the door, hoping it was vacation and he wasn't doing a take on sleeping with the fishes.

She walked back to her bedroom, taking slow breaths, hand on the wall just in case. She slipped inside of the room and closed the door before going to her bed. Back to the wall, she kept her eyes closed and breathed.

Everything is alright. I have insurance. I need to call the landlord. That is the first step.

A plan, a course of action pulled from the chaos.

She reached for her phone.

"Hello, you've reached Blue Tree Property Management's answering service. Are you having a maintenance issue?"

"It's Sunday," Zeta groaned.

"It sure is ma'am!" the operator said brightly. "Is this an emergency or would you like to call back during business hours between eight and six on Monday?"

"No, this is absolutely an emergency. There's a leak." Her head was spinning, her heart was beating too fast, too hard. Tears were welling up in her, but she couldn't cry because then she wouldn't stop until the world stopped. She had to keep it together.

"Most leaks are non-emergencies. Can you turn the water off to the affected appliance?"

"No. It's not." Deep breath. "I'm sorry, I'm not explaining it well. Something has gone wrong upstairs, and it is flooding my apartment. Also the ceiling fell in."

"Oh my! That does sound like an emergency! Let me take down your information and get this over to maintenance to send someone out right away!"

"Thank you," Zeta said.

She was feeling better in her room, a call made. She pulled on a pair of shorts and a T-shirt. She didn't usually wear shoes in her house but also didn't want to step in the dead fish water anymore. She found a pair of thick-soled sneakers, not her favorite, but they would keep her feet dry. She called Pixie.

"Hey, why are you calling me so early," Pixie asked, groggy.

"It's almost noon and I am not having a good day," Zeta sighed.

"What's wrong?" Her voice perked up, awake now.

"I don't really know what happened, but I woke up to my apartment covered in water. Most of my stuff is completely destroyed.

"Your computer?"

"Super destroyed. The only room not under water is my bedroom." Zeta wrinkled her nose. The smell was starting to come through the door, or maybe it was on her now. She didn't know.

"Oh my god, what are you going to do? Are you OK? When did this happened?"

"I guess last night, after I want to bed. I thought I heard thunder."

"That's really scary! You could have gotten hurt."

"I don't want to think about that. I'm waiting for the landlord's people to come over and look at everything. I think I'm going to have to move."

"Is it really that bad?"

"Yeah, it's really that bad. I'm going to need some help, later. Do you think you could come by? I'll probably need to go to a hotel."

"You can stay with me," Pixie offered.

"I know, but it's going to be for a while, and you've only got the one room. Thank you though, means a lot."

"Well if you change your mind, offer stands. And I'll come over and help you."

Another call came through on the line. The landlord. "I gotta go, Pixie. I'll keep you posted."

Zeta switched over, explained again what she'd found. He promised to be out in the hour.

It took two.

He was an old Black man. Wiry, with a thick white mustache to match his curly white hair. Somewhere in his seventies, she thought. Mr. Simon had owned the building all three years that she'd lived there, but she'd only met him once. "What's the problem?" he asked, no smiles, clearly annoyed.

Behind him trailed two men, one in his forties, the other probably in his twenties at most. They all looked similar and were wearing dress pants and shirts.

"Pulled me out of church," Mr. Simon said gruffly.

Behind him the middle-aged man smiled apologetically, and Zeta shrugged.

"Well, I mean, come in," she said, stepping out the way.

Mr. Simon stepped in, and his foot sunk into the marsh of the carpet. "What the hell happened in here?"

"I honestly don't know," Zeta replied as calmly as she could. "But you should have a look for yourself."

The men went through the apartment, and she could tell when they reached the back room by the string of curse words the old man let flow. "What the hell happened in here?" he hollered down the hall.

"Again," Zeta sighed, meeting them at the door to her once office, the carnage made of her livelihood and prized collection less shocking the second time around but still an unwelcome sight, "I really don't know."

"Where's the upstairs guy?"

She shrugged. "I woke up to this."

"Bryce!" Mr. Simon called the young man forward. He took a keyring out of his pocket and handed it over to Bryce. "Go upstairs. Knock first, count to ten, and then go in."

"Yeah, but Pop-Pop, what if he's, you know?"

Suddenly Zeta didn't feel so weird for thinking it earlier.

"He's not. If he were, we'd smell him over this fish mess. What a mess."

She didn't want to know how her landlord knew that with such certainty. "Why don't we stand in the hall away from the fish smell."

"What a mess, what a mess. This was a beautiful apartment!" Mr. Simon mumbled down the hall. "Can't fix this ourselves, going to have call in. A mess."

In the little vestibule that led to her apartment and the stairs for the neighbor, the smell was less intense. Zeta stood with her arms crossed, back against the wall, ready to take whatever blow was coming. She guessed she probably looked relaxed, but she'd found that without someone to catch her, the wall would at least slow things down if it was too much. She was already teetering on too much.

"You can't stay here," Mr. Simon said, shaking his head.

It was what she was expecting. "I figured. So, can I get my deposit back?"

"Deposit? You don't have to move! We're going to fix this place up. You'll just have to stay in a hotel for a few weeks."

"Are you . . . sure?" she asked haltingly, thinking of the mess of her office. "It's kind of a big job in there."

"Look, you're a good tenant. You pay your rent on time, don't cause problems for anyone, for me. There's insurance: it'll just be a couple of weeks. You got insurance, don't you?"

"I do." She breathed a sigh of relief. She wouldn't have to move. That was something. But not everything.

"Ey, Pop-Pop, he ain't up here. But there's a lot of broken glass and everything is wet. Smells awful. Looks like the shelves holding all his fish tanks broke or something. It's really trashed up here."

"See, this is what I mean. Tens of thousands of dollars worth of damage. What a mess! Bryce, come down from there before you hurt yourself! We're going to deal with this in court. A mess! Came out of church for this." Mr. Simon seemed to have forgotten her.

"Sorry," she said slowly, unsure of what else to say.

"You'll have to find yourself a hotel or room to stay in. File a claim with your insurance about it. I'll be in touch to let you know when the workers will be out, but you should be out of here by then. Pack up whatever you want to keep."

"Knock, knock, cavalry's arrived!" Pixie sang from the open door.

"Pixie!" Zeta sighed, surprised and pleased.

"Hadn't heard from you again, came to make sure you were OK. What's that smell?"

"Dead fish." Zeta sighed. Pixie frowned, and Zeta pointed into the open door. "Go see for yourself."

"Nothing else we can do here right now," Mr. Simon said. "You should collect yourself, find somewhere to stay."

"Alright, thanks," Zeta said, seeing them off. The middle-aged man was already outside on the phone with someone, probably insurance. She'd have to call her own. She'd have to find a hotel.

She'd have to pack. She watched her landlord leave, clear at least on the next steps.

Pixie was standing in the living room looking at the mess of photos. She turned to Zeta's splashing footsteps and held open her arms. Zeta walked into the hug, let herself be held.

"This sucks," she said.

"Hey, at least you got laid last night," Pixie said brightly.

"I did, but I don't want to talk about that either," Zeta sighed. There was something tickling at the back of her memory, but she couldn't remember exactly what through all the mess and upheaval. She'd think of it once things settled down. "Come on, help me pack. I gotta find a hotel."

"What about an Airbnb? You can get one with a kitchen!" Pixie suggested, following her into her room.

"I don't know if insurance will pay for that, and I don't want to get stuck with a bill or some weird scammer. There's like, no oversite with those things, and I don't need *more* stress." No, better to stick to the paths she knew. She'd gone off book last night and gotten her feelings hurt. She didn't want to think about it. She had to focus on the problem at hand.

Pixie had already dragged out her suitcase and was folding underwear. Zeta started looking up hotels.

Ash could still smell Zeta on his skin. The light, almost candy scent of whatever she used in her hair, the sweet scent of her lotion, and under that the rich smell of her skin and body that was all her and nothing else. It clung to him, filled his nostrils every time he moved, and Ash let himself believe that Zeta was in bed with him, wrapped in his sheets. The scent was deceptive—he opened his eyes to his own empty bedroom.

His curtains were still parted, but the sun hadn't been enough to keep him awake as it poured in with an orange, late afternoon light. In front of his bed was his dresser, dark wood, clean lines, drawers closed. The top was covered with his to-be-read pile. Above it hung a black-and-white print of a seedpod photographed by Karl Blossfeldt. His bed was low, a wooden frame with a mattress on slats. Nightstands on both sides, a set to match the dresser.

He rubbed his face, swallowed the guilt of Zeta. He'd known her for a handful of hours, but she was the first thing he thought of when he woke up. But then, he reasoned, it was because he *was* guilty. She'd been amazing, and the way he'd left was not one of his proudest moments.

He had panicked. Now that he had a moment to breathe, to think, he could admit that. He hadn't wanted to tell her that it was his mother, that there was an emergency with his father. They'd just met, and then there was the issue with the condom; he didn't want to put that on her too. It would've sounded like a lie, but he had to say something, had to leave, and in all that he fumbled, grabbed the easiest excuse he could think of. That he had to leave in the morning. She must hate him.

He'd call, explain things. He reached for his phone, fully charged. No messages. *No news is good news, right?* he thought, but dread still pooled in his belly.

He cleared his throat, called his mom. She didn't answer. *Probably sleeping*, he reasoned. He felt bad about leaving her at the hospital, but she was right—he needed to rest. He had been up all night and he smelled.

He ran down a list of all the things that still needed to be done. He'd reassigned his trip already. That had been easy; Scott had handled new branches before and could be counted on to do it again. It would be efficient and unremarkable for him to do, so Ash had thought very little about the change in his plans once the first phone calls and emails were done.

He moved on to other things. Claire was coming. She needed to be picked up. His mother needed to be given relief. He needed to address the office.

His father, head of Cross Construction, had had a heart attack in the early hours of the morning, leaving the running of his company to his son, Ashford. Him. He couldn't say he wasn't prepared for it. He was always expected to take over. But this wasn't the way that he'd wanted it.

He needed to get Claire. Not much longer until she landed.

Ash hauled himself out of bed, took himself across the room to the bathroom, and turned on the shower. He looked at himself in the mirror while he undressed. He was haggard. He considered shaving and then decided not to. Tomorrow he'd put himself back together. He was allowed a day, wasn't he?

Hot water, soap, and whatever traces of the night clung to him were gone. He looked a little better but not by much.

Drop off the rental, get Claire, come back for my car, drop Claire at the hospital, take Mom home, get Mom fed, switch with Claire. He ran through his list again, memorizing the steps, making sure that nothing was left out while he threw on a pair of linen shorts and a T-shirt. Between every item the creeping thought of *Call Zeta* tried to insert itself. He hated that he'd panicked. Hated that he left it like that. He wanted to fix it, but there were other things that needed his attention more.

He walked out into his living room. The low, sleek blue couch sat in front of his TV. The coffee table had another stack of books. There were bookcases on the walls where more books shared shelf space with plants. The end tables next to the couch were covered in greenery as well, and he walked past them to the jungle of his kitchen.

It's watering day, he sighed to himself. There was no time. He'd have to see to it tomorrow or the day after. *They won't die overnight,* he thought, scanning all the plants on their shelves while he stood between his kitchen island the fridge. A sick feeling twisted in his stomach as what he had just thought dawned on him.

"Doctors said he was going to be alright," he reminded himself, turning to the fridge. He stuffed a handful of lunchmeat and cheese in his mouth before grabbing a bottled smoothie and gulping it down. Fed and clean, he was out the door and into the rental.

Within forty-five minutes, the car was returned and he was at the gate just in time to meet his sister.

"Ash!" Claire called as soon as she spotted him. She was wearing dark glasses over her eyes, but he would know her anywhere. His big sister. She had his same blonde hair but it was longer, and his features but prettier, and she was nearly as tall. "How is he?" she asked, pulling away, frowning at whatever she saw on his face.

"The bypass surgery went well. The doctor said that he would recover," Ash answered. "He was still out when I went home."

"That's good." She let out a shuddering breath, took the glasses off, and wiped at her red, puffy eyes.

"It's going to be alright, Claire. Come on, lets get out of here."

"OK, OK. I've gotta get my luggage."

"I hope you packed light," he teased.

"I did not," she said.

"How long are you planning to stay?" he asked as they walked to the carousel.

"I don't know, however long I need to. If he's alright in a few weeks then that's fine, but I can stay a couple of months."

"What about the season?"

"I'm not in any shows this year. I was taking some time off, teaching."

"I remember, sorry, wasn't thinking," he said. They caught up while he got her bags, not light as she promised. Together they walked out into the summer heat, and he went to hail a cab.

"Where's your car?" she whined.

"I had to return a rental. I was supposed to fly out this morning. Figured I could just take care of it now. Besides, your luggage wasn't going to fit in my car."

Claire grumbled like a child while Ash and the cabbie loaded the trunk and the backseat with her bags. Ash squeezed into the space that remained and was glad he washed before he set off to get her.

He dropped her off at their parents' house, promised to be back soon, and returned to his own apartment for his car. Sighing, he settled into the driver's seat of the little black BMW, put his head on the wheel, ran through the to-do list again, and there at the top was *Call her.*

Ash ignored it. Claire, hospital, his mother. He started his car, drove to the hospital, and didn't realize that he'd skipped getting his sister until he was almost in the ICU. He sent a message, apologizing.

No big deal, he's still out right? I'll go in the morning. I'll spend time with Mom tonight, she replied.

He didn't let himself dwell on it while he focused on the next steps. His mother needed a break. She needed to go home. He was supposed to drive her, but then his father would be alone. He'd get her a car. He braced himself as he opened the door, guts twisting, muscles tightening.

The lights were low, windows closed in the room where his father slept post surgery. He was hooked up to monitors and IVs and everything in Ash's body released, unspent. Nathanial Cross had always been a giant in his son's eyes, physically and emotionally. He was a big man with dark hair and eyes, gone steel gray in his later years. He was a force that his son had always been trying to live up to, but now he looked sunken and pale in the bed. It was the first time Ash had seen him since the ordeal had begun. Friday he was fine, and now he was not. Next to him was Ash's mother, Bridgette, who was model pretty with the same blonde hair as her children. Her eyes were as red as Claire's.

"Hey, Mom," he whispered. "Claire made it in. I dropped her off at the house."

Bridgette nodded, smiled. "Did you come to visit?"

He shook his head. "No, I'll stay now, you go head home. You need to rest."

"There's a chair that I can sleep in they said. I'll stay, you go. After you visit of course."

"You've been here since this morning. I'm not going to make you spend the night in a chair. Come on, you need to sleep. I've got this."

His mother looked at him for a moment and then sighed. She stood up and wrapped him in a hug that he returned awkwardly. It was unexpected. "You're a good boy," she said. She pulled away, held his arms, and looked at him, her expression serious. "Ash, I know that you and your father have had a difficult relationship, but I want you to know that he loves you. He thinks very highly of you."

"Thanks, but Mom, he's not in a coma. He'll be awake soon. It's going to be OK."

She nodded. "Of course. The doctor said it went well. Everything is fine. Well, as fine as it can be."

Ash didn't let her sit down. He knew she wouldn't get back up again, so he led her to the door as he spoke. "It's fine, Dad's going to be alright. I can drive you if you want."

"No, no, I don't want to leave him alone. What if he wakes up and no one's here?" she said. Ash didn't remind her that the doctor had said he would be out for hours yet, that there were nurses, that it would only be a short while.

Instead he said, "Alright, do you want me to call you a cab?"

"I know how to use the apps. I'm not that old," she huffed.

"Then go get some rest. I'll pull the night shift," he laughed.

She looked like she wanted to argue but finally shook her head. "Alright, then I'll leave you to it. You call if anything changes."

"I will, and I'll be here when you get back first thing in the morning. Love you, Mom."

"I love you too." And then he was alone, just him and his father.

In the silence, their last conversation came to him. There was no mental to-do list to distract him. It had been meaningless, business over dinner, even though it was his mother's birthday and could have waited until the morning. It was supposed to be relaxed, but there was always work for Nathanial Cross, so there was always work for his son.

Ash had brought his mother a small sculpture from an artist that she was fond of. She cooed and awed over it, a perfect choice of gifts. His father was less impressed with his recent judgment on partners.

The three of them were eating at the dining room table. Even on her birthday she had cooked: salmon and fresh vegetables with rice, all laid out on the table between the three of them. She sat at the head—it was her day—and Ash sat across from his father.

His mother was chatting about running into one of her friends, Ash was nodding along, and then his father spoke.

"I decided not to go with Langly and Fellows. They had an impressive portfolio, but Frontier showed more growth. It was a move toward the future."

Ash dropped his fork. They hadn't even made it through the meal; his plate was still half filled with food that he'd suddenly lost the stomach for. "Do we have to do this? We're here for Mom."

His father shook his head. Of course, he knew why Ash had chosen to partner with Langly, but it didn't matter. Ash clenched his hands at his side, feeling like a teenager caught with a bad report card. He knew why his father had overridden him; he didn't need him to tell him.

"Brian Lees is the man over there at Frontier. Good man, has a son around your age, little older I think. He went into another business. Known Brian for years, we came up together in a way. The world is a small place, I keep telling you that. Better to have loyal, solid partnerships. Create a solid foundation. That's what you still haven't learned."

"Langly was solid, if you would just—"

"They're just another company. This is a relationship. I'm not going to be around forever, and you've got to learn that—"

"Every business is a relationship," Ash growled, his father's creed ingrained in him since he was a boy. "I know. But I'm trying to build my own relationships—"

"Not with my legacy!" Nathanial bellowed, standing up from the table so violently that the chair fell. His cheeks had reddened, his eyes were stormy. "I built this! Your grandfather may have started it, but I moved it forward. Your time will come but not if you keep pushing it in the wrong directions!"

Not with his legacy, Ash thought, staring at his father. He couldn't look him in the face over dinner, just stared at his own plate like a child, and he left soon after, claiming he had an early meeting. His mother looked so sad, and Ash was so angry that his father had ruined the meal. But maybe it was him all along. Maybe.

He sat in the hospital chair his mother had vacated, put his elbows on his knees, and leaned into his hands. He didn't want to think about the scene before him, couldn't stop thinking about the last night, so he turned to the only thing left: work.

We'll need to announce this. I need to get a handle on things in the office . . . The minutia was calming. He was doing what his father would want. He needed to stay focused. But his mind strayed off course in the near silence and stillness of the ICU room, where the only thing to look at was his dad. He couldn't not feel the lump in his throat.

He took out his phone, intending to read, but his mind couldn't focus on the words. They kept swimming in front of his eyes. He closed the book, almost put his phone away. Then he saw the apps. All of the little games that he'd downloaded on the deck the night that felt like a thousand years ago but in that moment, a gift.

Cozy games, she'd called them. He opened *Eden Apartments*, and a pastel-colored diamond-shaped creature popped up on the screen.

Hello, new tenant, it read. *You're a little early, and we're not quite ready, but we could use a hand actually . . .*

He'd never been one for video games, but maybe it was the novelty of the little creature and its list of tasks and puzzles. For the first time in hours, Ash relaxed.

6

Zeta stood in the vestibule in front of her door, hand on the knob, and took a deep breath. She opened the door.

The smell of fresh paint filled her nostrils, and she breathed a sigh of relief. She'd been back a handful of times with the insurance company and again with her friends to pack up whatever she could salvage, but she hadn't seen it since they'd finished the repairs. Brand and Cody had delivered all of her new furniture and moved her boxes, the pitiful few she had, out of the storage unit while she and Pixie picked out new dishes and towels. She wheeled her suitcase inside and left it by the door with her shoes. The carpet was dry.

The landlord had done, from what she could tell, a full renovation, and she wondered if he was going to reflect that in her rent when her lease ended in a few months. She walked into her kitchen, looking over the shiny new stove and refrigerator with their black finishes. The cheap brown bargain cabinets had been replaced with a light wood that matched the new pale yellow paint job. The new set of dishes and glasses sat on the counter waiting to be put away.

Her new table was bare and she put her purse on it, but it didn't make the place look any more lived in. *This has been my apartment for years, but it feels like I've never been here before*, she thought.

Brand and Cody had also set up her TV for her. The new couch was golden mustard yellow, and she'd had them put a green area rug over the sandy-colored carpet that covered the apartment. Her wall was bare, but she'd ordered reprints of all of the photos. She'd sort them when they got there. Boxes were stacked neatly waiting for her to unpack, make her apartment hers again. She would put things back together. She knew all about putting things back together.

She could do this. She just wished she felt better.

The last few weeks in the hotel had been an awful slog. It had taken them two months to make the repairs to her unit, and the landlord had said the upstairs one wasn't ready at all. She wondered what the man who used to live there had done to it, how all those fish tanks ended up all collapsing at once, but she didn't want to get into it with the owner. She was just happy that the neighbor was gone.

She could play her new games with the volume turned up.

Zeta left her living room and went to her bedroom. She'd kept her dresser but decided on a new mattress. The other had been from when she first moved into the city before she started working, and it was time for an upgrade. "Aww, they made my bed for me! Thanks, guys!" she said to the empty room. She was grateful. Without the guys' help, she would have been stuck depending on movers and "expert installers" who she'd have to watch over, so she wouldn't have been able to make the last minute runs to replace the odds and ends she'd forgotten. **You two are the sweetest**, she texted them. Now all she had to do was actually unpack and put things away.

The bathroom had been ripped out: new tub, sink, and toilet. Plus, to her delight, a stacked washer and dryer. "No more laundromat for me! Apartment glow up," she laughed, opening and closing the unit. She'd have to add detergent to her grocery order.

The only place left to look was the worst room. Her office. Zeta took a deep breath and walked the short distance down the hall. She pushed the door open, prepared for the sobering view.

Her posters weren't there; there really was no way to get them back. But she had at least been able to replace her computer, and she sighed in relief to see it set up. She hated working from her laptop—she needed the space of a desktop, multiple monitors, options. She turned it on, it booted up, and she was met with the factory settings, demanding her personalization. The laptop had gotten the job done, and she was happy to have had it during her stay in the hotel. She'd spent it guest writing blogs for extra money while she slowly ate through her checking account balance in takeout. She could have done her regular job, but she hated working on such a small screen.

That's probably why I feel like crap, she thought. Between her renter's and her landlord's insurance, Zeta's hotel stay and all the new things in her apartment were paid for. But she still had to eat, and she didn't land a hotel with a kitchenette. Not that she cooked much at home, but by the third week she was tired of her menu selections.

Which is why she had scheduled a grocery delivery. Zeta was turning over a new leaf. She was going to cook more, be around people more. She'd become such a shut-in since the spring. Her home literally collapsing was a sign. Of what, she wasn't sure, but she'd figure it out.

"OK, detergent, before I forget." She went back to her living room, pulling up the app for the delivery, and saw her battery was low. She thought about digging the charger out of her suitcase but decided not to. It would be easier to use the extra one from the nightstand. Besides, the one she'd been using in the hotel was dying and needed to be replaced anyway. *I should have grabbed one while I was out*, she frowned. Even more reason to break out the new one.

She sat on the edge of her new bed, enjoying how it gave under her weight. She pulled open the drawer of the nightstand and was confronted with a roll of bills. "Oh," she said picking them up. "That's what I forgot."

She wasn't feeling well most of the time. Her stomach was upset. She was crabby, emotional, and—had she gotten her period while she was away? She couldn't remember. Everything was out of sorts, she was out of sorts. She had tried not to think about anything but dealing with her housing disaster during those weeks, especially not him. Her head was swimming.

"Deep breaths, calm down, this is silly. What are the chances?"

Probably about the same as a million gallons of saltwater flooding your landlocked apartment, but here I am. Zeta plugged in her phone, saw that her shopper hadn't started, and added detergent and a pregnancy test.

Her life was in boxes. She left the phone plugged in and started unpacking. She found her clothing, dug out some fresh pajamas, and changed. More comfortable, she took the phone and charger and relocated to the living room with her new couch and TV.

She picked up her new Switch and started playing *Cuphead* to distract herself from any and every thought.

Her groceries came and she brought them in, stomach already in knots. Zeta put them away, forcing herself to mindfully stock her shelves, reminding herself of her new, thoughtful lifestyle until she came across the little pack. She'd ordered the kind with the lines, but the shopper had subbed the digital type. Zeta didn't remember approving it, but she checked the messages and saw that she had. It would be simple to read at least.

She didn't let herself think about the process. The mindfulness of putting away groceries was gone, and she tried to focus on anything else at all. She scanned the directions, told herself she was being silly, that it had been too much takeout and not being in her own bed for weeks.

Zeta left the test on the bathroom sink. Set a timer on her new, shiny oven and finished putting away her groceries. The timer went off just as she closed the refrigerator.

"This whole silly thing is almost over," she hummed, returning to the bathroom and picking up the test. She'd laugh about it with Pixie. She hadn't told her about the condom, hadn't thought about it, and they hadn't talked about the man from the deck again. Ash hadn't come up since their text message exchange about him after it was over.

The world was spinning. She gripped the sink with her free hand. "I'm pregnant," she said to the stick in her hand. "Shit."

The world dipped and she dropped the stick. It clattered in her sink as she caught herself on the edge. "No, come on, pull it together. If you faint, you might hurt the baby. Let's sit down."

She slid to the floor, back against the sink cabinet. She closed her eyes and waited for everything to stop spinning. Legs crossed, hands in her lap palms up, she looked like a monk. "I'm pregnant," she repeated out loud.

What am I supposed to do? She couldn't tell the father—she had no idea where he was or even who he was. So that was out. Zeta touched her belly. What did she want? She was worried about hurting the baby if she fell, so that meant that at least part of her did want it. But could she handle it?

Zeta had lived with her traumatic brain injury for all the life that she could remember. The thing that had rewired her neurons and given her a lifelong case of vasovagal syncope defined her normal. She could faint over anything, and she'd learned to live with it. But that was her life. A baby?

She needed advice. It was too big to think about on her own.

Steady, she got up from the floor, walked back to her couch where her phone waited, and called the only person who could help her.

"Hi, baby! How's the apartment? Did they do a good job?"

"Auntie," Zeta said sucking back a sob. "I'm pregnant!" And then she did start crying because she didn't know what else to do.

"Well calm down, no reason to cry. Women get pregnant some-times. I didn't know you were dating anyone," Aunt Josie soothed.

"I'm not! There was this guy at Cody's witch festival party, back in August? Right before my apartment got ruined, and that's why I forgot. The condom broke and I was supposed to get Plan B and he got a phone call and suddenly he was going on a trip and ran off! And then my apartment flooded and now I'm pregnant!" As everything came out in one big rush, her tears dried up as quickly as they came on. "What am I supposed to do?"

"What do you want to do, baby?"

Zeta lay down on her couch, stared at the paused TV screen. "I don't know. I want to eat something that doesn't make my tummy hurt and sleep in my own bed."

"Then do that. Try some yogurt and fruit. Chicken. You're going to be OK. You don't have to decide anything right this minute. It's OK to sleep on it if you need to."

"Auntie, please. I am disabled. I cannot have a baby."

"Says who? That's eugenics talk, and you know we don't stand for that in my household." Aunt Josie was many things, a womanist was one of them. "What have I always told you since you came to live with me?"

"That I can do anything I want; I just need to do it my way."

"That's right, baby girl. So decide what you want to do. But right now you probably need to eat. Do you want me to come up?"

"No, you don't have to. I'm OK, I just need to think about all of this."

"Well, I will whenever you need. Don't stress yourself. It's just a baby. It's not even properly that. It's a fetus, and it's up to you to decide what you want to do. But my dear, if you want this, don't be afraid of it."

"Yeah, I know, thank you," she rubbed her stomach. "But this is insane! What if the baby cries and I freak out and faint? What if I'm sleep deprived and cut my hand making breakfast and hit the floor? What if I'm holding the baby when that happens?"

"You've heard babies cry and never once had an episode. Stop making up problems for yourself. Use some of that fancy computer

money you've been saving from living in that raggedy apartment
to hire a night nurse. This isn't like you at all! Where's little Miss
I'll-Figure-It-Out?"

"My apartment isn't raggedy." The accusation pulled a smile
out of her though. Aunt Josie hated the little duplex, wanted Zeta
to rent something downtown with a doorman. But not being rent
burdened gave Zeta room to relax. "It's actually really nice now. I'll
send you some pictures. You said fruit would be OK?"

"Fruit, yogurt, chicken. Eat some crackers and try not to let
yourself get too hungry. You get into those games of yours and
completely forget to feed yourself. You let me know what you're
doing."

"I will. Thank you for not being, I don't know, mean about it."

"Mean? Have I ever? What were you expecting? Me to yell at
you? For what? Fucking?"

"Auntie!" she gasped, all giggles.

"I may be your auntie, but you are grown woman who lives her
own life that I assume at this point includes entertaining lovers.
You didn't sneak that boy in through *my* window, so it's really no
concern *of* mine. All I care about is that my little girl is happy."

"I love you, Auntie."

"I love you, too. Go get something to eat. Call me when you
know what you're doing."

"I will. I'll call you in a few days." Zeta sighed as the call ended,
feeling better but still completely unsure of what she was going to
do.

Food, she thought. She went to the kitchen. She hadn't ordered
much fruit, but she had some apples, so she cut them up and ate
them with peanut butter like a child. Her stomach thanked her,
and she sighed in relief.

It was far too early to sleep, so she sat back down and unpaused
her game. There was time to figure it out. Later. But sitting back
in her own home, she was pretty sure she knew the answer. Zeta
had put together the life she had now. She could adjust, make the

changes she needed to. She put the controller down, lay back on the couch, and raised her phone to her face. A peace sign and click.

She edited the photo name to "two months pregnant." Zeta added *Find a doctor* to her mental to-do list.

The call to Pixie could wait. Zeta would let everyone know about it later. For now she needed to sit with it, get used to the concept. *I'm going to have a baby*, she thought, testing how it felt to think it. The idea was fine; it sat in her mind as a vague but not unpleasant thing. She'd never thought it would happen. She had tried to be careful.

But then, she hadn't been *that* night—she'd gone home with a stranger unprepared, trusting his condom and his smile. For the second time in weeks, she let herself think about Ash. Not the Ash that rushed out of her room but the sweet man who shared her bed before that, the man from the deck. "I thought we could have had something," she said to her ceiling. "Well, I guess we do. I think I need to admit I have bad luck with men."

Zeta had only had a handful of relationships. She was careful, felt the edges of people before letting them in. That's why the night with Ash had been such an exception. Zeta really did not do things like bring men home. It was too risky. *But then again, I knew Ian for a while before we got serious, and look how that turned out*, she thought. *Maybe I am just a pushover.* Ian took every inch he could. She thought it was endearing at first, how he touched on every part of her life. She thought it was care.

There was nothing wrong, not really. They played games together, had things in common. He had his work, she had hers. It was alright, but it was just that. Brand asked her if she was happy. Pixie said she wasn't sure about him. Cody offered to write the "Dear John" letter himself.

"You're not into him," they told her over drinks, and they were right. But he was *safe*. Maybe there was no passion, but it was familiar and easy so she stayed. It was never like Ash, on the deck with all those sparks and butterflies. But that just went bad differently.

But Ian stayed and he was. . . fine. Alright. And because he was alright, she went along with it, let him control the relationship at his whims, pushed against her own comforts to meet his. They went out when she wanted to stay home. Stayed home when she wanted to go out. Worked when she wanted a break because they needed her to. Spent money on vacations she didn't care for. It was alright. She didn't care about the money or the work. It wasn't until she realized what she wanted never seemed to be what he wanted—and they always did what he wanted—that she accepted what everyone had already told her. That the relationship was all wrong.

That it was bad.

She moved out of their shared apartment with five months left on the lease. She emptied out her savings after the moving expenses, her new rent, and paying out those last months. The whole thing had been exhausting but worth it. Now she could breathe. She had only just started to feel better about everything, three years later, and now, well now there was Ash. And that was different too because it wasn't really Ash.

There was a baby.

The one time she decided to be carefree, have fun, she'd gotten pregnant. What luck.

Zeta tried to think of a way to find him, to see if anyone knew him. Maybe she knew someone who knew someone. But she didn't think they were from the same circles. He didn't even tell her his last name. All she had was his picture, and that wouldn't do her any good if no one recognized him.

"Maybe though," she said slowly, "maybe I shouldn't." He'd left. Couldn't run out of her apartment fast enough. Maybe it was a girlfriend calling to find out where he was. Maybe "business trip" was really "I'm about to get caught."

Maybe she should leave well enough alone. Take it as a blessing and not think of it at all.

Pulling herself up, she turned off the game and padded back through her apartment. *It is going to be alright*, she reminded herself, soothing herself. But there were things that had to be done. A tiny list—problems for now versus problems for Future Zeta—started forming in her mind. Doctor would wait until Monday. It was Friday afternoon; she couldn't start making phone calls now. Things she could do now: The brand new computer that needed set up before she could start searching for a new gig. The insurance money and all the funds she'd squirreled away from previous "fancy computer" jobs wouldn't last forever. And she was sure babies needed things.

Life was running smoothly for Ash except for two things.

One, his father would not stop checking in on him. The man was home and doing well, all things considered. And he was very, very annoying.

"Yes, Dad, everything is fine here. Yes, I have heard about the issues with the leave program from HR. How did you hear about them? Well, you're not supposed to be reading emails, but I will see to that first thing Monday morning. No, Dad, people deserve their weekends. Dad, please, you're going to upset Mom."

Ash cut off every sentence trying get his father off the phone. He was a man who was never satisfied, and his nervousness about leaving his company in the hands of a son he'd never quite trusted to be capable didn't help.

He heard his mother in the background. "Is that Ash? Please let him work, darling."

"I have to get back to things here. I'll speak to you again soon, Dad. Goodbye." He hung up the phone before the man could reply, find another thing to pester him about. Ash leaned his head into his folded arms and took a deep breath, forcing himself to relax now that the call was finally over.

He'd stepped into his father's role as if it were made for him and, truthfully, it was. Taking over the company had always been what he was supposed to do. And even though this father was out of the hospital and recovered at home, he wouldn't be coming back, and Ash didn't know how he felt about that.

He thought he would have the Scotland trip to finally prove himself to his father, and then the old man would hand things over to him. That there would be some sort of triumph in finally taking his seat. But there was nothing. He'd stepped in during his father's medical emergency, and now he was just *here*. Ash didn't feel anything about it other than obligated and guilty for not being more excited.

It didn't help that Nathanial Cross did not want to give his company over. Even after the heart attack and the surgery he still wanted to be in charge. If it were up to Ash, he'd just let his father take it back, but it wasn't. So instead he came in every day and sat in the chair that his father left behind, and they both acted like it was a temporary situation.

It wasn't. His father's heart was bad, and it was time for him to retire. And Ash didn't know what to do with that either because it meant his father was old and unwell and although he wouldn't say they were close, his feelings were a complex mix of love and guilt that he couldn't untangle. So, he worked instead.

Worked and thought about his second issue: Zeta.

He hadn't called. He meant to; he wanted to. All of those mobile games had given him something to do while he was sitting in the hospital and later when his father was in the rehabilitation center to recover before returning home. He got hours and hours of distraction, but then, when his father was on the mend, there was time to think about how he had gotten those games to begin with.

Zeta.

He'd successfully pushed her out of his mind for the first two weeks when everything was chaos and uncertainty. And then life calmed down, and she started to enter his thoughts. Slowly at first—just her smile, the way her eyes crinkled up when she laughed—but then there was more. The feel of her touch on his arm. The way she smelled. He dreamed of that scent, like jasmine tea but not. Woke up still smelling her like she'd just left his bed.

The way she kissed him, the careful, eagerness of it that matched the measured way she moved. He imagined kissing her again, holding her, never letting her go. It had been months, but his desire for her only increased, like he was possessed. And still, he didn't call. Couldn't quite bring himself to after what he'd done. He never knew what he should say, and every day that passed made it worse.

But he couldn't stop thinking about her. Two months was a long time. Even it was just to apologize, to explain.

He called his sister.

"Hey! What's up?" Claire was still staying with their parents.

"Don't ask any questions. Just answer me. If you were really rude to someone for a good reason and you want them to give you a second chance, what do you say?"

"I don't know? I'm sorry I was awful, let me explain and make it up to you?"

It didn't seem like enough. "Are you sure?"

"Yeah, what else can you say? What did you do?"

"Don't worry about it. I'll talk to you later." He hung up, no more questions.

With a deep breath, he pulled up his contacts, rewriting Claire's lines in his head to make them seem more personal, more apologetic, and then stopped.

There was nothing there. Ash did not have her number. Or her email or anything about her at all in his phone. Just the games she'd downloaded, the only proof that he'd met her at all. "This can't be right," he mumbled. He scrolled through every contact and didn't find her.

He thought back to that night, ran through their conversations, their lovemaking, all the way to the bitter end, and realized that he had *meant* to ask for her number before he left but had never actually gotten the chance to. And she'd taken him home but never given him her phone number or social or something.

She put her her address into my GPS! But then the excitement died. It was in the GPS of the rental. *There has to be . . .* he thought frowning at his desk. "She took pictures, she must post them somewhere. How many Zetas can there be in this city?"

More than he thought, it turned out. The next hour and a half was filled with searching social media pages, and not a single one turned out to be without a doubt her. She either didn't have an online presence or was so locked down she was impossible to find. The only one he thought was close had a cartoon picture of a grinning girl with a pair of headphones on, hands posed in two *V*s. The profile name was Zeta Graydaze, but that was all there was, besides the month and day of her birthday, December 7. But he didn't know what Zeta's birthday was, so that was no help. Ash frowned at it, unsure if it would be better to accept defeat or send a message.

Wouldn't that make me look like a stalker? But maybe if I said I was just checking to make sure she was alright? Would she even believe that? Would she even answer? What if she doesn't?

At a knock on his door his personal assistant, Ben, came in fiddling nervously with his brown hair, his normally olive complexion looking a bit pale. He stopped in front of Ash's desk. "Sorry to bring this in last minute, but I only just got it. It's about the leave system."

"This again? What's the problem?" Ash sighed and reached out his hand for the folder. He hadn't gotten into the gritty details of what was happening in that department. It had been on his father's to-do pile, but up until his hospitalization, it had been a very low priority. Since he'd been able to make his daily check-in calls, it was all he appeared to care about.

"Well, it doesn't really work. HR has been burning up a ton of overtime hours to catch up on the leave paperwork manually because the software just can't handle it."

He knew that part. It was the story he had used when Zeta asked him why he had to go to work on Sunday. The knife of guilt slid in deeper. "Yeah," he confirmed, and then looked at the paperwork in the folder. A budget request. "This is from IT."

"They want to hire some freelancers to fix what's wrong with the software. From what I understand, it was custom built, but the company Mr. Cross hired went out of business during the dot-com crash."

"Ben, that was twenty years ago, at least."

"Yeah, this thing is older than I am. It's backed up on a floppy disc. You see the problem then. When do you want to meet about this? You've got some free time on Thursday."

Ash didn't read all the paperwork, just scanned it quickly and signed off. They would make up what they spent on fixing it. It shouldn't have been allowed to go on that long in the first place, but it didn't surprise him either. It wasn't part of the business that made any money, and his father was not overly concerned with human resources.

Maybe the heart attack had changed him. *Well, at least tomorrow I can tell him it's finally getting taken care of.* "We don't need to meet about it, it's fine." He handed the paperwork back to Ben to file. "Have a good weekend," he said, dismissing him.

It was no use waiting.

Hey! I don't know if you remember me but we met at Tiki Max back in August. I'm sorry I had to leave in such a rush. We didn't get a chance to exchange numbers and I wanted to make sure you were alright. Is there any chance we can talk? I'd like to explain things better and make up for how I left. Here's my number.

He finished the letter with his direct cell and hit send. That was it; that was all he could do.

7

The job from *Cross Construction* had seemed like a godsend at the time, but now, two weeks later, barely 10:00 AM and reeling with morning sickness, Zeta wished she had given it a pass. Her phone was blinking madly at her, and she knew without looking where all the messages would be from.

It had seemed perfect when it landed in Zeta's email a handful of days after she'd found out she really needed a job. A sign. She had come recommended to them. The pay was good and they agreed to her three very simple rules.

One, remote work only. She wasn't going to any offices.

Two, no video calls. Phone calls were a last resort. Communication should be through email and chat only.

Three, she set her own hours on a day-to-day basis.

They had agreed and outlined the project: an internal leave system where employees could put in their time and HR could approve or deny it. They put her in charge. And then the messages from the *boss* boss started.

Mr. A. M. Cross, Director of Operations, was a major pain in Zeta's ass and had been for the last two weeks. She imagined, after a few interactions with him, that he was a late middle-aged man, a boomer with too high of a position and too little to do with his days. She was surprised she had to deal with him at all to be honest. She'd been interviewed and hired by the IT department. She had assumed that they would be her contact going forward.

Zeta had been wrong.

She pulled herself up in bed, swung her legs over the side, and rubbed her face. She felt awful. Nauseous and tired. She pulled her phone from the nightstand, opened the chat app, and typed back without looking, **I thought I made it clear I wasn't in until 11 today, Mr. Cross.**

Then she scrolled up. Demands for an update from the work the team had done, which she was set to review today, and an outline for the work going forward. Noise, noise, noise. She sighed, rubbed her face, and reminded herself that babies had needs and she needed money to take care of them.

I'm going on vacation after this job. Two whole weeks and then nothing but easy gigs after. Small companies. Going to set up online shops for old ladies' boutiques until a year after the baby is born.

Zeta cupped her hand over her still much-the-same belly. The only bump was the pouch she'd had before. She had told her friends about the pregnancy a week after she found out, when she felt confident in her own choices. Pixie had held her hand at her appointment when they'd gotten their first looks at the baby. She had gone to the ob-gyn and been declared healthy. Everything was fine, fit as a fiddle. Sick was normal. Her phone chimed, and she put it down without looking. It was not eleven yet.

Instead she stood, went to the bathroom, and started her day. She tried to get some food down before dressing, but it came up a few moments later, as usual. She didn't even pause, just pulled on her leggings and a baggy T-shirt adorned with a faded image of

Sonic the Hedgehog. She made a cup of tea and was at her desk a few minutes past the hour.

Sipping slowly, she opened the chat program on her computer and confronted the digital "face" of her boss. She had some sense that this project was important to him, more so than to the company at large for some reason, and she didn't care.

It is now past 11 Mr. Rogers, do you have any answers for me?

Zeta wondered if Mr. Cross thought he was being polite or reasonable. She also knew it didn't matter. He signed the big checks.

I will in about an hour or so. The last of the reports came in at close and need to be reviewed.

I assumed you would work late to make up for your late arrival today. Curt response.

A wizard is never late or early. Annoyed, physically worn down, she let the mask slip. Unprofessional.

You're very good but you are not Gandalf. Please have my reports by one, he answered, somehow, blessedly, satisfied.

"That was almost a compliment." She fought the urge to reply with *nerd* and won. Despite getting the reference, she didn't think the Tyrant would laugh at the jab. She sipped at the tea. Ginger and lemon to settle her stomach. It wasn't working, but she liked to pretend she was doing *something*.

Another message in the chat program. Ben. **My apologies, I did inform him of your schedule for the day. Please send me an update as soon as you get a free moment.**

Zeta made a mental note to respond when she was finished. More minutes passed as she finished the report, and then she sent it to Mr. Cross with a half hour to spare. Her tea was finished, her stomach settled. She responded to a handful of chats and emails from the team, including Ben's. Got to work.

The loud growl coupled with the sick feeling in her belly let her know she had forgotten Aunt Josie's advice: don't let herself get hungry. Zeta was very hungry and, now, also very sick. She glanced at her clock. Nearly five and she hadn't eaten more than a few snacks she kept around her desk. She took a deep breath, swallowed some water, and found some crackers to munch on. They went down easy and sat well for her. Mr. Cross sent another message.

"Fuck," she mumbled opening it.

I'd like to touch base with you about your latest report. Can we schedule a meeting for later?

She looked at the clock again. It had only been two weeks, but so far, he'd tried weekly. **No**, she responded. **Need I remind you per my contract, I do not take meetings. Please email your concerns and I will look over them this evening.** She frowned at the clock. She had started late: it only made sense to end late. **My response will be in your inbox in the morning.**

"Babies need things," she reminded herself, singsong, resting her hand on her belly again as she dragged herself to her kitchen to dig up some leftovers to eat while she looked over the Tyrant's email.

Ash sighed and settled into his chair at his kitchen island with his Chinese takeout plated in front of him, steaming and fragrant. He'd left the office, made it home, lost his jacket and tie, and planned to eat while he finished his book. His face was in his phone though.

The annoyance from his day had followed him home.

His fingers traversed the map; he tapped on eggs and chests and tried not to be so annoyed. His father had called, early, 10:00 AM, requesting updates because someone, he still couldn't figure out who, had told the man that there would be an update. He'd call again first thing in the morning, again, tomorrow.

Zeta hadn't responded. Hadn't even looked at the message. He opened a chest. Forced himself to think about something else.

The project was going smoothly. The programmer, Gary, was doing a wonderful job. He was quick, responsive, and, even with his peculiar demands about communication, seemed more or less accommodating. Ash's bad mood had nothing to do with him.

But he still wanted that response. So that in the morning he could tell his father and wouldn't have to listen to his . . . scolding.

He was far too old for his father to treat him the way he did, but Ash knew that it was his father's own fears that he was letting out. His father meant what he was saying, but he also, in another way, did not. Ash was doing the job that his father had been so worried about him taking over, and he was doing it well. Everything was steady. There was nothing to complain about.

Except the leave program. The overtime that was still piling up. The inefficient process of it all. Ash was fixing it, but it wasn't *fixed*. And that wasn't even the only thing that needed to be handled. The new branch needed to be checked on, and his own previous position needed to be filled. He couldn't keep doing both jobs. Even with the duties moved around, something had to give.

Ash was exhusted.

Gary had said the response would be in overnight, and Ash trusted he would make his deadline. His father would be asleep soon. So there was no need to stare at his phone.

Except. Zeta hadn't seen the messages.

It had been weeks. He thought of sending another.

Thought about hiring someone to break into her account. To find her.

Thought he was going crazy.

"You need to forget her," Randall said when they'd met up for dinner the week before, after Ash had admitted that he couldn't stop thinking about her.

"What?"

"It's guilt. You just feel bad, but you can't fix it. Just forget about it. You probably don't even really like her, you just feel bad."

"I mean, I do feel bad, but I do like her. She was . . ." he let it drop. He couldn't explain the easy, soft feeling that filled his chest and belly when they were talking. The way his heart felt when they touched.

But Zeta was gone. He'd missed his chance. Ruined it.

"Fuck," he said, putting down the phone, closing the app. "I should delete those games. They're just a reminder." His finger hovered over *Pretty Pretty Dragon Ranch*, but he stopped. He couldn't do it.

Ash put down his phone, picked up his fork, and started to work his way through his dinner. He ran through this day. He focused on all the things that were left undone, started planning. Tried not to think about the unread message.

8

The craft party was fun even if Zeta felt tired and unwell the entire time. Nothing was wrong; it was just an ambient offness in her that she swore could be fixed with a nap. But she'd taken a nap already, and it was time to be social. She swallowed down her discomfort. First trimester pregnancy was harder than she thought it would be, but she was making it through. She'd even put on a cute outfit—a pair of mustard-yellow wide-leg pants in a soft fabric, a form-fitting purple tank, and a long-sleeve crop sweater with colorful coin boxes all over it. She was starting to show, but it was still cute. She snapped a photo of Cody gluing cut-up magazines to his collage, bits of pages stuck to his big fingers. One for the wall.

She almost hadn't come, but it was her birthday party after all. "Let's go do something fun and easy" had seemed like a good idea two weeks before. Now she wished she'd opted for a movie night instead. She was tired of sitting in the house though.

Her only real outings had been to see her doctor twice. They said she was doing well, that everything looked good. Zeta was healthy, and the baby seemed happy where it was at. If only it would let her eat. She couldn't even properly enjoy her aunt's cooking over Thanksgiving after traveling the three hours to see her.

"Why is this so difficult? I swear this was easier. Is it my brain? It's glitter!" Brand complained in his attempts to create a glitter glue design on a Christmas card.

"I don't think you're using enough glue. You gotta lean into it." Zeta laughed.

"Don't lean in as much as me," Cody cautioned, pulling glue-damp magazine scraps from his fingers.

"I don't know what you're talking about. Seems pretty easy to me," Pixie said, holding up a picture-perfect card with HAPPY BIRTHDAY ZETA across the front in black and gold glitter.

"Oh man, I should have made a birthday card too! Shit!" Brand complained. "I saw crafts and I just thought 'make something for Mom.'"

"What are you doing anyway, Cody?" Pixie asked.

"Trying to make something funny to hang up in the bathroom." He turned his work to show it off. It was all body builders and letters cut from a magazine that spelled out, LOOKING GOOD, HOT PANTS! on a piece of construction paper.

"I'd laugh," Zeta confirmed.

Cody held up his sticky hand for a high-five, and she obliged.

"You still going to that meeting tomorrow?" Pixie asked, putting the finishing touches on her card.

Zeta was working on a Popsicle-stick picture frame with pipe cleaner accents. "Yeah, I think it might be a good idea. I think they might be offering me a job. Like a permanent one, with benefits and all."

"Boo, I was hoping you were going to take some vacation. I got promo tickets to go to this ski lodge and didn't want to hang out alone."

"Hmm, ski adventure, good wholesome '80s fun!" Zeta chuckled.

"Well I was thinking more hot cocoa and cute outfits. Girl's trip!"

"Maybe. I'll see what they want first."

The gig wasn't over. There was still an immense amount of work to do, and they'd only just started on it. The contract was for six months, and the program really needed to be rebuilt from the ground up. An entire international company's HR department's functionality was hanging by an unraveling thread. Their target due date for the first receivables was the end of the year, and although the small freelance team hadn't quite solved all the issues, it looked like they would be able to make it. Even though it was a grueling process of many late nights and weekends trying to piece together workable parts from a relic of a system. Her best guess was that Cross was now looking to hire someone full-time to maintain the damn thing until they could build or buy something better.

There were so many reasons she didn't want that kind of position, but she had to think about the bigger picture. It wasn't just her. A steady job with a new baby? It was worth looking into.

Working for the Tyrant wasn't even so bad anymore. She'd figured out his MO. He wasn't displeased with the work, he was just an asshole.

And if the benefit package was good enough and they let her keep working from home, well, an asshole boss wasn't the worst thing. At least while the baby was still small, the stability could be good. One less thing to worry about, she reasoned.

The Tyrant had been requesting a meeting weekly, but this one was different. It wasn't him.

It had come from the CEO, Nathanial Cross's office. Which explained the Tyrant.

He must be his brother or cousin or something, she thought after looking him up and finding a picture of an intense older (not unattractive) man with gray eyes and hair. He reminded her of someone, but she couldn't place it. She tried to find a picture of A. M. Cross, but there was nothing on their website other than a short bio about where he went to school and his contributions to the company. The name made it pretty clear they were related though; it was too much of a coincidence. That was not her problem though.

"Zeta?" Brand called, and she snapped back to attention.

"Sorry, my mind was wandering. What were you saying?"

"You OK?" he asked.

"I'm just tired. I don't want to work. What should I put in my frame?" She held up the Popsicle-stick creation. The first one that came to mind was the surprise image that had come with her order of prints the week before. She'd just uploaded the camera roll from her phone and her favorites from the cloud to replace what was lost. And there, mingled with her new apartment and progress selfies and takeout parties was Ash. Smiling into the camera.

It was a shock seeing the picture. Just as he was that night, just as he existed in the memories she tried not to think of but couldn't help, the version of him that had been so sweet and good. The man who she wondered what life would be like with now. But that man was gone. Maybe not even real to begin with.

She couldn't stop wondering now that she'd seen him again.

Maybe she'd been right all along that he just wanted to fuck her and leave. That is what happened after all.

Zeta thought about trashing the picture, but she couldn't bring herself to do it. It was the only one she had, and maybe the baby would want it someday, she tried to tell herself. She put it in her nightstand, tucked next to his money that she didn't know what to do with.

"Duh, your first baby pictures!" Brand laughed.

"Shit, that's a great idea. I should have thought of that," Zeta hmphed, but she smiled. Of course that was a good idea. Better than her trying to make an excuse to treat his picture as something more than it was. A memory. One that was better left forgotten.

"It's OK, mommy brain is real," Cody said, frowning at the dried glue now flaking off his hands. "I hate this; let's never do this again."

Zeta chuckled. "No, it was fun. I had a good time. Thanks for coming out with me tonight."

"It's your thirtieth birthday! We had to do *something*," Cody said. "But I wish we had gone with the escape room."

"After the holidays, I promise we'll go do puzzles with you," Zeta said sweetly.

"Pinky swear," he said, holding up his finger.

Zeta wrapped her own around it. "I'll be done with this job by the spring, so I'll have lots of time. You know, before the baby."

"You're not going to work?"

"I'm not doing anything like this. I'm too tired. It's back to blog posts and setting up family websites and shop pages. At least for a little while. We'll see how I feel. I thought it would be a good idea, with the baby, when I said yes, but the more I think about it the less appealing it all is."

"So, you're *not* taking the meeting?" Brand said slowly.

"No! I am, I gotta see what they want. It's not good to burn bridges. Who knows how I'll feel a year from now. You never know what can happen, so it's better just to go, politely turn it down. Is there going to be cake at this party or just the crafts?"

"There's cake!" Pixie announced. She waved to one of the craft studio attendants and gave them a thumbs up.

"I've gotta wash my hands. I can't eat like this," Cody complained, heading toward the restroom.

The attendant brought over a white box, and Brand cleared off a spot on the table.

"You know, there's a lot of glitter around to be having food here," Zeta hummed.

"Live dangerously, sparkle on the inside," Pixie laughed, and she moved to open the box.

"Hold on! We've gotta wait for Cody!" Zeta exclaimed.

He returned a moment later, and finally Pixie opened the box with a flourish, revealing a half dozen orange-cream cupcakes. Zeta's favorite. "There's two extra for you to take home."

"They look so good!" Zeta said.

"Wait, wait, wait, we got you a gift too!" Brand said. "We all chipped in. And this was not easy to find."

Cody reached under the table and then passed a gift-wrapped box to her. It was square, light. She opened it slowly, and her heart pounded as the first corner released. There was a lump in her throat when she pulled the wrapping completely away. "You got me another copy of *Time of Calypso!*"

"Figured you could start your collection over again. We know how much that game means to you," Pixie explained.

Zeta felt like crying, and then she was. "Hormones! Gah! Thank you!"

Later, when Brand dropped her off at her apartment, she put her ultrasound photo in the little frame she'd made and put both the game and picture on the shelf by her work desk before turning in for the night.

Ash frowned at the selection of jewelry the shopkeeper had pulled out to show him. "I don't think any of these are really what I'm looking for. They're too flashy, and she's more conservative," he explained.

The young woman nodded, smiled, and said, "Let me see what else we have!" She whisked the tray away, placed it back in the display case, and went on the hunt for a piece that would satisfy Ash.

Are you coming? It's not MY mother, Ash texted Randall, who replied that he was stuck in traffic. He'd asked Ash to help him pick out a gift for his own mother because Ash was "so good at that sort of thing." Apparently last year's Christmas present was not a hit with his mom, and he was losing a silent battle with his brother over who was the best son. While he waited for the girl to come back with another tray of options, he switched over to his social media account to check the messages. His attempt to get Zeta Graydaze to reach out was still unread. Two months and not a peep. He looked at the counter again, wondering what Zeta would like from it. He'd buy them all if it meant he could see her again.

A silver bracelet with an alternating pattern of stars and moons. *Maybe that*, he thought, before looking away.

The year was ending. He would have to move on from it soon, have to accept that she was gone and he'd ruined it for himself. At the time it seemed so reasonable. It wasn't what he had wanted to do, but it seemed like the best option of the not-great ones he had available. But with time and space he wished he had made any other choice.

He sighed, switched over to *Pretty Pretty Dragon Ranch*, and tapped his screen idly to set off tasks.

"Ash, is that you?" a woman's voice asked from his side.

"Hmm?" He looked up and found a smiling woman with dark hair. Very pretty, a soft smile on her face prompting a flicker of recognition in him but not enough to pull a name. Just that he'd met her somewhere. He quickly ran through possibilities: Was it work? Was it social? Did they live in the same building? He smiled to be polite, started to open his mouth and apologize because he couldn't place her.

"Regina," she laughed. "You probably don't recall, it was so quick! Randall said something came up and you had to leave suddenly. I hope everything was OK!" She smiled warmly. She seemed so different from his hazy memory of her. Her face was clear, paler; it was winter now. Her hair was pulled into high ponytail, a light blue peacoat buttoned to her throat.

"No, my father had a medical emergency," he stumbled to say something, to explain because he felt like he needed to explain and he couldn't say *I ditched you for another woman.*

"Oh no! Is he OK? I had no idea!" she gasped, lifting her gloved fingers to her mouth.

"It's alright, he's doing much better now." *Randall. This must be him.* Ash swallowed his anger. It wasn't the woman's fault. She had no idea. His phone vibrated in his hand. *It's him—"Something's come up"—I'm going to kill him.*

Traffic's terrible, I parked in that garage on 8th and I'll take the train. Pick whatever, I'll meet you at Jimmy's.

The bar down the street. Of course.

The salesperson came back with another tray filled with more suitable ideas. "Sorry for the wait! These are more conservative, but they have a little extra something," she explained, setting the tray down.

Ash glanced at the new options, settled on a pair of gold earrings.

"Oh, who are those for?" Regina asked brightly, leaning toward the counter.

"Randall's mother," Ash answered.

"That's so sweet! You must be really close. He speaks so highly of you. Actually that's why I'm here! He recommended this shop to fix some old jewelry I inherited," she explained.

"Can I help you?" a second salesperson asked. An older man with snow white hair.

"Oh yeah! I'm here to pick up some jewelry I had repaired. Regina Stocks, let me get my receipt," she said turning away from Ash to dig in her purse.

"Anything else?" the woman who was helping him asked, pulling his attention back.

Ash scanned the counter in front of him, thinking of his own mother and sister whom he still needed gifts for. Not to mention his father. He had to make time to do his own holiday shopping.

"Need help?" Regina asked, poking her head into his line of vision, her gaze on the same counter.

"No, thank you. I was just doing a friend a favor," he answered.

"I see," she said, eyes flicking back to him.

"I'm sorry, I really have to go," he said. Randall had probably planned for them to meet, to chat, and then to go to the bar, a second chance after the first failed attempt. He didn't give up easily.

"Of course, you must be busy. Let's meet up some other time. Maybe go for drinks," she said, voice brimming with hope. "Let me give you my number."

She was pretty; she seemed nice. There was nothing wrong with her, could be so many things right with her. He should say *Sounds great, maybe next weekend.* "I'm sorry," he said instead. "It's not a good time." He didn't want her. He wanted someone he couldn't find.

"How thoughtless of me! Because of your dad," she said, voice full of care.

He smiled, passed on confirming, let her believe what she wanted. "Thanks for understanding. It was nice seeing you again. Happy holidays!"

"You too!" she said, voice gentle. Accepting, no hard feelings.

"Ma'am?" the older man called, a tray in his hand with a bracelet, ring, and necklace, a matching set in gold inlaid with bright blue gemstones.

Regina turned to the tray, gasped in delight, and Ash slipped away to the register while she started to look over the pieces. His salesperson rung him up; he paid for the earrings, gathered the gift, and headed to the bar.

Jimmy's was a comfortable old-style bar with booths and high stools, a couple of pool tables, and few patrons on Sunday night. Ash ordered a bourbon on the rocks, had it served to him at the booth where he sipped at it while he sorted through his accumulated junk mail and waited for his friend, who he was sure wasn't coming.

"Hey, man, sorry I'm late. What'd you get her?" Randall said, sliding into the booth as Ash finished his drink.

"Earrings." He pushed the bag over to his friend.

"Great, I'll send the money for them over when I get home. Do you want to get something to eat?" he asked, waving over the server, a young man with silver hair, who sauntered over to the table.

"Our friendship is over if you ever ambush me like that again."

"What can I get you?" the server asked.

Randall furrowed his brows. "What are you talking about? Yeah, two orders of wings, french fries, another bourbon for him, Coke for me."

"Regina," Ash supplied.

Randall looked at him strangely. "I didn't do anything."

"She was at the jeweler's."

Randall's frown slowly changed to a grin, then a laugh. "Oh shit! I told her about that place a while back. She had some antique pieces that needed fixing up. Guess she finally got around to them. What a coincidence. I swear I didn't have anything to do with it."

"Here's your drinks, hon," the server said, depositing the bourbon and soda, taking Ash's empty glass. "Your food will be out soon."

"Maybe it's fate, your second chance," Randall laughed.

"I don't have time for this. I need to concentrate on the job. We need to promote someone to take over my position, and I need to—" He stopped, couldn't say it. "Anyway, I'm busy."

"Yeah, well, maybe after the holidays," Randall shrugged.

"Maybe," Ash agreed, and sipped at his drink. They changed the subject, caught up with each other while they ate.

Ash had two drinks and a basket of wings before going home on the subway and turning in for the night at a very reasonable hour.

And it was nearly eleven when he finally woke up for work the next day.

9

Zeta climbed out of the car, the winter air biting at the exposed skin of her face. She pulled the hood up on her lavender-gray wool coat to cover her ears and hurried into the building, wishing she'd worn a scarf. At the door she caught sight of her reflection, hair protected from the wind, the little cat ears on the hood standing at attention.

She checked in at the security desk, giving her name. When the guard couldn't find it, she corrected herself. "Oh, it's under Gray Rodgers, sorry," she said, shaking her head and handing over her ID. *Pregnancy brain is real, just like Cody said.* She had worked under her middle name since she started freelancing—gender neutral helped get resumes through—so she wasn't sure why she'd made the mistake. *I'm going to take such a nap after this meeting.*

Zeta met the guard's indifferent expression with a bright smile, and he pointed to the elevator bank. "Top floor," he said as he handed her a visitor badge.

"Man, security's really tight around here," she laughed, but the guard's expression remained the same.

Zeta took the plastic card and walked to the elevator bank, the air already getting a little too warm. She unzipped her coat and slipped it off. Underneath she wore a baggy black sweater with thick white lines designed to mimic the look of a doodle, as if the sweater had been drawn on. Under it she wore a pink long-sleeve T-shirt, the bunny rabbit running along the bottom hidden by the sweater. Her pair of loose pants were made from knit material. She thought it looked business casual enough and hid the small but definitely noticeable bump of her belly. With clumsy fingers, she attached the badge to her sweater, adjusted her purse, a gray floppy messenger bag, and her coat in her arms, and hit the call button. She stared at her reflection while she waited. She'd pulled the thick mop of her hair back into a bun, and although she seemed a bit pale in the blurry reflection on the elevator doors, he shouldn't notice. He'd never seen her before.

Also, he didn't seem like the type that would care. She remembered the photo, a stone-faced man with steel gray hair and stormy, dark eyes. And now that she was there, and thinking about it, it was strange that *he* had asked for the meeting and not the Tyrant.

The elevator dinged, the end of the ride. She stepped off into the bustle of an active office. "Excuse me," she said, stopping at a reception desk.

The Black woman working behind it looked up with a blank expression, eyes flickering over Zeta, a match for the guard below. "Can I help you?"

"I'm here for a meeting with Mr. Cross? The CEO. Can you point me in the right direction?" Zeta asked.

She looked at Zeta strangely. "You need an appointment," she said.

"I have one. It's in a few minutes. Zeta, I mean Gray Rodgers." *I'm tired*, she assured herself. She'd been working hard. Maybe she did need more rest.

The receptionist tilted her head, gave Zeta that *Now, sis* sort of look.

"I swear," Zeta said, trying to inject some calm into their interaction, lighten things up. *Is it my outfit? Maybe this wasn't a good pick.*

The woman looked at her screen, her expression faltered, eyes darting between the screen and Zeta. "You said Gray Rodgers?"

"Yup. One o'clock. I'm about to be late."

"Alright," she said slowly. "It's just down this hall and to the end, the glass doors on your right. But they're running a little behind today. Mr. Cross apologizes for the delay and hopes it's not a huge inconvenience. If you'd like, you can reschedule."

I am not coming back out here, Zeta thought. Already she could feel her body starting to revolt. She hadn't had enough rest after her party the night before, as low-key as it was. She'd come, she'd hear them out, see what this was all about, find out if they would continue to let her work as she had been, and no, she wouldn't be coming back for another meeting. One was already too much. "No, that's fine! I can wait a little."

The woman, still looking at her strangely, like Zeta had somehow tricked her, motioned toward the hall, and Zeta waved as she walked past.

There were cubicles and other offices with open doors revealing a bustle of business operations. Zeta followed the directions she had been given, walked to the end of the hall, and was confronted with the CEO's office suite.

Another receptionist sat at a desk just behind the glass doors. Past her stood another door, dark and heavy.

"Hello, I have a meeting with Mr. Cross today," Zeta said brightly as she stepped inside.

The woman looked up. She looked to be middle aged, with light brown hair styled into layers around her face. "I'll take his delivery."

"What?" Zeta asked, thrown off, confused.

"His lunch delivery?" She stood, hands out.

Zeta pushed her coat to one arm and held up her empty hands. "I'm not a delivery person. I'm here to see Mr. Cross. I'm—"

"You need an appointment," the woman cut her off. "Please call and make one."

Zeta frowned. "I do have an appointment. It's at one."

"I'm sorry, you're mistaken. Mr. Cross has another appointment at this time," the woman said. "Please call and schedule one for yourself."

Zeta's cheeks turned hot and her heart sped up. Pulling in a deep breath, she calmed herself. Quickly she read the name tag on the desk and tried again. "Hi, Margaret, it's nice to meet you. I do have an appointment. My name is—"

"Ma'am, if you don't leave, I will be forced to have you escorted out." Margaret stood, her hands on the desk.

Zeta stared at her, wide eyed. A tremor started in her hands. Frustration coursed through her. Anger following it. *I should leave, before . . .* She closed her eyes, tried to breathe.

The phone rang on Margaret's desk. The secretary listened for a moment before speaking, "There's a woman here who claims to have an appointment with you, sir." The voice on the other end gave some instruction, and Margaret responded. "No, he is not, sir. I will let you know as soon as he arrives." A pause. Margaret looked up at her. "Yes, alright."

She hung up the phone and looked back at Zeta. "Mr. Cross will see you after his one o'clock. You can wait there," she said, pointing at a row of three chairs along the wall.

He's not here yet, Zeta thought, putting the pieces together. Zeta had let them call her Gary for weeks, what she assumed was a typo. It didn't bother her. But now she realized that her name was wrong, and they were looking for a man. Which she was not. *Should I message Ben? Try to get this sorted?* she wondered, taking the seat she had been directed too. Frowning, she decided not to. She didn't want to drag him into this mess and she was too angry.

Zeta needed to calm down. She took out her phone, opened a match-three game. They'd figure out "Gary" wasn't coming soon enough.

The minutes ticked by, building on each other until it had been nearly half an hour. Two men walked out of the office, both laughing good-naturedly, and closed the door behind them. They walked past her without a look, and the room was silent again. Finally, the phone rang.

"Yes, sir," Margaret said in response to the call before hanging up. Five more minutes passed before she turned to Zeta. "Mr. Cross will see you now."

"Thank you so much," Zeta said, exiting out of her game to conserve the battery. She still had to order a ride to get home. The secretary closed the door behind her.

Zeta slipped her phone back into her bag as she stepped further into the office. *I'll thank him for the opportunity, pass on the job if offered, but let them know to keep my number for future work. Ten minutes, tops. Then home, hot cocoa for being so brave, and a nap. No more work today.*

The office was modern and sleek. A heavy desk sat in front of large windows overlooking the city skyline. In the center of the room stood two couches, facing each other, a glass table between them. Tasteful art adorned shelves and walls. He was typing, his face turned from hers, but she could see it well enough. Zeta stopped at the table because . . . it couldn't be.

"My apologies for the," he said, finishing whatever he was typing and finally looking up at her, the last word a whisper, "delay."

Blond hair, broad shoulders, tall, blue eyes, and a straight nose. Dressed in a gray shirt and darker pants and tie, his hair longer— but still him. "Ash," Zeta said slowly. Part of her wanted to laugh. Another part wanted to yell, because how dare he show up in her life, suddenly, unannounced, after months and months. After he made her think that there could be something only to disappear without a trace. She tried not to think about those feelings, those ideas. There was no room in figuring out a life for them now that it wasn't just her. With every new day bringing its own issues to her door. She badly needed to sit down—her face was too hot, the world was wavering at the edges of her vision.

"What . . . are you doing here?" he asked, standing, walking around the desk, confused but his expression soft—soft as it was on the deck, in her apartment, looking down at her on her bed. Before it all changed.

Zeta's head spun. "I had a meeting." Like that explained everything, anything.

Ash crossed the room to her and he smelled like sage and his voice was exactly as she remembered it. "How did you find me?"

She couldn't catch her thoughts or her breath. "The security guard told me." *No, that's not right, that's not the question.* She needed to do something because she was teetering on the edge of *bad* and she needed to be careful because of the baby, but Zeta couldn't quite hold on to what things that meant. Her thoughts were all foggy. The world was too bright, and the only thing that she could think was that he was there, and she needed ten minutes to understand it all, to calm down. But she couldn't think of the words to ask for it, so instead she said, "I should go. I'm not feeling well." The only thing that made sense was leaving. If she left, the panic would stay in the room, with the impossibility of him, and she'd be gone from here. She turned, moving away from him, back toward the door.

"Security told you? How did you find out who I was?" Ash moved closer. He didn't block Zeta's way, but he reached his hand out, an unfinished gesture. The smell of him filled her nostrils, and sweat broke out along her back. She had no idea what to do. She didn't know him, didn't know how he would take her pregnancy, had no kind of speech prepared to explain why she was pregnant, and she couldn't think.

"No, I'm sorry, this was a mistake." Nausea rose in her.

Ash caught her arm. Her elbow rested in his palm, and he looked distressed, as lost in all this as she felt. "A mistake? Didn't you come here to see me?"

Zeta blinked. Time skipped a few seconds. She came to almost instantly, caught in his arms. The hand that held her elbow had moved to hold her, to catch the weight of her body to keep her from falling. His chest was hot under her cheek, his heart pounding. Zeta's own chest and belly pressed into him, and Ash stared down at her, realization flickering across his face. "Zeta?" The question hung in the air between them.

Panicked thoughts, hot and irrational, coursed through her. She pushed him away, hard, and he released her. Zeta stumbled back, acid burning in her throat for half a second before her body followed through on the threat, stomach cramping, and she bent over and threw up—no time to stop herself or find a better place. She stood straight up quickly, embarrassed, the motion too sudden, and her vision blurred. She fell blessedly backward, avoiding her own vomit. Ash reached for her, but his fingers caught her purse and it slipped from her arm as she collapsed.

She came back to herself, and now he was kneeling over her, hands frantic and hovering, afraid to touch. "I think I hurt my head," she said, lifting her hand. Blood dripped from a slice along the side of it. "And my hand."

"Don't move!" he ordered. "Margaret! Call an ambulance!"

She tried to sit up, the world flickered again, and instead, she reached for Ash, gripping his shirt in her fingers, drawing him back to her. "Listen!" she hissed.

"Zeta, it's OK, stay still. They'll be here soon," he soothed, kneeling in glass, untangling her fingers from the fabric to hold them.

"No, listen! It's important! You have to tell them to sedate me! You have to, I can't," the words were slipping away, panic. *The baby*, she thought frantically trying to collect herself to tell him what to do.

"I'll tell them, I'll tell them," he said. "Relax, please, you'll hurt yourself."

Zeta didn't have time to protest. Overworked and overwhelmed, the lights went out before she could try.

10

Ash drove as fast as he could to meet Zeta at the hospital, her coat and purse in the seat next to him. Traffic moved at a crawl, and he didn't have the benefit of a siren. He was left with his own thoughts in the stop-and-go line of cars as he gripped his wheel so tightly he thought it would snap. *This is my fault,* he thought. *That last meeting could have waited. I should have seen her right away. Why did I send that email? If I'd been looking, maybe . . .* He knew he was being irrational. There was no way for him to know that it was *Zeta* sitting outside his door, but he couldn't help it. The guilt settled over him like a blanket. *She looked so pale; I should have offered her a seat! Maybe then she wouldn't have fainted.*

But another thought was swirling too: Zeta was pregnant.

And with just as much surety, he knew it was his baby.

Ash had fantasized about the moment he would see her again. He would kiss her, apologize for leaving so suddenly, and they would start over. Do things properly. Making her throw up and faint was not in this fantasy scenario. *Did she find me to tell me about the baby? Has she been looking for me this whole time? Why didn't she look at my message? Why didn't I just leave my number to begin with?*

More guilt. It wasn't all his fault, he knew that. He had been a jerk, but then, his father was in the hospital and his mother hadn't been able to reach him because he was buried in a woman he'd just met. It was understandable, but still. His reasons for not taking a couple of extra minutes all those months ago seemed flimsy and thoughtless to him now. All he could see was Zeta searching, scared, pregnant with his child, while he sat in comfort, completely clueless about her situation, the situation he caused, because it was his condom and he had thought of nothing but his own life, his own problems. He should have made sure that he could get in touch with her, make sure that it was all alright.

But even before the phone call, he hadn't exactly been honest. He didn't tell her he was going away, what his job was. He was playing pretend on the deck so that she wouldn't think *anything* of him, in the hopes she just see a nice guy, and for what? He had found a treasure and lost it in the same night.

He hadn't been thinking long term on that deck. And isn't that what his father always said? That he didn't think about building relationships, that he was shortsighted, and here he was, making those exact mistakes. If he'd been more aggressive, if he'd done *something* different. He didn't know what, and in his guilt and shame he forgot what he had been dealing with for those months. The only thing that mattered was Zeta.

And all the things he'd missed. It had been four months. She would have gone to the doctor. Had she gotten an ultrasound? Did she know if they were having a boy or a girl? Was she alright?

The Zeta that found him looked so pale, so worn and tired. He wanted to hold her, take her home, and tuck her into his bed, breathe in the scent that had haunted his dreams. The scent that wrapped around him when she fell into his arms. When he felt the firm curve of her growing belly against him.

"Fuck," Ash cursed as he pulled his car into the hospital parking lot. He rested his forehead on the wheel and took a deep breath. "No more of this. No more wasting time on regrets. I need to focus on her."

It was his second chance.

He jerked opened his door and climbed out of his car, pulling her coat and purse with him. At the front desk of the emergency room, he said, "I'm here for Zeta Cross. She was brought in by ambulance."

The woman checked her records. "She's being treated. We'll let her know you're here if you want to wait until she's finished with the doctor."

"I'm her husband," he said quickly, without thinking. It was so effortless, natural. *I'm her husband, father of her child, she's my wife, that's my baby, please let me see them, I need to see them.* He didn't even realize that it wasn't true himself; it felt so right. The lie was already set up. He had been the one to give her information to the EMTs. The information he had, her first name. The rest he filled in with whatever came to mind. Last name? Cross. Age? Twenty-seven. Condition? Four months pregnant and currently resting in the glass from his table. He explained that she fainted, had a stress disorder, that she needed to be sedated for treatment.

"Oh, of course, so sorry," the receptionist said. She tapped a few keys on her keyboard. "I've paged someone to take you back. It'll be a couple of minutes. She's getting an MRI."

Ash paced back and forth by the reception stand. When a nurse appeared, all smiles and gentle natured, he shuffled behind her as she led him to Zeta's room, still in the ER floor but private. She parted the curtains to let him in, and Ash's breath caught in his throat, hands cold.

The lights in Zeta's room were low, and she was laid out in bed like a painting. Ash took in all of her at once. She *was* pale, her cheeks washed out, and there were bags under her eyes. On her temple was a bandage. The bump of her belly, clear under the thin blankets, was made even more evident by the monitor attached to it by the medical staff. Her injured hand had been wrapped neatly while an IV line stretched from her other. Ash's heart ached. He closed his eyes, suddenly saw his father, the shrunken way he moved in the world now, and there was Zeta again when he opened them.

It's not what he imagined. Never in a thousand years what he wanted. *Is she alright, will she be alright?* In his dreams he swept her into his arms. In the real world, he was afraid to touch her.

"It looks worse than it is. She and the baby are perfectly fine, just a few bumps and cuts," the nurse said.

Confirmation. There was a baby and, more important, it was fine. She would be fine. Relief.

"The doctor is working on figuring out why she fainted, but we'll be able to tell more when she wakes up."

"I told the EMTs, she's got a condition, something with her brain," he tried to remember from their brief discussion. She hadn't given him many details, just that her heart was fine. "A stress response; I gave her some upsetting news. She faints; it was my fault," he said quickly.

"I'm so sorry, I'll mark that in the charts," the woman said brightly.

"Thank you," he said softly.

Concern flicked across the nurse's face.

"I just saw her fall . . ." He pushed his hand over his hair.

The nurse's smile returned, her eyes filling with sympathy. "Of course, this is a lot to take in. The doctor will be in in a few minutes to talk with you."

Ash nodded as the nurse left. He set Zeta's things down in one of the empty chairs, then pulled up the other to sit by Zeta's bedside. Cautiously, Ash caressed her face, and in her sleep she leaned toward it. He wanted to kiss her, tell her it was OK, that he was there for her. But instead he cradled her hand in his, mindful of the IV, and waited.

A knock at the door before it opened, and the doctor swept in. In a low voice he assured Ash that the baby was fine and in no danger.

"What about Zeta?" Ash asked.

The doctor nodded. "She'll be fine. She did hit her head, but she doesn't have any sort of concussion. The cuts aren't nearly as bad as they look. They sedated her in the ambulance. She's just sleeping it off now. Aside from the stitches, she looks great."

Ash nodded. "Thank you."

"We are going to admit her and move her to a new room in a few moments. Just to monitor her overnight to be sure. Fainting isn't uncommon for pregnant women, and it's likely nothing, just bad luck that she hit that table, but we would just like to keep an eye on her given her condition."

Ash nodded and the doctor left. He turned back to Zeta, her face serene in her rest. Tentatively he reached forward and placed one hand over her belly, finding a space on it unoccupied by monitors. It rose and fell under his palm with her breathing. She made a small sound, not waking but dreaming, sleeping. "Is this mine?"

He didn't need to hear her answer. He already knew. Knew when he caught her first fall and felt the press of her belly against him. *Of course it's mine. Why else would she be in my office?* Ash ran his thumb over the gentle curve of her. He was surprised to find himself pleased with the thought, excited even. He wanted a family. And he knew he didn't know her, but she felt right. His fear turned into a tentative happiness. His breathing slowed, the tension in his shoulders released as he watched her. There were questions, things that needed to be discussed, but they could figure it all out later, together.

When she woke up.

Zeta stirred under his touch, a small, questioning, nearly waking sound coming from her throat, and Ash stilled. Held his breath, waited. Though she stayed asleep, Ash couldn't tell if the jittery feeling in him was nervousness or relief. Didn't let himself think about the moment she *would* wake up and they would have to talk.

Another nurse came, this time to move her, and reluctantly he pulled away from Zeta, gathering her things and following them to her new room. Once the bed was parked and the lights dimmed, Ash settled into the open chair while the nurses flitted about, reconnecting her to various machines.

Outside the window, the sun dropped lower. Another woman, not a nurse, came into the room. She quietly explained she was from administration to get Zeta's billing information but would come back when she was awake. Ash stopped her, handed over his credit card, and was happy to see her leave again.

Alone, he held Zeta's hand, and with the other he played *Pretty Pretty Dragon Ranch* until finally she stirred.

Zeta made a small groan, a little sigh, shifted, waking, and he released her hand. Her eyes opened slowly, dark pools in the low light. They swept from side to side, taking in the room before landing on him.

Ash held his breath, prepared for the worst, that just the sight of him would send her into another spiral.

"Is the baby OK?" she asked, voice creaky and small.

He smiled slowly. "The baby's fine. Everything is fine, Zeta."

11

Zeta woke slowly, opened her eyes to find herself in a dim hospital room. Her head felt fuzzy and sore. She lifted one hand, felt the IV needle, and stopped, switching to the other. She curled her fingers and sucked in her breath. Also sore.

The baby was alright though. Ash had confirmed, and the monitors tracking them both beeped steadily away. Still, fear filled the empty spot where her memory of what happened should be, and she wondered if she'd lost the ability to remember, if the dark in her mind would spread over years, eat everything. She'd remembered the baby though, the tiny life in her.

Then events started spilling into her head, delayed just a few moments. Her hand hurt because she cut it on the glass. She touched her head and found it bandaged too. The fall was more of a known fact than a real memory, but everything else she could see clearly. Ash, who she thought she'd never see again, standing in front of her, his office all around. The surprise, the panic.

But now, relief. It would be worse if she was alone. Worse if he wasn't there to tell her that the baby was alright.

"You're finally awake," Ash said, his voice low and familiar. Like she had heard him say that exact phrase that morning, every morning enough times that it sounded cozy and unexceptional. But it had been months and months and he had never seen her wake up. But his voice was warm and his expression gentle. She tried to push them away, the feelings she felt in herself. She had to figure out what was going on, how he was there, real and warm and staring at her so . . . longingly.

She had felt the baby move before, at least she thought she had. She had read about the flutters, and now Zeta felt something like them again, but these were different. These were her own butterflies.

"Where am I? And don't just say the hospital. I know I'm in the hospital." Her voice cracked. "My mouth tastes horrible."

"You did throw up. I'll get you some water. You're in Luther Memorial," Ash explained, standing and crossing the room to the waiting pitcher. When he returned with a full cup, he helped her sit up and handed it to her. "You fell through my table and cut your head and arm on the glass. You told me to have them sedate you."

"I'd keep fainting otherwise," Zeta said before she took a long drink, hoping to use the time to settle and recalibrate. The events after the table came back to her as a sort of dream; she'd been sedated and not unconscious but not far from it. He had listened; she remembered, in that same dream way, that she'd told him to tell the EMTs that. But there were gaps. The ultrasound when she got there and then, an MRI? Her mind was fuzzy and she was tired, but the baby was alright, which was the most important thing. Ash was there, and it was all unexpected, and it didn't feel terrible. She looked toward the window and noticed that the day had gone to complete darkness, sunset long since passed. "What time is it? How long have I been here?"

"It's not that late, just after six. Winter, you know? Are you hungry? What would you like to eat?" His voice was awkward, unsure. Like he had been the night they met. The same sort of rapid fire questions. Not the rushed, slightly formal goodbye he left her with that night.

Zeta frowned at him. She turned her head and saw her bag. "Hand me my purse." She tried to sound cool. Was aware that he had seen her throw up and faint into his table. Was decidedly trying to ignore that he knew, without a doubt, about the baby. *Is he going to make me pay for the table? God, I hope it's from IKEA or something and only **looks** expensive.*

Ash moved to do as she asked, drawing her attention back to the room. Back to the here and now. He handed her the bag, and she dug her phone out. Missed calls and dozens of texts awaited her. She didn't bother to read them. **I'm fine, I fainted, I'm in Luther Memorial.** A single message to the group text. She'd explain better after she dealt with Ash.

The responses came flooding in. She scanned them, letting out a long breath. She knew they would be worried, but she didn't want them to come. She was still drowsy from the sedation, and there'd be so much fussing. And she needed to do *something* about Ash, who would probably want an explanation. Everything was a lot, and she just wanted to sleep. Just ten minutes.

I know you all want to come but I'm ok! I hurt my hand and needed stitches but me and the baby are good. I'll text you when I'm done talking to the doctor to let you know what's going on. She put the phone down and looked back up at him, Ash, the man she thought she would never see again.

"How did you find me?" He scooped up her injured hand, holding it delicately in both of his. Ash's brow was furrowed, but his eyes were wide and earnest. Not the face of someone who was trying to get out of being sued. Not the actions either.

"Who are you?" she asked slowly. She was there to meet with an older man.

He looked confused. "What do you mean? You don't remember me? Your head, I'll get the doctor!"

"No," she said, gripping his hand to hold him still, the shock of pain reminding her of her circumstances. He noticed her reaction, shifted his hold, and waited. "Who are you? I was supposed to be meeting with Nathanial Cross. The big boss."

He held his free hand to his chest. "Ash. Ashford Cross."

They favored each other a little. The shape of their jaw, the nose. "What does the *M* stand for?"

"*M*?"

"Your middle initial."

"Milton," he answered slowly, clearly trying to piece together what was happening. "How did you know what my middle initial was?"

"You're the Tyrant," she sighed. "Your email signature says you're the director of operations."

"I am. I mean for now. I have to talk to you," he stumbled before taking a deep breath. "It's complicated. I need to explain. Tyrant?"

"I wasn't looking for you. You asked me to come today." Zeta wanted to melt into that touch but slipped her hand out from his. It was too much.

He looked at his empty hand, frowning, but curled his fingers closed, accepting. "I haven't. I didn't. I thought about you. I sent a message to a profile I thought may have been you, but I never heard anything. I couldn't, the way I left things . . . I'm not making sense. But I didn't ask you anything, Zeta."

"This is so stupid!" she said, laughing at the impossibility of it. It didn't feel funny, it felt cruel. To know he was there, right there, the whole time and she didn't know. He didn't know. "You have no idea who I am, do you?"

"What do you mean? Of course I know who you are, I've been thinking about you for months and, oh god, I'm sorry. I'm such an asshole, you've probably been looking for me. I'll—"

Zeta pressed her fingertips against Ash's lips, cutting off whatever promise he was about to make. "Stop talking. I wasn't looking for you. I figured that night was all there was going to be between us, and I couldn't spend time being concerned about it."

Ash's eyes were wide. Zeta wasn't sure how she felt about any of it. She wasn't angry, but she wasn't happy to see him either. *Hurt, maybe?* she wondered. She hadn't considered that she would ever see him again, even by chance. The city was big, their meeting a random encounter to begin with. Now it all seemed so impossible, a series of once-in-a-lifetime coincidences. The day had already been too much, and she wasn't sure if it was the drugs in her system or the pregnancy or just that she was working too much, but her head spun.

It did not occur to her that she was touching his mouth, how intimate that was.

His fingers circled her wrist and pulled her hand away from his mouth but didn't release her. He was so careful to avoid the bandage. His touch was firm and warm, and she didn't fight it because only when he moved her did she realize what she'd done. "If you weren't looking for me then how did you end up in my office? What other reason did you have to be there if not to find me and tell me about—"

"I had an appointment!" she spit out quickly, cutting him off and pulling her hand away. She didn't want to talk about that. Not yet. She didn't know what to say, how to explain. "I told you, I was scheduled for a meeting with the CEO, Nathanial Cross."

"That's my father. I'm acting CEO while he's out. There must have been a mistake with scheduling. Wait, who are you?"

"I'm working on your leave system. I'm Gray Rodgers. Z. Gray Rodgers."

Recognition flickered over his face as the pieces slid into place. "You're the programmer."

"I'm the programmer," she confirmed.

"I wanted to offer you a job," he said slowly, the information still processing.

"Even if that offer were still on the table, I don't think I'd take it," she said frowning, remembering what it had been like when she finally did go into the office. "Everyone was kind of an asshole. And besides, things are a little complicated now."

"A little, yeah," he said slowly. "We need to talk."

Zeta rolled her eyes, a sick chuckle escaping her. "You think? Anyway, I can't do this right now. I need some time to . . . think about things. Thanks for sitting with me in here, but you can leave. I'm alright." *I just want to go back to sleep.*

"Is that my baby? Am I a father?" His voice was soft, warm. There was no accusation in it, just surprise. "I don't mean to push you, and you have every right to be upset with me, but Zeta, I really need to know. I need to hear you say it."

And Zeta had no idea how to respond.

A soft knock came at the door and a woman walked in, breaking the tension. "You're awake!" she said brightly.

"Yeah," Zeta confirmed drily, unsure if she was annoyed with the woman's bubbly demeanor or that she'd interrupted whatever it was that was happening between her and Ash.

"I'm Dr. Nickelson, one of the doctors on shift tonight. How do you feel?" she asked, checking Zeta's chart.

"I feel fine. I'm just tired and ready to go home," Zeta replied.

"Didn't your husband tell you? We're keeping you overnight, just as a precaution."

Zeta shot "her husband" a sharp look. "We didn't get that far."

Ash smiled sheepishly, face turning pink. "Sorry."

"Your chart says you have an underlying health issue," the doctor went on, ignoring their "marital" squabble.

Zeta nodded. "Yeah, I've got a brain injury, from childhood, and developed an overreactive vasovagal response. I just had a little bit of a shock today. I'm really fine."

"I see. No need to worry, the baby's vitals are good, so you can relax, Mr. Cross." Dr. Nickelson gave Ash a smile that said *All that fuss for nothing*. "He's been so worried the entire time you've been here! He must really love you, lucky girl!"

Ash's face went from pink to red.

"Oh! Thanks for telling me that. It's really nice to hear how much my *husband loves me*," Zeta replied sweetly.

The doctor went over the tests they had run, and Ash listened intently. He was so earnest and focused, and she was softening to his care.

"Well, if you need anything, just press the call button. I think they're bringing dinner up soon as well," the doctor said brightly before patting Zeta's leg and sweeping out of the room.

Ash looked at her, red faced but smiling and adorable, and she didn't want him to leave at all. Her emotions and desires were all over the place, and she hadn't answered him.

"Husband?" Zeta asked finally, voice soft.

"It was a spur of the moment choice. I needed to give them a name, so I gave them mine, and then when they said I couldn't come back, it slipped out. I can't believe it worked, honestly." He was still smiling. That same smile from the deck. It tipped her heart and mind fully over to disarmed.

"Why? You don't even know me. You literally did not know who I was."

"Because you're pregnant and we both know who the father is," he said gently. "But I still want to hear you say it. I still want you to tell me yourself."

Zeta wrapped her arms around her belly and considered lying. Knew how ridiculous that would be and had no idea why it felt so catastrophic. "I . . ." she started, and then stopped, unsure of what to say. And then, too worn to think of anything else, "Yes. It's your baby."

Zeta watched his face, tried to read his expression, but she didn't know him well enough to know if it was happiness or guilt or what his parted lips and round eyes meant.

"When is our baby due? Do you know if we're having a boy or a girl?" *Our baby.*

"The end of April," she said. "I don't know what they are yet. That appointment isn't until next month."

He turned away, his cheeks puffing out as he let out a breath. "We really do need to talk. But I don't think right now is a good time."

"OK," she said slowly, wary.

"I shouldn't have left that night like that, I'm sorry. I want to make it up to you if you'll let me but not right now. Right now, I am here. I am with you and I'm not going anywhere. So don't push me away. Alright? Can we do that at least for tonight?" He was firm but still warm, still open.

"I don't know. I'm not really sure," she stuttered.

"Alright then." He stood up.

Oh, he's leaving. I'll probably hear from his lawyer. Would that be better? Her stomach dropped at the prospect, and she thought it was fear for a moment until it settled and started pulling her down into it—disappointment. There was fear there too, but it had nothing to do with him leaving and everything to do with the prospect of him staying. But that was the good sharp fear that tumbled into warmth. Everything in her was mixed up, emotions leaping over each other.

He didn't leave. He took off his jacket and settled on the edge of the bed, his thigh aligned with hers, and he took up her hand again. "Let's start here then. How are you feeling?"

"What kind of question is that? I'm in the hospital," she chuckled, disarmed because he was charming and she was tired.

"True, but I meant in general. You look very, very tired, Zeta," he said softly.

"I am tired," she sighed. She pulled her hair out of the bun, ran her fingers through it, and then parted it into two. She took up one thick side and started braiding. She grimaced at the pain the movement caused in her hands. It disturbed the stitches, pulled at the IV.

Ash shifted on the bed, lifted the hair from her fingers, and took up the braid. After a beat of silence, "Sorry, I should have asked, do you mind? You're hurt."

"You don't—"

"You're hurt," he repeated. "Let me help. It's probably not as nice as what you're used to; I haven't done this in a while. But it should be OK for tonight."

His hands were light, careful. He didn't pull; his fingers combed her hair delicately, parting her curls before firmly twisting them together.

"There," he said softly, sitting back down.

She reached up and touched his hair. The last time she saw him it was cropped close, but now there were at least two inches, enough for a little wave. "You grew your hair out."

"It's winter." He leaned into her touch. A puppy.

Zeta wanted him to explain more. She wanted to understand what happened, find out who he really was so that she could make a choice about what to do. She'd spent four months pretending not to think about him, pretending not to care at all. That their meeting had been one of those funny things about life, like her apartment flooding with seawater. But here he was—a cosmic collision, her aunt would say.

Her head was swimming. Exhaustion, hunger, and him staring at her with such concern, his face warm against her palm. "Ash," she said slowly, unsure of what she was going to say next.

"Zeta, what do you want to eat?" Ash asked.

"They're going to bring something, remember?" Zeta yawned and checked the time on her phone. It wasn't even very late.

"I'll bring you whatever you want," he said in a way that didn't sound like an offer, more like a promise, and it made her face warm.

What she wanted was to be held, and she was dangerously close to saying that. "I'm tired, Ash. Thank you, but I really need a little time to myself. You should go," she said. "We can talk more tomorrow."

"I'll come get you in the morning then. We'll get breakfast," he offered.

"Why are you always trying to feed me?" she laughed. "No, it's OK. I'll get a Lyft or something."

"Is it because you don't want to see me?" he asked, more serious than she liked. She liked him awkward and sweet, not troubled. The realization made her feel strange because she shouldn't like any of him. Not after the way he'd left—and he could leave her like that again. But right then he was all of the things that made her like him in the first place.

"No, this is all just a lot? I need a little time."

Ash smiled. "Ten minutes, right?"

Her face heated, the memory of their night together rushing up, charmed that he'd remembered such a small thing. "A little more than ten minutes today," she said.

"Fifteen then," he teased, lighthearted and sweet. "You need my number anyway."

"Not going to make the same mistake twice? All new and exciting mistakes this time?" Zeta said, meaning to tease as she unlocked her phone and handed it over.

Ash didn't laugh. "Do you have a charger?" he asked, his face unreadable, his tone neutral.

Confused, she shook her head. "No."

He turned her phone, showing her the face, "Your phone is going to die before you wake up."

"Shit. You're right. Oh well." She'd been playing on it while she rode to the appointment and while she waited for it. By now she would have charged it again. Nothing to be done about it. She shrugged, accepting it.

"How are you going to call for a ride?" he asked, confusion on his face.

"That's a problem for Future Zeta. Present Zeta can't do anything about it. I'll just use the room phone to call a cab. Actually, I can catch the bus. I'll just jump on the thirteen, switch to the one-oh-eight, and it'll drop me off on my corner," she said. A plan in place, problem solved. It wasn't like it was the first time in her life she'd had to get around without a phone or car. She knew how to handle it.

"I'm not letting you catch the bus home from the hospital and especially not in December." His tone had changed but not in a bad

way. He sounded focused, set. Ash stood up, looking at her phone
again for a moment before returning it to her. "I'll be back soon."

"Just go home! I'm OK, really. I don't need anything, and I
promise I'll call you in the morning," she said, embarrassed at his
attention.

He picked up his jacket, put it on, and Zeta sucked in her breath.
She hadn't had time to notice it before, but a tailored suit took
him from handsome to godly.

"I'll be back in an hour or less. Do you want anything special?"

Zeta shook her head and Ash bent, pressing his lips against her
forehead. Zeta felt the kiss all the way in her to the tips of her fingers, warm and electric. She touched the space his lips had marked,
skin hot under her fingers, stared at him in shock.

"You can use up the rest of your battery dealing with that mountain of messages. Your friends really care about you."

"They do," she confirmed.

"I'll be back soon," Ash said.

"Wait," she called while he was pulling his coat on.

"Hmm?" He turned, and she took a picture of him.

"That's it, bye," she said.

"I'll be back soon," he repeated. He walked out of the room,
taking all the heat with him.

Her body still tingled from his kiss, and she tried to remind
herself to be wary. But she looked at the picture of him that she'd
just taken, head slightly tilted, brows raised. Even in the dark suit
he looked exactly like he did all those months ago. Soft and eager
and adorably handsome.

"It's been a very long day, Baby," she said softly, running her
hand over her stomach. Inside of her the child moved, a flutter in
her belly. Zeta sighed and prepared to update Pixie on the whole
mess.

12

Ash dropped into his car and put his head on the steering wheel. He didn't need to see his face to know that it was bright red, and he thought he would both throw up and suffocate from laughing too much. His heart felt like it was going to beat out of his chest. It was her, it was really her. His lips were still warm from the brief kiss against her forehead, an indulgence that he hoped let her know that he cared. Not just for their baby but for her.

When she first woke, asked him if the baby was alright, it had been so hard not to do more than just tell her they were fine. He wanted to take her in his arms. Kiss her for real. Make her understand how much he missed her, how sorry he was right there, right then.

And that little kiss felt good. *Really* good. Just to touch her felt like heaven. She was there, she was real. His fingers still smelled like her hair. The car was freezing but Ash's face was burning. He ran his hand through his own hair, scalp tingling where she had stroked a few strands. It almost erased the memory of Zeta fainting into his arms and then crashing through the table.

Almost.

It is my fault, I should have asked her to sit right away, he realized, turning everything over in his head. *She was pale and clearly exhausted. Is that my fault? Did she work too much? Tyrant?* He didn't want to ask about that; instead he ran over everything she'd said about work, putting it together. She was Gary, he emailed Gary.

Zeta-as-Employee had never complained about anything. Had been responsive to his messages, fulfilled any request that Ash had given. He ran through their communication in his memory. He'd only been so involved with the process because his father was obsessed with it, but maybe he had been too overbearing, too intense. Especially given that she had ensured her group produced the results he requested. The only thing she'd ever turned down was his request for meetings.

Except for the one he sent from the CEO's office.

The meeting was scheduled because his father insisted that he make sure there were good people on the project. It was so important to him, all he talked about, but Ash couldn't figure out why. Ash didn't have time to figure it out, he was too busy. He just stuck "meeting with the programmer" in his calendar, had the offer put together, and was going to see what happened to make his father happy. *Would she have come if it was my name on the meeting request?* He didn't think so. She didn't seem to think highly of A. M. Cross, but maybe there was still hope for Ash.

He started the car.

And there's the baby. A baby that would be coming into the world in five months, give or take. A baby that he would be the father of. The condom breaking had been an accident, but this, the baby, he couldn't bring himself to see them as a mistake. He had thought about children, of course. He'd been married before. He and his ex-wife had the type of misty future plans that weren't anything but notes on a maybe. They had not been married long enough for anything to really come of them, and he hadn't thought about it since. He'd never been so lax with protection, and it'd never come up before. He'd never been in the position of possibly being a father, let alone actually. But from the moment Zeta fell into him in his office, he wanted to hear that the baby was his. It filled him with a giddy, wild joy.

He drove until he spotted a chain pharmacy and allowed himself the entire time to think about what their baby would be like, what their life would be like. He tried to guess who the baby would look like, him or her (he hoped it was her), whether they were having a boy or girl. A house outside the city, what kind of family they would all be together. Him and Zeta and their baby. Then the yellow light of the pharmacy broke through the darkness, and his thoughts abruptly turned to the present reality.

When Dad finds out about this . . . Ash knew exactly how his father would see things. See her. As a mistake, a costly one that people would judge him for. A baby after some random hookup. Not to mention the absolute scandal of her then coming to work for him. He'd probably think the fainting and the table was some scam to extort them.

Nathanial Cross would be disappointed beyond belief in his son. All his life his father had been critical of him: He wasn't the focused strategist he wanted in a son. Ash wasn't much for the nitty gritty of the office. He didn't want to oversee everything down to the finest detail. And Nathanial thought he was lazy and shiftless for it. Ash had wanted to go to school for architecture, which he did against his father's wishes. But ultimately he ended up right back where his father wanted him because he had no choice, not if he wanted his father's love. And now it was good that he hadn't been stubborn, because they needed him. His father needed him.

I'm getting ahead of myself. I don't have to say anything. Everything is still settling. Next month, after the New Year, when I've made things up to Zeta, I'll introduce her. And I'm not a teenager. It's alright for me to have a kid.

It was a plan. He would have time with Zeta, and by then every-one would have forgotten the woman who fainted in his office—he hoped. Then he could bring Zeta over for lunch, say he had been keeping the relationship to himself until things settled. No one would care, not when there would be a grandchild to fawn over. It would have to happen fast, before the baby arrived, and he'd already lost four months. He and Zeta could come up with a better story for how they met between now and then.

"Charger," he grumbled to himself as he climbed out of the car.

His phone rang as he walked in. *He knows*, he thought, staring at the screen. Every fear he had came rushing forward. His head pounded, his face went cold. He had to get a handle on himself. *No, wait*, he corrected. There was no way he could know. No one knew about Zeta at all except for Randall, who didn't even know that he'd found her again. "Dad."

"What happened? I heard that there was an accident in your office today?"

Ash clutched his phone. "Yes," he confirmed. "There was an accident." *I don't need to tell him anything else. Someone came in for a meeting, had a health scare, and that was it.*

"I heard that she was upset about something. It was a girl, wasn't it?"

Where did he hear that? It had been months and Ash still couldn't figure out who was contacting his father, but he always seemed to know what was going on. "No, she wasn't angry about anything. Really, Dad, it had nothing to do with the company. It was just a fluke." Ash almost said *like a heart attack* and caught himself, sick with his own thoughts.

"Gossip then. You've got to be careful with that; people will say and believe anything. Good thing you weren't hurt."

Ash thought he'd misheard, ran it back through his memory. "Thanks, Dad, I'm fine," he said finally, the care so casual and unexpected he had no idea what to do with it.

"It's good that the leave system is finally being taken care of. I've been meaning to for a while, but there were always more important things. I'm sure you see that now."

He was talking about work, but all Ash could think of was Zeta. Zeta in the moment of asking if the baby, their baby, was OK. The total relief when he could tell her that, yes, it was. He didn't know how his father, who had been lying in a hospital four months ago, who was still healing, could spend any time thinking about work. Wasn't that why Ash had taken over? So his father didn't have to think about it? And Ash didn't want to think about it now. But his father had said a kind thing to him, and even now, he was being reasonable. Maybe things had changed? That would make everything easier. If his father was softening toward him then maybe introducing Zeta and the baby wouldn't be so hard. Maybe he could convince his father it was all just another piece of the puzzle—a successful business, a solid family. It was destiny that they met and that they had stumbled back into each other's lives. But no, even he knew he was being too hopeful. His father had been the way he was for years; *softened* was not *changing*. Ash needed to think about things carefully, plan them thoroughly.

"I'm actually about ready to settle for the night. It's been a day." He wanted the call to end, didn't want it to start going badly.

"Are you just leaving the office?"

"Ah, no, I'm grabbing some things from the store," Ash replied, hoping he wouldn't ask any questions.

His father hmphed, started coughing, a harsh wet sound through the line.

"Dad? Dad, are you OK?" Ash asked, trying not to sound panicked.

"I'm fine! You and your mother! Claire's the only one that doesn't act like it's the end of the world every time I so much as fart."

"I'm just worried."

He made another noise. "I've got to go. Don't have time to sit around on the phone. You get home safe." The line went dead.

As always, he felt instant relief when the call was over. But there was guilt all mixed in for feeling that relief. He seemed to be collecting guilt.

Charger, he reminded himself, pushing his thoughts away from the phone call. His father was fine, and right now it was Zeta who needed him. *A problem for Future Ash, as Zeta would say.* Ash dug through the charger options before picking one with the longest cord. *Will hospital food be enough? I'll get snacks, just in case.*

Ash stood in the middle of the aisle, singing quietly to himself and eyeing snacks with no idea what Zeta liked at all. He tried to guess, recalling what he could from their conversation months ago but finding nothing about food. He remembered her offering drinks and having a bare fridge—she didn't have any food in her house at all. *She said she was sick*, he thought, frowning at the assortment of cakes and candies, wondering if that was true. Not whether or not she was sick but if that was the reason for her empty fridge. "Has she been eating well?" he mumbled to himself. *There's so much I don't know about her. Is she on a special diet now? Do pregnant women have special diets?* He decided to grab a little of everything. There was bound to be something that she could eat.

An hour later, Ash was back at the hospital, just as he promised, treats and charger in hand. He sped down the hall toward her room, noting that visiting hours would soon be over when it hit him: *They think I'm her husband. I can stay all night if I want.* The idea sounded even better as he slowed to a walk and took his time, enjoying the play of their relationship, the privilege it could buy him.

Zeta had turned on the TV but the sound was low, just the light flickering over her. The promised tray had been picked over and put to the side, half eaten. Ash took pleasure in his own foresight. Zeta herself, though, was fast asleep.

Ash set the bag down and fished out the charger. As quietly as possible, he removed the packaging and then reached for her phone. The device was dead. *So she couldn't even play her games. I hope she was able to contact her friends.* He could and would fix that for her, plugging it in and leaving it the nightstand next to the bed, near enough for her to reach when she woke up. Ash considered turning it back on, then he remembered the series of notifications she'd had before he left. No doubt her friends would want to check in with her all night. *No, she needs to rest. It's OK if it stays off.* He organized the snacks on the same table her abandoned tray sat on. They would be there when she woke up too.

Then he allowed himself to take in Zeta.

The light from the screen cast dancing shadows all along her face and body, like the night they met. And she was beautiful, just as she was then. His eyes rested on her parted lips and he touched his own absently, the memory of what hers felt like playing in his mind. He forced himself to move on from them, to the curve of her cheek, lashes resting on them. And above her closed eyes was the bandage covering the cut on her head. Guilt, worry, something like pain twisted in him, and he wanted to touch her, feel her warm skin, her breathing, and know that she was alright. Her chest rose and fell with every breath, but looking wasn't enough. He wanted to be closer.

I shouldn't leave her, he thought, remembering his mother by his father's bedside holding vigil until he was well enough to leave. Ash wanted to do that for Zeta—it felt wrong to leave, wrong to let her wake up alone. It felt like making the same mistake all over again.

It's the last time, he promised silently. Ash wouldn't wake her; she needed the rest. And as much as he didn't want to leave her, didn't want to slip out while she slept, he couldn't stay. They weren't in a place between them where he could stay. *She's OK,* he told himself.

He bent, brushed his lips over her temple. He turned off all the lights he could, and with one last look at Zeta, he left.

There's probably a stack of emails, messages I need to respond to, he mused as he unlocked his apartment door, but his thoughts wandered back to Zeta. Now that she was settled and there was nothing else for him to do, his thoughts filled with a thousand questions. What happened? Had she wanted to find him at all, ever? What about her condition? Did she want to try being with him as much as he did her? Would she hate him? Would he be a good father?

He tried to cook himself dinner but couldn't think straight. He needed to talk to someone, get it all out of him.

The phone rang three times. "Yeah?" Randall asked, half distracted, TV going on the background.

"Are you busy?" Ash asked.

"No." Randall drew the word out slowly. The TV went silent. "Was just watching a movie."

"Good, OK, I'm going to be a father and I think I'm having a panic attack," Ash said in a rush, emotional floodgates opening. His hands were trembling and he felt lightheaded. He abruptly sat down on his floor, back to the kitchen sink cabinet.

"Who?" The question was sharp, surprised. "You're not dating anyone. Is it Hope?"

"No. Why would you think that? I haven't seen her in years."

"I don't know, I thought maybe you had one of those baby deals or something. Anyway, if not her, then who?" Randall asked again.

"It was Zeta. It is Zeta. I found her. I found Zeta." He wanted to lie down, right there on the floor. It looked cool; it felt cool against his back when he lay down. He threw his arm over his eyes, blocked the light.

"The girl from the deck?" Randall snorted, like it was a joke because it couldn't be anything but a joke.

"Yes."

A long pause while it all sunk in for him and finally: "Where are you right now?"

"My kitchen."

"Are you lying on the floor?" Randall sighed.

"No," Ash lied.

"Get up and tell me what's going on."

He did not get up, but he explained it all in a jumble of words, more or less chronologically.

"Well, I have no advice. I've never been in this position." Randall Maximilian Forsyth III had never so much as held a relationship for more than six months. "You're sure she's not just . . . lying?"

"She's really pregnant," Ash said.

"Yeah, but are you sure it's *yours*?"

Ash thought of Zeta's mouth pursed nervously, her clear, focused stare as she confirmed that it was his. "I'm sure," he said. With a hollow laugh, he said, "This is impossible, isn't it?" Ash ran his hands through his hair and remembered the feel of Zeta's fingers on it, the hot sting of desire rising from his belly. He was never cutting it again. "It's just like it happened before. I met that woman from your office, turned her down, and there she is. Again. How is that possible?"

"Ash, don't rush into anything. I know that there's the baby and all, but take your time with this."

"I'm not a lovesick teenager."

"You are not a teenager, but you are lovesick. I can hear it in your voice."

"No, I don't know her. I just . . . I don't know what to do with this."

"You don't have to do anything right now. I'm serious. Don't just do this because you think you have to. If it's about the kid, then work it out so you can be part of their life, but don't force this just because you think it's the right thing to do. I mean, do you even want a kid?"

"Of course I want the baby. The baby is here—well, it's coming. Why would I force anything?"

"Because that's what you do. You're Ashford Cross, Mr. Reliable. Always willing to work hard and meet expectations, even if they're not yours. That's why you're still slaving away for your dad. And what are you going to tell him?"

"Randall, I have enough on my plate without dealing with that," he sighed. Randall was right though. And now he had asked the question: Did Ash want this because he wanted it or because he thought it was what he *should do?* He wanted to meet her again, date her for real, but this was something different, something more serious. "I don't know. I can't tell," he said quietly.

"Seriously, do not rush into this. Look, why don't I come get you? We'll go out, get a few drinks, and talk this out more."

"No, I was already late for work today. It can't happen again tomorrow." He frowned at the memory. *Maybe if she hadn't had to wait*, he wondered. "Besides, I need to pick her up tomorrow. No, I can't, not tonight."

"Are you sure? Maybe you shouldn't be alone on your kitchen floor."

Grumbling, Ash pulled himself back up to sitting, calmer now. "Do you think I'll be a good father?" he finally asked, nervous.

"I think Ashford Cross is good at whatever he puts his mind to. If you want to be a good father, you will be. But maybe give this some more thought. She could have a boyfriend who thinks that baby is his. You know nothing about this woman."

All the memories Ash had of Zeta flooded his mind. He picked through them and came up lacking. But still: "I don't think she has a boyfriend."

"How do you know?"

"Because she didn't call him when she woke up," Ash said. She messaged her friends, never mentioned another man. "If she had a boyfriend, wouldn't she call him? Wouldn't she want him there with her?" The only person who was there at all was him.

"I guess, but you should ask, you know, really talk to her," Randall warned. "Sure you don't want to go out?"

"I'm sure. I need to eat and get some sleep. It's been a long day." The call ended, and Ash finally got off the floor.

"He's right, I have to think about this," Ash said to his empty apartment. He forced himself to make a real dinner, pan-frying chicken and roasting sweet potatoes and squash before throwing it over a bowl of rice. He remembered the picked-over tray in Zeta's room and swallowed a forkful of his own dinner along with the urge to reach for his keys.

He sat down on his couch and opened his laptop to start sorting through the work emails that had come during his unexpected absence. He put his phone down next to it and tried to ignore the disappointment when the notifications turned out to be from games and not Zeta. He didn't even notice when he stopped answering emails and started reading up on what the first trimester was like, how big the baby was (about the size of an avocado), and what he could do to be useful.

13

Zeta stared at the ceiling, hand resting on her belly, and thought about the day before. It seemed like a dream. He was there, suddenly, just like the night on the deck. She didn't want to focus on that, couldn't focus on that, because cute wasn't enough to be safe. And she had to think about more than herself, there was the baby.

They didn't talk enough about anything that mattered. But not because he didn't seem willing, just that he'd been focused on her, her comfort, her needs. "We'll talk more today," she said patting her belly and attempting to turn but giving up on it. The monitors, the IV, everything was so uncomfortable.

"He said he found me on social media. Let's see if he was right."

Sitting up, a dull pulse of pain in her hand reminded her of the long gash down her palm and arm. There was no memory of the fall itself, only the aftermath, surrounded by glass—and, of course, the pain of it was real. She touched her belly again, knew it could have been worse. *I'm just tired,* she thought. *This isn't normal.* Her phone sat on the nightstand, plugged in. On the table where her dinner tray had been, there was a line of snacks. She reached for the phone.

It vibrated like a bee when she turned it back on. A legion of texts, friends checking in mostly, and game notifications all alerted at once but she let them sit.

The social media app opened with a host of notifications. She ignored them and went to her inbox. In the main there were only the expected messages from her friends and other mutuals. She went to the unknown sender box and scrolled through it. *How long ago did he say?*

It didn't matter because there he was. She knew it was him because the photo matched the same one he had used on his phone background. A plant that she only recalled now, looking at it again. **Hey! I don't know if you remember me** . . . from two months prior.

"Well, I guess I'm the asshole," she frowned at the screen.

Sorry, looks like you did find me. I never check this box, it's full of weirdos and porn bots. She added a little cartoon of a pudgy animal that looked like a crossbreed between a cat and a hamster, hiding its face. Message sent, she followed up with a friend request.

The message chain from Pixie was just under his now in the inbox, and she thought about messaging her, catching her up on what was going on—that he had tried to find her, *had* found her, but his bad luck was that she didn't check that box. But if Pixie was up, she'd come straight to the hospital when she saw the message.

And if Pixie came, then there was a chance that Ash would not, and she still hadn't decided if she wanted him to.

"I need to talk to him more," Zeta said to the empty room.

Later she would message, when she got home. She'd check in and sleep some more. A message popped up.

Are you alright? Why are you up so early? Ash.

I'm OK, what are you doing up? Casual, friendly.

I'm always up this early. I left snacks, didn't look like you ate much last night.

Zeta yawned, checking the time. "Ugh, it's barely 7 AM." She looked back at the table. "He didn't have to do that. He didn't have to do anything," she hummed, amused at the spread. **I see. Dinner was kind of gross. Really dry chicken tenders and very bland mashed potatoes. I was tired anyway,** she wrote back with a throw-up emoji.

Her stomach growled. She hadn't had much of an appetite in weeks, but suddenly the plastic-wrapped processed goods seemed like the most delicious things she'd ever seen.

"Your daddy left us food," she said to the baby without thinking. Zeta paused, surprised at the ease with which the words came out of her mouth. They were comfortable; she was comfortable. She touched her belly, still hooked up to the heart monitors, her life and the baby's beeping along. She thought it would be just them, but now Ash was there. Someone else to think about, to consider in her life. Did she want that? *I shouldn't be so comfortable. Remember how he left, how he treated me when I was "Gary."*

He accepted her request, and Zeta dived into his profile.

And found nearly nothing.

Zeta couldn't say she was surprised, but she still growled at it, annoyed. All his profile had were happy birthday wishes, a post here and there about holidays, and automated updates from the book app he used. She could tell that he read a lot, that he had been telling the truth about that on the deck. The only photo was the plant.

Her stomach growled, louder.

"Alright, alright, guess he's not really online. Let's see what we have here." She reached for the tray, pulling it back to her. "Donuts, fruit cups, no spoon—oh wait, here's a spoon—two different types of jerky, pastry, granola, four mini boxes of cereal. And three different juices, room temperature." She opened the donuts and started eating. **Did you grab everything that was shelf stable,** she wrote back.

Sorry, I didn't know what you wanted. I can bring you something else. His message came back almost immediately.

"Hmm," she hummed to the phone. The jittery, twisty warm feeling stuttered gently to life in her chest. She was trying to keep their history in mind. It was less that he had left and more the change in him, the cold that covered him. That cold, uncaring nature he'd shown her as the Tyrant. He had been nothing but sweet and attentive, thoughtful since they met again, but that didn't erase what happened before. He'd shown her how quickly he could change. She opened a fruit cup and turned over her options.

No, it wasn't good to let her guard down. She had to be smart, careful.

It's fine, thanks for thinking of me, she wrote back. She didn't want to make him feel weird. She liked how he was treating her, and she didn't want it to change, but she didn't want to get used to it either. She put the phone down and focused on picking over the all the little packs of food he'd left for her.

Stomach settled and mostly rested, Zeta found the thoughts she'd tried not to think, had hoped would hold off until she was home at least, bubbling to the surface. It had been a while since she'd had an attack so bad. Working as much as she did with the pregnancy was a terrible idea and an unignorable sign that, yes, a baby really does change everything, a fact she had been actually trying to ignore but couldn't anymore.

Will I have to move back home? She had no way of really knowing if it was just the panic of the moment or something else, and the worry sat in her stomach. She knew she was being reckless, but she thought she had more time, that it was better to take chances now before it got harder later. But it was all hard. She had told everyone it was normal to be tired, to be ill. Tried to smile, hide how hard it was, but now she was paying for it. She touched the bandage on her head, looked down at her arm. The real question, the big fear since it had all started: *Can I take care of my baby?*

A nurse came into the room, disrupting her thoughts. "Oh, good morning! Just coming in to check on you! I'm Callie, and actually we can take all this off you."

The woman quickly went about her work, explaining that the doctor had already peeked in on her while she slept, which Zeta was vaguely aware of. It's what had woken her to begin with. Even though she'd tried to go back to sleep, her exhaustion had subsided enough that she couldn't just return to slumber and decided to get up. The doctor, Zeta was told, would be back to discuss discharge after breakfast.

"I'm surprised your husband isn't here," Callie said as she removed the IV from Zeta's hand. "I would have thought you would have to tear him away the way everyone was talking about him!"

"I made him leave. One of us should get a good night's sleep," Zeta said, keeping up their little ruse. It was silly and harmless and felt nice, easy to slip into.

Callie nodded and saw herself out, leaving Zeta alone again. Free from all the wires, she stood up, walked around the small room, and brushed her teeth before she snuggled back on the bed into a more comfortable position. She reached for her phone, planning to play something to distract herself, but it rang in her hand.

"Hello?" she said, answering it without looking, expecting Cody. He worked night shift and would be leaving.

"Hi. Thought it would be OK to call, since you were up." Ash, again.

"Yeah, it's totally fine," she answered, surprised, stumbling.

"So, you didn't answer me."

Startled, Zeta cycled through everything they talked about the night before, trying to remember the question she missed. Was it something about the baby? Her? "What question?"

"Why are you up so early? If I remember correctly, you like to sleep in," he chuckled.

The tension went out of her. "Oh," she said, lying back in the bed. "The doctor came in and I just couldn't quite get back to sleep after that."

"You were pretty deeply asleep when I left you last night," he teased. "Did they say anything?"

Her cheeks tingled with embarrassment. Hearing him admit that he'd seen her sleeping was somehow more awkward than everything else he'd seen. Zeta was aware of how silly it was. He'd been there when she came to in the hospital, but this seemed more exposed. "Well, I'm not anymore. They're going to discharge me. I told you, I'm fine."

"Do you want some company?"

"You can't come; it's not visiting hours!"

"I'm your husband, remember?" he replied, the smile clear in his voice, the little game still in effect. The little lie.

"Alright." She heard herself agreeing before she could think about it, stop herself.

"Good, because I need your help with something," he stretched, groaning, on the other end of the line.

"What?" she asked.

"I'll explain when I get there. You should try to sleep more. I'll be there soon."

They exchanged goodbyes and hung up the phone. She leaned back, telling herself they needed to talk, that it was better to do it now than later. But her mind wandered to the little puzzle he'd dropped in her lap and could only come up with one thing that Ash, A. M. Cross, the Tyrant, could possibly need from her at seven in the morning.

Work. It had to be.

Boundaries. She had to set boundaries.

But if I can't perform, is he going to fire me? A stray thought. *I'm pregnant, and he knows that; am I a liability? Is it ethical for me to work for him now? Is this against company policy? But we're not in a relationship. I haven't saved up enough!*

The swirl of worry, nearly divorced from the first thought that had caused it, surged in her, all ideas of his kindness replaced with the man she'd actually known for the last two months. Making up a reason to let a pregnant person go seemed like exactly the type of thing the Tyrant would do to avoid any issues.

She tried to play games to distract herself, but the idea just kept coming back, irrational but the only thing she could think. *How will I take care of the baby?*

The plan was to work the job, save the money, and move her little apartment around, but if he was going to fire her . . .

The door opened and Ash walked in, bundled in a scarf and hat against the cold, a paper bag in one hand and a cup holder with two hot drinks in the other. He smiled at her, his blue eyes shining in the early morning sun. "Good morning," he said.

"I can't drink coffee, sorry. The baby. And— And I can't answer anything about the project, I don't have anything with me."

He put the bag and drinks down. "Alright. I wasn't going to ask anything about . . . For god's sake, Zeta, you're in the hospital! Why would I ask you about work? Although," he said slowly, frowning, "that *is* something we'll have to figure out."

"Are you going to fire me?" she asked, gripping the blankets, eyes closed to keep the world from spinning, her heart pounding.

"No! Absolutely not. You're an excellent employee. I was trying to hire you yesterday, remember? You don't need to worry about that." He chuckled and she looked up at him. He held the disposable cup out to her. "You can have some caffeine. I read about it last night. But this isn't coffee. Well, yours isn't. I got you hot chocolate."

That was my reward for going to the meeting. Zeta sniffed, and then tears rolled down her cheeks, hot and fat. It was perfect. She was trying to put on a brave face, trying to keep the events of the last twenty-four hours small, compact, contained, but that was impossible. Things had changed, rapidly, and she was struggling to stay ahead of them.

But then Ash had brought her hot cocoa, like he knew, like it was always supposed to happen. Her Aunt Josie would say it was a sign; she would say she shouldn't ignore it, should lean into the universe. Zeta didn't know what she believed, but there was comfort there. The universe saying, *Sorry, it's alright.* Or maybe it was saying that *he* was alright. Or maybe she was reading too much into it, but it didn't matter because hot cocoa was the exact right thing at that exact right moment and he had brought it to her.

"What's the matter?" he asked, putting the cup down, pulling off his coat, and settling next to her, hands on her knees.

She looked away. "No, I'm sorry, please don't freak out. It's just, I was going to get myself hot chocolate yesterday, so it felt like something else, but you're just being nice. I'm sorry! I'm just emotional. Hormones."

Now that she had started, she couldn't stop. It wasn't about the hot cocoa anymore. Now it was about everything. Tears brimmed over in her eyes, her own stress and anxiety, feelings she worked very hard to keep from experiencing that she had in fact built a life focused around avoiding completely, bubbled over and spilled down her cheeks. The kind of cry that isn't about one single thing, that's about everything and nothing at all. She was crying about the hospital, her apartment, the last four months of being sick and uncomfortable. About him and the weird way he'd left, about not seeing his message for two months. About her asshole boss and all his meeting requests that she never took but maybe if she had . . . She wiped at her tears furiously; her cheeks hurt but wouldn't dry. She felt even weaker than she had after she fainted into his arms the first time.

"Zeta, it's fine," he said softly. His fingers, cold as ice, wiped at her tears before he bent forward and kissed the wet streaks along her cheeks. Then her eyes and forehead, his touch gentle and reassuring against her skin.

He was so close, the scent of sage mingled with the lingering wool of his coat and something else fresh and light. Ash's nose and cheeks were still red from cold, his hair a mess from the hat. His lips brushed over her face, little feathery kisses, unsure but landing anyway. He held her closer, his hand on her bare back through the slit of the hospital gown, cold but warming against her skin.

She tilted her head up to him, his kisses bolder on her cheeks, her chin, the corner of her mouth.

In the hazy soft pleasure of his touch, she wasn't sure if she turned or she was turned so that her mouth met his, tasted winter for a moment before his lips parted, the hot touch of his tongue begging entry which she granted with a sigh. There was no hesitation in his kiss. No hesitation in the way he wrapped his arms around her and dragged her into his lap. Pulled her from the tangle of blankets and placed her against him so that she had no choice but to straddle him.

It was different, the feel of him between her legs, than she remembered. Now the swell of her belly pressed against the flat plane of his, and she faltered, embarrassed, realizing what she'd done. But her retreat was halted by his arms, his mouth that refused to be parted from hers for more than a breath. For more than the two-syllable space of her name, the sound sending shivers through her, and she remembered how it felt when he moaned into her ear.

It was different, they were different, but the desire was still the same. Sparking, flickering, burning back to life under his touch.

His hand, warmed by her back, shifted and found its way to her breast as his mouth found the tender skin of her neck. Her body rocked against his, her softness met with his hardness. The space low in her, below her belly, began to shift and twist in on itself, tighter and tighter as she moved against him.

"Ash." His name slipped from her mouth, a single breath, between a question and a statement. "I . . ."

His hands moved to her hips and Zeta wrapped her arms around his shoulders, losing her warning, let herself be moved, each mock thrust bringing her closer and closer to the edge. She bit down on his shoulder to drown out her cry as she felt the flood of release. Ash sucked in his breath at the press of her teeth through fabric. Zeta's legs loosened; the world felt heavy.

Ash hugged her to him. Stroked her hair, turned his face to hers, and laid kisses along the shell of her ear, the curve of her neck. "I have to put you down."

Zeta nodded, untangled herself, and slid back into the bed. She pulled the blankets up and peeked over the hills of her knees at him. He looked dazed.

"I . . ." Ash started slowly, and her guts clenched tight with worry. "Have to go to the bathroom."

Bathroom? It completely overrode the apologies she had waiting on her tongue. She couldn't figure out why he'd said that, what it meant, and then, "Oh. Oh!" Heat ran to her face. "It's right there," she pointed at the door just past the bed. "Take your time."

"I don't think I'll be long. I brought you some breakfast. You can start eating."

"Why are you always feeding me? You know they have food here, at the hospital?" she asked, forcing the joke to cover her embarrassment. To swallow down her real question: *Was that alright?*

"But you don't like the food here. And besides, I thought pregnant women liked to be fed," he teased, matching her tone, her forced mood. Ash reached into the bag and pulled out a foil-wrapped package like they hadn't just dry humped on her hospital bed. Like he wasn't about to go finish himself off or clean himself up in the bathroom. "Breakfast burrito. Eggs, peppers, and sausage."

Presented with the food, all care about what he was about to do and what they had done left her. Her mouth watered at the smell. She found she was starving even after the snacks. She snatched it from his fingers and unwrapped it quickly, taking a huge bite. Still warm, it made her hum in pleasure. Mouth full, Zeta gave Ash a thumbs up, and he slipped away, closing the bathroom door behind him. He returned ten minutes later, but by then she'd already finished the burrito.

"I'm sorry, I should have waited for you to eat," she said guiltily.

"No, don't worry about it. Did you like it?"

"Yeah, you didn't mention the sweet potatoes though."

He handed her the hot cocoa and sat down to eat his own meal. "I forgot. I have a lot left over, and I'm trying to use them up before they go bad."

"You made that? I thought you picked it up on your way here."

"I got the drinks on the way here."

"I don't think you can get from downtown to here *and* cook a meal *and* stop for coffee in half an hour. How long have you been planning this?" she teased, chuckling.

"Since I left last night," he responded.

Zeta smiled into her cup. "If I had known you were that determined, I would have told you to bring me a change of clothes."

"I can get you some now if you want." Ash was smiling, playful but serious.

Zeta felt a little burst of warmth in her, his care not quite unexpected at this point but still surprising in its own way. "No, I think I'll just wear what I came in. They're letting me out soon."

"What else do you like to eat?"

Zeta chose to ignore the chance to make an obvious innuendo of the question and answered it straight, hoping that it steered them back to more neutral territory. "I'm pretty adventurous usually, but since I've been pregnant I've had to be more careful. Half of what I like is on the no-no list, and I can't stomach what's left."

"So tell me anyway."

Zeta listed off her favorite foods while he finished his breakfast. He responded with his own, and it all felt like that night on the deck. Ash gathered their trash and then slid in the bed next to Zeta, wrapping his arm over her shoulder, his phone in his hand. She couldn't stop herself from leaning into him, resting her weight against his chest, and he shifted until they were both comfortable and curled up against one another.

Her phone was sitting on her lap, and she realized he'd never seen the baby. He hadn't been there when they checked her over at arrival. "Here, look," she said, pulling up the picture she took of the early scans. A small, gray figure with tiny limbs.

He took the phone from her, face slack, lips parted. "Is that?"

"Yeah, not much to see. It was pretty early on. Ten weeks," she explained.

He moved his free hand over her belly. "This is them?"

He was grinning, excited. His hand was heavy on her, like a blanket, and it radiated warmth through her, made her feel comforted and settled. She pulled against him, thoughtlessly, breathing him in, letting his body support hers. "Yeah, that's them."

"Send it to me," he said softly, and then kissed her head. "Don't fall off to sleep yet, Kitten."

Butterflies, a sea of them, erupted in her. Her cheeks tingled and bubbling giggles started to form. "Kitten?" she repeated flatly to keep them from escaping.

"Your coat has cat ears," he responded simply as he shifted his phone in front of her. "Look."

"You're playing *Alone in the Multiverse?*"

"Yeah, this girl I met told me it was really good."

Zeta could feel his words through his chest where she rested her head. He'd kept playing them; it really hadn't been just a pickup line. *He did like me,* she thought, and then, *He **does** like me.* He had looked for her. It was Zeta who hadn't bothered, and now, lying in his arms, pulled close, she didn't know why she hadn't at least asked for his number, had let him just go. He settled his hand over her belly, as natural as anything. "What do you need help with?" she asked sleepy, hopeful.

"I'm stuck," he said as his game started. "I can't get past this puzzle. You need two people, and as the title indicates, I'm alone."

Zeta recognized the level, about halfway through the game, when everything changed. "You have to use the call button. Did you find it?"

"Show me."

"You're never alone in the multiverse," she said. She tapped the call button on his screen, and another player, a random person from the network, joined him. Together they pressed the panels to open the door. The call button wouldn't do anything in the first half of the game. It only unlocked after you ascended into the outer plains where the gameplay became "endless." Players could call on anyone at any time to help then. Zeta liked ending up in other games, even if it was just for a moment. The trick then was figuring out the puzzles before the timer ran out and you went back to your own game. "There's an endgame," she explained, "but from here on out, you can get called into other games, even if you've beaten your own, as long as you're logged in. Is this what you needed my help with?"

He hummed yes and then he played on, keeping her close to him, his chest rising and falling under her. Zeta closed her eyes. She slept through the arrival of her terrible breakfast and only woke when Ash shook her gently to speak to the doctor.

She was so groggy, she missed the doctor's name. The man before her went over her chart, what she needed to be aware of at home, and what to do for the injuries she had sustained, but he agreed to discharge her with instructions to follow up with both her primary care doctor and ob-gyn. She'd have to come back to get the stitches taken out of her hand.

Once the doctor left, Zeta, regretfully, sat up fully. Ash let out a little whine, which Zeta pretended to ignore. *Puppy*, she smiled to herself. She slipped into the bathroom to change and swallowed a knowing giggle at the sight of the damp washcloth on the sink.

A few minutes later she was done dressing and fully ready to go home. The discharge nurse came and went, to Zeta's relief, handing her a bundle of paperwork and wishing them both luck on their baby.

"It's too cold," Ash said, draping his scarf around her throat as they rode the elevator in the parking garage. "Your coat isn't warm enough," he added.

"That's why I wear layers," she responded. He looked so serious and concerned with his brows pulled together she almost laughed. He was so cute. *Yup, just like a puppy.*

On the ride back to her place, the silence was comfortable, Ash keeping his hand on her thigh as Zeta floated through consciousness, not asleep but not quite awake. At the entrance of her apartment building, Ash grabbed her hand as she opened the door to get out.

"Wait, this doesn't feel right," he said softly. "I don't like just letting you go like this."

She understood. Those same feelings were in her. That *this* could not be how things ended. That she should bring him up, sit him down, work things out but, no. "I don't think we should rush into anything. It's obvious that there's something between us. I mean, more than the baby. I mean, ah, this is so awkward."

"I understand." He chuckled. "I'll see you again, soon then," he promised. "Maybe if you're feeling better, we can have dinner this weekend? Or lunch? Or anything."

"Yeah, I'd really like that actually. Have a good day at work!" she said brightly. *This doesn't have to be weird.*

"Get some rest," Ash responded before leaning over and brushing a kiss over her mouth. A clear message of his intentions. Before she could stop herself she was kissing him back, swallowing his contented sigh. He pulled away, grinning.

"I need to go," she said, embarrassed.

"If you need *anything*, call me. Anytime, alright?"

In Zeta's mind there were reasons why not, rebuttals and reminders. They'd just reconnected, they still had to talk about boundaries and plans, she had a support network. But the baby moved, a fluttering wave, and she just nodded. "Alright. I'm really going now."

Zeta slipped out of the car before he could hold her again. The cold air bit at her face, and she fumbled for her keys, crossing the distance from sidewalk to door.

She turned back as she unlocked it, saw him still watching, waiting, and passed through the door, back inside her quiet apartment. Through the wood she heard him leave.

Zeta was in her apartment before she realized she still had his scarf. It smelled like him, and she stood in her doorway, breathing him in, her cheeks hot, lips still tingling where he had touched them.

14

It had been twenty-four hours since he'd dropped Zeta off from the hospital, and Ash was still in a daze. He'd texted with her throughout the day, checking in, offering his help at every turn, but she declined, politely, gently. He offered to stop by after work, bring dinner, and she told him that she had company coming.

He wanted to ask who, suggest that she should rest, and stopped himself. Zeta had her own life and he shouldn't intrude. They weren't anything yet but two people in strange circumstances—but then his shoulder ached from the bite she'd left on him and he remembered her body on top of his and he didn't know what to think. The spot where she had sunk her teeth into his shoulder was bruised and burned with his every movement, sending hot waves of remembered pleasure through him. *There has to be something here,* he thought idly as he went through the morning.

Ashford Cross had never had this problem before. He was driven, motivated; he should be able to walk into the room and proclaim them a couple and have that be it. But he couldn't, and he felt awful and wrong for having the thought. He hadn't even explained everything properly to her. There was so much they needed to say to each other, but it had only been two days since she fell through the table.

"Right, she needs to recover. She probably is *also* figuring things out on her end," Ash said, trying to convince himself and failing. He checked his watch, saw it was nearly lunch, and gave in to his impulses.

"Hi!" Zeta said, picking up the call. "What's up?"

"Nothing," he sighed at her bright voice. "I just thought I'd check in on you. I hope I didn't wake you. It's almost noon; have you had lunch yet?"

Laughter. "I know I told you that I sleep late, but I meant, like, I get up at nine. I've been up and working for a little while now. But I guess I do need to eat something."

He frowned. *Is this because of me?* "You're back to work already? You were in the hospital yesterday. You should be resting."

"I'm fine. If the table hadn't been there, this would have all ended yesterday." She sighed, and the sounds of her shifting in her chair came through the line. His guts tightened at the idea that they could have ended yesterday. "And this won't get done on time if we're down a full body."

"It's not important, Zeta," he said gently. He didn't want to talk about work but, "We can adjust the timeline."

"You don't have to. It's not right to give me special treatment," she replied.

"You could have told me you weren't feeling well," he said.

"And then what? It's my job, Mr. Cross," she responded, and he wasn't sure if it was anger or just annoyance, but the edge of it sliced at him.

"It's my job to see that things run smoothly. I was wrong and I'm sorry."

"Why are you saying this to me?" She shifted again, focused.

"I don't want you to think that I don't care."

"I don't want—"

"I'm not giving you preferential treatment," he said, cutting her off. "I didn't present myself as someone who you *could* come to, and I apologize for that. You had a medical emergency. I *know* you did because it was in my office. You should not be working today. It doesn't matter if you're ten feet from your bed or you feel alright. *I am not allowing you to work for this company until after you've recovered.* So, Ms. Rodgers, please log off and take a few days for yourself."

Silence, and then, "Oh."

"Oh?" he echoed.

"You were very professional sounding. Did you call me today as my boss or as . . . whatever it is we are?"

He opened his mouth, didn't know what to say, nervous. He had called for a reason. It was not to talk about work; he wasn't expecting her to be *working*. He thought she would be in bed, soft and sleepy, resting.

"Because you know, you're not supposed to call me about work," she said slowly, testing the conversation, testing him.

"I didn't call you to talk about work. I called you because I'm worried about you. I wanted to make sure you were doing alright."

"Ash," she said, voice heavy, hard.

"Zeta, I—" he tried.

"If you want us to . . . see where this goes, do not ever speak to me like you're my boss again. If it's about the job, then send me an email or a chat message. But do not ever, *ever* talk to me like that again, or it will be the last time we ever speak."

There were arguments on his tongue, that they had to discuss that dynamic, that he would need to speak to her *as her boss*, but he stopped, swallowing them. "I called to ask if you were busy Saturday night, Kitten."

"Kitten," her turn to echo. "It's weird." In his mind he saw her nose wrinkle.

"Do you not like it?" He'd upset her again.

"I don't . . . dislike it. Like a date?"

His heart sped up, ears burned. He'd never been so nervous about asking someone out, even though the woman he was asking was currently pregnant with his child. "It doesn't have to be? If you're not comfortable, I mean. I thought we would go to this place, Remy's? It's nice." The words spilled, a nervous ramble.

"You're taking me to a nice restaurant and it's not a date?" Zeta asked, laughter in her voice.

"I don't want you to feel pressured. We can go somewhere else!"

"Well, that depends. Are you asking me on a date or are you just wanting to talk to me? Because if you just want to talk to me, we're doing that right now, I don't have to go out with you."

"It's a date! I want to take you on a real date!" he blurted out. He felt like a teenager but she was laughing, the upset of a few minutes ago passed.

"I'm sorry, I didn't know you were going to get so nervous. A real date it is then."

He leaned back in his chair, stared up at his ceiling, blew out long breaths, and waited for his heart to stop racing. "I thought you were trying to avoid me," he admitted.

A questioning hum. "Why did you think that?"

"You keep turning me down whenever I offer to come see you."

"It's been a day. Chill," she scolded, playfully.

"I've been wanting to spend time with you for longer than that though," he said, shifting back, tucking the phone between his ear and shoulder and pulling up his email.

She sucked in her breath. He'd said something vulnerable, but he couldn't help it. He didn't think it would help him to hide anything, not from her. He hit send on the email to Zeta's department letting them know she'd be out for personal reasons until Monday.

"There is one thing though," Zeta said, snapping him to attention.

"One thing?"

"I'd like to know you why you ran out on me that night. I think we should talk about it now, so we don't have to talk about it later."

"Why don't I come over then? To tell you in person," he offered, alert, focused, ready to leave the office right then. He had to get this right. It was his chance to set things back on the correct path. He shouldn't do it over the phone.

"No," Zeta said. She didn't sound upset or nervous that he could tell. He couldn't read her voice as well as he wished. She always sounded calm, collected. "You're too pretty. That will influence my opinion of what you say. Tell me over the phone."

Ash was torn between being flattered and anxious. It wasn't how he planned to tell her. He was going to explain over dinner, hold her hand, apologize. But that wasn't what she wanted from him, and he had no right to force his perfect setting on to her. "Do you remember, I got a phone a call?"

"Yeah, it was more like five phone calls, but I remember," she replied.

"It was my mom. She was calling because my father had a heart attack. That's why I ran out of there. It wasn't you at all." There, it was out. Not as he planned but out all the same.

"Is he OK? Your dad, I mean."

"Yes, he's getting better. That's why I'm in charge right now." *Right now*, he thought. Even to her he couldn't just say *forever*.

"And why his face came up in Google. You must look like your mom."

"I do." *Who do you think our baby will look like*, he almost asked but stopped himself. *Let her lead. I have to show her how sorry I am, that I'm accountable for this, that she can rely on me.*

"Why didn't you just tell me? You were babbling about a trip." She sounded like she was eating. Good.

"It felt like too much to say to a woman I'd just met. Especially after what happened. I mean, why would you believe me?"

"OK, that's fair, I would not have. But I thought you were, like, a secretary."

He put his face in his hand. "I really liked talking to you, and I knew if I told what I really did and that I was supposed to be traveling the next day, then the conversation would have been about that instead. And I didn't want to talk about that."

"Or did you think your odds were better for a hookup if I thought you were just some guy?" She sounded so matter-of-fact, no accusation.

"I *am* just some guy. And I never wanted it to be just a hookup, I swear. I wanted you to like me."

"Hmmm, that's a really weird thing to do then, Ash."

"I know! I thought I could explain things later. Like in the morning? And then my mom called and I panicked and I'm sorry. I'm really, really sorry." He closed his eyes, gripped his phone so tight his fingers hurt.

"You're so weird," she sighed.

I'm not; it's only around you. I can't get my head together around you, Zeta. Which meant he was weird, he couldn't help it. "I am. I'm sorry."

"It's alright. About being weird. I'm weird too. I don't think I'm upset about it, what happened. I mean, not now? I'm glad we talked about this before our date, it would have made for a depressing first date conversation." She chuckled.

"It would have." He matched her laughter. "I want to move on from this. Can we start over? I know how that sounds. I mean, we're having a baby, but can we?"

"I think we can try? I have to finish my food and get back. You know you can, like, talk to me more if you want. I check my messages. You don't have to be so nervous."

"I'll do that then. Can I ask you a question too? I was going to ask when I saw you again, in person, but maybe it's better to get it out of the way now."

"Sure," she answered.

Ash's mouth was dry, and he cleared his throat. The question had been rolling around in his head since she fell into his arms, but he still hadn't figured out how to ask it. "I'm not upset. I don't want you to think that I'm upset," he started, clumsy, stuttering, aware that he'd already made multiple bad impressions. He rubbed his face, tried to clear his mind, settle his thoughts, but there was no way he could think of to ask that didn't sound like an accusation. "Why are you pregnant?"

"Oh," she laughed. "I guess it makes sense to talk about that too. You're not going to believe this!"

Ash closed his eyes, took a deep, shaky breath. Laughter was good. "It can't sound worse than my reasons for leaving that night."

"It can! Remember my upstairs neighbor?"

A flicker of a memory, her worry of being too loud. "Yes."

"Apparently he kept, like, a lot of fish. Something happened upstairs and all those tanks fell, broke, and flooded my apartment that morning while I was asleep. I had to move into a hotel for two months while they cleaned and fixed everything and I just . . . forgot to get the pill."

"You're right, that does sound less believable. And you decided to keep it?"

"Yeah. I knew it would be hard, but it was one of those *I didn't know I wanted it until it was happening* type things, you know?"

"I do," he said softly, wishing he had waited so he could touch her, feel her warmth. Wished she could see his face, how sincere he was. "I really do."

He heard her breathing through the line. "Good," she said finally.

Face hot, he cleared his throat again and scrambled for something else to say. He couldn't think of anything worthy, so he stumbled back into the safety of pleasantries. "You probably need to get some more rest. Please call me if you need anything, anything at all."

"I'm really OK." The faint click of a mouse. "Hey, did you email everybody about me?" She growled, sounded like she would protest.

Ash took a chance, leaning into that soft space that was growing between them. "Kitten, please," he said softly. "We're not talking about work anymore."

Silence. He held his breath. And then, "Alright, *fine*. But," her voice softened, came out quiet, "really don't do that again. I don't like when guys are too pushy."

His intent hadn't been to force her, only to take care of her. Take over a small responsibility. He'd overstepped. "Noted, it won't happen again."

"It's alright. We're still figuring things out, and besides, you probably thought you were being helpful, right?"

"Yeah, actually," he laughed. "Didn't work out the way I wanted."

"Not everything will, Mr. Cross," he heard her smile in her voice, relaxed. It was alright, everything was alright, but he wished she called him something else. Something to match his *Kitten*, build the soft space between.

A mumbling voice in the background. Then Zeta again, "Be out in a minute!" To him, "Sorry, I've gotta go."

He didn't want to let her leave the call. He swallowed the desire. "Can I call you more?" he asked, stomach twisting.

"Sure, just don't go overboard. I get the feeling that you would call me every time you had a free minute if you could."

I would. "I'm not free that often."

"We'll see. Goodbye, Ash."

"Goodbye, Kitten."

Zeta giggled as she hung up the phone, and Ash leaned back in his chair, letting the jittery, nervous energy run out of him. She'd said yes to their date, and she hadn't pulled away when he explained what happened that night. She was willing to see where things went. Ash couldn't have asked for better circumstances. He picked up his phone, looked at her profile to see her smiling face again.

All the recent posts were happy birthday messages, and he checked the date. He'd just missed hers. It felt too close to be a coincidence.

"I have to get her something," he mumbled to his empty office. But he couldn't think of what. Randall's mom, his own mother and sister, easy. He knew them, knew what to get them, but he didn't *know* Zeta. Not the way he wanted, to give her something that would garner more than "Oh, thanks" or "That's nice."

He didn't know her taste in clothing or purses. He didn't think she wore perfume and he didn't remember any art from her apartment. Just photographs and . . . games.

He didn't know what games she had, but he knew what kind of phone she owned and what she played. He purchased a gift card for the Play store.

Something to entertain you until our date. Happy birthday, sorry I missed it. He pressed send on the gift card and hoped it sent the right message. To help it along, he took a screen shot and sent it as well. A start.

Zeta stuffed the last of the muffin in her mouth. She hadn't felt like eating it before she started working, but Ash was right, she did need to eat, and she did feel at least a little better after she'd started. She didn't want tell him that, overall, she still felt like she'd been hit by a truck. She was exhausted. The cut along her hand ached but looked like it was healing. The stitches wouldn't be coming out until the following week. She looked down to see her belly standing out. "I guess I really am showing now. You couldn't wait, like, one more week to become a big deal?" she chided before rubbing it. "I guess not. At least you aren't evicting everything I eat still." The muffin wasn't making any rumblings.

She rested her hand on her belly, let herself sit with the conversation that had just ended. *Kitten, please*, her memory played, Ash's voice a low rumble that she felt all along her spine and into her belly. He had sounded so comforting, and she wished she had waited until they met in person again. But she wanted the distance in case it didn't go well. And now she regretted being so cautious.

His "I do" had been so full of care and warmth it made her heart skip. But it was better that they had talked, had gotten those things out of the way. He hadn't been perfect, but he didn't push against her boundaries, at least not knowingly. They could move forward.

"OK, let's get an actual meal," Zeta said. She shut everything down and grabbed her phone, finally opening the door to her office.

The air smelled savory, meat and spices. "It smells great!" Zeta sang, coming down the hall and around the corner into the kitchen.

"I cooked because I knew you wouldn't," Pixie confirmed, still in her T-shirt and short-shorts that she'd slept in. She'd shown up an hour after Zeta got home to sit with her and make sure she was alright. "What did you have for breakfast? Nothing."

Maybe I should have mentioned that to Ash, so he wouldn't be so worried. "I had a muffin," Zeta said, sitting at the table.

"This morning though?" Pixie asked, making a did-you-really face.

"Just . . . now. Anyway, I thought you were going to work?"

"I am, I have to leave right after we eat. Who were you talking to?" Pixie sat a plate with chicken and gnocchi covered in a creamy sauce in front of Zeta.

"Ash. He called to check in on me. We were talking about what happened."

"At the hospital?" Pixie asked, sitting down with her own plate.

"No, the night we met."

Pixie paused, fork halfway to her mouth, tone serious. "Tell me."

Zeta explained what had happened over the phone call, leaving out that her brain had turned into goo when he called her kitten, twice. She had no idea why that little nickname, *pet name*, had such an effect, but it made her warm and jittery in a good way. Maybe it was the irony that she'd been thinking of him as a puppy since they met on the deck. Either way, she kept it to herself. Pixie listened, fork unmoving.

"That sounds like a lie. His dad just suddenly had a heart attack, and he just didn't tell you he was leaving because he didn't want you to think it was a hookup," Pixie said, finally eating. "I don't know if you should trust him. Of course he'd say he wanted the baby *now*. What choice does he have?"

"I thought the same exact thing. But it would be a wild thing to lie about. It's not like it's something that I can't find out about. I can ask someone about his dad *at the company that we both work at*. And no, he doesn't have to be happy about the baby. I mean, he could just walk away. But he's not."

"Good point," Pixie said, face twisted in thought. "You guys had the worst luck after you met."

"I know! It's ridiculous! Maybe we're cursed?"

"Don't start that woo woo shit, you sound like Josie. We already have Cody, and that's enough manifestation and praying to old gods," Pixie made an *X* with her fingers. "Don't think about it. Bad luck is just bad luck. It doesn't have to mean anything."

"I know, I know," Zeta sighed, nearly convinced to call her aunt and ask about magical interventions just in case.

"So what are you going to do?" Pixie asked.

"What do you mean? I'm going to go on the date of course!" Zeta answered. "Free food!"

"I meant about him. I don't want you to get hurt," she said slowly, unsure. "I don't think you should rush into anything. He seems very nice but . . ."

"I know, he's so nice, it's too perfect, isn't it? He could be hiding something, or maybe I'm just falling into this because I'm pregnant and he's so easy because he's . . ." *a puppy*, she stopped herself from saying.

"Pretty? He's *very* pretty," Pixie said wistfully. "He could have a whole other family that he's hiding!"

"Hey, stop that! This is not one of your K-dramas. There's no dark secret. He is a normal man."

"So are you going to take him to the ultrasound?" Pixie asked.

The appointment was right before Christmas. She hadn't had time to think about it. "I don't know. Everything is happening so fast and I don't want to spring it on him."

"Girl, spring *what* on him? He knows you're pregnant! Just ask him," Pixie said, rolling her eyes.

"Yeah, but we haven't actually *talked* about the baby. Like, not really. He's *saying* all the right things, but I don't know if he's going to *do* them."

"And you can't know until you give him a chance," Pixie said, pointing her fork. "What are you scared of? You have to deal with him either way."

"I know, you're right. I'm just . . ." It wasn't fear really. "It feels irresponsible to rush into things. I have to think about more than just me. What happened to 'Don't trust him'?"

"Yeah well, he's really pretty. And you have to deal with him either way," Pixie repeated, and shoved a fork of food into her mouth. She looked at the stove and jumped up. "Is that time right?"

"Yeah."

"I have to go to work!" She stuffed more food than Zeta thought possible in her mouth, grabbed her overnight bag, and ran into the bathroom.

Zeta picked up her phone, eating her own food more calmly, and found a text from Ash. Two texts, but the picture grabbed her attention.

You got a peach fire stone dragon! You must have spent a fortune! she texted. A smile worked at the corner of her mouth that after their heavy conversation he would want to talk about such a silly thing.

This was mostly farming. I had a lot of time on my hands the last couple of months.

I got mine in an event. Remembering that he didn't know anything about mobile games, she explained. **You should do them sometime. If you get the chance. It's silly but worth it. It's basically just interactive ads for stuff.** She really had made an impact on him. First, *Alone in the Multiverse*, which wasn't proof of anything, really; it was fun, engaging. *Pretty Pretty Dragon Ranch?* Complete waste of time and money, and the only thing worth it was collecting digital assets. Made to be addictive but entirely possible to walk away from. But he played it because she said she did, and now he was showing her how far he got.

She melted.

Then she looked at the other message. It was a link. To a gift card.

Much better than flowers, she hummed, accepting it. **You didn't have to get me anything but thank you**, she wrote back with a sea of hearts and smiling emojis.

He's been offering to help. Maybe this is just something he does? **I'm going to buy this cutie**, she messaged. She attached a picture of a dragon-like creature with a furry sheep body and curling horns.

I've got a lot further to go before I can get Sweet Dream Dragon, Ash replied. **The recovery bonus would be nice though.**

I'd kill for a recovery bonus right now, she responded. **I'm going to go lie down.**

I wish you all the Sweet Dream Dragons your heart desires.

Zeta smiled at her phone as Pixie came bursting out of the bathroom dressed in blue skirt and a yellow blouse. Her hair was under a black wig fashioned into a bob. She dashed to the table, stuffed more food in her mouth, and somehow managed to talk around it. "Sorry to leave this for you! Do you mind cleaning up? Ugh, I suck, but I'm about to be late!"

"It's OK! Thanks for making lunch! And dinner! And I'll see you later. Get out of here before you get fired."

Pixie left in a whirlwind. Zeta finished her food while she played games with the other hand. As she put away the leftovers, she realized Pixie had gone out to get groceries in her pajamas because Zeta's refrigerator had been bare as always. She made a mental note to order groceries; she was supposed to be trying to do better about that. She went to rinse out the pot and realized she couldn't do her own dishes. The renovations to the apartment didn't include a dishwasher. And she couldn't hand-wash them with her stitches.

"Problem for Future Zeta," she grumbled before leaving the lot of them in the sink and going back to bed. *Buy gloves*, she added to the mental checklist that she forgot as soon as her head hit the pillow. She thought she'd fall right to sleep, but she tossed and lay awake, worrying over what to do about the man who was sliding into her life and if it was OK to just *be OK* with it all. Tired and unable to sleep, she picked up her phone and started reading *The Time Machine*.

15

Ash froze at the sight of Zeta. It wasn't the first time that he'd seen her in a dress; he'd met her in one. But it wasn't like this. A lavender that leaned toward gray, the dress seemed to shimmer. The waist was high, and a deep V neckline showed off the gentle curve of her breasts. The sleeves were long and loose until they cinched at her wrists. She held a little gold purse shaped like a coin. The skirt was flowing, reaching to her knees covered by sheer black stockings, feet in a pair of low black heels. Her lips shimmered, glossy, the way they had the night when they first met, and simple square, gold studs adorned her ears. Her hair was braided into a crown around her head.

There was a change in her, subtle, from when she had come into his office. Her skin richer, bright, her lips fuller, softer. Everything seemed softer. *Glowing.*

She wrinkled her nose at him and his heart skipped. "Do I look OK? Sorry, my belly is sort of noticeable, but I didn't have a lot

of time to find something and I started showing, like, overnight."
She smoothed her skirt and inspected herself, frowning.

They'd agreed to meet at the restaurant. Ash had tried to convince
her to let him pick her up, but she'd declined for reasons unknown
to him. He'd booked a room for them so they would be alone, and
now she was standing at the door. Beautiful. He felt underdressed
in his maroon sweater and brown slacks.

He crossed the short distance between them and took her hands,
forcing her attention back to him. "You look beautiful."

Ash bent, brushed his lips over hers and inhaled her scent. The
same sweet scent that had filled his nostrils when he had pulled her
into his lap in the hospital and before that on the deck. Flowery,
jasmine tea, she smelled like summer. Warm air, sun. His hands
found their way to her belly; he couldn't stop them as they traced
the firm swell of it. She covered his hand with her own, and when
he met her gaze, she wore a dazzling smile. He'd never seen her smile
like that, couldn't have imagined it, but now his heart fluttered in
his chest, breath quickened. Her hand, so much smaller than his
own, was grounding. Ash ached to pull her closer, hold her and
get lost in that scent, feel her breathing and her heat all along the
length of his body, their growing baby rising and falling with every
inhale and exhale under his hand.

"I guess it's OK then?" she said shyly, still smiling.

"Perfect," he breathed.

"I'm glad," she said, looking down at their hands.

His face went hot, tingling, and his breathing was heavy. He
pulled away, reluctantly, the world freezing over without her touch.
"Let's sit down," he said, stepping away, needing to break the spell
of her closeness, her warmth.

"You know," Zeta said, staring at the private room he had
reserved, "you really didn't have to do this. You could just take
me to a diner or something."

He picked it for the view and because it was a cozy space where
they could be alone. Where they could talk outside of either of

their apartments. The room was the size of a bedroom, with a wide window that showed the closed courtyard of the restaurant, making it seem almost like they weren't in the middle of the city. The walls were covered in bronze damask wallpaper, a large floral still life hanging on one wall. The table, flanked by cushy chairs, was set for two. No candles but the lights were low. Zeta stared out the window into the courtyard. Lit by false gaslights, the bare trees and short path that led to the small fountain in the center hinted at a world beyond. It made their small room more intimate in the cold winter night.

"It's our first date," Ash replied, smiling at her. "It should be nice."

"It is! Funny. Since we're already having a baby and all. We should talk about that," she sighed, her smile started to twist into a thoughtful sort of frown.

No, he thought, taking her hand, *don't*. "We will. I want to learn more about you first. Here, come sit down." He put his hand on the small of her back, gently nudged her toward the table.

He pulled her chair out, and Zeta slid into it, showing him her back, and his breath caught for the second time.

The back of her dress had a deeper V to rival the front, held across the top by a thin tie. The smooth skin and the line of her spine were revealed and his mouth watered with the desire to bend and move his lips over her shoulders, trace the road of her back with his tongue.

She hummed, question in the sound, turning to look up at him.

"This dress is very nice on you," Ash said slowly, letting himself indulge in her, slipping his fingers into the opening, her back warm against his touch. She gasped in reward.

"I don't think my dress is the important thing here," she said, turning away, flustered, making him want to touch her more. He pulled his hand away as she kept talking. "We need to figure things out."

"That's exactly what I want to do, Zeta," he said, taking a seat at his own chair. His leg brushed hers beneath the table and his heart fluttered. He kept talking, ignoring the tingling sensation that radiated from the touch, focused on what he was saying. "I already know I love the baby—it's my child, how could I not? I plan on being an active parent. Nothing that happens between us changes that. What I need to figure out is if I love you." He stopped, realized what he had said, but it was too late, it was out. He held his breath.

"That's a lot riding on dinner." Zeta chuckled, smiled. Relaxed, easy, and he couldn't tell if it was an act or if what he had admitted really had rolled over her. "You don't even know if you like me."

"I do like you. I like you a lot. I thought that was clear."

"Then I don't know if I like you yet." She frowned and looked out the window, and he wanted her attention back. He wanted to prove that he was worth liking. Wanted more than anything for her to be in the same place he was. Wanting, falling all over himself, to see her smile, to hear her voice. He knew that Zeta must like him on some level—the way that she'd kissed him in the hospital was proof enough—but was it anywhere near what he felt? He didn't know at all, and the not knowing dug its claws into his guts, twisted until his stomach hurt.

"Zeta," he started, unsure. "I hope I can show you how sincere I am about this."

"I'm sure you will; you've been nothing but thoughtful and kind. But you know . . ." She poked out her lips, choosing her words. "I don't know if it's really you. You're saying and doing all the right things, but—" She stopped, covered her face, and then looked over her fingers at him. "I'm sorry, this is our first date, right? I'm making it . . . not fun."

He stilled; his stomach flipped. *Does she think I'm here because I think I have to be?* Randall's words echoed in his memory. He didn't want Zeta, his child, to be just another thing that he did out of responsibility. He wanted to be in their lives; he wanted her to know that he *wanted* to be there. Responsible, yes, but he wanted the joy of it all. "No! Tell me what you're worried about! I want to know. I need to know. Tell me whatever you want."

A shy smile. "Let's pretend that this is a real first date. At least for a little while, OK?"

He nodded, reached for her hand, and squeezed. "Explain to me why you faint."

She laughed, loud. "That is a *terrible* starter for a first date! You're supposed to ask me about my job or favorite movies or something!"

He almost said, *I know where you work*, and stopped himself. "We're not supposed to talk about work," he reminded her, smiling, trying to seem funny, light. Not sure if he was succeeding.

She pointed at her temple. The long cut from her fall was still there, slightly red but fading. Ash fought his frown but Zeta grinned, unbothered. "I have a brain injury. It's not very exciting. I climbed really high up a tree when I was four, the branch broke, and the next thing I knew it was two weeks later and I was in the hospital. I don't remember a lot of it. There were a lot of things messed up after it. I couldn't walk or talk; I was like a baby again. And my memory wasn't great. I actually don't remember most of my life before I was six."

"The pictures," he said, thinking of her wall, the one she snapped of him as he was leaving the hospital. Slowly it dawned on him what that must have meant, that she, in that moment, wanted to remember *him*, and it settled in him, warm and alive, proof that there was hope. "It's why you take the pictures."

"Yeah," she smiled, pleased. "Old habit. I don't have memory issues anymore. I pretty much fully recovered. The technical term is vasovagal syncope, which is just fainting, but it happens a lot, more than most people, so I have to be careful of the kind of things that trigger it. You know, nose bleeds, getting up too fast or short of breath, running into the previously totally unknown father of my child. Everyday stuff." She laughed. "Who knows, maybe the last fall fixed it? Brains are weird."

"You seem very relaxed about everything for someone who could faint at the hint of stress. I would have guessed you would be the type of person who liked everything planned out, step by step."

Zeta grinned. "See, that's where most people mess up. Life happens whether you plan it or not, and the more you plan, the more you have to worry about keeping it on track. Not that I don't have plans or goals or dreams, but keeping things fairly simple is step one to living a faint-free life."

It was not the type of response Ash was expecting. "So you just wait for things to happen to you?"

"No, I know that it can seem that way. Think about life like a trip itinerary. Some people plan every little thing, and if there's a late bus or it rains, then there's a domino effect and everything is ruined. But then there are people who have just a general idea, a list of things, and every day they'll decide what they're going to do, and sometimes you have tickets to an attraction that you can't move around but it's not such a big deal to plan around them."

"I think I get it," he said.

"So which one are you?" she asked

"I think I'm the first type."

Zeta made a small hmm sound, and Ash wondered if that had been the wrong answer, and why he thought there could even be a wrong answer. He was about to ask, and then the waitstaff came delivering water and asking what they'd like to drink. Iced tea for him and a ginger ale for her. Two plates with three fragrant stuffed mushrooms in front of each of them. And then they were alone again.

"Shouldn't we have menus?" she asked at their departure.

He smiled. "The menu was already chosen for us. I hope you don't think I'm being pushy. I took into consideration what you told me while we were in the hospital, and it should be alright. And if it's not, we can go wherever you want instead. We can leave right now if you want."

"Low stakes surprises! Exciting! I *like* this kind of thing," Zeta said, her enthusiasm genuine.

Ash's heart fluttered at making her happy.

"It's my turn to ask a question," Zeta said, picking up a mushroom, inspecting it. "How did you get a table here on short notice? It's fancy."

"My sister is one of their investors. Tables on short notice is one of the perks."

"The one who taught you how to braid?"

"Yes, Claire. We're ten years apart. She's older," he explained. "She's actually in town right now. She lives in Greece."

"That's nice that you guys get along. Are you close to your family?"

A natural first date question. She'd asked before, on the deck, and he hadn't really answered then. His fingers twitched; he didn't know if she remembered or if she was asking now because it mattered. "We have our own lives," he said slowly, trying to frame the truth. "My sister has her career and is away a lot, and I'm busy too; my parents have their commitments. Since my dad's health scare we've been having dinner together a few times a month. We spend time together on holidays."

"Sounds like no one really has much time for family with work and . . . commitments," she replied, tilting her head, slight frown on her face.

"It was different when we were younger," he rushed to explain. "We're older now, and no one has children. I mean, mine isn't here yet!" He stopped, took a deep breath, and started again. "I know how it sounds, but I always have time for the things that are important. You?"

Zeta raised an eyebrow and smiled softly at him. "Promise you won't get sad and apologetic on me."

"OK, I won't," he said, relieved that she seemed to find what he said acceptable enough to continue.

"I mean it! No sorrys or pity looks! Or I will get up and leave."

"I promise."

"My parents passed away when I was five, and I don't have any brothers or sisters. My great-aunt raised me, Aunt Josie. We're pretty close. We went on vacation together right before I met you, to the beach! But we don't visit very often because of the distance, and you know I don't drive."

"I'm," he started, caught himself. "I'm happy that you had family who could take care of you when you needed it. I think I remember seeing a picture of her. On your table."

"Yeah, it was a really fun time."

"So you like the beach?"

The conversation flowed easily between them like it had on the deck, and he relaxed into it as they traded more details about their lives. They talked about how she'd gotten into programming (she'd heard she could do contract work from home) and that he'd gone to school for architecture. Places they'd like to go, places they liked to eat at, what they did on their days off. Little everyday details, and Ash was enraptured with Zeta. Her life seemed so colorful and full, and he wondered as she tried the second course, a soup, if he had ruined it.

Guilt, near constant, triggered by everything he did recently, rose in him, clawing at his belly, climbing into his throat.

Zeta picked up her spoon. "Is this the right spoon? Are you judging me on my spoon choice?"

"It's the right spoon if that's the spoon you want it to be," he said, forcing his thoughts away from the dark corner they were trying to slip into. "So where did the name Zeta come from? It's unusual."

"I picked it myself! I had it changed legally when I was twenty, so it's been ten years?"

"Why Zeta? Why not something more common?" He leaned forward, tried to read her expressions. She was as relaxed as she had been on the deck. Relaxed as she had been when he left her later that night. The only change he had seen in her was at their unexpected reunion and then when she woke and asked about the baby, their baby. Brief flashes of whatever was below her surface, and he wanted to know that woman, wanted all parts of Zeta. But wanted more of her to trust him enough to show him those things.

"Same reason I moved. For the adventure. Doesn't Zeta sound like she's on an adventure? That's how I want to sound even if I'm just at home playing games. I'm still on my own little adventure, and I need a reminder of that. I can be a little, hmm, insular." She looked up at him, her lips pulled into a small smile. His heart clinched in his chest, a not-unfamiliar feeling now. With every one of her smiles, laughs, and small signs that she was showing him the real her, his body reacted like a teen with a crush.

"Now you tell me something I really need to know about you." She'd pushed the soup away, put her elbows on the table, and rested her chin on the shelf of her hands.

Something important? He scrambled to find something to rival any of what she'd told him. Ran through college, his family and friends; everything seemed basic, familiar, unimportant. And then, "I was married!" The words came out in a rush. He never really thought about it; it'd been so short and so distant. "We were divorced seven years ago. It only lasted a year."

"What happened?" Curious, soft.

Ash forced himself to keep his hand on the table, match her mood, even though his whole body was tight with the need to move, fidget, do something to relieve his nerves. "I wasn't happy, and I knew she wasn't either. It wasn't arranged but it was expected? And it ending was for the best."

She wrinkled her nose. "Sorry, I don't follow. What do you mean expected? You didn't ask her? Or vice versa."

"No, I did. But it was one of those things." He paused, frustrated at his clumsy communication. It was unlike him, except, when it came to her. "It just felt like what I was supposed to do next at the time."

Zeta's eyes flicked over him, considered what he said. "And were you happy after it was all done?"

"I don't know. Happier, I think. But I know I'm happy right now. With you."

She smiled, soft and inviting. "You're getting too gushy for a first date!"

"I'm out of practice," he said, all the tension leaving him.

"Me too," she admitted. She looked down at the bowl. "The soup is not my favorite."

"Well, lets hope the next course is better for you. You're eating for two," he teased.

"Tell the baby that. I had terrible morning sickness."

"You're feeling better now though?" he asked, hearing the anxiety in his own voice.

"Much better. I think I'm out of the woods."

"Good," he smiled, wondering how she had felt all those weeks, ill and alone. While he badgered her about later start times and reports. "There's something that I'm confused about though," he said suddenly, to stop thinking about work, about Zeta tired, which would only lead to the pale reappearance of her in his office and everything that happened after.

"What?" she asked, head tilted, the bare length of her neck exposed, drawing his attention, making his fingers twitch with the desire to touch, his tongue to taste.

"You wear bright colors. The night we met you had on these cute socks and underwear, and your dress now, but you told me your favorite color is gray. You love playing video games, mobile games, and you are an excellent programmer, but you don't make games. Why is there so much . . . distance between you and the things you love?"

She tilted her head the opposite way, slight frown on her lips, brows furrowed, and his stomach dropped. He'd upset her and he started to apologize, but then she spoke.

Zeta's voice was soft, thoughtful. "Don't say it like that." She chuckled low. "It's not distance. I just don't want to overwhelm myself with them. Moderation. Besides, are you doing the things you love? Was your little boy dream to write cold emails, or was it to build houses? We all make choices." Zeta's voice was soft, thoughtful, a reminder that they couldn't go backwards and had to deal with the reality they'd created.

"We do," he agreed. *Choose me* he thought. Almost said out loud,

Another set of waiters appeared with their main course. "I hope this is alright then," Ash said as they set the food before them, a plate of savory risotto with chicken breasts sliced and artfully arranged like a flower in its center.

Zeta smiled at it, took a thoughtful bite, and he held his breath, anticipating her review like it came from his own kitchen, because the last thing he wanted was to give her something else she didn't want. "It's yummy," she said, taking up another forkful.

"Good, I was worried I was going to have to stop for burgers," he laughed.

"Oh, now that you've said that maybe we should do that anyway," she teased. "So, any other secrets you want to reveal?"

"I'm sorry to disappoint you, I'm very boring," he said, picking up his own fork. "I spend most of my free time at home."

"Oh, yeah! I read *The Time Machine* the other day," she said, surprising him.

"What did you think?"

"It was good; different. I don't think I would have read it on my own. What are you reading now?" she asked.

She remembered, he thought, skin tingling all along his leg where it still brushed against her. "*A Long Way to a Small, Angry Planet*. I just started it, I haven't made it very far yet. What are you playing?"

Zeta's smile was small, sweet. "*Disco Elysium*, kind of different from what I usually play but I'm trying new things."

"Look where trying new things has gotten us so far," he said without thinking, the joke rolling out of his mouth before he could stop it.

Zeta laughed, covering her mouth. "Yeah, it's definitely been trouble, but I'm willing to give it a second chance. I mean, I can't get double pregnant."

He laughed despite himself, embarrassed but amused, her carefree attitude infectious. Like a curtain had pulled back, they began to talk about what had gone on in the last four months. She told him more about her apartment, the renovations, and he mentally added getting the place inspected for safety to his list of things to do, asked her if there was anything he could do. She declined and told him what she'd been up to with her friends. He told her about his father, the hospital, the work in settling things around his health, but he couldn't bring himself to talk about their relationship, to explain how strained it was. He showed her pictures of the new plants he'd brought, of his mother and sister.

The waiters took their plates, replaced them with a dessert of poached peaches, and he barely noticed, enraptured with her laughter and warm personality, again, just like he had been all those months ago. Like nothing at all had happened. He wanted to ask about the baby but he didn't want to lose the easy back-and-forth that was happening between them. *Later*, he told himself, pushing his questions back. Right now, he just wanted to learn more about her.

Zeta looked out the window again. "I heard it might snow tonight," she explained, turning back to him. "But it doesn't look like it."

"You didn't take a picture of the view," he said slowly, recalling all the places she had on her wall.

"No, that would be rude," she responded, brows crinkling, question in her eyes. "We're on a date. I can't just have my phone out."

He took out his phone, captured her, eyes focused on him, lips slightly parted, hands unconsciously resting on her belly. "There, now you have one," he said, sending it. *And so do I.*

She shifted, pulling her leg back from his as she settled in her chair. She must have done that dozens of times that night as he did the same, but it felt different then, noticeable, because he wanted to reach for her, hold her hand, hold her, and just then, the minor contact that they had shared was broken. She'd turned back to the window, staring at the empty courtyard.

"Kitten?" he said.

Zeta drew in her breath, sharp, eyes widened. "Yes?"

"What's got your attention out there?"

"Nothing. It's just getting late. We can't stay in the restaurant forever. And I am having a nice time with you."

"We can go to a different restaurant. Nurse a cup of coffee for a couple of hours," he suggested, playful.

Zeta chuckled, "I can't have coffee."

"You can have hot chocolate."

"But," she said, looking out the window again, "it's supposed to snow."

"It's only snow."

"Then," she said slowly, "I want some hot chocolate."

"I can make it for you, from scratch if you want. No powdered stuff," he leaned forward, hopeful.

Zeta smiled, "I'd love that."

16

The first thing Zeta noticed was that Ash's apartment was bigger than hers. His living room was twice the size, her kitchen tiny compared to his, and she didn't even really have an entranceway. Even adding her bedrooms and bathroom she was pretty sure he had her beat for square footage. Before the renovations from the "flood," yeah, in comparison Aunt Josie was right, her spot did look raggedy.

The second thing she noticed was that it was covered in plants. A little jungle.

Ash took her coat. "Make yourself comfortable," he said, stashing the garment in a closet along with his. He didn't take his shoes off as he strode across the carpet into the kitchen.

The floor plan was open. She could see from the kitchen to the living room where he did indeed have a TV that sat in front of a blue couch. The coffee table between them was covered with potted plants and books. As were the matching end tables. She knew nothing about plants; she couldn't name them and was afraid to touch them at all. Behind the TV the walls were covered with bookcases full of more books. Paperbacks, hardcovers.

Upon closer inspection they were all science fiction and fantasy novels. The shelves were neat, free of dust. Everything in the apartment was neat, put away.

From the kitchen she could hear him moving pots and pans. He was, as he had offered, really making her hot chocolate from scratch. There was one door across from the couch and it hung slightly ajar, just enough that she could see inside to his bedroom, the corner of his bed a dark silhouette.

Zeta took another look at the living room. There were no pictures. No family, no art, nothing at all on the walls that were free of shelves. They were as blank as his social media profile, though the apartment wasn't without personality. There was something comfortable and lived-in about it. It was all very utilitarian, minimalist without the trappings of the aesthetic.

Everything was set, neat, with no room for anything else, even with all the extra space. It was as he liked it, and she couldn't imagine a playpen or crib or anything else there. She went to the kitchen.

Here too everything was neat. His cabinets were dark, and she bet if she opened them she'd find matching dishes. The appliances were new and shiny, the only mess was the one he was making now, his back to her as he worked. It smelled of melting chocolate.

There was one window, and all across it hung the vines of the plants that sat on shelves around it. There was no curtain and the city sprawled out beyond the panes.

"Is it snowing?" he asked, looking back at her, catching her staring out the window. He turned back, whisking together milk and chocolate over the heat.

"No," she said, but there were clouds now, the kind that said the weather was turning. She sat at the counter, stared at his back. "Are the only things you buy books and plants?" she asked.

"Yeah." He chuckled. "I told you, I'm not very exciting."

"There are none in your office," she said, trying to remember what she'd seen in that brief moment before the world came crashing down. "If you like them so much, why don't you keep them there? You have plenty of light."

"Because when I'm work all I have time for is work. I tried keeping plants there years ago, but they all died because I didn't have time to care for them. Even the most hardy plants need attention, even plants that usually do OK in offices," he explained.

"Are all of these real?" Zeta asked.

"Yeah, of course. There are no plastic plants in this apartment."

"Do you know what they all are? To me they kind of all just look . . . green." She reached forward, brushed her fingers along a waxy green leaf that belonged to a cute little plant in a white ceramic vase in the center of the island. "They're pretty though."

"Yeah, that one you just touched is a Chinese evergreen. The one over the window is philodendron. Those are money trees in the living room. That one hanging from the ceiling—"

"Wait! I know that one, spider plant," she said.

"Yes! I can give you some clippings. Grow your own."

"I'm not very good at keeping things alive." She chuckled, waving away the idea.

"I don't think that's true," he said softly, placing a warm mug of chocolate in front of her. "Careful, it's hot."

She blushed, realized what she'd said. "I meant green things!" She wasn't ready to stop pretending, wanted to let this play out like it had the night they met and hope for a different ending—but she couldn't. "Ash, I'm having a baby."

"I know." He stopped rinsing his pots and sat down across from her, his elbows on the island, chin resting in his palms. "I've wanted to talk about it with you more, but I thought maybe we needed to get to know each other a little first."

"You don't have to do this," she said all in a rush.

"What?" His brows drew together, lips frowning, confused more than angry.

Zeta wrapped her hands around the cup, warmth soaked through it, still hot. "You drive a sports car and live in a bespoke apartment! This place looks like a Pinterest mood board. Your life is totally put together, and I'm a contract worker who only has matching dishes because the last set broke. You don't even take your shoes off in your house!"

"I'm not sure what that has to do with anything, but I can start taking my shoes off," he replied. "And I did figure I'd have to get another car."

"It's not about the car or the shoes . . . Sorry, that was weird. It's just, you have a life that is going perfectly well. You don't need . . . this." She looked down at the cup to avoid his eyes.

"What do you mean? The baby? I don't think having a child is a needs-based decision even when you're planning it, Zeta."

"No, you know what I mean. This isn't a great time to make a joke." She couldn't look at him. Her face was burning, a lump was forming in her throat, and she didn't know why she'd come, why she hadn't just gone home. *Because I like him*, the thought came. But he couldn't like her; she didn't fit into his perfect Pinterest life. Her gold coin purse stood out glaringly in his plant-lined kitchen with its copper pots. A warning.

"Actually I don't know what you mean. At all. Explain it to me." Ash's tone was unreadable. She couldn't tell if he was angry, She wasn't trying to make him angry. She just wanted him to understand.

"I'm not a very put-together person. It's like, OK, you're Pinterest, right? I'm Tumblr. You're organized and perfect, and I am a messy collection of random posts and reblogs."

His hands reached around hers, cradling them against the cup. They covered hers, fingers past her wrists. "Zeta, I do not get that reference, but I think I understand. I really like you, Zeta. I like who you are. I liked you on the deck. I've liked you this whole time."

"Ash, I'm disabled. And you haven't had any time to really see if you're OK with that."

"I don't care, Zeta. You told me, I know, and I like you. I want to be with you. I don't care. I'm really nervous about a lot of things but not that."

Her head snapped up, met his eyes. His smile was awkward and sweet.

He continued, "I'm so nervous about everything. I'm worried you won't like me, about how I can make up for the past four months, how I can be there for you for the next five, if you even want me there. I'm worried about the baby. I've been reading, so many things can go wrong! And you!" He reached up, ran a finger over the cut on her forehead, the scar hot under it. "You got hurt because I didn't catch you."

"No, you— I pushed you away. And I'm— We're alright." Her face was hot, and an odd tightness sat in her chest, but he was the one that looked like he was going to cry.

"Then don't push me away now. You had a life before we met, and I changed that. If you need me to take off my shoes or get a different car or buy an ugly couch to feel comfortable, I'll do it. Just give me a chance." His eyes were wide, begging under wrinkled worried brow.

"I don't want you to think you have to do this. I don't want to feel like—"

"I'm not here because I think I have to be. I want to see where we go."

Her heart felt like it beat strangely for a moment, her cheeks tingled inside of her mouth. He was so sincere, and she couldn't ignore what she wanted—that she wanted him. She moved her hand away from the cup to reach for Ash. He put his cheek in her palm, leaned into her touch. "Puppy," she sighed.

"Kitten," he answered back, kissed her palm, and she reached, rubbing away his worry lines.

"It would help if you took off your shoes," she said, accepting him. Accepting trying.

Ash pulled away. "I'll do it right now!" He reached down, took off his shoes, and came to her side, squatting to do the same for her. "Drink your hot chocolate before it gets cold," he said, his fingers running over her stockinged foot.

She gave a surprised gasp as her stomach jumped, and she jerked her foot away. "Ah, sorry, don't do that, it's too surprising." She looked down at him. He was staring up at her, eyes wide, but his gaze was heavy, her foot still in his hand.

"I wasn't thinking," he apologized. He wrapped his hand around her ankle, traveled up the curve of her calf. "Is this better?"

Heat pooled between her thighs. "Wait, don't move," Zeta said, reaching for her bag. She grabbed her phone and took a picture of him.

He chuckled, didn't say anything, and stood up with both of their pairs of shoes. As he walked away she took a photo of the hot chocolate. When he returned she was taking her first sips, and he sat on the stool next to her, hand on her back.

"How is it?" he asked, voice low. His free hand came to rest on her belly, rubbed the curve of it.

"It's good, better than the powdered stuff."

"Good." He sighed, resting his forehead on her shoulder. Close, comfortable. She leaned against him, his hair brushing against her cheek and releasing sandalwood and the familiar sage that must be his soap.

His fingers moved lightly against her back, like feathers against her skin. She felt it through her belly, high between her thighs, the tingling touch of arousal.

"I didn't have any whipped cream. It probably would taste good with that," he hummed. His hand moved up her back, his other rounding her hip, holding her in place while she drank. His fingers slipped into the opening at the back of dress, ran up her spine. She leaned into it, couldn't help herself.

"Yes," she agreed, almost a purr.

"Drink up, I don't think it will taste as good reheated, and I made it just for you." His fingers found the bow holding her dress together, pulled it, releasing the tension. The sleeves fell, revealing her back, the tops of her breasts. His fingers traveled over her shoulders, pushed the fabric away further.

Ash leaned toward her, placing a kiss on her bare shoulder. A shiver worked through her body. She sipped slowly, the drink still more hot than warm. She could feel his smile against her skin. Another kiss, his fingers testing the give in the fabric, finding how much of her he could expose. It caught against her breast, showed only the top of her bra. But it was enough.

Ash's mouth moved across the space of her shoulders. He left small kisses in a line that tickled and sent a jittery communication through her belly and thighs. His tongue on her spine made her arch her back in surprise, nearly drop her cup.

"Careful," he breathed, voice throaty and deep. He was so close she could feel the length of him, ready, against her hip. "You'll burn yourself."

"Don't you want any?" she asked, dazed by his touch.

He kissed her, met the slight part of Zeta's lips with his own, his tongue sweeping over hers quickly, firmly, and then they were apart. "It is good. Very sweet."

Ash had made that switch again, from the puppy waiting for her lead to a wolf. Capable, willing, but still collared. His hand brushed over her back, pulling another shiver from her while he teased her lips, moving over them with his own but not quite kissing her. "It's snowing," he said.

Zeta turned and saw fat flurries swirling outside. Thick, wet flakes that turned to water against the glass. There wouldn't be anything in the morning if it kept up the same way. "I guess I'll have to stay the night. Is that alright?"

He stared at her, shock that stretched into a smile. "It's alright," he said. He plucked her cup, half finished, from her fingers, and an annoyed growl came from Zeta's throat. "I'll make you more," he said, swallowing any further protest with his kiss. He pulled away, kissed her forehead, and took her hand to help her down off the stool.

He turned off lights and led her through his apartment in the near dark to his bedroom. He shut the door, took her into his arms, and kissed her. Hungry, needy, his mouth trapped her while his hands roamed up her skirts, squeezing, petting. Her own hands traced the lines of his throat.

He pulled away, and she sighed, heat racing through her, pooling between her thighs and twisting around her stomach. *More*, she thought, just as hungry, her fingers hooked into the soft weave of his sweater. "More," she said.

She pressed herself against him, and he obliged, his hands wrapping themselves around the curves of her body, holding her tightly, pressing a deep, lingering kiss to her mouth before pulling away, breaking their contact. The smallest whimper escaped her, and he laughed, touching her lips with his finger.

"I'm not done." His voice was a low hum, and she remembered the last time he had said something similar and how it felt. Her body was weak with need as he released her, taking her hand and setting her on the bed she'd seen in silhouette. A soft click and a low light flooded the space.

The room lacked the plants that had taken over the rest of the apartment, but there was a single picture—a black-and-white print of some sort of pod, it looked almost alien. It hung over a dresser covered with books. The bed she sat on was soft, king size, the comforter dark blue and plush. Four pillows at its head. Nightstands flanked either side, but there was only one lamp; the other nightstand sat bare and unused. Another wide window, this one with matching blue curtains, still open, showing off more of his beautiful view. On the opposite were two doors. A bathroom and a closet she assumed. There were no clothes on the floor, no shoes left out. She looked at the dark, rumpled comforter and sheet, the pillows piled at the head. *His bed is soft. I thought it would be hard*, she thought.

"I wasn't expecting company," he smirked, following her gaze.

"Bold of you to bring that up," she said. "Aren't you worried that I'll remember how terrible you were and get upset?"

"I can't change the past, and I don't want to ignore it, but I can make this time different. Better, make that one not hurt so much because we have this one."

"You don't have to keep trying. I understand what happened. It's not your fault," she said, and then looked away as she realized what she'd brought up. "And it's our first date anyway," she added to distract, to hold him in the space with her.

He pulled his sweater off, tossed it to the floor. "I'll never stop trying to make up for it," he said, dropping to his knees between her legs. He pressed himself between them, spreading her thighs. He covered her mouth with his kiss, pulling gently at her lips with his teeth before his mouth returned to hers, the position easier with him on his knees, between her legs. His hands slipped under her skirt and over her stockings until they reached the swell of her stomach and he stopped, broke their kiss, and looked down at them.

Nerves tingled all along her body, worry in her belly, the failures of make-believe presenting themselves. His body, after all these months, was exactly the same, and hers . . . was not. *Of course, I'm bigger now and I'm starting to get stretch marks and that dark line . . .*

"Is this alright?" he asked. "I've never . . . this is new territory for me. Am I allowed to? Should we talk to your doctor first?"

Ash's lips were twisted into a frown. He was very clearly worried. Laughter bubbled up in her and spilled out, breaking the tension. "I don't think I'm the first woman to ever have sex while pregnant. You don't have to worry."

"I do, though. I do have to worry. You're not just *any* woman," he hummed, his fingers stroking the rounded expanse of her. He looked up at her suddenly, his expression serious. "What can I do to be good, for you?"

The question settled over, already answered in the asking of it. The way he touched her, adjusted around her instead of pulling back. Desire spread through her, lightning fast. Her mouth watered and the laughter that had been sitting in her chest died. A thousand replies fizzled away to leave only one, the only thing she wanted from a lover. "Fuck me like you aren't afraid you'll hurt me."

Ash smiled darkly at her. "I can do that."

There was no warning. His position shifted, her dress lifted. His hands were a hot press on her hips as he hooked and slid off her panties and stockings in one movement. Her bra came next and her heavy breasts fell free, her nipples already taut and ready for his attention. Ash ran his thumb over one, and Zeta's body shivered at the touch, pleasure flooding the space between her legs.

The heat of his hand moved from her and she gasped, opening her eyes, to find him staring down at her. She tried to cover herself with her arms. "Is something—"

"Stop. I want to see you."

She forced her arms down, felt vulnerable in a way she hadn't before. In her apartment when they had been looking at each other, making their judgments, it seemed fair. But, now it was only him looking, really looking, at her. *What if, what if,* played in Zeta's mind, her face hot, fingers clenching the dark comforter to keep her arms still. Her body didn't matter as much before, but now it was different, now it was serious.

"I can't believe you're here, with me, right now."

Zeta's instinct was to push his desire away: *You don't have to lie.* But it was wrong, because he wasn't lying. He looked at her exactly the same way he had months ago, exactly as he had when she walked into the room at the restaurant, entranced. And she wasn't sure at all how to handle it. She looked away to avoid his eyes, nerves raw and tight in her.

"Look at me." Ash's voice had a hot edge to it that she couldn't resist. "I want you to know exactly why I'm going to do what I'm about to do."

"What?" Zeta's mind stumbled, trying to catch up, his desire dragging her out of her own insecurity, forcing her back to him. The dark, mottled mark of a bruise graced his shoulder. A few days old. "What happened? Are you OK?"

"You happened," he said.

"Me?" And then she remembered. The hospital, the feel of him between her thighs, the noise she stifled by biting down on him. Her face went hot and she could feel her own wetness between her thighs, need and embarrassment all tangled together. "I'm sorry, I didn't mean," she sputtered.

"Don't apologize. It's my turn," he replied.

His kiss came quickly, arms on either side of her so she was forced to hold on to him or fall back completely. He captured her, held her, his hand cradling her head as he pulled his mouth from hers to attend to her exposed throat.

Ash's teeth pulled at her flesh, toyed with the delicate skin, a playful mockery of what her teeth had done to him. He licked and sucked at her neck, traveling downward to her chest and then to the soft hills of her breasts. He cupped one with his hand, running his thumb over her nipple, sending a shock of pleasure through her. Zeta expected that he would cover it with his mouth, but the same nibbles and pressures that he covered her neck with he applied to her breasts. One, then the other, his fingers teasing, making her pant and squirm on the bed.

"Ash!" Zeta gasped, staring down at herself, dark marks blossoming all over her.

"Breathe, Kitten," he said, lazily stroking her nipple before flicking his tongue over it, making her jump. He shifted, took her face in his hands, and repeated himself. "Breathe."

The command made her shiver, bite her own lip. Her mind was a haze, putty in her arousal. "You're teasing me too much," she pouted. Her breaths were shallow, fast, more gasps than breathing. Her body felt so sensitive, pulled tight and wanting more of his touch. On the edge already, it was going to her head, making it swirl and swim.

"What do you need, love? Tell me."

"I want to see you," she said.

Ash stood and reached for the buckle of his pants, pausing as he undid the belt. He rested his hand on her jaw, and his thumb stroked a line along her tender lips to send flares of jittery shocks through her. "Are you alright?"

Her head felt light, dizzy but in a good way. She was drunk on his touch, intoxicated with pleasure. She licked his thumb and he groaned. "I'm alright. Show me."

Ash's arousal was already apparent through his clothing. He undid the buckle on his pants, releasing the hold on him, and his cock pressed against the front of his boxers, pulling them down enough to show off the edge of his pubic hair. He slid his pants and boxers off of his hips, exposing his cock fully erect.

He was shaped exactly as she remembered, jutting up toward his flat stomach. A shaft that was slightly darker than his skin, a vein running down the center to a head the color of his blush. A bead of precum sat at the tip. She smeared it with her finger and Ash groaned above her as she ran her fingers down the velvet shaft of him, letting herself calm down, giving herself the time for her head to stop its spinning.

"Kitten, you don't have to . . . let me . . ." His voice sounded strangled, like he was holding something back or holding himself back, but she didn't want him to hold anything back.

"You told me to tell you what I want." Her fingers moved along the underside of his cock and down his testicles. Not quite a touch, but in his arousal, the light press of her nails and fingers were enough to make him drip and jump.

"I want you to want me. I want to be the only man you want."

"I do want you," she replied, and took him in her mouth.

Above her she could hear his surprised gasp, felt him stumble when his knees went weak before he could catch himself. She looked up as the head of him passed over her tongue, pressed against the back of her throat. He filled her mouth, the fresh taste of his skin mingled with the salty precum that dripped from him. Zeta rested her hands on his thighs, felt his muscles tense under them, remembered how his back felt when he thrust into her that first night. She pulled back slowly, his head popping out of her mouth, resting on her lips. She licked the shaft, the musky scent of his pubic hair mingled with his soap, filling her nose. She slipped her tongue back along his shaft, covered his head with her lips and sucked gently at him before swallowing as much of his length as she could, wrapping the rest in her hand, stroking in time with her mouth. He watched her, mouth open with panting breaths.

He let out a groan before touching her head. "God, you're so fucking cute. You have to stop, or I won't last much longer."

Zeta released him, pleased that she had pleased him, that she had caught him so off guard. He leaned down, arms on either side of her, kissing the smile from her face.

"Move to the pillows, love," he said close to her ear, voice low, deep.

"Is it bedtime?" she teased. "Are you all done?" Zeta leaned forward, wrapped her arms over his shoulders. "You don't look done."

"You asked me to fuck you, and I'd rather be in my bed too. Now." Ash's voice was a low growl, filled with a need that made Zeta shiver and follow.

Ash slid onto the bed after her, met her at the pillows, and wrapped her back into his embrace. Zeta welcomed his heat, the press of his body against hers. She pressed her lips against his, and he pushed her back on the bed slowly until her head touched his pillows and he pulled away.

She huffed, impatient, unhappy with the loss of his warmth.

"I've barely touched you," he said, hand running down, moving to cup her breast. "I've changed my mind."

"What?" Her muscles tensed, body ready to jump up and out of her playful bliss.

"I'm not going to fuck you just yet," he said, inspecting her body, his fingers traveling over her ribs and belly, find the divot of her hip, tickling, teasing. "You like to be touched here," he said.

"Yes," she breathed as he bent and stroked the sensitive skin with his tongue. The touch changed her breathing to gasps and sighs.

"And here," he said, running his hand along her inner thigh before pulling her leg over his shoulder, his mouth traveling over the hidden skin, tasting, nibbling. Her gasps turned to moans and she covered her own mouth to stifle them.

His hand circled her wrist, pulled her own away from her lips. His hair was messy, falling over his forehead, eyes dark, intense. "You don't need to do that here. Let me hear you."

He released her, leaned back, and slipped his fingers through the wet folds of her pussy, teasing them, exploring the contours of her sex. His fingers sunk into her slowly. "Beautiful," he said, eyes still on her.

Small moans escaped Zeta's mouth as his fingers moved in her, his thumb searching through her slick, wet folds for her clit. Finding it, he pulled a sucking breath from Zeta with the stroke of his thumb. The muscles in her thighs tensed, tried to close her legs against the not unpleasant but shocking pressure, and he held them open effortlessly, lightened his touch. Pressure was building just below her belly, her face was hot, she gripped the sheets under her.

Ash pulled his fingers out of her and she whined, suddenly empty. He smiled at the sound of her frustration and then leaned forward, lowered his face to her and dragged his tongue over her clit. Electricity ran up her body from his touch on her already teased and swollen sex, the feeling of his tongue shot through her like a bullet. Her fingers dug into his hair, pushing him away and pulling him close all at once. He circled her clit with his tongue, waiting for her body to relax before again dragging it over the hard point.

Zeta couldn't control her body. Her moans were loud and low. Some part of her mind was embarrassed, but it was drowning under the unrelenting pleasure of his touch. Her legs shook and he stroked them, held them open

"Oh, baby, baby, baby, I'm about to, it feels," she gasped and moaned, head spinning.

"Not yet, stay with me," he said, pulling his face away from her.

A low whine came from her throat. Zeta could feel herself at the edge, so close, and he was pulling away. Words escaped her but she pulled at his hair, tried to bring him back.

"Trust me, trust me, love," his voice was a growl against her, not angry but desperate, needy. Hungry.

Do I? The question shimmered briefly across her mind, but then his hands were on her, firm, hot pressure, and she leaned into them, accepting their guidance, the absolute freedom of falling into the pleasure of their lovemaking.

He turned her and pulled her back against his chest, one arm still under her, squeezing her breasts gently. With his free hand he lifted her leg, and she felt the tip of his cock press against her opening for a moment before he worked himself inside in small thrusts, her body taking him inch by inch.

She gasped as he filled her, accepting the full length of him.

"Tell me if I'm hurting you," he said, releasing her leg and returning to her clit. He stroked her in time with his thrusts, deep and slow and Zeta gasped with each movement, waves of heat and pressure breaking through her. She gripped his arm, needing to hold on to something as the pressure started again in her belly, picked up where it had left off, expanding upward. Her breath shortened as the heat crept up her body, nipples pulling into tight points begging for touch. Ash kissed her shoulder, his free hand cupping her breast, squeezing the taut peak. A burst of pressure released in her and she cried out, wanting more. It built in her body, blossomed and rolled through her stronger, heavier than what he had drawn with his fingers.

"There," he groaned as he moved, his thrusts shortening in time with her harried breathing. "Tell me what you want." He bent and took her shoulder in his mouth, his teeth grazing skin. A threat, a promise.

"You," she gasped, unsure if she meant just then or if she wanted him all the time but knowing that it was right, that it was true, "I want you." And the world shattered, a wave of pleasure swept up, through, and over her, pulling her body tight. Ash stilled his fingers, leaving the pressure as he matched her, falling into his own climax. Zeta's cry was animalistic, joyful and relieved, tapered into panting. Ash tightened his arms around her, holding her closer as his body emptied into hers.

"You aren't as loud as you think you are," he said. His voice was low and sleepy as he pressed a kiss to the crook of her neck.

Eyes closed, Zeta felt like she was floating. Vaguely she was aware that Ash had shifted, was kissing her shoulder, asking her something, but she couldn't catch it, couldn't make sense of the words. She pulled herself from the edge of sleep.

"Are you alright?" he whispered low and hot in her ear. One hand stroked her belly while the other rested across her. "Was that alright?"

"Yes," she said, settling against him. "Yes."

He turned off the light, found her again in the near dark, covered them both, and pulled his body against hers. Ash's arm was comfortably heavy against her side, his hand on her belly, fingers lazily petting. He breathed sleepily above her, his breath slowing as his hand stilled. She stared out the window, watching fat white flakes gather and stick to the pane until she joined him in deep, comfortable sleep.

17

Ash smelled tea, dried lavender, chamomile, jasmine. It filled his nostrils, and he thought it was a dream as he shrugged off sleep. Then Zeta shifted next to him and the night flooded back hot and wonderful and real. The blue early morning light came through his still-open window, illuminating Zeta curled around a pillow, fast asleep. Her hair was coming out of the braid, and he brushed his fingers over it. She sighed at his touch but stayed asleep.

He smiled, played with the soft curls that had escaped in her sleep, traced the warm slope of her shoulder, fingers feather light as he watched her sleep, comfortable, content. Dawn was breaking, the room illuminating, and her brows pulled together, waking.

No, not yet, he thought. She needed rest. It hadn't even been a week; she still had stitches in her hand, the cut on her head was still red. He stopped himself from running his fingers over it; it wouldn't make it disappear.

Carefully he got out of the bed, the world turning to ice away from her. He pulled the curtain mostly closed to keep the sun from waking her. Quietly he went to the bathroom, shut the door, and thought about what to do.

His mornings started early. Gym, wash up, breakfast. Work during the week; Saturday he spent on errands, Sunday he tended to his plants. Today was Sunday, and Zeta was sleeping in his bed. *Should I make breakfast?* he wondered, brushing his teeth, and then rejected that idea. He didn't know when she would get up, didn't want her to wake up alone. The gym was not considered at all.

He climbed into the shower, hot water not a replacement for what he was missing. He ran through ideas of what he should do. Get her clothing? Maybe she had something to do that he could take her to? Did she need something for the baby? He didn't know what her morning routine was or her plans for the day. He had no to-do list for Zeta, no tasks, and it made him feel clumsy and ignorant when he wanted to prove that he was capable.

But he wanted to be honest with her, and now that she was there, really there, he could see how much there was for them to sort through. In his fantasy it had been as simple as being together, that once she was there he would become more resolute and purposeful, not so awkward and nervous.

More like his father, who would never have admitted to his mother that he didn't have everything under control. But Ash couldn't help but be honest with Zeta, the words spilled out of him before he could stop them.

Puppy, she had said. His face burned with the memory of it. He wasn't his father. And he wasn't sure he knew how to be one, but she'd called him puppy and it didn't seem to matter that much.

But it did. He needed, wanted, to be good for her. For them.

We need to spend more time together, he thought, but he didn't know when that was possible. He'd already made plans and had responsibilities from work and his own family. She probably had the same. He had to start thinking of the future—wasn't that what his own father was always saying? That he didn't think past the present? And maybe that was true. *This month is too busy but next month?*

He hummed to himself. He needed to introduce her to his family soon, but he knew he would need to prepare them. His relationship that wasn't really a relationship would be too sudden otherwise.

Then the first step would be to figure out where they stood. He and Zeta.

Clean, he looked around his bathroom while he dried. One toothbrush, his towel in his hand. A bathroom for one. He hung his towel up, then went to his linen cabinet and retrieved another one. He hung it on the rack next to his, gray. He kept extra toothbrushes to replace his own, and he sat a fresh one, still packaged, on the sink for her.

Finished, he turned off the light, stepped naked back into his room. Dawn was further along, the light brightening, and she had turned over, still sleeping. He crossed the room more conscious of the sound of his steps on carpet then he had ever been. A skill he thought he'd have to perfect. He wouldn't want to wake the baby.

A smile crept across his face at the idea. *His* baby sleeping, warm, real. He'd be able to hold it soon, five months wasn't long, feel it move and kick before that. His palm itched with the urge to caress Zeta's belly and he fought it. He mused about early mornings when he could take their baby while she slept, spend time with the infant.

Be a good dad.

Is that all? He wasn't sure. It seemed too simple, but he wanted to have a better relationship with his baby than he had with his own father. He thought about his mother telling him in the hospital that his father really did love him, about what she saw in them that made her say that at all. Maybe it wasn't just his father, maybe it was him too.

His alarm started to go off, and he snatched his phone up to stop it. In the bed, Zeta made small complaints, tiny whines in her throat.

"Shh," Ash said, settling onto the bed, rubbing her back through the blanket. "It's too early."

Her breathing deepened. He looked at his phone, six thirty, sleeping in for him. He made a mental note to turn his alarms off when she was there. He turned the weekend ones off altogether. Then remembered her phone.

"It's going to die, again," he mumbled, getting up from the bed, leaning into the distraction of the task. He shivered at the kitchen tile cold under his feet. "Would she mind slippers?" he wondered, picking up Zeta's phone from where she'd left it on the counter. He breathed a sigh of relief that it wasn't in her purse.

He stopped and looked around his apartment. Something she'd seen here had upset her, disrupted the comfortable air between them. In the elevator she'd leaned against his arm, but after walking around his apartment she was unsure.

Something had made her doubt him, made her think he couldn't or wouldn't shift his life, make room for them, but all he saw were his plants, his books. *I need to fix it*, he thought. For now, her phone.

Ash looked out of his kitchen window at the city encased in white.

Back in his room, he put the phone on the extra nightstand. He only used one, but they both had built-in wireless charging. A few seconds and then her phone lit up, battery at 3 percent, charging. *I should get another lamp*, he thought idly. Sliding back into bed, he lay down next to her, kept himself from touching her. She was already too close to waking, so he just looked, listened to her breathing. Enjoyed the warmth of her. Not a dream. When the urge to kiss her rose too high, he took up his phone and checked the weather, brow raising at the screen. He touched her shoulder and she sighed. Worried it was too much, he pulled the blanket over her, smiled as she snuggled into it. Then he farmed gems for dragons and completed puzzles in the multiverse on his phone until the light coming in through the slit he'd left in the curtains was strong enough to read by.

He let himself fall into the book, but he remained conscious of the warm weight of Zeta next to him, looked up every time she shifted and sighed in her sleep, until she yawned, stretched, and woke. She rubbed her eyes, breaking out of the deep sleep she had been in as she rolled over to face him.

"You're awake," he said. An echo of the hospital before. He put the open paperback down on his chest. "Good morning."

"Good morning," she replied. She shivered, pulled the blanket up to cover as much as she could. "What time is it?"

"You're cold! I'll turn the heat up," he said, moving to throw the blanket off, solve the problem.

She reached for him, touched his bare stomach, her hand hot, the touch holding him. "So are you," she said, voice full of sleep still.

He smiled down at her, wanting more of her touch, but first, she was cold. "Hold on, let me turn up the thermostat," he said, pulling himself out of the bed, exposing his own nudity, thankful that the swirling heat he felt in his belly hadn't traveled farther.

"What time is it?" she repeated.

"I'm not sure. Around ten? Your phone is on the nightstand," he said, crossing the room to his dresser.

"It's probably dead," she frowned, and then stared at it in confusion.

"The nightstands have wireless charging. I'll start the shower for you in a minute."

Zeta's face lit up in a wide grin. "Neato!"

He pulled on some dark sweatpants, swept out of the room while she checked her messages.

His face tingled with embarrassment. Of course she was cold. *He* was cold. He turned up the thermostat, heard the furnace kick on. It wasn't freezing, but 68 degrees was too cold outside the covers. He put it on 73 and went back to the bedroom.

Zeta was looking at her phone, biting her bottom lip.

"Is something wrong?" Ash asked.

Zeta looked up, startled. "No, I was just looking at the weather, why?"

"Because you're making a face like something's wrong." He came back to the bed, sat down in the single strip of light, frowning. "What's wrong?"

She wouldn't meet his eyes. His heart beat deer fast, panicked.

"I'm being anxious," she said finally. "I know I am, but it feels like you're trying to get away from me. You got out of bed really fast."

She didn't know how he'd hovered over her, that he'd been up for hours. "I haven't been!" He grabbed her hand, kissed her knuckles, "I'm—" He stopped. His face was hot, his ears burned. He covered his eyes with his free hand, embarrassed by himself, his lack of control, but the woman in front of him was so beautiful with her sleep-messed hair. Zeta's eyes were soft, her lips pink. The blanket had fallen, and her chest was covered with the marks he had left there, and she had no concept of how she looked to him at all.

He felt her moving, inching her way up to him on her hands and knees, which made it worse.

Zeta pressed her hand to his thigh, "What's— Oh."

"I'm trying to control myself, but . . ." She was so close and he could not. Ash kissed her, her tongue meeting his. Her mouth tasted sweet, sleepy, *good*. He laid her down, pushed his pants back off so that he was as bare as she, and pulled the blanket over them both.

"I'm going," he said slowly when they were both satisfied, forcing his breathing back under control, "to start your shower, and then I'll make you breakfast."

"I can do it myself," she said, voice dreamy and soft, pleased.

"You do not have to," he said, kissing her temple before pulling away. *Breakfast*, he thought reluctantly. The bed was warm and he wanted nothing more than to stay tangled in her arms, but her needs came first and she needed to eat.

Ash left, taking his warmth with him, and Zeta snuggled back down into the blankets, reluctant to be exposed to the air. Her phone was mostly charged, and after their brief intimacy, their morning-after redux, there was only one irrational thought in her mind.

Auntie I need you do something to make bad luck go away.

A couple of minutes later, a response. **Why? Did something happen?**

*Yeah, something happened, things **keep** happening.* A series of catastrophes followed their first meeting. Zeta didn't want another. She thought there *would be* another when she woke and there was that strange distance between them after all his passion the night before. **No. Just want to make sure it doesn't.**

Say no more. Can't wait to meet that boy.

Aunt Josie would light candles or burn some herbs or *something,* and even though Zeta didn't believe in it all, there had to be *something* to it. How else to explain everything that had happened? And now that they'd made it past the morning, she didn't want to fall asleep and drown in the tub or fall down an elevator shaft because the universe had it out for her. For them.

The idea of *them* felt comfortable and easy and far, far too new. *Do not rush things, Zeta. He's nice now, but . . . it's only been two nights, really.* She looked back at her phone, tried to distract herself.

The notifications were mostly games for later, but Pixie had texted.

How was the date???? She'd sent the message late the night before, expecting Zeta to be coming home, in bed to gossip.

It was good. It's sort of still happening? I'm at his place.

The response from Pixie was immediate. **You went home??? With a BOY????**

Stop it, I've stayed over with people before. She tried to think of when, of who she'd let take her home so easily. It was true it wasn't her habit, but she had before. Maybe once or twice. **I'm leaving soon.** The snow had stopped, she could see the sun, and she couldn't stay in his bed all day. She crawled out of it, suddenly aware of her state of undress, and hurried to the bathroom.

The room was done in green tile with black granite accents. There was a claw-foot bathtub and a stand-alone shower with a clear glass door. The wide shower head was pouring water, already starting to fog up the room from the heat. She had forgotten that he'd started it for her, wondered how much longer the hot water would last. On the dark counter, she saw his comb and brush, one toothbrush in the holder—a brand new one on the sink, package unopened. The bar on the wall held two towels, the damp one blue, the other dry and gray. And her reflection in the mirror.

Her hair was coming loose from the braided crown, face flushed, chest and neck spotted with dark petals left by Ash's mouth. She ran her fingers over them, the skin sensitive, her whole body sensitive from the lingering rumbles of Ash's lovemaking. She shivered at the memory, turned to the shower.

She stepped into the hot water, tried to avoid getting her hair wet, and reached for his soap, expecting the bar to smell like sage, like him, but it didn't. It smelled like any soap, fresh. She washed slowly, mind a haze still tingling from pleasure. She wrapped herself in the towel, brushed her teeth, and didn't know what to do with the toothbrush. She put it back in the package. *I'll just take it with me*, she frowned. It felt too soon to put it in the holder next to his.

Zeta touched the hairbrush—soft bristles—and the comb's teeth were too small. She took out her damp hair anyway, brushed it as well as she could, then braided it into four parts, the stitches in her hand not painful but irritating with every movement.

Finished, she went back to the bedroom. All the clothes were gone from the floor; a robe sat on the bed, black and made of something soft. It was so long it dragged on the floor, the sleeves past her hands. She rolled them up, tied the sash, and, picking up the sides like skirts, made her way into Ash's living room.

Someone was singing, and she stood at the door listening to the rich voice carry across to her. She knew the song, but something wasn't right, the voice wasn't right. It couldn't be the radio, it was live. "Ash?" she whispered to herself before stepping across the floor.

He was at the stove making pancakes. The kitchen was bright, filled with light and the buttery scent of breakfast. He'd found his pants.

"Are you singing Florence and the Machine?"

He paused and thought, like he wasn't aware that he was even singing at all. "Yeah, 'Hunger,' I think."

"You sing," she said, taking her seat across from him at the island again, putting the phone next to her bag.

"I sing. Do you?" he asked.

"No. I can play a few instruments. Guitar and piano, a couple of other ones. I can't sing at all," she said.

"So I'll be in charge of lullabies then. You changed your hair," he said, putting a plate with two perfect pancakes, sausage, and eggs, sunny-side up, in front of her. "I didn't know how you liked your eggs. I hope that they're OK." He handed her a fork.

"These look great, thanks. I did the best I could with my hair. I used your brush, sorry I didn't ask. Oh, I didn't know what to do with the towel; I don't know where your dirty clothes are. I couldn't decide what to do the toothbrush either. I figured I'd just take it with me? It's brand new, so it would be wasteful to toss it. Also, where are my clothes?"

He sat a glass bottle of syrup on the table along with his own plate. "Just put it in the holder; the towel can go back on the rack. Your clothes are in the washer."

"There's a washer in here?"

"It's behind the kitchen. You probably missed the door."

"I can't leave a toothbrush in your bathroom. I'm not your girl-friend. I shouldn't do that."

"Why not?"

"What if you want to bring someone else home? They'd notice. And then you'd have to explain, and that would be awkward for you."

"Why are you explaining to me how to manage my imaginary future relationships?" Ash laughed while Zeta looked guiltily at her plate.

"I don't want to cause you any problems," she mumbled to her food.

"Zeta, I am not going to date anyone until we are *not* dating. If that's what you've been worried about, you can stop. I'd much rather talk about our baby. What were your plans?"

Our baby. She smiled shyly at the idea, at him. "I'm going to take a couple of months off," she said, trying to collect her thoughts. The baby. "I've been saving to pay up my bills. My aunt is going to come down for a couple of weeks to help. After that I was going to hire a nanny to watch the baby during the day while I worked."

"Are you putting them in the office?"

"I don't know, I haven't figured it out. I might give them my room and take the living room? They'll stay in there with me at first anyway and we'll probably just share for a while. I think I might move when they're a little older."

"You can live in this building. There are three-bedroom units," he suggested. "Then I'll be close too."

She chuckled. "That is not an option for two reasons. One, I cannot afford this place. I don't know how much it is, but there's a doorman and I don't make doorman money. And two, it feels too, little kept family that you can pop in and out of whenever you'd like."

"That is absolutely not what I want, Kitten," he said softly. "I can help you look for something else, somewhere you'd be comfortable."

"It's a while off. For now I'm just staying put. Problem for Future Zeta."

"Future Zeta, sure. What about . . . baby stuff? Car seat, bottles, are you breastfeeding? Clothes? A crib?" he frowned, clearly trying to think of more baby related items and failing.

"I was going to try at least, breastfeeding. But no, I haven't gone shopping yet. Aunt Josie says its bad luck to bring anything in too early, so I was waiting until after the ultrasound."

"Do you believe in that sort of thing?" he asked.

Zeta looked away, embarrassed after her frantic morning text. She shrugged, tried to come off as chill. "Everybody believes in luck."

"Yeah, I guess that's true," he said softly, and when Zeta looked his eyes were focused on her, making her feel shy and small. He cleared his throat, looked back at his plate and moved his eggs around with his fork. "When is that? The ultrasound," he asked, his tone shifting into something more focused, more businesslike. She hadn't realized how relaxed he was, how relaxed she was, until he wasn't quite anymore.

"It's in January. The ninth, I think, I have to check."

"Can I come?" he asked, eyes back on her.

"Sure. I was going to take Pixie, but I'm sure she'll understand," Zeta said, shrugging, keeping to herself that Pixie suggested she take him to begin with. She took another bite of her pancakes.

"Let me know what time. I'll pick you up. What are you doing this month, for the holiday? Maybe we can spend more time together."

"I'm going to visit my aunt, and there's a couple of holiday get-togethers that I might go to. You?"

"I'm not going away, but I've got a few business functions. My father will kill me if I skip them; he goes to all of these things, so I've got to go too. How about New Year's? Can I take you out then?"

New Year's was weeks away, but she didn't have plans. She usually went out, but the idea of hanging out in a crowded bar all night didn't seem appealing then, and she didn't think it would get any better when she was even more pregnant. But a night with Ash? "Sure," she said. "I'd like that." A flutter in her belly grabbed her attention. She placed her hand over it unthinkingly. "Oh," she breathed.

"What is it?" he asked concerned, standing up, already rounding the island to her.

"I think the baby moved," she said. "I mean, I've been feeling them move around in there, but this time it was a little stronger."

"Really?" His voice was light with curiosity, and he put his hand on her belly. "What does it feel like?"

Inside she could feel the soft, feathery movements of their child, like they too wanted to voice their opinion. "Like being tickled a little, but inside. Almost like when you get butterflies in your belly but it's only like, one. Fluttery."

He stood behind her, both hands on her stomach now. "Where?"

"Here," she said, leaning back into him, placing his hand where she'd felt their baby. "You won't feel anything though. It's too early."

Ash didn't say anything. His hand on her was warm, his arm sturdy, breathing even and comfortable. He smelled like pancakes, but underneath was the same sage smell, not his soap or aftershave—he hadn't shaved. It was just him.

He kissed her head again, fingers lingering on her neck. "Eat up," Ash said finally, breaking his embrace. "It'll get cold. When are you getting those stitches out?"

She looked at her hand. It had been a week since they'd met again. "Wednesday. I have an appointment in the morning."

"Good, I'll take you. We'll go to lunch after."

"It's at nine thirty," she said.

"Brunch then," he said, smiling.

"It's a date," she laughed, taking up a forkful of eggs, surprised at her own delight over going on a second date with the man from the deck and hoping that Aunt Josie did whatever she was going to do to make sure everything remained well.

18

It had been a week since Ash had seen Zeta for more than a few hours. He'd taken her to the appointment to remove the stitches from her hand, had brunch with her, and then dropped her off at home, gone back to work, and regretted it.

He missed her in his bed even though she'd only been there once. They met for dinner a handful of times; she came over once but didn't stay—work in the morning. They had both been busy this past weekend, and he was trying not to be too overbearing, trying to take things at her pace. Now it was Wednesday again and they didn't have any upcoming plans. But he was considering them. *Maybe I'll just show up with dinner. Should I make something?*

He opened the door to his apartment and smelled popcorn.

Zeta, he thought, excited, smile rising only to drop instantly. "Claire?"

"Hey!" she said from his couch. A bowl of popcorn sat in her lap; the TV was on and some '80s action movie was playing. "When did you start buying microwave popcorn?"

He hadn't. He'd begged some off one of the other people who lived in the building the day after Zeta stayed over. The snow had kept her with him, the streets miserable until the evening. They'd talked and cuddled. Later in the afternoon she'd suggested a movie, a low-budget thriller that she promised would likely be more funny than tense. She insisted that a movie wasn't as good without popcorn, and he wanted her movie to be good, wanted everything to be good. He'd signed up for the neighborhood app in desperation. The next option was walking through the snow to the nearest corner store for a box. Which he would have done. Barefoot.

"What are you doing here?" he asked Claire.

"I've had enough of our parents. Now that Dad isn't at work, all he does is talk about what you are and aren't doing there."

"Yeah, I know. Although I was wondering why he stopped calling every day at four. That's been nice. I still can't figure out who's emailing him." Not that he'd spent much time on that mystery since Zeta had come back into this life.

"You should have gone into theatre with me. You wouldn't have to deal with this."

"I think he would complain about that more. And besides, I don't want to live the rest of my life identified as 'Claire Cross's younger brother' every time I do anything worthwhile."

"But you are going to be my younger brother for the rest of your life. It's not too late!" she said, in mock support. They both knew Ash was locked into his life. And besides, he had more to think about than himself.

"I didn't want to be on stage anyway. I wanted to build houses." He hung his coat up and took off his shoes. Dropped his keys, wallet, and phone on his kitchen island.

"Not too late for that either!" she said brightly.

"How'd you get in here?" he asked, changing the subject.

"The doorman, George. I'm still on the list."

I have to add Zeta, he thought to himself. "How long have you been here?"

"I don't know. A couple of hours? There's a Van Damme marathon on."

"I guess you're staying for a while. I'm going to go change," he said.

She gave him a thumbs up as he passed by the couch and went into his room. He shut the door, pulled off his tie. He walked into his closet and turned on the light, illuminating his rows of organized shirts, pants, jackets. He started to take off his shirt.

"Hey! What's your code?"

"Code?" He poked his head out of his closet to find Claire poking her head into his bedroom.

"For your phone. I want to order a burger," she said, waving the device at him.

Maybe I can send Zeta dinner. Let her know I'm thinking about her? "Use your own phone."

"I'm not downloading another app. There are too many apps in this country. That's what's wrong with the place, the gig economy. I'll get you something to eat too."

"If you're using my phone, I'm the one paying," he said, rubbing his face.

"You're going to buy me dinner? Thanks!"

Ash rattled off the code, shooed her out of the room, and finished unbuttoning his shirt. *She talked about a burger at Remy's. Would she like that now?* He stopped, breath catching, cold sweat down his back. "Fuck."

He dashed out of his closet through the door of his bedroom to find Claire standing in his living room, staring at his unlocked phone.

"Who," she said slowly, turning his phone to him, "is this?" Zeta's picture from the restaurant was his background.

"Claire, give me my phone." He held out his hand, an adult.

The smile crept to her face, cheeks rising up, eyes twinkling. "Ash has a new girlfriend," she sang.

"Please don't do this," he begged.

She shook her head. "Let's see what you're hiding."

He lunged and she danced out of the way—an old game. He'd gotten bigger but he'd never gotten better at it. He chased her around the apartment and she jumped out of the way, dodged his grabs like they were children again. The only thing that it was doing was slowing down the inevitable.

"Oh, she's so pretty!" she said, teasing him with the photo he'd taken of her the next day looking out of the window in his robe. "Do you have nudes on here? No," she answered herself. "You don't do that." But there was something he didn't want her to see.

He caught her by the couch and she toppled back onto it, throwing her legs up to catch him, keeping him too far to grab the phone from her, laughing hysterically. Her finger swiped to the next image and she stopped, the laughter died.

He pulled himself up and she stared at him, mouth in an O, eyes wide as she sat up. He took a seat on the couch and held out his hand again. Claire put the phone in his palm this time. The black-and-white ultrasound image Zeta has sent him was on the screen. He closed it.

"Ash, is that?"

"Her name is Zeta, and that is our baby." He looked at Claire and smiled, lump in his throat. There was nothing he could do now but tell the truth. "I'm going to be a dad."

"Oh my god! Congratulations!" She threw her arms around him and he hugged her back, laughing shakily, all the tension leaving him. "When's the baby due?"

"The spring, end of April," he answered.

"Wait," she said, the math running through her mind. "She's like, three or four months along now! Why haven't you told anyone about her?"

"It's complicated."

"Complicated? It's a baby. Mom and Dad will be ecstatic. Well, maybe not Dad, but maybe he'll stop complaining about the mess you're making of his company."

"I found out about this two weeks ago."

Claire stared at him blankly, and he gave her a watered-down version of what their relationship had been so far, ending with the agreement to see where things go.

"Hey, do you need to take a couple of deep breaths and lie down on the kitchen floor?" she asked when he finished.

Yes. "No." He leaned back on his couch, stared at his ceiling. "We're still figuring things out. That's why I haven't brought it up yet. I don't want to say anything without having a plan."

Claire shook her head and frowned. "You're overthinking it. You just told me and it's fine. It's a baby—things happen, and it's not like you're a kid. You're allowed to have a baby."

"It wasn't you I was worried about."

"He's going to be grumpy either way."

"It's not really his mood that's the major concern, Claire." They were all being careful around Nathanial Cross. He was recovering, but he was not the same. The heart attack had been serious; decades of work before everything, including his own health, had finally taken their toll.

And besides that, things with Zeta were too new, too unsure. He wanted things to be steady between them. Settled. In the hospital he had thought they would just *be* together, especially the morning after they'd found each other, but reality was more complicated. She had a life without him, a life he needed to fit into.

"Right, but you have to tell our parents eventually. I won't say anything, but I'd do it soon, get all the hard stuff out of the way before the baby's here. When are you guys seeing each other again? When can I meet her?"

"We've had lunch or dinner together a few times a week so far, but we're so busy right now, the holidays. We're going to spend New Year's together, but I have no idea what to do."

"Why don't you just take her to the carnival?"

"What carnival?" He looked up from his phone, their order on the screen.

"The one cousin Doreen used to take us to. She likes games, right?"

He thought back. Doreen was their father's cousin who had nevcr had children. She took them for the holiday every year while their parents went to a formal party. It was hosted by some club she was part of as an annual fundraiser. The details were hazy, but he remembered it being fun. Lots of games, dancing, a very casual affair. Doreen had moved down to Florida for the weather two years ago. Ash hadn't spent New Year's with her since he was fifteen. "Do they still do that?"

Claire shrugged. "I don't know, you should ask her. But probably. They've been around for forty years. When is the food going to be here?"

"Half an hour," he said, pushing himself off the couch. "I'm going to finish getting changed."

"Ash, it's going to be OK. You'll be a great dad," Claire smiled.

He closed his eyes, could feel his face tingling, turning pink. "Thank you," he said, and left before the tingles turned to heat, escaping into the safety of his room. *I hope I will be.*

Are you home? he texted Zeta. He went back to his closet, shed his shirt and pants into the hamper.

His phone beeped. **I'm not! I'm shopping with Cody.**

For what? Cody, she'd mentioned him. A friend.

A Christmas gift for my aunt. You home yet or are you working late? I can come by after I'm done if you want. Maybe another hour.

The idea was more than appealing. But. **I'd love that but Claire is over. I want to send you dinner. Tell me when you get home.**

She sent a photo of herself giving a thumbs up in a store surrounded by crystals and little idols. He smiled, heart blossoming into a thousand small suns in his chest. "She's so cute," he said to her image before putting the phone down and getting dressed to meet Claire on his couch for what would be an all-night marathon of bad movies and junk food.

———

Claire is his sister, Zeta thought. A funny feeling that she couldn't quite place churned in her stomach, made her a little nauseous. Jealousy? Worry? Fear? She wasn't sure and tried to suppress it with logic. He'd just found out about the baby, of course it was way too soon for her to meet anyone in his family. Did she even want to? Was it *that* kind of relationship? She had no idea, and she reasoned she shouldn't read too much into things.

The feeling lessened but was still there.

"Should I get him a Christmas gift?" Zeta asked Cody suddenly.

Cody looked up from the display of Buddhas. "Who?"

They were in a little metaphysical shop, Eternity's Messenger. Every inch of it was lined with shelves that held crystals, amulets, tarot cards, and herbs. Books about aliens, chakras, and numerology were stacked on tables and in bookstands. Handmade goods from local spiritual artisans dotted the store here and there. Cody's body took up almost the whole little aisle they stood in.

"Ash," she replied.

"Baby daddy Ash? Did he get you a gift?"

"Is there another, secret Ash I don't know about? And I have no idea." She thought about it. "But probably. He got me a gift for my birthday, I don't know why he would skip Christmas. Besides, he seems like the type who would."

"What does that mean?" Cody asked.

"I mean he seems nice and thoughtful? But it's been literally two weeks so I don't know. But, like, remember when I stayed over at his place? He made a pie and then showed me how to make quiche. I should have asked for the pie; it was really good. And I mentioned popcorn would be nice and he was like BRB and came back ten minutes later with a box from a neighbor."

"So he made sure you didn't starve? I think you should raise the bar on what's nice a little bit," he laughed.

Her face said *I am not amused*. "It was more than that," she tried to explain. "It's like he's always trying to figure out what I need or want before I ask for it. And when I do ask for something there's this second where he looks guilty, like he should have known so I wouldn't have to ask. But not in an infantilizing way."

Cody's mouth twisted, brows furrowed, *sure*.

"He just texted me so he could order me dinner!"

"In that case tell him you want an order of the vegetarian chicken parm from Leo's," Cody said, all smiles.

"No. I want tacos," she laughed.

"If he was as thoughtful as you say, he would know that," Cody teased.

"Whatever. So, should I?" she asked, picking up a brownish crystal, trying to figure out which one said *I love you, sorry I don't call more* for her aunt.

Cody hummed, thinking it over. "Probably not."

"Why not?"

"Because you've only known him a couple of weeks, you're not in a relationship, and it sends a message that you *are* in a relationship," Cody explained. "Not that one," he added, pointing at the crystal.

She put it down. "We are in a relationship," she said, putting her hands on her belly. "A developing one. He's not seeing anyone else. I mean, I'm not either, and we are sleeping together."

He crossed his arms, hunched over to her height, face full of concern. "You don't buy Christmas presents for your fuck buddies."

She felt the words in her chest. *Is that all there is?* she thought, running through what their relationship had been. A one-night stand, two weeks and a handful of hours, and in that time it felt like most of what they did was fuck. They had dinner, they met for lunch, sure. But it just seemed like every chance they had, they were wrapped around each other. Maybe not actually going all the way every time, but physical, everything was very physical. "OK, but we are having a baby. This one?" A pretty piece of rust-colored crystal with many small, faceted faces sparkled in the light as she held it up.

"Vanadinite! Good choice! Creativity and manifestation. She'll love it. And OK, think about it this way, if you weren't knocked up, would you be thinking about buying this man a gift?"

She wrinkled her nose. "Of course not, it's only been two weeks. But this is different!"

"No, babe, you hope it's different, but you don't know that yet. I'm not saying don't date him, and maybe he is, magically, The One. But you can't jump him ahead in the process just because you're expecting. Take things one step at a time."

"You're right," she sighed as she turned around, found of a rack of hand-woven shawls. She started picking through them, turning over the interaction. He was nice and sweet, but it was new. People change; it was better, smarter, to take things slow and not send the wrong message. "One of these, and Aunt Josie is all set for the holiday. Thanks for helping me."

"Anytime, Z. So, you wanna get some tacos?"

She paused. What would it mean to get dinner with Cody instead? Would Ash see that as a message? *No, I'm overthinking it. He knows I'm out, of course I'll get dinner.* "Yeah. Want anything from here?"

"Not today," he said. "Let's go, I'm starving."

Later, belly full of tacos, Zeta put her purchases on her table. She ignored the pile of dishes in her sink. The stitches were out, but she didn't have the energy. Tomorrow.

Went out to dinner with Cody. She added a taco emoji surrounded by party poppers.

Do you want dessert? I still have some pie. I can run it over, spend a little time with you.

The sweet taste of pear and apple flooded her memory; her mouth watered. Then she looked at her messy kitchen and grimaced. No, he could not see that. **No,** she wrote, frowning, shoulders heavy, **I'm pretty full.**

Let me know when you're settled then. I want to call, see how your day went. Thoughtful.

Aren't you visiting with your sister?

She's watching Bloodsport.

Alright, hold on, I'll call you.

She changed out of her sweater and thick leggings and into a flannel, long-sleeve nightgown, grandma style. Comfortable, she dialed him.

"Kitten," he said after the second ring.

"Hey," she responded, giddy from the breathy sound of the pet name. *Do fuck buddies have pet names?* "I didn't know you liked those kind of movies," she said.

"What movies? *Bloodsport*? What do you mean? Action movies?" His voice was light, amused.

"Yeah, I thought you liked twisty science-fiction mystery stuff. Like *Inception*."

"I do," he said. "But I think those are still broadly categorized as action. But I don't really. It's Claire. There's a marathon and she loves those movies."

"She sounds fun," Zeta said, testing the conversation, seeing where he went with it.

"She can be. How was your day?"

Oh, she thought. She had hoped that he would say something to her about Claire, but he moved from the topic quickly. Zeta knew she should ask, be clear, but she was too embarrassed to admit that she cared, that it mattered. *He just found out; of course he's keeping it to himself.* "It was good. I got a lot done. Hey, were you going to buy me a Christmas present?"

He chuckled. "Is there something you want?"

"Don't."

She heard his breath catch. "Why?"

"We haven't been seeing each other very long," she said quickly. "It's too much pressure for an already busy time." It didn't seem like reason enough, but she'd already said it. "I'm just not comfortable with it."

Silence and then: "Alright, if that's what you want."

"I know how much you like providing, so this probably really bothers you. Don't take it too hard, there's still Valentine's Day. And you did give me a birthday gift."

"Did that make you uncomfortable?" he asked nervously.

"No," she said, thinking back to it, that little moment between them. "But that was different. Things hadn't started between us really. Now we've been on a date, we've talked more. It's just different." She was making excuses—they didn't even make sense to herself.

"How about when I send you meals; does that make you uncomfortable?"

"No, it's nice," she mumbled.

"So it's just this one thing," he asked slowly.

"I . . . guess."

"I respect your wishes. No Christmas gift this year."

She let out a breath. "I know it's weird. Thank you. And don't you have a visitor?" Her words came out awkward. She covered her face, skin burning.

"It's just my sister."

"Nah, don't be rude. I wanted to play the new Legend of Zelda anyway."

"Alright," he said. "I'll let you go."

"One more thing!" she said, the sadness in his voice echoed in her belly, pulled her throat tight. "Can I come over for a piece of that pie tomorrow? Maybe we can watch something you actually like."

"I would love that," he said, lighter, smoother.

"Great! Goodbye, Puppy."

Softly, almost a purr, he said good night in return, and the sound of it tickled her ears, spilled into her belly, and spread warmth all through her.

19

It was a Christmas party, but *party* was a very loose explanation of what was happening. There were people, they were gathered, there were drinks and decorations, but Ash didn't think anyone was having fun, least of all him. But the Cross Holiday Gathering was a tradition that had been happening since before he was born: his family, the caterers, and a selection of business partners or their proxies.

Ash stood in front of a man whose name escaped him and nodded, not sure what he was agreeing with but understanding that it was the proper time to agree with something in the conversation. Whatever they said, it was idle chatter, meant to remind Ashford Cross that they existed so that when it came time to do business, he would think of them.

He was bored and tired, exhausted really, and wished that they could have had a small, quiet family dinner. But they had always had the party and his father wouldn't stop it that year. Definitely not that year. He didn't want anyone to think that anything had changed.

"It'll make people worry. It's a tradition," Nathanial had claimed when Ash floated the idea of cancelling the party over Thanksgiving. Before he knew about his own personal life surprise.

Dutifully he showed up at the cabin, the same place they'd hosted the party every year of his life. The cabin, his parent's place just outside of the city. Far enough out so that they were in nature but not so far that his mother couldn't dip into the city for shopping. And more than close enough for a bunch of enterprising business associates to come for drinks and "Christmas cheer."

The cabin was really a miniature mansion with a log exterior. The main hall had been done up with a huge tree, lights strung all over the place and sparkly snowflakes hung from the ceilings. A delightful setup, all it needed was a couple of kids running around and a Santa. But there were no children, and certainly no Santa. Years ago when Ash was young there had been, along with other children, the heirs of other company families that his father wanted to impress. As the years went on they all got older, but Ash always had to be there, even after Claire had left for her own life. They were the company's children and he had grown to be the company man. Like his father. The decorations were a show of wealth and nothing else. The people were the same and they were all still trying to impress each other.

Is this how I want to spend my child's holidays? He thought of Zeta, wondered if she was doing alright at her aunt's. If she had gotten enough rest.

"Excuse me for a moment," he said, pulling himself out of the conversation. The other men, their wives and girlfriends at their sides, nodded and wished him well as he slipped away. He passed servers, hands full of trays. None of them paid him any attention as he turned down the hall and slipped into his mother's sitting room.

He turned on the light and shut the door. No decorations here. The room had off-white walls and original, bright paintings ranging from abstract to realist. Part of her collection. Plush golden-brown couches and quirky armchairs. She held book club meetings once a month in the room.

No one would leave the main hall; they weren't there to explore. The party would end promptly at eleven, everyone would line up for their drivers, and that would be that. Ash would stay the night with his own family; they would all wake at a reasonable time. They'd open gifts and he would be home by noon.

Zeta wouldn't have a gift from him and he didn't understand why. It had been bothering him the entire time. There was a gift. He'd told her there wasn't, but he'd known as soon as he saw it. He just hadn't known he would have a chance to give it to her.

A bracelet of stars.

It was sitting, in a little black box, inside his dresser drawer next to his underwear and would stay there until he figured out how to give it to her without making her uncomfortable.

He picked up his phone, cleared a handful of game notifications, then stopped himself. *She's out with her family. I shouldn't bother her.*

He put his phone down reluctantly, leaned back on the couch, and closed his eyes to keep from staring at their previous text messages. It didn't work, and the phone was back in his hand, the texts on screen.

The door opened.

"I'll be out in sec," he sighed without looking, expecting Claire.

"Oh, don't rush out on my account. By all means finish looking at your email or whatever."

"Mom," he said, looking up.

She stepped into the room, her red holiday dress sweeping the carpet with every step. Her hair was pinned up and decorated with a comb shaped like holly. "And why are you all alone in here, mister? You're supposed to be mingling."

"Just checking my email, like you said," he said, waving the phone in front of his mother.

She tilted her head. "And who is that?" she asked, voice playful.

Fuck, he cursed himself. He was terrible at secrets. "It's, I mean— Her name is Zeta."

"Zeta, oh my. Interesting name. Well let me see!" she hummed, reaching for his phone.

He showed her the picture, trying to figure out how he would tell his mother about the baby, about everything.

"She really is a looker! So pretty!" Bridgette handed the phone back, smiling softly. "You'll tell us about her when you're ready. Claire said you were seeing someone but you weren't ready to share her yet. I can wait."

Claire! He cursed again. "We haven't been seeing each other that long,"

"Bring her over for dinner when you're ready. Right now, it's time for the toast."

He looked at the time. "Is it that late?" he asked, standing. The party was almost over; he'd lost track somewhere.

With his mother he left the room, joining his sister and father in the main hall. Someone handed him a glass of champagne, and his father started his speech.

It was always nearly the same: A brief history of Cross Construction. The highlight reel of whatever big projects worked out well, a nod to any new business they'd brought in. Thanks to everyone for another prosperous year in business. Ash was only half listening, which is why his father's words caught him off guard.

"Ashford, I've watched you grow your whole life. Your toddling first steps all the way up to right now. The way you stepped in, the dedication and loyalty you've shown. I'm proud of you. And I think it's time to hand over the reins."

"Dad?" Ash asked, head spinning.

Nathanial laughed, patted him on the back with a big smile while the gathered crowd applauded.

Ash looked at them, remembered himself, and smiled. "Thank you," he said. "It's only because you raised me so well."

They hugged for the show of it, his father just as tall but thin, thinner than Ash ever remembered him being. Then his mother kissed his cheek. A hug from Claire. A sea of congratulations and handshakes.

And then it was eleven. His family stood at the door, waving goodbye, wishing everyone a happy holidays and thanking them for coming out to celebrate with them.

"Come sit with me," his father said, pulling him back through the house to his mother's sitting room.

Alone, his father turned to him. "This is a big step." His voice was solemn, eyes hard. "You're taking on a legacy. Your focus needs to be on this company. You've got a bit of a head start, but changeover is hard. People will try to take advantage. But stay the course we've been running for almost a century. I'm leaving this to you. One day you're going to have your own family and you'll have to set the path for them. Make sure they're taken care of like I've done for your mother, your sister, and you."

His father's eyes had a softness he'd never seen. *Do you understand*, they asked, but the question was bigger than that moment, bigger than the company. It wrapped around their family. The legacy, Ash's family.

His family. His child.

"I understand," he said. He would do exactly what was expected of him. Ash was reliable.

The older man hugged him again and he returned it. "Go on to bed. You know your mother likes to get to the gifts early."

"In a bit."

Nathanial smiled, agreed, and clapped him on the shoulder, leaving Ash in the room to his own thoughts.

Ash rested his face in the steeple of his fingers and thought about the last few weeks. He had known this was coming. Had to come. Even though he hadn't filled in his old position quite yet. Even though he still hadn't really settled into the office. He told himself he delayed because he was busy with everything. Or maybe, he didn't want to replace his father.

Now that the company was his, though, he realized that it wasn't any of that. It was that he didn't want to be in charge of Cross Construction. He didn't know what he *wanted*, but now that he had it, he knew it wasn't that. *I should tell Randall, I should let him know*, he thought. Randall had said it was coming soon and he was right. Ash wondered what else he had already guessed.

He called Zeta.

"Hey!" she answered brightly. "Aren't you supposed to be at a party?"

"It ended a little bit ago. Are you busy? I'm not pulling you away from anything?"

A soft splash. "No, I'm just soaking in this bath."

A bath. Did she prefer baths? Should he run her one the next time she came over instead of the shower? Or was it more practical? The trip was long, maybe she was sore? "I didn't know you liked baths," he settled on.

"They're fine I guess, but this isn't for hygiene. Aunt Josie insisted. To wash off the negative energy."

"What?"

"You know, from my apartment falling in and the . . . table."

"Right, that negative energy."

"You're getting a box with directions to take one too. She *insists*."

"I wouldn't think of passing on the opportunity. I, too, would like to wash off negative energy." He chuckled. "How's your visit?"

"Fine, some of my cousins stopped past and we ate. But really the big stuff isn't until tomorrow. We're going to dinner at my one cousin's house."

"We do a family lunch. My mom cooks. Most of my family has moved out of the area though."

"Small gathering," she hummed. "Something the matter?"

His heart jumped. "Why?"

"I don't know," she said, the water splashing through the line as she shifted. "You sound . . . down."

I should tell her, he thought. Then, *No, that's too much; we're just figuring things out.* "I'm just tired."

"You should get some rest then. It's late."

"It is. Why are you in a bath this late?"

"It's a good hour for the work," she said by way of explanation.

Work, he thought. "My dad is stepping down," he said in a rush.

"That's great! Congratulations! Isn't that what you wanted?" she said.

Had he told her that? His head was spinning. "How's the baby?" he asked suddenly, wanting, needing to change the subject.

"They're fine. Just hanging out. I don't know if it's because I wasn't doing much today or what, but they were pretty active. Are you sure you're OK?"

"That's good, and yes, I'm sure. I just wanted to check on you, but I should probably let you get back to your bath."

"And you should get some rest. Good night, baby."

He leaned back on the couch, stared at the ceiling, heart exploding. "Good night, Kitten."

For the child. He had to do it for them.

He couldn't walk away from it.

20

Aunt Josie stood just in the doorway, fur coat still on, her eyes sweeping the space of Zeta's apartment while Zeta stood in her kitchen, hands clasped under her belly, waiting.

Zeta's weekend bag sat on the kitchen chair. Her aunt had insisted on driving her back home, all three hours, even though she already had her bus ticket. Zeta had napped through the ride, the holiday busy with family visits and outings with her aunt, and now she had that rested-but-off feeling that sleeping for a long time in a car after a trip causes.

She wanted to lie down. In her own bed in comfortable clothes and not nap, but sleep.

But first, Aunt Josie wanted to make sure she really wasn't living in a thrown-together apartment that should have been condemned. A concern that Ash had voiced more gently.

"It's nicer, I'll give you that," Aunt Josie said slowly, stepping into the kitchen, turning her attention to the cabinets. "The cabinets are still the cheapest they could get. Probably need replacing in three years. Appliances are nice."

"It's nice having a new stove," Zeta admitted. Not that she cooked much, but when she did, it was *nice*.

"You need to clean up though," she sighed.

The kitchen was trashed. Everything was trashed. The backlog from her stitches and then work and then just too tired all the time. And then the holidays were upon her and it was a problem for Future Zeta. "I know!" she said. "I just got busy," Zeta explained, embarrassed.

"No dishwasher," Josie tutted. "I'll help you get it sorted some before I leave."

"Thank you, you don't have to," Zeta said. "I've got a cleaner coming."

Josie raised an eyebrow, amused, "When?"

"Next week, for the New Year," Zeta said, hoping the older woman didn't catch her lie. She was embarrassed and didn't want her aunt to help, to think that she couldn't take care of it on her own. Now that she'd said it, it was an excellent idea. *Someone to come in, get things back in order.*

"Why don't you ask that new boyfriend of yours to come help," Josie teased as she walked back through the place, checking the hall, giving a little whistle at the washer and dryer.

"He's not my boyfriend. We've only been seeing each other for a few weeks, like, really. We barely know each other."

"I see," Josie said, ending up in Zeta's office. "Looks bare in here without all your things."

"Yeah, that's the worst part. Turns out some things really are irreplaceable." She'd tried. Digging through pages of eBay listings turned out to be a good distraction from work stress and the OMG-I'm-having-a-baby panic that settled over her from time to time in the first weeks. Some of her games she'd stumbled upon, but she passed on them to save the money for said baby. The posters, collected free from game stores at the end of promotions, were harder to find still. But when they popped up she convinced herself to spend the money so the walls weren't so empty.

"It looks better, I'll give you that, but it's still a rinky-dink little place. You're thirty years old! Don't you think it's time for you to get a little house? If it's really about the money, I can help you," her aunt said, crossing her arms giving her that *Come on, now* look.

It was the conversation they had avoided having over the holidays when everyone was cooing over Zeta's growing belly and saying how surprised they were that she was having a baby! Gifts and holiday cheer. And Aunt Josie was supportive and understanding but she knew that Zeta was stubborn.

"I like it here. It's a nice neighborhood, the rent is low, and it has everything I need. The bus stops at the corner, and delivery drivers have no trouble finding it. Plus, I sort of in a very literal way just moved in."

"Well you can sort of, in a very literal way just move out." Josie laughed. "How are you going to fit a baby in here?"

"I don't know yet, but I'll figure it out." Zeta shrugged. "There's time."

Aunt Josie shook her head. "Alright, I'll let you be for now, but you can't just let this sit. After you get that ultrasound, it's time to go baby shopping."

He probably wants to go, and he probably wants to pay for every-thing. She didn't know how she felt about that. If she should let him or if it was too soon. Everything seemed to be happening faster than she thought, like the world started speeding up when she crashed through his table. "Yeah, I'll hop right to it," Zeta agreed.

"You go sit while I take care of things," Aunt Josie said, shooing her out the office. "Back-to-front work," she said solemnly before adding, "even though it really should be cleaned up in here first."

Zeta walked out the room while her aunt pulled out bundles of herbs to burn. "And don't change your clothes!" she added. "We've got another stop to make!"

Baby shopping, Zeta thought to herself. She went to her bedroom, and as soon as she lay down on her bed, her phone rang.

"Hello, Puppy."

"Kitten," he returned, the soft sight in his voice she'd come to expect and crave. "How was your trip? Did you make it home?"

"Were you timing me? I just walked in the door a few minutes ago."

"No, I had cameras installed while you were away." He laughed. "You told me what time you would be back."

"I forgot. Pregnancy brain. You didn't really have cameras installed, did you?"

"Of course not! Why would— Do you think I'm a stalker?"

"Well, you did find my locked-down social, so . . ."

"I was trying to find you. Does that bother you? I swear I wouldn't—"

She giggled at his panic. He seemed so sure of himself but got flustered so easily. Never angry, a little anxious, ready to correct. "I was just teasing a little." Down the hall she could hear her aunt repeating a psalm, she wasn't sure which one, the scent of the herbs flowing into her bedroom. "My trip was fine."

"Good, I know you just got back, but I'd really like to see you. I can bring some food over."

She almost accepted but remembered that her aunt wanted to go somewhere. "I can't. My aunt came down with me and she wants to go somewhere. Sorry, I can't have friends over today."

"I'll let you go. Will you call me later?" he asked.

Thoughtful, she smiled. Tried to ignore the desire to have him come over. "Yeah." They'd just met, a call was fine.

He said goodbye and hung up, and when she looked up, her aunt was standing in the door. "Is he home?"

Zeta looked up at her aunt's grinning face. "Auntie, no."

Ash lay on the length of his couch, his book open and facedown on this chest, and finally decided that he would see Zeta that night. He knew he shouldn't, but he needed the reassurance of her physical form. That she was real, that he had found her, that she was alright.

He wanted to hold her.

The bell for his apartment rang, dragging him out of his daydreams. *Claire*, he thought, probably to avoid their parents for an afternoon. He was trying to convince her to rent a place if she insisted on staying. Before it was about their father, but now she planned on waiting to go back to Greece until after Zeta had the baby.

He dragged himself up from the couch. He hadn't bothered to get dressed, having nothing to do this weekend but wait for Zeta to arrive back in town. A pair of green pajama pants and a T-shirt covered his body, and a dusting of stubble covered his chin.

Zeta's smiling face met him on the other side of the door, and his mind cleared of all thoughts, leaving behind nothing but joy. "Zeta!" he breathed before bending down, sweeping her into a hug, and planting a kiss on her lips that she returned, before pushing him away.

"Hi! Sorry," she said.

Which is when the rest of his mind clicked back to life and he recognized two things, nearly at once. One, he looked like shit, a state he had planned to change before leaving, and two, Zeta was not alone.

Standing behind her was an older woman, She was tall with clear, hard eyes and dark hair that was streaked with silver, pulled into a braid, and laced through with various earthy-colored ribbons that matched the skirts that peeked out from her fur coat. Her face was mostly smooth, with the barest of wrinkles just around the eyes and mouth from laughter. She looked like she was in her late fifties, early sixties at most. Right around the age of his own parents. "Aunt Josie," he said.

She smiled. "He's quick. And excited to see you," she laughed, looking back at Zeta before returning her gaze to him. "And nervous. Good signs."

Aunt Josie bustled her way into his apartment, stripping off her coat. "Would you look at this place!"

"I'm sorry! I'm so sorry! She insisted!" Zeta explained as she thrust a bag into his hands.

He looked at it, confused. "Insisted on what? If you told me, I would have made something to eat. Cleaned up a little. What is this?"

Zeta shook her head. "She wants to get a real sense of you. And that is for your bath. You can do that after we leave."

The bath, she'd mentioned it.

"Zeta, baby, this is what kind of apartment you should have!" Aunt Josie said, looking around Ash's living room. "He's a reader, and he takes his shoes off at home."

"Y-yes," he said. "Do you want something to drink?"

"Auntie!" Zeta nearly yelled, stepping into the apartment. Introductions. "This is Ash."

He held out his hand and she brushed it away, wrapping him in a hug instead. "It's nice to meet you," he sputtered, returning it, worried suddenly that he smelled.

She released him and went back to the apartment, nodding her head. "The energy here is, hmm," she said, turning back to him. "I see what Alice meant about the ears now."

He reached up, touched his ear. "Is there something wrong with my ears?"

"No," Zeta said. "Don't worry about your ears." She touched his arm, "Relax," she whispered, "she's not scary, I swear."

Everything was so wildly out of his control that all he could do was nod and smile, which was strange because it was his apartment.

"Zeta doesn't usually bring her little boyfriends around, so I know you must be serious."

"We are having a baby, ma'am," he said, unsure if he should mention that it was his apartment or if the encounter was some sort of test.

Aunt Josie laughed. "You think that matters?"

"Auntie!" Zeta drew out the word, and he could feel the eyeroll in her voice. "You're making him nervous."

Zeta was right. He *was* nervous.

"He should be. So *Ash*, what exactly do you do."

"I'm the CEO of a construction firm. We deal in—"

"Stop right there, it doesn't matter. It's not what you want to do anyway! What about your family?"

How did she . . . ? "Family?"

"Your mom, dad? Did you find him on the street?"

"In a bar, but I think you're stressing him out," Zeta sighed. "She's teasing you."

Still. "Wait," he said, taking a deep breath. "I don't think I properly introduced myself," he said, finally getting his feet under him in this little play that Josie was putting on. "Please have a seat. Welcome to my home," he said, pulling out the chair at his kitchen counter."

He poured water for them both, not knowing what Josie wanted. "My name is Ashford Cross. It is my greatest pleasure to be dating your daughter."

Her aunt smiled, his wording having the desired impact. "And it's nice to meet you, finally. What did you really want to do with your life?" Josie asked.

"This is a carnival trick, Ash," Zeta said, rolling her eyes. "I can't believe you're doing this," she said, frowning at her aunt.

It was a playful sort of look, annoyed but also accepting. Ash relaxed; whatever he was doing, it was correct.

"This is how it goes in my line of work too sometimes. Someone comes in, flashy, tries to throw you off balance. I wanted to be an architect."

Josie sat back and whistled. "There he is. Give me your hand."

Ash held out his left hand.

Aunt Josie took his in her smaller, dry hands, traced lines on his palm with a finger, clucking at whatever she found. Josie motioned for his other hand; he gave it to her. She treated it the same and after a moment looked up. She considered him as she sat back in her chair.

"Earnest, family oriented, which is good, considering. A romantic. Hmm," she considered. "As I was saying, the energy in here is stale."

"Stale?" he repeated.

"You need to loosen up." She laughed. "I do like the plants though."

"They're my hobby," he replied.

"I wish this one would do something besides play all those games." She laughed. "Do you play them too?"

"She's teaching me about them," Ash said. He looked at his palms, turned them over, and wondered if she saw anything or just made it up on the spot to flatter, to test. To give him something to live up to. He didn't believe in palm reading, but it didn't matter because he knew *she* did and he wanted her to like him.

"Well let's get this done then," Aunt Josie said, standing up and digging into her purse. She pulled a fresh bundle of herbs and a lighter.

"You can't smoke in here," Ash said quickly. "Especially not around Zeta, sorry."

Both women giggled. "She's not going to smoke it! It's called smudging. To cleanse the negative energy."

"Do you mind if I go into your bedroom?" Josie asked.

"No?" Ash answered. The woman left to do her work, and Ash turned back to Zeta. "Do you believe in this?"

"If I said yes, what then?" she said.

"Then I know."

"Well, not really, but we've had a lot of bad luck and it can't hurt."

"You want us to only have good luck from now on?"

"Don't you?" she smiled, and he wanted to wrap her in his arms, promise her that there would be nothing but good from that moment on, but her aunt was in the other room chanting.

Instead he said, "I'm going to make lunch." And was rewarded with her smile.

21

Zeta handed her coat over to the attendant at the coat check and took her ticket with a thank-you before turning back to Ash who stared at her, eyes dazed, smile wide. "Do you like it?" she asked, risking a little twirl of the sparkly, fluffy dress she wore.

When he'd told her to wear something "fun and fancy," she didn't know what to make of it and went looking for "a dress to make her eight-year-old self proud." Which resulted in this dress, with a sparkly black bodice and plunging neckline held up by thin straps. The dark marks of his kisses had finally faded, leaving behind smooth, rich skin. The skirts were made of poofy tulle that fell to just above her knees. Her stockings were sliver fishnets that sparkled with the dress, the shoes black ankle boots with a low heel. She wore her hair out, the curls bouncy and tight, hair thicker than ever, which she'd read was because of the pregnancy. Silver earrings with dangling crystals peeked out through her curls.

"You look amazing," Ash said, handing her shawl back to her. His long legs were encased in dark slim pants and his shirt was white, no tie, unbuttoned at the collar. A long jacket, black with dark flowers all over it, hung from his shoulders. His hair was brushed back from his face.

"You look like a vampire, and I mean that in a very positive way," she said, digging her phone out of her little handbag covered in dark sequins to match her dress. "I'm taking a photo and sending it to Pixie."

"If you want to," he said, standing still.

"Wait, wait, not like that. Turn a little to the side and lean back. OK, now look toward me. Don't smile! Perfect. Kind of put your hand in your hair like you're brushing it back, elbow up, don't move!" Zeta took the photo and turned the phone toward him. "See? Vampire."

He pulled her close and bent down, nibbled on the sensitive skin of her neck, making her jump. "I vant to suck your blood," he teased.

"Ah, we're blocking the line." She giggled, the mood between them light. It had been good since the surprise meeting with Aunt Josie. She'd been worried that he'd think she was strange, that something in him would change, but he had been nothing but sweet and respectful. Her aunt had nothing but praise for him when they left, except that she thought he was holding something back. To which Zeta shrugged, reminded her they'd only known each other for an amount of time that was literally measured in weeks.

"Come here," he said, guiding her away from the coat check. "One more thing. Give me your wrist." He lifted it himself, and out of his pocket appeared a silver bracelet. He fastened it around her wrist.

"Stars," she said, looking at the thin sliver chain made up of stars and moons, a dainty piece of jewelry. Her heart fluttered. The metal was warm from his body and sat on her wrist like it was made for her. "I should be mad at you. For being pushy."

He smiled softly down at her. "It's not Christmas, Kitten."

"That's— You're being," she stumbled, trying to find the right words, but her mind was too charmed, her heart fluttering.

He bent to her ear. "Let me give you the stars, love." He kissed her cheek, and when he looked down at her again she swore he was about to ask her to marry him. Zeta wasn't sure what she would say. "Don't be too mad at me."

She wasn't. It wasn't a test; she didn't feel any disrespect in his actions. It felt like telling someone not to worry about waiting up for you and they do anyway because . . . they care. And the bracelet, no doubt expensive but just a trinket all the same, was something nice and sweet. Something to say, *I was thinking of you.* "I'm not," she huffed, guilty. "I didn't get you anything though." She dropped her eyes. "Sorry."

He tilted her chin back up with his finger. "I don't care. I'm happy to just be with you. Come on, let's go in." He pulled her down the carpeted hall to the main ballroom of the hotel.

Ash hadn't told her at all what the plan for the night was, only an idea of what to wear and when to be ready. When they parked at the Grand Landing Hotel, she thought fancy dinner and dancing. When they entered the massive hall, the reality was not what she was expecting.

A crowd of people, children and adults, dressed in evening wear meandered between booths set up with different games like ring tosses and darts. A fishing pond for prizes, silly guess-my-height and strongman contests. Clowns and jugglers moved through the crowd alongside waiters with trays full of snacks and drinks. The air smelled of popcorn and cotton candy.

"It's a carnival," she said, bubbling with delight.

"It is! It's the yearly fundraiser for the Fish Choir Society."

"The . . . what?" she asked, looking up at him as he took her arm.

"Honestly? I have no idea what they do, but my cousin Doreen is a member, and I thought you'd like this more than the other formal dress events I was invited to this year."

She grinned. "I love carnivals!"

"Really? The games, maybe, but I didn't think you'd like rides," Ash said, moving her into the room toward the ticket booth to wait in line.

"Carnival rides are really chill. Tiny rollercoasters, bumper cars, Ferris wheels. I tolerate them surprisingly well. Are there bumper cars hidden somewhere?"

"I don't think so—and I'm not really a fan. I'm a little tall."

She laughed behind her hand, imagining Ash squeezed into a tiny car. "Now I really want to see it."

"I'll do it for you." He smiled back. "I'll have to tell Claire she was right."

"Right about what?" Zeta asked, keeping the frown from her face. The weird, sick place in her still ached. How he handled his own family was up to him, but she couldn't help but feel worried about it, like it meant something more about them, about him.

She had told her own family about him. Showed Aunt Josie his picture and she had one of her friends, Alice, "read" his face. They said his features pointed to someone trustworthy but he had fearful ears. Which Josie evidently agreed with upon meeting him. Her baby cousins joked about how clean cut he was. Everyone was surprised that she was really having a baby. She was still surprised sometimes. They asked if they were getting married, and she told them they were figuring things out.

She assumed he hadn't told anyone anything. It had only been a few weeks. Zeta knew how she felt about that—jealous, angry, bad—and it didn't make her proud. She felt weird and ashamed of her feelings. They were dark and nasty things. She didn't want to obsess over it, especially not there with him, didn't want to let it color the night.

"That you'd like this place. She suggested it."

Her arm tightened around his. "You told her about me?"

"Yeah, I did."

"I didn't think you had talked to anyone about . . . this."

"It wasn't exactly how I planned to bring it up. I wanted to wait until after the ultrasound, and I am waiting to tell my parents until after we understand more about each other, but she's excited. And my mom did see your photo and knows I'm seeing you but not about everything. She thinks you're very pretty."

"That's— That's good. I'm really happy to hear that," she stuttered, face hot. *Why did I let Cody get in my head?*

"If you're worried about something you can just ask me. Don't keep it yourself," he said, looking up at the moving line.

She leaned into him. "Alright."

At the front of the line finally, Ash bought a bundle of red tickets that were handed over by a smiling young man in a yellow shirt. "Enjoy your night!" he said as Ash pulled her away.

"What do you want to play? Or do you want to eat something?"

"I want to do a ring toss!" Zeta's excitement bubbled, spilled out of her.

Up close, the booths were all designed to look like they rolled out of the 1930s. The ring toss game was set up with dark-colored bottles, row upon row of them. Three other people were already throwing rings. Ash traded a ticket for a pile of plastic rings from the attendant. Zeta picked up the first and tossed it. It bounced off a bottle with a ping.

"Close," Ash said. He tried his hand at it with the same result.

"Same to you," she said, bumping him with her hip. "What do we get if we win anyway?"

"Green tickets. You can trade them in at the prize booth," the man running the game explained.

"Oh, nice. I want a bear," Zeta said laughing, tossing another one with the same result.

"Then I guess I have to work harder to get you one," Ash said. He tossed his ring and it landed, swinging around the bottle. The other players stopped to clap, and Ash looked embarrassed as he accepted his green tickets.

"I think you'll have to land more than one to get that bear for me," she teased. She tossed again, missing along with the others who had thrown theirs.

"I don't think I'll get lucky like that again," he said. He missed. "See?"

"Well there are a lot of other games." She laughed as she tried again. It collided with another person's toss, somehow landed perfectly on the bottle, and she raised her arms, squealing softly.

Ash put his hand on the small of her back and kissed her cheek. She grinned up at him, letting her weight rest on him.

The ring toss man handed Ash her green tickets as well, and he slipped them into the inside pocket of his jacket. "Where next?"

"Oh, they've got the racing horses!" She wrapped her hand in his and tugged him along. They took second and third place. More tickets added to his pocket.

Zeta's insides vibrated as she moved from game to game, Ash beside her, teasing and cheering as she did the same. They threw darts and popped balloons, fished for plastic fish in a little pool and spun the wheel of fortune. Zeta dissolved cotton candy with sparkling grape juice, the world sugar filled, and Ash drank champagne while they watched a juggler perform complex stunts with pins and balls. He fed her popcorn and little meatballs and cheese while he tossed balls at a cat rack game, managing to knock over all three.

"I thought you didn't play sports," she laughed, taking the string of tickets.

"You think I'm good enough for the major leagues?" he joked in return.

"Let's get our picture taken!" she said suddenly, spotting the photo station. "We don't have one together."

He paused, lips parted, brows raised. Then a slow smile crept along his face. "No, we don't."

The person manning the open-air booth was a woman who smiled brightly and told them to get into a comfortable pose. The backdrop was a piece of fabric that looked like a circus tent with a sign above them that said HAPPY NEW YEAR!

"I'm going to decide how to stand this time," Ash teased, pulling her close.

"This feels like a prom picture," she said as the operator started the timer.

Ash's arm snaked round her waist, rested on her belly. His other grabbed her hand, and she looked up him, smiling just as the flash went off.

"Oh no! I think I ruined it," Zeta said, laughing. "Can we go again? I promise I'll be still."

"Actually, I think you should keep it. Look," the attendant said. The picture was still on the screen and it had captured them smiling at each other.

He looks like he . . . she stopped the thought from forming. That was fantasy; she didn't know him well enough to even think something like that. But she looked so comfortable in his arms, at peace. "It's really good."

"It's perfect," Ash confirmed, and gave the woman his email address for the photo. He slipped his hand into Zeta's, laced their fingers together. "Are you having fun?" he asked, but it didn't sound like he was talking about the night, didn't sound like it was the question he wanted to ask.

"I am," she said, forcing herself to stop reading into things. To take them as they were. Take him as he was.

He checked his watch, gold sparkling on his wrist to the silver he'd given her. "It's almost midnight. Will you dance with me?"

A jazz band played in the back of the room in front of a small dance floor inhabited by mostly older couples and young kids darting around high on sugar and the excitement of a late night. Zeta smiled at them as Ash gently moved her onto the floor, into his arms, and started swaying to the music with her.

"Do you think our baby will be like these kids?" she asked, still distracted by their antics as they played and chased around them.

"I hope so," he said bending close to her. "I hope our baby is happy and healthy and does nothing but run and laugh." He put the hand he was holding on his shoulder, stroked her belly, then wrapped his arm around her. "I hope they always feel confident and safe. I hope their days are filled with singing and drawing and games and friends. I hope they know they're loved."

Zeta relaxed into him, sighed, her whole body melting at his words. Inside of her she could feel the fluttering touch of their baby, stronger by just a breath than they were before but growing. Warmth radiated from her chest, spread all through her, and she let herself be supported in his arms. "I think they know," Zeta said. "They're moving; maybe they can hear you."

"No. But they feel you," he said, the smile in his voice.

She wanted to ask what he meant, but the MC started talking, dragging her attention to the stage. "OK, kiddies! It's almost time for the big event! Annnnnd! Ten! Nine!"

Zeta turned away from the stage back to Ash. His eyes were sparkling in the light. The count reached zero, the crowd shouted "Happy New Year!" and from above gold confetti dropped, fluttering down.

Ash kissed her, pulling her closer, his hands on her back. She wrapped her arms around his neck, opened to him. He kissed her deeply, his tongue caressing, familiar. Sweet champagne taste flooded her mouth, mingled with sugar, made everything sweeter, sharper.

When he pulled away, leaving small tapering kisses on her lips, her ears were ringing from the cheers all around her. Her lids felt heavy but her lips were tingling. The MC was saying something, but she could feel Ash's chuckle through her hand on his chest and couldn't concentrate on the words.

"My love is tired," he said softly, brushing one of her curls back. "Let me take you to bed."

Just a pet name, it didn't mean anything, Around them the games were still ringing but the children were returning to their parents. The house lights would come on soon. "I didn't get my bear," she said.

He held her hand as he walked to the prize booth. "I don't know what you can exchange for this." He laughed. "I was just going to give them to a kid."

She touched her belly, his soft hopes still playing in her ears.

The prize counter was stuffed with all manner of small toys. Stuffed animals hung from the wall; on shelves below were boxes of bouncy balls, key chains, sticky hands, and whistles. They'd won seventeen tickets, and the exchange rate at a private event turned out to be better than either of them anticipated. The paltry amount of winnings, enough to get a whistle or small ball from a standard arcade, was enough there to claim one floppy, soft brown bear.

They collected their coats, but instead of turning to go back to the parking lot, Ash took her to the main lobby and the elevators.

"Where are you taking me?" she asked as they ascended.

"To bed. We're staying here for the night."

She hadn't slept over or had him sleep over since the first date. Her apartment was too much of a mess to be seen, especially by him, and she didn't want to get too comfortable at his place. They had just started seeing each other; it felt like rushing things. "I don't have anything to wear," she said.

"Don't worry, I took care of everything. I wanted you to have a good time tonight. Did you?"

"It *was* a good time. Thank you."

He smiled, placed a kiss on her forehead as the elevator stopped, and they stepped into a hushed hall. A few feet and he was sliding a keycard into the lock. She was half expecting candlelight and rose petals, but inside there was only a bed covered in soft-looking white blankets and pillows, ready to be climbed into. A decorative wardrobe in dark wood. A TV hidden behind a cabinet. A very refined space illuminated by a single lamp.

He sat her on the bed, kneeled at her feet. "Your feet must hurt; you've been on them for a couple of hours. Are you feeling alright?" he asked, unlacing one of her shoes.

"The shoes are more comfortable than they look," she said as he slipped one off, revealing her foot.

"Still we have to be careful. I don't want you to hurt yourself." He wrapped his hands around her foot, rubbed it, pressing away soreness that she hadn't even been thinking of. His fingers caressed her arch, circled the sphere of her heel, and then moved up her ankle and shin. She sighed, letting him work his fingers against her. He removed the matching shoe, did the same to the opposite foot.

Zeta yawned and he kissed her knee.

"There's a change of clothes for you in the bathroom." He stood up, helped her to her bare feet, and gently pushed her to the bathroom door.

She went inside, closed the door. Hanging on the hook was a nightgown. It wasn't sexy, not to her anyway. It was long and flowing with thin straps made of shimmery silver fabric. *Is this what he likes?* she wondered, feeling it between her fingers. She took off her dress, swapped it on the hanger for the gown. She stripped her stockings and put them, rolled up, on the sink. She took off her earrings and left them by the stockings. She looked at the bracelet and decided to leave it on; it was so small.

She stretched and noticed the bonnet sitting, still packaged, against the mirror. She chuckled, unwrapped it, and pulled it over her curls.

Zeta opened the door to find Ash already in bed, undressed, lights off. She leaned against the door frame and pointed at her head. "How'd you know?"

"Lucky guess," he said. Ash raised his arms and held them out to her. "Come to bed."

She reached back and turned off the light. Yawning, she met him in bed, sliding into his arms, and he laid them both down with a sigh. In the dark he was solid weight beside her. He kissed her gently and stroked her hip, arm wrapped around her.

She started dozing without realizing it, yanking herself from the edge of sleep. "Sorry, give me a minute and we can—"

"My love is tired," he repeated, and kissed her forehead.

There in the dark, nestled in his arms, his breath a feeling against her, she heard his words differently. Felt them differently. "I am tired," she said. "Is it really OK if we just . . . sleep?"

"As long as you're by my side, I don't care what we're doing. Sweet dreams, Zeta."

"No, call me . . . something else," she said, her voice a soft whine.

"Then sweet dreams, Kitten."

"That's better," she mumbled, already falling.

22

It was a wave dragging shell-filled sand back to the ocean. Over and over, a steady rhythm, the sound filled his ears. A heartbeat, his baby's heartbeat, and Ashford Cross had never felt more protective of anything in his life. He thought that moment holding Zeta in his arms in his bed was the strongest he could feel for another person, but he had been wrong. He was sure the moment he heard their child's heartbeat for the first time trumped that.

When he saw the baby's form on the ultrasound, that feeling doubled, squeezed his heart in his chest so tight he thought he would die. Knew he would die for that child.

"Do you want to know the baby's sex?" the technician asked, bringing him back to the world. "Or I can put it in an envelope for you?"

Does she want to know? He turned to Zeta, waiting for her response.

"I am dying to know!" Zeta said, smile blooming on her face, and his heart and head turned into a sunburst. His heart pounded like a drum; he crossed his arms, clutched his own biceps to keep his arms from wrapping around Zeta. They weren't done yet, but his cheeks ached from holding back his smile.

"Alright, let me see here. Looks like you're having a girl!"

A girl! His mind started to spin in a thousand directions. Ashford Cross did not know the first thing about babies except that he was having one and that she was a girl. Zeta was carrying his daughter. *Will she look like her? A combination of us?* He tried to imagine her but there was just a vague feeling, warm and tingly. There was a layer of very practical thoughts about her physical needs: blankets, bottles, a crib, a nursery—a list of tasks, of needs to be met that his brain was attempting to build. But overlaying that was a sea of possible experiences. Seeing her after work, watching her learn to walk, talk, become her own person. Reading, playing, enjoying *his* daughter as she grew. And then the worry came—he'd never done those things, would he be calm enough, present enough? Could he make the time? Ash was in his father's place now, and he had few memories growing up with him that weren't wrapped around special occasions.

"Ash?" A tug on his sleeve.

He turned to Zeta. Her hair was out, pushed back by a headband, a dark halo around her face. His first instinct was to pull her off the table, cover her in kisses, hold on to her until the tremor that was running all up and down his body stopped. He had to get himself under control. He pulled himself back.

"Are you OK?"

Am I OK? I should be asking her! "I'm fine." He forced a smile, tried to regain his composure. He leaned over and kissed her cheek, hoping it made her stop worrying about him.

She smiled back, and he felt the tightness in his chest explode. *What is this?* he thought, and then there was nothing because Zeta was smiling and his daughter was well and everything was alright. The tech was talking, and Ash forced himself to focus on the man's words.

"I'll let you get cleaned up and then the doctor will see you to talk about the results. Congratulations!"

"Thank you," Zeta replied as she started to push herself up.

Ash steadied her, helped her the rest of the way as the tech handed her some paper towels to wipe off with before sweeping out of the room.

"Oh man! It got on my pants! This stuff gets everywhere! I'm taking a shower as soon as I get home," Zeta looked up at him suddenly. "Are you sure you're OK? You look a little out of it."

Ash leaned forward, pressed a kiss to her mouth. "No," he said. "But I am happy, so don't worry." He pulled away, crossed the room for more towels, and handed them to her. "I need to pull myself together." *I don't want to ruin this appointment for her.*

"You don't, though. It's OK, I already know you're a softie." She smiled.

He calmed instantly, like she'd willed it, but she hadn't done anything at all. He leaned his forehead against hers. "Only for you. For our daughter." He helped her down.

A nurse came in just then. "Dr. Tuttle is with another patient but I'll take you to her office."

Ash held Zeta's hand as they walked down the pale pink halls. It felt like the night they'd first met and he held her hand tighter, completely unwilling to lose her ever again. The nurse sat them in in two chairs in front of a closed office.

"She'll be done soon!" she said brightly, and disappeared.

"A girl! I didn't really care but . . ." Zeta paused and cradled her belly. "It's nice, isn't it?"

"It's very nice," he agreed, tucking her under his arm, pulling her over to rest against him. "Can we go shopping now?"

"Yes," she hissed, mock annoyance. "We can go shopping. Maybe next weekend. I want to relax."

"All burnt out from the holidays?" Aside from their New Year's date, they hadn't gotten to spend much time with each other. Both of them were playing catch up with work, and the weather had been miserable, keeping Zeta at home—and she wouldn't let him come over either. The roads were bad, she said. Now he wished he *had* come to see her more. The time they spent together wasn't enough. Texting and phone calls weren't enough, and he wondered if she felt the same.

He brushed the little hairs that curled at her forehead, "Don't fall asleep, Kitten."

"You can't tell me what to do," she yawned, snuggled closer.

"Hey, looks like I wore the right shirt today." He laughed.

Zeta pulled herself from her dozing, leaning back to look at his shirt. He'd come from work to pick her up at her apartment. He hadn't thought about the gray suit and tie or the pink shirt that he'd dressed in that morning, but it had turned into a coincidence too perfect to ignore. Maybe he had really wanted a daughter. Zeta giggled. "How'd you know?"

"Just lucky," he said, kissed her forehead. The way she touched the spot his lips had brushed and looked upward made his breath catch. She did it every time.

Stretching, yawning, she pulled herself up. "It's been a long day," she complained.

"It's only three," he soothed.

"Yeah, but I'm keeping time for two people so it's, like, six in my body," she replied.

"Your math doesn't make any sense," he laughed.

"Hello! Hello again!" The doctor sang, bustling down the hall. Dr. Tuttle, Zeta's ob-gyn, was a middle-aged Black woman with straight hair pulled back into a ponytail and huge glasses. She looked cozy and friendly, and Ash could see why Zeta had picked this doctor. Dr. Tuttle opened her office door, ushering them both inside.

Ash helped Zeta to her seat and took his own. There was a change in her at the doctor's arrival. They hadn't gotten any bad news but there was still a chance, and he could feel her nerves over it even as she held the same smile, could hear it in the change of her breathing—longer, deeper breaths, preparing for the worst. He reached for her, found her hand, and wrapped his around it, squeezing gently before letting it rest on her lap, his knuckles against her belly. He felt her relax, and his chest swelled with pride in having comforted her. It was a sign that she trusted him.

"Alright! Well, I had a look at the ultrasound and baby looks great! Congratulations on your little girl!" Dr. Tuttle said, taking her seat behind her desk.

"Thank you!" Zeta smiled wide. He could feel the tension release through her hand. Ash grinned at her, happy that she was happy.

"Also, just a neat thing, you were exactly right on your dates. Usually people are a little off, but you were right on it. Good job keeping track."

Ash's ears burned.

"Yeah, I was really on top of that," Zeta said, tight smile plastered on her face.

"Now we've got to make sure mom is taking care of herself," Dr. Tuttle tsked.

"Is something wrong?" Ash asked alert.

"No, nothing yet. Zeta, you're doing well, but I am worried about your condition. As the pregnancy progresses, you might become more susceptible to episodes like the one that happened last month."

"That was a fluke. I was very surprised that day," Zeta countered. "It won't happen again."

Never again, Ash thought, swearing to himself.

Zeta was trying to push past the subject, but the doctor wouldn't let her, and Ash fought against his smirk silently cheering her on.

"Yes, but you were also, I believe, overworking. I know it's hard, but you have to take it easy, make sure you're getting enough sleep, enough to eat," the doctor explained.

The doctor spoke directly to Zeta, but it felt like her words were meant for Ash. It was his fault. He hadn't known it was her, hadn't known what she was going through. He could have been far kinder.

"I know, but my morning sickness is much better now and work calmed down so I can rest more."

At least there's that, Ash thought.

"You're looking really good though. The baby's growth is on track and you're gaining weight well. The baby looked great on the ultrasound. I know you saw her, and they'll have some pictures for you up front. You can download them from the portal too."

Dr. Tuttle changed the subject to the next few weeks. "I want you to try walking around a bit every day; I know your work keeps you at your desk. Be careful though, your joints are going to be looser and I don't want you injured!"

Ash made a mental note to make sure she took a walk. With him. He'd have to figure out a time. *Lunch? I can take long lunches*, he thought.

"No problem," Zeta said. "There's a park close by."

"Perfect." The doctor smiled. "You might start feeling some heartburn and that can be normal. Constipation is a normal complaint as well."

He felt Zeta stiffen, embarrassed about discussing that in front of him, but he ran his thumb over her hand.

"You might get some gum irritation," Dr. Tuttle continued. "Even a little bleeding from them because of the hormones. This is normal as well, so don't worry too much. Some women get nosebleeds, so be careful but don't panic, nothing is wrong."

Her hand twitched in his, but she only nodded. *Bleeding*. He squeezed her palm in his, let her know that he was there, that he understood.

Done with the things to look out for in the coming weeks, she moved on to what Zeta could expect going forward. "Mostly what you need to remember now is that you've got the glucose test to check for gestational diabetes soon. They'll schedule you, but you need to fast for that one and it is four hours. But things look good and you're doing so well!"

They thanked the doctor, said goodbye, and checked out, scheduling the next appointment.

"What are you singing?" Zeta asked as they got into the car.

He hadn't realized he had been singing, not really, the edges of the song were still there. "'Some Kinda Fairytale,' Tori Amos."

"You listen to Tori Amos? You were in elementary school when she was big, I think."

"My sister had all her albums and listened to them every day. I know all of her songs," he explained.

Zeta giggled. She was bundled up in her coat with cat ears, the hood up to protect her from the cold and the edges of his gray scarf sticking out. He'd gotten her gloves but they were still balled up in her pocket, the hands that rested on the slope of her belly were bare.

"Hey, we have to pick a name," Zeta hummed as they started to drive.

"Did you have a list that you liked?"

"Of names? No, I couldn't decide on any."

He smirked. "You picked your own name but couldn't decide on one for your baby?"

"Well, I don't really know them very well, the baby I mean," she huffed. "You've known about this for a month now. What were you thinking? Did you want to name her after your dad, like Natasha? It's Nathanial right? What's your mom's name?"

"Yeah, it is, but I don't want to do that. And my mom's name is Bridgette. What were your parents' names? If we're doing parents, I think it should be yours."

She paused, and he swallowed the sudden pain in his throat. He hadn't been thinking ahead—would she want to talk about her parents? He didn't even really have the whole story on their passing; he'd never asked. There never seemed to be a good time to bring it up.

"Their names were Alan and Fatima." She looked out the windshield, a frown on her face for a moment before speaking again. "You know, it's weird, you never asked me what my name used to be. Most people ask when they find out that I've changed it. Everyone's always curious about it. I don't ever tell anyone, but most people try to guess. But you didn't even ask."

Her gaze had returned to him. He wanted to turn to her, give her his full attention, but he was driving, "You told me your name was Zeta and that is your name. I don't need to know what it was before. You'll tell me if you want me to know."

She smiled, closed her eyes, and leaned back. "Alright. I still don't have any ideas."

"We can look at baby name books. Put a bunch in a jar and just pick one," he suggested, shrugging.

"You know, I don't hate that idea."

"I kind of thought you wouldn't."

She frowned, her thinking face. She always frowned when she was puzzling over something, the corners of her lips turned down, brow wrinkled. Cute. "Something on your mind," he chuckled.

"I guess I should meet your parents soon," she said slowly, unsure.

"Do you want to?" he asked.

"Have you talked to them about this?" she asked motioning to her belly.

"No," he said slowly. "I was waiting until I had a bit more information."

"I don't know. It feels too soon." She sighed. "We're still figuring things out."

"But you introduced me to your aunt," he said, attempting to figure out what she wanted before she told him. To know her.

"That was different," she laughed.

"How?" he asked, confused.

She shrugged, smiling, "It just is. Just feels like we should have things really settled before . . ."

"They get involved?" he finished chuckling. "They're just people."

She eyed him. "I don't know, they seem like they have high expectations."

"Zeta, I'm an adult. The only opinion that matters on my relationships is mine," he said, unsure if he was trying to convince her or himself.

She leaned against the window. "Sure, but there's no rush." She yawned. "I'm so tired today," she mused, changing the subject.

"Rest. I'll wake you up when we get there."

"It's fifteen minutes away."

"Cat nap, Kitten."

She smiled, closed her eyes, and leaned against the door. He put his hand on her thigh, let the interaction replay, tried to understand what she wanted from it and came up blank. When they arrived at her apartment, they walked in together.

"I can't wait to shower! My belly feels tacky," she complained at her door, turning the key. She suddenly stopped. She put her hand on her head. "I'm sorry, you can't come in." Zeta turned, blocked the door. "Sorry! I'm just, I'm really tired, so you, um, you have to go." She was stumbling over her words, eyes on the floor.

He frowned, took her face in his hands. Her eyes wouldn't meet his. "Kitten, what's the matter?"

"Nothing!"

"It's something," he said, frowning at the sudden distance, the strange panic in her.

"It's not," she started, stopped. "This is silly. I mean, it's not a big deal."

"Whatever it is, it's fine," he hummed.

"OK, OK, you can come in," she said, frowning, but didn't move.

He reached past her, turned the knob, and pushed the door open.

"I'm so embarrassed!" she said, stepping inside, finally letting him in. It was messy. The kitchen was piled with dishes, two full trash bags, and a can that needed emptying. "It was my hand! I couldn't do the dishes because of the stitches and I kept forgetting to buy gloves and everyone was busy for the holiday and I've been so tired it just got a little out of control and I swear I'm not like this all the time well you've been here you've seen it I swear—"

"Shhhh," he said, wrapping his arms around her, breaking off her panicked confession. "It's fine. Is this why you haven't been letting me come over?"

"It's too messy. You don't think I'm gross?" she asked, hiding her face in his chest.

"I think," he said, bending to kiss her lips, "that you're very pregnant and I haven't been taking good enough care of you." He'd planned a long lunch. He wasn't returning to work. "Go shower. Don't worry about this, I'll clean up."

"I can't ask you to do that. It's so much!" She looked stricken.

"Why not?"

"Because you're not my, I mean, we're not," she stopped, pressed her lips together, frustrated. "You know what I mean!"

He did. They were still "figuring things out." The same reason why she couldn't say if she wanted to meet his parents or not. The reason he wasn't sure if he was ready to tell them. "I still want to help you. You didn't ask, and it's not as much as you think," he said, slipping out of his shoes and coat. He put the coat over one of her chairs. Turned back for hers.

"Are you sure?"

He kissed her cheek. "Very."

Zeta slipped into her bathroom, and he, rolling up his sleeves, began to work in her kitchen, singing quietly to himself.

23

January was ending before Zeta was able to meet up with her friends. Brand had gone out to California to visit his own family and got delayed but had made it back. Cody finally wasn't working extra hours, and Pixie had a break from events.

And Zeta's apartment was clean.

It was the perfect time to have everyone over to celebrate the news that she was having a girl. She ordered a pizza, and Pixie brought a pink cake. They'd spent the last hour catching up with holiday stories and how each other's family was doing. Zeta took the last bites of her cake and shifted on the couch, pulling her feet under her.

"It smells like," Brand sniffed and waved his hand in front of his face, "lemon in here."

"Ash cleaned," she explained.

"Did he buy the groceries too? Because I'm really into this 'single mom with all the good snacks' thing we're doing right now,"

Brand said, tossing a fruit snack into his mouth and looking at the package. "Fortified with a daily dose of vitamins."

"Yeah, he found out I wasn't taking my prenatal ones—they made me too sick. I told him not to worry about it, I'm already five months in, but he insisted, so now, fruit snacks."

"So it's going well. Maybe he's not a fuck buddy. Maybe he's actually a boyfriend. Zeta, is he your *boyfriend*?" Cody asked from the table, grabbing another slice of pizza from the box.

"Oh yeah, did Dio get you a present?" Pixie asked.

"Dio?" Cody asked.

"Yeah, because he's a blond that looks like a vampire," Pixie explained.

"Not Spike?" he asked.

"He's too tall, and he doesn't look like that type of vampire," Pixie responded.

"He got me this bracelet," Zeta said holding out her wrist, the little silver stars sparkling.

"Oh, that's cute!" Pixie said.

"I know! But I feel terrible about it!"

"Why?" Brand asked.

"Because I didn't get him anything! He took me on this fun date and got me this cute bracelet, and I didn't even get him a card."

"That was my bad," Cody said. "That sounds like a boyfriend."

"No, he's not my boyfriend. We're just . . . figuring things out."

"Why not?" Pixie asked.

"Aren't you supposed to tell me not to rush into things? I haven't even met his family or anything yet."

"Most people don't actually meet their significant other's families before they decide to date, Zeta." Brand laughed.

"Well, most people aren't five months pregnant," she snapped back, and then regretted it. "Sorry, that was a lot harsher than I meant it. It's just, am I making a mistake?"

"I don't know, are you?" Brand asked with a shrug, unbothered by her tone.

When he'd offered to clean up her apartment, when he *insisted* that he clean up, she couldn't quite say, *You're not my boyfriend.* Because wasn't he? It *felt* right, the idea, but she had a lot of feelings these days. She worried that Ash was one of those temporary feelings. Everything with him was so *easy.* But she'd learned from being with Ian that easy wasn't always the same thing as right. "I don't know, everything is so different with him. But it all feels so sudden and I'm pretty comfortable with how things are."

"Things are going to change in a couple of months regardless of how you feel," Brand laughed. "What's so different than any other guy? Other than the obvious," he asked.

She thought for a moment. They'd only been dating a few weeks really. Everyone was nice in the honeymoon phase, but were they clean your kitchen nice? Buy expensive jewelry nice? Yes. But just cuddle on New Year's in a fancy hotel nice? Do the grocery shopping nice? He didn't just purchase them, he did the labor. Made a list, went to the store, brought it all back, and put it away. She couldn't remember anyone she'd ever dated doing all of that. But "he's actually helpful" seemed more like a bare minimum, and she didn't know how long it would last. The memory of him that very first night floated up suddenly: *Why wouldn't anyone be good to you?* "It's just different. He's trying."

"What does that even mean?" Pixie asked. "Get me another slice of cake," she told Cody before continuing. "Trying what?"

"To be a good partner. He cares." She was getting flustered, dancing around the things that were really bothering her. The single thing that was scratching at her, crawling under her skin.

"That's what he's supposed to be doing," Pixie said, laughing.

"So what's the problem? Come on, spit it out," Cody said. "Judgment-free zone."

She sighed. "He hasn't told his parents about this. Like, at all. Shouldn't he do that? Like, isn't that a big deal?"

"Depends, is he close with his parents?" Brand asked.

"He eats dinner there twice a month."

All three of her friends grimaced. No one said anything, but all of their faces said *yikes*. "He should have said something then?" Zeta asked.

"Family is complicated," Cody offered.

"*So* complicated," Pixie echoed, clearly trying to soften the blow. "Maybe he's waiting. Did you ask him?"

"Sounds like he's taking his time. Maybe his parents are assholes," Brand offered. "You *should* ask him."

"I can't ask him if his parents are assholes, Brand."

"Why not?" Cody shrugged.

"Would you want someone to ask you if your parents were assholes?"

"They wouldn't need to, that's first date conversation," Cody responded.

"Honestly, Zeta, all you can do is talk to him about it. This is probably a misunderstanding. He's been nothing but great otherwise," Pixie said.

Pixie was right. When she was with Ash, everything was so perfect. And that was part of the problem. She wasn't sure if she was overlooking reality, because he made everything around him so dreamy. Zeta cradled her belly in her hands and sighed. She wasn't going to get any answers from her friends. She had to get them from Ash.

"So when are we going to meet him?" Cody asked, leaning back on his chair.

"Yeah, it's been months and except for a couple of pictures, no one's seen this dude. Maybe he really is a vampire," Brand said, rolling a fruit snack between his fingers.

"Eat that or I'm taking it away," Zeta said without thinking.

"Oh my god, you sounded just like my mom! Your maternal instincts are kicking in!" Brand laughed.

Zeta let a few chuckles slip. "He's not a vampire. There just hasn't been time." It sounded like an excuse even to her.

"I want to meet him before the baby comes," Cody said.

"Me too. He sounds good, but you know, I wanna check him out. Make sure. You know, what's he doing now? Can he come over?" Pixie agreed.

"I don't know, what time is it?" Zeta dug her phone out of the couch cushions. Past ten; it had gotten late and it was a weeknight. She had to stop eating anyway, the glucose test was in the morning. **What are you doing?** she texted him.

At work. The message came back quickly.

I'll let you go then.

There was no reply, the message was clipped, short. *He's busy*, she thought. "Sorry guys, no visit tonight, he's working late."

"Sounds sus, like your girlfriend who lives in Canada." Brand laughed, standing, stretching.

"Aunt Josie met him. You can confirm with her he's real," Zeta said, rolling her eyes.

"She might be in on your little con," Brand said. "Come on, let's clean up. Don't want to undo all 'his' hard work."

The three of them cleaned up the empty pizza boxes, wrapped up the leftovers. Swept paper plates and napkins into the bin. Washed cups, put everything away while they joked and chatted. Zeta sat and stared at her phone, wondering at the curtness of his text, remembering his emails as A. M. Cross, worrying over his lack of reply.

"Hey," Pixie said, getting Zeta's attention. "Don't worry so much. There haven't been any red flags. It's OK to just enjoy something."

"I know, you're right, I'm just being cautious," Zeta said, standing, hand on her belly.

Everyone filed out of the apartment, saying their goodbyes and leaving Zeta alone.

She changed her clothes, turned out her lights, and went to her own bed, planning to clear out her notifications and get some sleep, trying to ignore the unease of the brief exchange. She'd been less tired recently, but she still found herself turning in early.

"He didn't call me today," she tutted at the phone. No messages, either, aside from the conversation they'd had that evening, and Ash usually called by nine. "He knew I had people over though."

Zeta called Ash instead. The phone rang and went to voicemail. She cleared a few levels in a match-three game and tried again with the same result. *Is he still at work?* It was so late.

The minutes ticked over and she began to worry. She frowned at her phone, changed to a more engaging strategy game, and waited.

Finally, forty minutes after her call, the phone rang in her hand, startling her. "Ash," she breathed, answering.

"Hey, Zeta. Sorry about calling so late. Work's kept me."

"Work? It's after eleven. You should be home." She almost teased that he wouldn't let her work this late before remembering that he *had* and would've continued to if he didn't know it was *her*.

"There were some international things that needed to get done. Don't worry about it." Distance, she could feel it. A hurried, cool response.

"I started to worry something had happened," she blurted out.

He sucked in his breath on the other end, she could hear him shifting. His voice was softer when he spoke next. "Sorry, I should have let you know. That's my mistake, Kitten. Nothing's wrong. I'm just at the office. Everything's backed up from the holidays," he explained, sighing.

"Do you want me to let you go?" she asked, frowning. There was something off. An unsettled tremor deep in her signaling *something*. Zeta tried to push it away.

"No, but I have to go," he replied.

Her stomach dropped. He never wanted to end their calls.

"It's alright, I'll let you go!" she said brightly, swallowing the burning in her throat, ignoring the twisting feeling in her guts. He had a company to run, he would be busy sometimes. She would be too. There was no reason to feel any way about it. They were adults, with work and family and friends.

"Kitten," he said softly. "It really is just work, nothing to do with you."

"Why'd you say that? I know you have to work," she said, trying to laugh it off.

"Because I don't want you to get the wrong idea. I'd rather be with you." On the other side of the line he sounded tired.

"It's really late," she said gently, "Maybe you should leave the rest for tomorrow."

"I've got to finish this," he sighed.

"I'm sure the company won't collapse if you go home for the night." She rolled her eyes and settled into bed, trapping him on the phone for a little longer. "And," she added, remembering, "you're supposed to be coming to take me for my test in the morning."

"I didn't forget, I'll be there at seven to pick you up. But I do need to get things settled here so I can take some time off for the baby. Did you know we have a paternity leave policy?" he asked.

"I did, I'm building the system that handles that. You may remember, we were supposed to have a meeting about it," she teased. "I didn't know you were thinking about taking time off."

The deep sound of his laughter carried through the line. "I am going to. I want to come stay with you for a few weeks. I want to take care of my daughter, take care of my baby."

The fluttering, tickling touch of pleasure from his words, the soft claim. *Kitten, baby, mine.* Too fast or just right for their circumstances? She rested her hand on her belly; she was nearly six months, impossible to hide, and maybe their relationship was the same. "Like a move-in trial," she laughed.

"I guess. I know your aunt is going to come up, but I want to be there. I need to be there," he said.

Zeta's smiled spread; the fluttering turned into a warm hum of contentment. "We'll talk about it. My apartment is really small, but it would be nice if you were here too." The baby moved, pressed on Zeta's insides awkwardly, and she let out a sound half between a yelp and groan.

"Zeta?" he called, instant panic.

She rubbed her belly in the spot the sensation had come from. "I'm fine, the baby just moved funny. I wasn't expecting it."

"She should be asleep. It's late. *You* should be asleep. I'm keeping you up."

"Well, if you'd called me earlier instead of working all night, we could both be asleep," she teased.

"I've learned my lesson. Forgive me, Kitten."

"Only if you come over now. I can't trust you to go home when we get off the phone, but if you know I'm waiting up for you, you'll come to bed."

He groaned, playfully, "Don't do this."

"I'm getting out of bed," she sang, throwing the blankets off and sitting up. Her head swam at the sudden movement, and she ignored it, closing her eyes to force it to stop. "I'm going to play *Animal Crossing* until you get here to put me to bed."

"You win, I'll be there soon."

The call ended and Zeta went back out to her living room. On her couch she closed her eyes again, breathed deeply, and waited for everything to settle before she retrieved the Switch and started tending to her animal community while she waited for Ash to come to her.

An hour later he was at her door, and she knew that she should ask him, tell him her worries, get answers, his plans, anything, but, late, she just leaned into his embrace, drowned in his sage scent, and let herself be put to bed.

24

"Why'd you come all the way out here?" Nathanial Cross asked from his seat across the sitting room.

The sitting room looked exactly the same as it did the night of the Christmas party except now it was filled with cold late morning sunlight. Claire was in the city for the day visiting with old friends, giving Ash some privacy to talk to his parents.

About Zeta.

When he arrived at her apartment she was upset in that quiet way of hers. It wasn't about his lateness or the lack of communication, there was something else. He'd woken up wrapped around her, three minutes before his alarm would go off. Her body had been warm and soft against his, dragged him back into sleep. While Zeta dressed for her appointment, he sent an email saying that he wouldn't be in, because in that time between wake and sleep he could only think of one thing that could possibly be on her mind.

Spring was coming, and at the end of April, maybe a little later, maybe a little sooner, his daughter would be in the world. He couldn't avoid telling his parents any longer. Telling his father. He would be responsible for another life, and it was time to put that out in the open. He was hoping the joy of it would override the vibration of worry that simmered just under the surface, but instead it only got louder. He tried to calm it by building plans and explanations. *This is what happened; this is what I'm going to do about it. This is the future. Here is the plan.* But all of that escaped him once faced with the reality of it: that he was having a baby with a woman that he he'd known for a few hours more than his baby had existed.

His mother sat next to his father and frowned softly at him. "Your hair is getting so long!" she said. "I'd forgotten it was so wavy."

Ash ran his fingers through it. It had gotten longer since December—since Zeta touched it for the first time. He tried to focus on her. He'd taken her to her glucose test, where she'd leaned against him, playing her Switch and frowning at the taste of the drink she was forced to swallow. He'd taken her to a diner afterward to get breakfast. The morning had been so nice that he thought it would be enough to carry him through this. "I'm growing it out," he said.

"I think it's out enough. It's going to start getting out of hand." She laughed.

The memory of Zeta on New Year's, with her hair all dark curls falling all over her head, how beautiful she was. He wondered how his own daughter would look. Would his mother say her curls were a mess? *I'll talk to her, but I need to tell them first. I can't get distracted, focus. Future Ash problem*, he told himself. They were waiting for his announcement.

His parents smiled at him, and he thought they looked different. Maybe it's because he was going to be a parent himself soon. Maybe it was just the light.

Between them the table was set with refreshments. Iced tea and cookies, a plate of fruit and vegetables that his father picked at, uninterested. Ash's stomach was doing flips inside of him.

"I've been seeing someone," he stumbled, unsure how to set it up correctly. His mother smiled, expectant after having seen the picture on his phone. He had planned—he always planned—but sitting in front of them now it seemed inadequate. They would have questions and he hadn't come up with good answers. The truth was embarrassing, and he was a bad liar.

"You took a day off work to come tell us you were dating someone?" Nathanial grunted, shifting in his chair.

"Oh stop," Bridgette scolded. "It must be serious if he's bringing it up to us." She rolled her eyes, winked at her son, *Go on*, and picked up her drink.

Thanks, Mom, he praised silently.

"Could have waited until dinner next week. Hell, he could have told us last week. What I want to know is why you've been so lax in the office. If we're going to have a talk, we can talk about that."

"What do you mean?" Ash asked, thrown off his script to explain that he was off because of the woman he needed to talk to them about.

"Everything's slowed down. The leave software was on track to be done by now, and you had them put the brakes on it. You've been putting off meetings, leaving contracts to sit until deadline. What's going on there?"

Work. What his father really cared about. What he wanted him to care about. The company.

"I thought the company could use a better culture. We've been pushing people too hard, too long; there's no reason for it. We're still meeting our deadlines, the board is still happy, we are still profitable, and our employees are happier." *This is not what I came to talk about.* "We don't have to run the company like a dictatorship."

"And who gave you the authority to do that?" his father asked, hands gripping the arm of the couch.

"It's my job. It's the job you wanted me to do. The job you just *gave me*." Ash could feel his frustration rising, boiling over into anger.

"Not so you could ruin it!" Nathanial shouted, silencing Ash, shutting down anything else he wanted to say.

His mother sighed and threw her hands in the air before crossing her arms across her chest, frowning, and settling in to listen to her husband reprimand their son as she always did, had been doing for as long as Ash could remember. Nathanial Cross was always given the floor.

Ash's throat tightened painfully. His heart pounded and his stomach pulled into a small, closed ball. His thoughts were flittering things he couldn't collect. Work wasn't what he'd come there for but he couldn't find the words to set the conversation back in order. Now all he could think of were the things he absolutely couldn't say. That if his dad wanted the job so badly he could have it back, have it all back. That Ash didn't want it at all. He couldn't say any of those things.

He wasn't Claire, who could do whatever she wanted. He was the responsible one. The one who was taking over the company. The one who would continue his father's legacy.

His phone buzzed in his pocket. He pulled it out to look, make sure it wasn't an email or text, and found a game notification. New play levels in *Alone in the Multiverse*.

Ash looked up from the device in his hand. Nathanial was talking at him, explaining responsibility, what he was meant to do, how he should handle things. The important things. Bridgette sat next to him shaking her head, used to his father.

Nathanial made a disgusted noise in his throat. "Your incompetence is going to cause more issues than you realize. Company culture! So you can take a day off work whenever you feel like it? I was too hasty in passing the torch, you're not ready!"

"You're right, I'm not," Ash said thoughtfully. "But that doesn't matter. Her name is Zeta."

"What?" his father said, sputtering to a stop.

"The reason I came to talk to you today. Her name is Zeta."

"I don't care about your girlfriend. Don't you think you have other things to be focused on?" his father huffed.

She's not my girlfriend, he almost said, because she wasn't. They were still settling on that and that felt strange and raw in him, but he pressed forward. "She's pregnant. We're having a girl."

Their mouths hung open.

"Well," his mother started. "What— What do you intend?"

"What do you mean?" Ash asked, still shocked that he'd managed to get the words out at all. "We're still working on all the pieces."

"Do you really think *now* is a good time for this? You've just taken over the company." His father. Work first. "You don't have to go through with this. There are . . . things that can be done."

There was no question of what he wanted. What his plans were, what *their* plans were. "She's due at the end of April," he said, still processing his father's statements.

Nathanial suddenly started coughing. Waving Bridgette's busy hands away, he pounded his chest and picked up a cup of water.

Ash didn't see his parents in the sunlight anymore. He didn't come up on the weekends when he was off until it was time for their bimonthly dinners. In the low light of the dining room he could see his father wasn't well, that he wasn't himself. In the sunlight of his mother's sitting room he could see more than that.

Nathanial Cross was old.

His father's eyes were watery; he had lost weight. His hair looked grayer, his body smaller. Nathanial Cross, the father that Ash had always on some level feared, was old and ill.

"I've got to go," Ash said, standing.

"Wait, honey, let's talk about this more. I didn't realize that this was . . . Nathanial, apologize, please."

His father shook his head. "He left work, during a vulnerable time for the company, to tell me he got into some trouble with some girl? Childish."

"This isn't," Ash started and then stopped. He didn't know what it was, he couldn't say that they would be together or that they were together. "I wanted you to know."

"Well, I'm excited! A granddaughter!" Bridgette sang, attempting to change the subject, to bring the conversation back around. To mediate.

"A distraction," Nathanial said, head shaking.

Enough. He'd had enough. "Goodbye, Dad." Ash stood and placed a kiss on his mother's cheek. "I'll talk to you later, Mom."

He turned and left the room without looking back. He stopped at the coat closet for his jacket, and as he closed the door, he saw his mother coming down the hall. She put a finger to her lips and shooed him forward.

"Don't let your father get you down," she said at the door, taking the edges of his jacket and straightening them like he was a child again. "He's just shocked, you know he doesn't do well with the unexpected, and honestly I would have never thought you'd announce something like this!"

"I didn't either. Zeta is really special to me," he said slowly, the words sounding inadequate.

"She must be. I'll talk to your father. He's just surprised," she repeated. "Bring her around for dinner soon. I can't wait to meet her! Do you have an ultrasound picture?"

Dinner? No, he thought. Impossible, not if his father planned to act like he had. "Sure," he said, pulling out his phone, opening it to the photo of the ultrasound he had taken. He turned it to his mother, realizing that he should have grabbed the physical one to show her.

She smiled gently, took the phone from his fingers, gazing at the image with soft eyes. "Oh, Ash, she'll be beautiful." When she returned the phone, her eyes were watering. "My first grandchild! My little boy is having a baby!"

"Mom, don't," he started, before his mother wrapped him in a tight hug.

"Don't worry, it'll be fine, just bring your girlfriend, Zeta, over for dinner soon."

There was so much he hadn't explained about the situation. That he needed to make clear, but instead he just said, "Yeah, I'll bring her over soon."

She cupped his cheek. "I'm sorry about today. Your father . . . Well, you know he likes to be on top of things and since his . . . little scare he hasn't felt himself."

He swallowed his denial. He didn't want to fight with this mother too. "I know."

She smiled, and he felt the anger and stress from his father melt. "I'm very proud of you."

Ash wrapped his mother in a hug. "Thanks, Mom."

His hands shook as he turned the key in the ignition. He gripped the steering wheel to make them stop. Ash drove back to the city, his stomach still rolled tight. Finally he tossed his keys on the counter and lay down on his kitchen floor, arm over his eyes, until he could breathe again.

He wanted to call Zeta, see her, hold her until his heartbeat matched hers, but he didn't want to explain to her what had happened, didn't want to burden her or give her any reason to believe that she should pull away from him.

He didn't realize what he had done until he was back at her apartment, ringing her bell.

"Back?" she asked, confused.

"I decided to take the rest of the day off."

"Well, I didn't, but you can hang out until I'm done, if you want?" she shrugged.

"I think the boss will be fine with you calling it a day."

"Hey, no work stuff," she scolded.

He wanted to feel better. Needed to feel better, and Zeta made him feel so much better. He leaned into her, laid a kiss on her mouth.

"Did something happen?"

His cheeks tingled. "No, I just didn't want to be away from you today," he said, kissing her, gently leading her to the couch.

His hand swept over the swell of her belly, under the shirt. He pushed it up to reveal the taut skin, traced the blossoming dark line that had started to arch across it, felt a burst of possessiveness and delight at the sight. "Every time I see you, there's something new."

"Don't stare!" Zeta pushed herself up clumsily and threw her hands in front his eyes.

"Why not?" he laughed around her palms, before kissing one and dragging her hand down to lick at her fingertips. Her hands that fit inside his so comfortably. Dainty and light. She inhaled sharply, tried to pull her hands away, but he caught one, kept it pressed to his lips, played over the digits with his tongue. "Why not?" he asked again, softer this time.

He watched her try to pull her shirt back down with her free hand. He stopped her, gently pushed her back before planting a kiss on the top of her stomach. "You're beautiful."

"You have a fetish or something," she laughed. "You're obsessed with my belly."

"Not your belly, you. You weren't pregnant the first time I met you and I still couldn't stop thinking about you. Maybe I do have a fetish. For Zeta."

He brushed his mouth over hers, pulled her eyes to his. Smoky pools, golden hour in a forest eyes, hidden in shadow until the light hit them just right and they exploded into perfect facets. He kissed her again, held his lips to hers, moved hers open, a quick, teasing kiss. Another, deeper, an urging for her to forget about his eyes, just enjoy his touch.

He moved smoothly, pulling up her shirt more to reveal her bra. He dipped his hand inside of the smooth cup and lifted out her heavy breast.

"Here too." He whistled, using his thumb to toy with the dark nipple.

"What?" she asked, already dazed.

"You haven't noticed? They're darker." He didn't wait for an answer before he covered the bud with his mouth, sucked it gently into a hard peak. He kissed a trail to the opposite side and did the same to the other.

Sitting up, looking down at her, hair a mess and her eyes already soft with pleasure, his mind floated, no thoughts, the lightness spreading through his body. He pulled off his own shirt while she inspected her breasts.

"I guess they have. I don't spend a lot of time looking at them," she said, laughing, sliding out of the shirt and bra herself.

"You should. Your hair is thicker; your skin is glowing. You're beautiful," he repeated, hooking the top of her pants with his fingers and sliding them, along with her underwear, down to reveal her thick, brown thighs and round hips. "And softer."

He squeezed her hips, ran his hands up the curve of her body. Slipped his hand between her thighs and she shifted, opened them for him, sighing when his fingers found wet. "Lean back, let me see," he said while he stroked.

"Enough?" she asked, teasing, the space between her legs still too narrow. A little game.

"Never enough." He tickled the space where her thigh met her hip, pulled a gasping giggle from her. "Little more, love."

She spread her legs wide, leaned back, and showed him the blushing lips of her sex. Here, too, the color was darker, her sex a little swollen, like a ripe berry, but he kept it to himself, a little secret. He slipped his fingers through her lips, revealed her opening and the pearl of her clit. He followed the path of his fingers with his tongue.

He dragged his tongue over her, her taste, a little tart, a little sweet, bathing it. He held her thighs open, kept them from snapping shut around him. Her fingers found his hair and tangled in it as she moaned above him. He pulled back, kissed her thigh. "Wait, not here."

"Why not?" she asked. Her wide eyes and full lips made his cock jump with anticipation.

"Because I'm going to make love to you until you fall asleep," he hummed into her ear.

"I'm not tired though."

"You will be," he promised.

He held out his hands and she put hers in them, trusting. He pulled her up to her feet where she wrinkled her nose. "I feel silly," she said her body hot against his.

"Why?" he asked.

"Because I'm naked."

"I'll join you," he teased.

The shades in her bedroom were still open, letting in the last of the afternoon sun, casting an orange light over everything. It had been bright when he left his parent's, still bright when he arrived here, but now it was all fading. Becoming late. The light made her glow with a low, warm fire, and he was thankful for the high fence that made it a sight for only his eyes.

"You look like a goddess," Ash said. He kissed her, holding her bare body against his, adjusting for the swell of her belly. His hands followed the curve of her back while his tongue explored the familiar caverns of her mouth. She shivered at the tickling trail of his fingers, sighed into his lips and pulled him closer, tighter while he maneuvered the rest of his clothing off.

Releasing her, he pulled her onto the bed with him, gathering her soft body into his lap, her side pressed against his chest. Met her giggles with kisses along her throat. Turned them into gasps as he gently nipped at her shoulder.

"I can bite too," Zeta said with a faux pout.

He teased open her lips with his finger, slid it between her teeth. "I remember. Do it again," he challenged, vibrating with the memory of it. He pressed his face to her neck, sucking at the delicate skin.

The pressure of her teeth increased, just shy of pain.

"Harder," her groaned. He wanted her to mark him. Claim him.

Zeta released him and shook her head. "No! I'll hurt you."

"You can't hurt me," he replied before finding her mouth with his. His fingers traveled lower to between her legs, already parting, already wet. He teased her, dipping fingertips into her opening while holding her still, keeping her from moving against him and pulling soft, begging sounds from her.

The throaty demands of her pleasure sent rolling, tickling waves of heat through him. He held her close, kissed her neck, and breathed in the scent of her. Flowery and rich, like the pages of a new book, like jasmine tea.

Ash held her captive, moved decisively, shifting her and forcing her to hold on to him, use his body as an anchor so that he could move his fingers over her clit. Pulling pleasure from the bundle of nerves and flesh, swallowing her soft moans and cries with his kiss as he stroked her, drawing her closer. His own body was tight with need. Her fingers squeezed against his skin, digging into his arm with her coming orgasm.

"Stop!" she gasped suddenly.

Ash instantly pulled away from her, slipping his fingers from her wet heat, as he pulled back to check over her, searching for the cue he missed, but her clutching hands held him close. "What's wrong? Do you need a break?"

"No," she said, shy and small. "Not like that. I want to be closer; I want you to kiss me." She turned toward him, kissing him slowly, her tongue pressing past his lips.

"Yes," he agreed, feeding on her urgency. He shifted her so that she straddled his thighs, spread wide. Steadying her, he guided himself to her entrance and lowered her slowly onto himself.

She moaned into his mouth as he gasped in response to the touch of her sex on his. Hot and welcoming, she swallowed what he offered. Inch by inch until he was fully inside of her. She rocked slowly against him, using his shoulders as leverage. He held her hips, accommodated the space needed for her growing body, and kept his eyes on hers. The memory of the hospital came to him, her body against his, her teeth on his shoulder hard enough to bruise.

The stone of guilt that sat in his belly melted under the heat of his adoration and pleasure. He floated, eyes closed, his body burning at each point where they connected, her short, gasping breaths a prayer in his ears.

Shocks ran up his torso as she moved against him, achingly slow. He matched his touch to her pace even as it drove him mad, pushed him toward the edge of his own release. Zeta tightened around him and he braced his arm against her back, holding her as she shattered on him, her climax pulling a shocked cry from her throat matching the hot gush of fluid around his cock, still buried deep inside of her.

He gathered her tighter into his arms, the press of her body against his skin bringing him closer to his own pleasure. A deep part of his mind wanted to apologize, beg her forgiveness for his selfishness, and he didn't know if he meant for the situation he'd created around their relationship or for taking pleasure in her whimpering body. It didn't matter, he couldn't voice it; Zeta held him too tightly, his thrust short and quick because she wouldn't release him, his thoughts turning into white waves to match the hot pulses that moved through him at every press. He rocked her hips faster and she held on to him, whimpering and gasping as he took her. He felt himself coiling tightly and then released, spilling into her.

Still connected, Ash held her, kissing her slowly, covering her cheeks and throat with the lightest touch of his lips, each kiss an offering, a promise. *I won't hurt you, I'll honor you, I'll protect you, I'll care for you.* All the things he couldn't say because it'd only been two months. Too soon. Too soon. He pressed his lips into her hair as her arms dropped. He stroked her back, her body becoming heavier in his grasp.

They stayed like that, the only sound their breathing. Beyond them, the sun set, the room darkened.

"Ash," she said finally, breaking the spell. "You should—"

Alarm. He could feel the distance growing, a physical thing. Tension twisted in him. "Zeta, don't—" *tell me to leave.*

"Put me down," she finished, pulling back, smiling at him and rubbing sleepy eyes. "I can't sleep like this."

He nodded, settled her into bed, pulling himself around her. "I thought you were going to tell me to leave."

"Why would I tell you to leave?"

"I don't know." He kissed her shoulder. "Do you want me to sing you a lullaby?"

"Sing to the baby," she sighed, pressing into him. "Music is good for her."

She wrapped her arm around his, the thin chain of the bracelet he'd gifted her sparkling. The tension fell from him, and he hugged her as close as he could along her back, covering whatever skin he could reach with kisses. Ash stroked her belly as he sang gently to his daughter, to her mother in his arms.

Her breathing changed, deepened with the coming evening, and listening to it, he began to plan, make decisions about things. He wouldn't tell her about his father. It would worry her, hurt her. He'd work harder, make sure there was nothing that the man could say about his work, clear the distractions from their relationship so that all he could see was Zeta, how serious and real it all was.

And then he would be able to say to her how he really felt. For now he held her, waited until their hearts and breaths came in sync.

25

Zeta was tired of being pregnant.

Her back hurt, her hips hurt; she was over the doctor appointments and tired of having to pee all the time. It felt cliché, but Zeta was learning, quickly, that people complain about those things all the time because the struggle was real. Really real. She didn't know what she would do if she had a physical job, but even the daily pressures of her labor-unintensive gig were weighing on her.

She'd gone out, despite the freezing temperatures, to clear her head, shock it clear, but it wasn't working. She was distracted with her own discomfort, and on top of it all, one nagging thought.

Something was off about Ash.

The change was subtle; he was exactly the same in many ways, but since the glucose test he was also different. After he'd come back that day, he stayed until the next morning. Played games with her, made dinner, and went to bed with her but left long before she woke in the morning.

And hadn't quite been the same since.

He worked more, he was busy more often than not, and yes, he had said that it was so things could be in place for when the baby came and she believed that. But still there was something *different* between them that she couldn't place.

"Hormones," Pixie suggested when Zeta brought it up. "You're probably just anxious because of that," she said, shrugging it off because Zeta really didn't have any reason to be anxious.

He was patient and calm and increasingly late for every meeting with her that he didn't cancel outright. It had been three going onto four weeks, nearly a month, since then and they *did* spend time together. He spent the night at her place, she hung out at his over the weekend, but there was this *staleness* to it all that felt more like this-is-what-we're-supposed-to-do rather than this-is-what-we-want-to-do.

Zeta caught herself staring at his ears, wondering what Alice saw in them, like they held the mysteries of his personality switch.

Distracted, she wasn't getting anywhere with work. It was Friday anyway. Defeated, she logged out, picked up her Switch, and turned it back on. She was trying to work her way through *Sayonara Wild Hearts*, but she kept losing the rhythm. Music wasn't enough to distract her.

She went out to the kitchen, forced herself to eat a sandwich, and tried a different game. *Pikmin* this time. Zeta curled up on the couch, played it on the TV, tried not to think about her not-boyfriend, if he should be a boyfriend. There were little guys that needed her direction on the screen.

He hadn't even *texted* her since the night before.

The baby kicked, more than a flutter in her. "Maybe I should go shopping, get out of the house." She mused. She could pick up a few small things at Target, she needed to get started on that anyway.

But. Shouldn't she be shopping *with* Ash?

A cartoonish bug creature wiped out all hundred of her pikmin. Not a game over but she'd have to start over on a new day. "God," she said, leaning back, confused about everything.

The doorbell sounded. She looked at the time. Just after six. *Package*, she thought. She'd ordered Ash's Valentine's gift and wasn't sure if it would make it on time and hoped it would be early. Either way, she'd give it to him right away.

"Coming!" she called, pulling herself up from the couch, hips protesting, pulling a frown from her. It was still there when she pulled open the door to find Ash smiling gently down at her.

"What are you doing here?" she asked, the frown softening.

He kissed her hello. "I came to see you. We haven't been able to spend much time together."

Her heart fluttered. "We haven't, I've been thinking about that." He was there now though, she didn't want to dwell on it; everything was already hard. She grabbed his hand, pulled him inside. "Are you going to cook?"

"Of course. Is everything OK?" Now he wore her frown. He stepped inside, shut the door, pulling her close and running his hand down her side, soft pressure against her.

"Hey, when are we going to go shopping? I keep putting it off. Since we know the baby is a girl there's no reason to wait," she explained, breaking away from his touch, locking the door behind him.

He didn't answer, and when she turned he was frowning. His gaze was thoughtful but far away. "There hasn't been time," he said finally. "Maybe this weekend. I got your mail out of the box."

"You don't have to go, you know. Aunt Josie and I can handle it if you need to work. Maybe we should just order online, there's probably a better selection? What do you think?" she asked as she led him back into her apartment proper.

He dropped her mail on the table and turned back, and he circled his arms around her, leaned his chin on her shoulder. Filled her world with his heat, his fresh, sage scent.

"I think I want to do that with you. This weekend. Just tell me where you want me to put it all."

The other problem. She let herself relax against him, tried to pretend that there wasn't an issue there. "Can you spare it for me? Are you sure Tokyo doesn't need you?" she said teasingly.

"I'll squeeze you in," he laughed, taking it lightly, and she smiled back, comfortable, but still, something was *off*.

"I think I've missed you," she sighed.

"I know I've missed you," he replied, the tickle of his breath on her ear spreading through her.

She turned, kissed his cheek. "Then come see me more."

Ash let her go. "I'll start dinner," he said, not answering her. Something was *wrong*.

She sat, unsettled, and picked up the pile of mail.

"What are you in the mood for," he asked, opening up the freezer.

"Anything," she responded, still distracted, unsure of how to say what she knew needed to be said. The first letter was addressed to the man who used to live upstairs. She sat it in a growing pile of mail she would write RTS on and put back out for pickup soon. It was getting large. The next was a bill for her, a catalog, a sales flyer for baby supplies, another bill, and then a letter from her landlord.

Dear Zeta Rodgers,

Thank you so much for being such a valued tenant these past five years. As you know, we recently did some major renovations to the unit, and in accordance with those updates, we will be raising the rent on the property. Your rent will be increasing May 1. Please see the chart below for the changes. If you have any questions, our office is open 8-6 M-F.

Thank you for your understanding!

She glanced over the numbers and quickly realized that the new amount would be well above what she'd calculated for her maternity leave savings. Her head swum in panic. *No, there's, OK, I just need to call, I just need . . .* She touched her forehead, closed her eyes, breathed deeply.

"Zeta?" Ash called.

"I'm OK, I'm just— Give me a minute." She wouldn't be able to take time off for the baby, just a couple of weeks. The number on the page was a nightmare.

Ash plucked the letter from her hand, scanned it, frowned, and then checked his watch. "When's your lease up, Kitten?"

"August," she answered.

"It's alright," he said, dialing the number and then holding the phone against his shoulder with his ear to finish preparing the tea.

"Hello, is this Blue Tree Property Management? Oh great, I'm calling about a letter we received." He gave Zeta's address, waited a moment. "I'm her husband."

She turned at the announcement, but all she could see was his back clad in a dark blue shirt.

"I didn't call to discuss my relationship. I did call because you've notified us of a rent increase and you simply cannot do that," he explained.

Us, she thought, the sparking touch of pleasure down her back. But it was a lie, like in the hospital, a way for him to bypass the barrier and move in her life. A magic word that unlocked doors and allowed him to *take care* of things, which was lovely, but was it too far?

"First of all, the renovations are basic at best. Second, and more important, you can't double our rent no matter what work you do. She has months on her lease. It's illegal for you to do this."

"Is it?" she asked.

He nodded. "I'm positive it is. So you can retract this or be tied up in litigation about it." He listened in silence. "I'm glad we were able to sort this out. I expect to see a written follow-up about this before the week's out or the next call you'll receive from us will be our lawyer."

He hung up the phone. "No need to worry; it's taken care of."

She let out a breath, pressed her hand to her chest. "Oh my god, I thought I was going to have to move!"

"You should move though," he said quietly. "You need the space, for the baby. She won't be small enough for your room for long."

"I know, but it's fine for a little while, don't worry."

"You should move in with me, Zeta."

She laughed, trying to avoid the conversation. "You only have one bedroom! There's no space for me and a baby."

"I meant we should find a place. Together," he said. His lips were straight, brows relaxed, but he was searching her expression, reading her. Serious. "We could get another apartment, or a house, find something that suits us."

"I can't move in with you, Ash," she blurted out.

"Why not?" he asked. "It would make things easier when the baby comes."

"Why? Ash, you haven't even talked to your parents about us. I can't move in with you after a handful of months when you can't do that," she said, torn in herself because it sounded nice, perfect even, but no. They weren't anything. He was not her husband, not even a boyfriend. They were just . . .

"I did," he said cutting into her thoughts.

"What? Why didn't you tell me?" she asked slowly, confused.

"Because it's complicated, but that doesn't have anything to do with us," he explained, leaning against her counter. Distance.

"What the fuck does that mean?" Zeta asked slowly, wary.

He rested his forehead on his fingers and closed his eyes. Zeta noticed the gray pockets under them. She almost reached to him and touched them before he spoke.

"It means that their feelings don't have anything to do with our relationship. How they feel about you, about us has no bearing on how *I* feel." His tone was hard, and she wrapped her arms around herself, sat up straighter.

"How *do* they feel about me? About this?" Zeta asked slowly.

Ash stopped, and she watched his expression shift, the realization dawn how far he'd come down the path of the argument. He looked around the kitchen then, like he saw it for the first time, realized where he was, what was happening, and sat across from her. "They'll come around. Please don't worry, Kitten."

Soft, gentle rumble, the pet name used to disarm her. He wrapped his hands around hers, and she wanted to be disarmed. It was *easier* to follow, to trust.

She pulled away from his touch, pulled her hands back into the floppy flannel shirt she was wearing and rested them on her belly. "Ash, tell me what they think."

"It's nothing bad, Zeta. My mother is looking forward to meeting you, the baby. My father just needs some time."

She felt the frown come to her face again. "OK, so why didn't you just tell me?" she asked slowly. "Why'd you hide it from me for so long?"

"I don't want to upset you. Kitten, listen don't worry about that. It's not important."

"It is," she said softly.

"Why do I need some sort of approval for you? If it were reversed, if your aunt didn't like me, this wouldn't be a discussion. You'd laugh about it," he tried, voice losing its softness. Tense.

"That's different," she shot back.

"How? Explain to me how that is different. Explain to me why you care about what my parents think! You don't care about anything!"

She sucked in her breath. She could feel it in him, that it had been anger, frustration that things weren't going his way, but she asked anyway. "Is that what you think? That I don't care?"

His eyes went wide, face pale. He put his hands in front of his mouth and looked away. "I didn't mean that, not like that, I'm sorry I said that. I know you care. I'm tired and I'm not . . . that's not an excuse. I'm sorry, I spoke out of turn. But I *don't* understand why this is where you're suddenly drawing a line."

"Because it matters *to you*," she said slowly. "If my aunt likes you then that's good, but it's not the end of the world if she doesn't. I told her about all this as soon as I found out, but you needed to wait for weeks to tell people you see every other weekend. I know this isn't an optimal situation, this probably isn't how you wanted to become a father, but I'm not naïve enough to believe that you were holding out on telling your family because you were waiting on ultrasound photos. And I think that the only reason you want to move in together is because it will make this look better to *them*."

She'd never seen him shocked, not really, and she didn't know if it was what she'd said or that she had said anything at all, so she continued to prove her point. "Why do you want to move in with me?" she asked slowly.

"Because it's easier for us," he said, and she could see that coldness coming on him again. A shift before he explained, logically, without question, the reasons for them to live together, for her to say alright, OK, of course of course. To take back everything she had said about him. And she realized then that part of her had gone along, to make things easier in hopes that he would take the space to find a way to make it alright for her, not use it to force what he wanted.

What she liked about him, the way he turned to her, let her lead, stepped forward when she wanted, was missing, gone, and it was more like those weeks working for him before they knew again who each other was. Cold, decisive, nonnegotiable.

"Easier for us or easier for you?" She could feel the edge in her voice, and her heart started beating harder. A hard trembling began to pull on her lips because this all felt familiar.

He leaned back, eyes closed, rubbed his head like he had a headache. "Do not do this. I didn't come over here to fight with you. I don't want to fight with you."

"I think I deserve an honest answer. Don't do what? Ask you questions? Why are you talking to me like this? Who are you right now?"

"What's that supposed to mean? I'm not allowed to be frustrated?"

"Frustrated over what? I don't think it's unreasonable that I'd like everyone to be on the same page before we move forward."

"And what page is that, Zeta? Every time I try to bring anything up with you, you tell me we're still figuring things out!"

"We are!"

"I'm not!" Ash said quickly, voice a stone, cold and hard. A force, and even then she knew what he meant to say next. "Zeta, I—"

She moved without thinking, snapping up from the table, throwing her hands forward and covering his mouth, stifling the words. Too fast—her condition or just blood pressure changes from the pregnancy; the world swayed and darkened and the only thing holding her up was his tight grasp on her arms across the table.

"Zeta," he said, softer. "Zeta?"

"Don't say that," she said. "I'm fine, you can let me go."

"No, listen, let's start over," he said.

She pulled herself away, the world still shifting around her. "It's a little late to start over." She wasn't sure if she meant the conversation, the relationship, or something else, and when she looked at him, found his hard gaze, under a furrowed brow, she knew he didn't know either.

She turned to move to the couch. A breath after he was at her side, hand on her lower back, ready to help, catch.

"I'm fine, Ash," she said, taking a seat on the cushion, pulling her legs under her.

He took a deep breath, started again. "I have a thousand things to take care of, including you and the baby. Is it really such a horrible idea for you to live with me?"

"I told you before, months ago, that you didn't have to change your life. I don't want you to feel obligated to do things; you have something else going on," she said slowly, a twisty sick feeling in her guts. It felt true but also wrong and awful. Cold moved over her, numbed her fingers, crawled down her back. She held her hands curled to her chest.

"Zeta," he breathed. "Do you not like me at all?"

Her head snapped up and she looked at him again. All the coldness had left him, and there was nothing there at all but that question hanging in the air. The question she hadn't really considered. Of course she liked him—who wouldn't like him? But that wasn't what he was asking, and he knew that she knew it.

"I just . . ."

"Need time," he finished. "But we're running out of time."

She thought he meant because of the baby. That made the most sense, but it felt more like an ultimatum, a threat, and she wasn't sure if that was real or just her own anxiety. "You should go."

"I don't think that's a great idea, love," he said softly, and it sounded different this time, not just a term of endearment but a title, and she wondered how long he'd meant it. Wondered what the problem was even though she felt it in the center of her chest and it spread through like the press of his hand on her skin.

"I just need to clear my head, think a bit."

"You just fainted," he said, stepping toward her. "This is why I want—" he stopped himself, started again. "We won't talk anymore about any of that. I'll make dinner."

"Ash," she said slowly, "I'm fine. I won't break and I won't do anything reckless, but I want you to leave because I don't know what to say to you right now and just, please."

She closed her eyes, heard him shuffling around her space and then: "Here."

When she looked he held her phone. "I don't want you to get up right away. Will you call someone to sit with you? If you won't let me stay, promise that you'll call someone."

"Alright," she said, taking her phone in numb fingers.

Ash was gone moments later. She listened to the sound of his car driving off on the empty street. She didn't call anyone. She played on her phone, thoughts scattered, confused, until the battery died and she fell asleep.

Hours later she woke, charged it, saw no missed calls or messages, and only then did she call Pixie. She started crying while she explained and couldn't stop.

26

Ash wasn't drunk but he was fairly sure he was on his way. He wasn't sure why he'd come out, except that at the time, getting some fresh air seemed like a good idea. But then the reality came and he'd rather be anywhere else but a bar full of strangers who were all having an excellent time. He certainly did not feel like being out.

Not after how he had left things with Zeta. Zeta, who only answered his texts in as few words as possible and none of his phone calls. It had only been two days since their fight and he was already going insane. He couldn't even call it a fight. He knew what it was—exhausted from working long hours, he'd been short, let his frustrations control him.

He had sounded like his father and he hated it. Hated himself for acting like that. But he was so tired. The company was eating him alive from the inside out. He was always meant to take over, and now that he had, he knew for sure what he had always known in the back of his mind: he didn't want it. He hadn't let himself think about it after school when he came to work for his father, hadn't thought about it when he took his last position, and not when he'd finally gotten to the top. And if he was being honest, it was partially because he never thought he would *have* to. He thought that his father would be in the position forever. That there would never come a time when Ash *had* to step forward, because by the time that happened there would be some other younger, better prospect to be appointed.

Someone who wasn't him.

The anticipation he felt was only at seeing it ended so that he could be freed from the space of waiting, but now he was trapped in being.

It was what he was supposed to want, what he had always been told would be given to him. And the truth of it all was, he wasn't interested in making it work between what his father wanted for him and what he really wanted.

He wanted Zeta and his daughter, but it felt like his world wasn't big enough for both things. It could only be either-or.

The glass touched his lips, the rum tasteless, the burn numbing the lump in his throat enough to speak. "I agree completely," he said to the man speaking to him. He wasn't sure what he was agreeing to, but it was the right answer.

"See! He gets it!" the man guffawed, and wandered off; Ash returned to his thoughts.

He had nearly told her he loved her, and she had stopped him, refused to hear it.

He needed to make it up to her, somehow, come back to what they were. He didn't know if that was possible, if they could, because she didn't love him. But it was so soon and maybe she would. How could he say sorry for pressuring her when what he had meant was that he wanted to be with her, had always wanted to be with her.

And she was right. He had wanted to move in with her primarily to make it easier on *him*. She did not need him in her space; he needed to be with her. He felt awful. He ordered another drink. He didn't think she'd really ever talk to him again.

We'll split custody, I'll have the baby a few hours a week, mostly weekends. I'll have endless time for work. He felt like crying. He checked his phone.

Where are you? Randall.

That bar down the street from my place.

No questions, just: **I'm on my way.**

Ash flipped through photos of Zeta. There were only photos of Zeta or photos of things he wanted to show her. Screenshots, passages of books, funny things he'd seen while he was out without her. He'd never shared so much of his inner life with anyone, couldn't imagine sharing it with anyone else.

Ash was finishing his third drink, ordering his fourth, by the time Randall made it to the bar.

"Hey, she still not picking up?" Randall asked, taking the seat next to him.

Ash shook his head. "She hates me."

"She doesn't hate you," Randall said.

"She's never going to speak to me again."

"You're having a baby together." Randall sighed. "And I think you're drunk."

"She's never going to speak to me about anything that's not the baby again, and yes, I am drunk."

"Come on, let's get you home," Randall said, moving to take the drink from him.

"I tried to tell her I loved her and she wouldn't let me."

Randall stopped, pulled his hand back. "Maybe you better drink that then."

Ash had already told him most of what happened. Randall had listened, nodded, and told him that he just needed to give her time to cool down, to talk to her during the week. Go on a date.

"I asked her if she even liked me," Ash said. "She told me to leave."

Randall patted him on the back as he downed his last drink, felt the world turn blurry and soft. "Now you're really done," Randall said, and helped him off the stool and back down the street.

The cold air shocked him back to a state of near sober. Sober enough to put himself to bed.

He kicked off his shoes when he entered his apartment, leaving them piled in front of the shoe rack. He stripped his clothing, dropping them on the floor as he entered the bedroom. He put his phone on the nightstand and slid across the bed. He picked up the floppy bear that they'd gotten on New Year's and buried his face into the pillows that might still contain a trace of her.

"In the morning, I'll call, I'll go to her house. I'll apologize, explain," he told the darkness. "I'll wait outside until she lets me in, anything I have to do." But it didn't feel like enough, and his stomach churned, the lump in his throat expanded, choking him in his half-sleep state until he fully succumbed to unconscious.

He slept through his alarms and woke groggy and smelly shortly before noon. *Shower first*, he thought, pulling himself out of bed.

27

Zeta was supposed to be working. It was Monday morning. Work happened on Monday mornings. Instead she was staring at the unopened box on her table and wondering what to do with it. It had arrived Saturday morning, and she hadn't touched it since she sat it on her table. She would know what to do with it if she could figure out what to do with him, with Ash.

She'd asked everyone. Pixie said dump him, which made her realize that she did not want to do that. Brand said talk to him—reasonable, but she didn't know what to say. Cody said find one of his friends and fuck them. Completely useless, but it made her laugh and stop crying at least. Aunt Josie said that her spirit would guide her to the right decision and also that she was coming up next weekend to kick his ass.

She put her hand on her belly, felt the baby move under it. "Maybe I overreacted. Maybe I should have just told him how I felt?"

She didn't know what else to do but put him out. In that moment everything was so jumbled. She knew what he was about to confess, but she didn't want to hear it, not like that, not then when it was colored with his frustrations. And she wasn't ready to respond in turn, but not because of how she did or didn't feel.

It would be easier to say yes. Ash had been perfect. On paper she knew the answer should be *Yes, OK, I'm sorry, you're right.* Because she didn't want to fight, didn't want to upset him. But she couldn't be like that—not again. It wasn't good for her baby or for her.

She had to be sure.

But is that what he was after? He had never seemed to want her to follow his orders so easily, only when he was working. And they didn't talk about work.

He'd called, but she wasn't ready to talk. His texts were gentle check-ins, reminders that he would talk when she was ready. But she wasn't ready. The baby moved in her, and a strange, heavy turn made her suck in her breath, not pain—odd but safe, natural. She rubbed her belly and looked back at the box.

"OK, first things first. We'll see if it's still any good." She was supposed to unpack it as soon as it arrived, but she hadn't. She'd left it on her table all weekend and pretended that it wasn't there at all while she played games and asked people what she should do about her relationship.

But only she could answer that.

She cut open the box.

Inside were soft lilac-colored petals encased in glass.

She pulled out the little glass lantern-shaped greenhouse to find the orchid she'd ordered Ash alive and well. It was much sturdier than she thought it would be. The plant had a tall curving stem with multiple flowers hanging from it. Lush green leaves grew from a cream-colored pot. It was fine despite her avoidance.

She looked at the time, 11:45, and made up her mind.

"OK, baby, we're going to drop this off with the doorman and call your daddy after work to talk. We'll get ice cream after this for being brave." She kicked inside of Zeta in agreement.

Zeta picked out a plain, black maxi dress with thin straps and a low neckline. She had it in three colors because the fabric was soft and forgiving and it felt comfortable on her growing waistline. She covered her bare shoulders with a loose, oversized sweater with a bright vaporwave print. She dug out a pair of thick, knee-high socks that had tacos printed on them in bright colors to match the sweater. As dressed as she was going to get, she ordered a cab and shoved her feet into a pair of flats.

Coat on, she replaced the plant in its box and picked it up. A red FOR RENT sign was pounded into her yard.

The trip was quicker than she remembered. Her heart pounded in her chest, and her hands shook. The morning was clear and blustery, pretty for February. Clutching the box to her chest, she walked into the lobby of Ash's building. The brown marble and wood was familiar after so many nights over.

"Ms. Rodgers!" the doorman said brightly. *George*, she thought, recognizing the portly elderly man with a huge friendly smile.

"Hello," she replied. "I have a package to drop off for Ash. I know he's at work."

"No problem! He's left very specific instructions to always let you up. Let me just call and see if he's in just in case," he said.

She tried to stop him, explain that she only wanted to pass the box off, but the man was already dialing. He smiled as it rang in his ear before hanging up. "Looks like he's not. Matt will run you up."

"I really don't need—" She tried to protest.

"No problem at all! You have a good day!" he said, all smiles.

She smiled back. It wasn't worth arguing over, she'd just drop it off in the kitchen. She rode the elevator with Matt, who whistled next to her the entire ride and then let her into Ash's apartment. The silence was sudden as the door shut behind her.

She slipped her shoes off and padded over his carpet to the kitchen island, where she sat the box down. *I should leave a note*, she thought. She looked for paper, found his neatly stacked mail next to a pile of baby books and paused.

Zeta turned back around and looked toward the door where she'd left her shoes. His shoe rack held most of his shoes, placed neatly, except for one pair that mimicked hers—kicked off on the floor. She walked away from the island and to the living room. There was a blanket thrown over the couch that hadn't been there when she first saw the apartment. She sat under it when they watched movies. He'd cleared the table of books for her popcorn.

And on the floor was his shirt in a pile. Which was stranger still because he was very neat.

His bedroom door was open. She could see his pants on the floor in a little heap, and as she stepped over it, she found his bed unmade and empty, the blankets on the side she slept on tussled.

The bathroom door opened and she turned to find Ash, not at work, fresh from the shower, his towel wrapped around his waist. It should have startled her, his sudden appearance, but instead there was a relief, swift and cool.

"Zeta," he said softly as he crossed the room to her. "Zeta," he breathed again, reaching for her, his hands sliding around her waist. "I had a bad dream."

"I," she started, but his kiss swallowed the rest of her explanation. That she'd come to drop off the plant, that she thought he was at work. His open mouth met hers perfectly so it felt like they had been already wrapped in a kiss. His tongue tasted like toothpaste still as it moved against hers.

The bed was soft and sudden under her back; her dress was hiked up to her thighs and his towel was gone. His body, hot, heavy, pressed against hers, a comfortable weight. He kept his mouth over hers, releasing her to breathe, swallowing any words that tried to escape. His hand found her breast through the layers of her clothing, slipped around her nipple.

"Ash," she gasped at the touch.

"It was horrible, I never found you," he whispered, low and sad into her ear. "I'm sorry, I'm sorry, I didn't mean to hurt you.

Please don't leave me, I'm not like that, I don't want to force you to do anything."

He looked down at her with those same soft, questioning eyes that he'd looked at her with all those months ago in the summer.

"I'm right here, and you, there you are" she sighed, her hands wrapping around his back, tight muscles under her palms, sage scent. Woodsy and clear. Safe. "No more A. M. Cross, just you, just Ash. My Ash."

"Yes," he sighed, voice thick, and then he was kissing her again, his tongue caressing hers, body close.

They knew each other's bodies well and shifted, lifted, moved with sighs and moans into a position where they could meet. He touched her deftly, pulling purrs and gasps from her throat. Her mouth on his skin, her hands against him made him stop, grip the pillows.

Zeta's legs opened for him, and Ash settled himself over her. Heat poured from him, covering her. He rocked against her while they kissed, his cock hard, sliding comfortably against her, sending shivering rolls of pleasure through her body. Under him, her body felt like an ocean, wild waves, alive with sensation.

He took up her hand, laced his fingers into hers. She could feel the need in him, her body rippled and sparked with it. She whimpered as he entered her, body still tight, gripping at him, not quite ready but wanting. Her fingers tightened around his, holding him, pressing him forward. His thrusts were quick, deep, hungry as the rest of him, but he held himself above her, control keeping her safe from the crushing weight of his body. Of the press of her own body on her. A stubborn climax came over her, stuttering pulses around his cock that pushed into one another until a final release. She bit her lip, focusing on the sensation until it became overwhelming, and she gasped, shuddering at the last of it. A moment later his body buckled, and they were both left behind in the static satisfaction of release.

Ash kissed her cheek, pulled himself away, and lay down next to her. He pulled the blanket over both of them before gathering her in his arms. They lay silently, wrapped in the sound of each other's breathing, Ash's fingers brushing her shoulders, down her back.

"Epsilon," he said suddenly.

"Epsilon?"

He put his hand on her stomach. "Epsilon. It matches Zeta."

Inside of her, a small foot or fist pressed against the side of her belly, against the palm of Ash's hand and stilled. She smiled, "Epsilon it is then. I think she likes it."

They lay in bed in silence save for Ash's low chuckling at catching Epsilon's movements in Zeta's womb, until her stomach growled.

"I'll make some lunch."

"What are you doing home?" Zeta asked, sitting up.

"I had too much to drink last night," he explained. "It was a very bad plan to deal with my feelings."

"Did it work?"

"Not even a little bit."

She chuckled, slid off the bed, and went to clean up. Her toothbrush was still there, but she was a mess. She straightened her clothes, finger combed her hair. Back in the bedroom she found a pair of clean underwear she'd left there.

In the kitchen he was already boiling water and melting butter in a skillet. "What's in the box?" he asked as she sat down.

"Your Valentine's Day present came. That's why I'm here. I just meant to drop it off, and I thought we would talk later about . . . what happened."

He pulled out the orchid, turned it in the light with a soft smile on his face. "You got me flowers."

"I did. I thought you could use a little color, and I read they were easy to keep, despite their reputation, so they wouldn't be too much extra work."

"I wouldn't care if they were the hardest plants to keep alive in the world. I would devote my life to their care because you got them for me." He put down the orchids, walked around the island, and wrapped his arms around her. "Thank you. I've never gotten flowers before."

Zeta leaned against him, listened to his heartbeat, steady, even. "Ash, what you said, I do care."

"I shouldn't have said that to you. It's not what I think or feel. I was exhausted. I know you care, love. I see how much you care in everything you do. So let's start over." He let her go, went back to the stove.

She wasn't sure what he meant. The argument about moving in with one another? The pot started to boil and he dumped in a box of noodles. "Start what over."

"You and I are going to have lunch, and then we are going to meet my parents."

"For sure! Yeah, that sounds great," she replied, head tilted in mock enthusiasm, eyes rolling. "One question, though: Why?"

He leaned across the table, and his hair was wavy and shining in the cold winter light. "Because you were right, I do care. I thought it was about what they thought, but it's not. I want to be clear that this is what I'm choosing, you are what I'm choosing. And so they won't be too shocked to see you next week for dinner."

"Oh," Zeta said, unsure of what else to say, her feelings a wild mix of excitement and fear. Finally she settled on, "I look like shit."

"You look beautiful," he replied. "That dress is cute, almost like the one I met you in."

"My socks have tacos on them, and my sweater literally says 'no future.'"

"We can stop so you can change if you want."

"I do, I really do want that. What's for lunch?"

Ash grinned. "Cheesy mac and apple slices."

"I'm not a toddler," she laughed.

"I'm practicing," he replied.

28

Zeta had changed into a knit tunic dress that she had forgotten about but was happy to have found. The long dress flowed freely around her hips and belly with three-quarter sleeves and a wide boat neck. The bodice and sleeves were brightly colored stripes while the skirts were dark slate gray.

She'd fashioned her hair into one braid and thought about adding earrings or a necklace but just wore the single bracelet that Ash had given her. She matched him well. He'd eventually gotten dressed in a V-neck shirt over loose pants with a long open sweater.

On the drive he gave her a crash course on this family, told her about the house, where they were going, and assured her that if she felt uncomfortable they could leave, no questions asked. But the way he gripped the steering wheel, she wondered if he was offering that for her or for him.

At their destination, Zeta snaked her hand in his as they approached the door.

His parent's home was huge. Made to look like a log cabin, the wood was a rich, reddish color, offset with stone features. If each window was a bedroom, there were at least six of them. All she could think as he knocked on the door was that she couldn't let Aunt Josie see this. She'd never stop talking about it.

A moment later, the door swung open and a woman, just slightly older than Ash and only a little shorter, met them. She was wearing a baby-blue velour track suit, her long blonde hair held back by a thick headband.

"I didn't know you were coming today." Her brows crinkled in the exact expression that her brother made when he was confused. "Why aren't you at work? And who—" She stopped, eyes flicking over Zeta. "You're her, you're Zeta!"

"Hi, nice to meet you," Zeta said, unsure.

Claire let a squeal of excitement slip before wrapping Zeta in a hug. Zeta returned it and Claire stepped back. "You're so pretty! I'm so happy to meet you."

"Can we come into the house? It's cold, Claire." Ash asked.

"Of course! Sorry, just, wow, I can't believe you're here. I've been looking forward to meeting you. Mom's going to be so excited."

Zeta smiled. "I've heard a lot about you too." Not a lie, Ash did talk about his sister, but she was sill surprised by what a bubbly personality she had.

"I'll get them!" Claire said.

"We'll meet them in Mom's room," Ash said.

They parted ways, and Ash led her through the house past paintings and statues. A den, a living room. "Is your childhood bedroom in here?"

Ash nodded. "Yeah, but my mom turned it into a guest room as soon as I moved out."

"Harsh, mine is still the same at my aunt's."

"I told you, it's complicated." He sat her on one of the golden-brown couches.

"She really likes art," Zeta said.

Ash nodded. "She's an avid collector."

"Are you OK?" she whispered.

"Yes," he said. "I should have done this from the start. As soon as I found you."

Someone cleared their throat, and Zeta looked up to see Nathanial Cross, the man she had only seen in photos online, standing in the doorway next to a blonde woman who looked a lot like Ash. Zeta moved to stand, to introduce herself, but Nathanial waved the gesture away. The two of them came and sat down on the couch across from the one that she and Ash occupied.

"Zeta," Ash said, "These are my parents, Nathanial and Bridgette. Mom, Dad, this is Zeta."

"It's nice to meet you," she said. And looking at Nathanial closer now, Ash did favor him too. His nose, his ears, the way his hair sat.

"So what do you do, Zeta?" his mother asked.

"I'm a programmer," she explained, wondering how in depth she should get.

"She's the lead on the leave program," Ash provided, and his father's eyebrow twitched and his head turned.

"So you met at work?" his mother asked brightly. "How cute!"

"No, we met before that," Zeta corrected and then stopped, embarrassed.

"We met at a party over the summer but lost touch. I didn't know she was working for us until recently."

"I work remotely, under a different name," Zeta explained.

"I don't mean to sound rude but I'm a little confused about the timeline," Bridgette said.

Zeta looked at Ash, unsure of what to say. She'd been honest, but she wasn't sure how they would take it. Besides, they weren't her parents.

"I didn't know she was pregnant until we reconnected," Ash explained their situation, a PG version that skipped the details of broken condoms and tables.

"You're the one that we wanted to offer the job to," Nathanial said slowly when Ash was finished. "Z. Gray Rodgers. Zeta. You're quite skilled."

"Yes," Zeta responded. "Thanks."

"Are you going to take it?"

She looked at him strangely, she could feel it on her face. "No," she said slowly.

"Why not? Didn't like the offer?"

"I didn't even see the offer." Ash's hand rested on her knee and she turned to look at him, but he was looking at his father.

"Dad," he said, voice low and hard.

"Honey, you didn't see the ultrasound!" Bridgette said suddenly "The baby is so pretty, wait till you see her!"

Ash reached into his pocket for his phone, but Zeta stopped him. "Wait, I brought an extra photo," she explained, reaching into her own bag. "I thought your parents would like one," she said, handing them the glossy paper.

It wasn't an original, she'd kept those, but had the one she handed over printed. His mother took it from her fingers like it was a holy relic, her mouth an O. She touched the image delicately before leaning toward Nathanial.

A strange thing happened then. Nathanial, who was cold and hard, *melted*. He tried to feign disinterest but kept looking at the photo every time Bridgette, who was fawning over the image, pointed out a different feature. The way the baby's nose was shaped or her lips. The little fingers held tight against her.

He sighed, and Zeta watched his entire body relax. "Give me that," he said, taking the photo. "What are you naming her?"

Ash shifted next to her, confused at the sudden shift, the break in the tension. "Epsilon," he said.

Nathanial nodded, crossed his arms. "The system you're working on. I had it brought in when I took over the company from my father. New technology. The company that built it went belly-up, and though it worked well enough for years, I'd always meant to repair it."

He tapped his chest. "When I woke up from this, all I could think about was getting that taken care of. Couldn't let it just sit anymore. Needed it to be done. And so they brought you in." He chuckled. "I think you should look at the offer. I want my granddaughter to be comfortable. And I have a feeling they still want to hire you."

Zeta looked at Ash, but he stared back, as confused as her.

"Honey, why don't you take Zeta to the kitchen and explain the floor thing to her," he said to his wife. "I need to talk to my son."

"The floor thing?" Zeta asked, and Ash's face was red.

"When he gets anxious he lays down on the kitchen floor, in front of the stove," Bridgette said. "He's been doing it since he was toddler. I thought he would grow out of it, but he never did."

Zeta chuckled. "That's cute," she said, and stood up to follow his mother out of the room.

"So what do your parents do?" Bridgette asked to make conversation. There was an anxiousness about her, and Zeta wasn't sure if it came from her husband or if it was something just in her.

"They passed away when I was a child," Zeta explained.

Bridgette held her hand in front of her face, embarrassed.

"Why don't we talk about hobbies. I heard you liked art," Zeta said.

"I do! Mostly sculpture but I do like some paintings here and there. Would you like a cup of tea? I'll call Claire."

"Great," Zeta smiled. They were strange, his family, like him. She could see why he was nervous, but they weren't so bad. Maybe it was the baby.

She sat at the kitchen table between the two women, Claire sharing stories from overseas and the stage, Bridgette gossiping about the local families and discussing her home decorating projects. They asked about the nursery, and Zeta danced around answering because she didn't have any answers. They asked about her plans after the baby and all the normal questions about feeding and care. They were earnest and sweet, and she wondered if he was alright with his father, who had shifted, let down his guard, but was, she could see, the problem all along for him.

She lost track of time, and Ash appeared at the door of the kitchen. "Sorry, but I've gotta get Zeta home," he said.

"So soon? We're just getting to know each other!" Claire whined.

"Here's my number," Zeta said, scribbling it down on a pad of paper that looked like it was used to make grocery lists. "Call me, we'll have lunch or something."

Both women stood, wrapped her in hugs, and promised they'd call soon.

"What did your dad talk to you about?" Zeta asked when they'd stepped outside.

"He asked me about work, about you," Ash said, leaning lightly into her.

"And what did you say?"

"I told him that I wanted to take care of you and I wanted to build houses," Ash said, opening the door and letting her in the car. He slid into the driver's seat and started the engine.

"What does that mean?" she asked, confused

"It means that I'm quitting my job," he said. "Is that alright?"

Zeta's eyes flicked over him as he drove. His shoulders were loose, the fingers that rested on her thigh stroked her gently. His jaw had no tightness in it. Ashford Cross was utterly and totally relaxed, which Zeta realized she'd only ever seen when he was sleeping. "It's fine, you look . . . peaceful."

"I am!" He grinned. "I don't think I could be here for you or the baby the way I want if I kept working there, so I decided not to."

Zeta's breath caught, eyes wide, "Ash."

"Don't worry! It's going to be a little bit, you don't have to worry about anything."

"I'm not worried." She covered his hand with hers and he shifted, held it.

"Good. Oh, he also told me that Scott was emailing him."

"Who is Scott? What emails?"

"Don't worry about it, love. Do you mind going one more place with me? I just thought of something."

She shook her head. She didn't mind going anywhere with him.

29

Zeta didn't realize where they were going until they arrived. "Tiki Max? Not exactly a big drinker these days."

"We're not here for drinks," he said, smiling.

Inside the bar was dead. It was too early for there to be much traffic beyond the regulars, and besides, it was a Monday night. "What are we doing here?" she asked again, confused.

He pulled her gently along, back to the labyrinth of private rooms, and just like before, the path spit him out at the deck, where a sign said CLOSED FOR THE SEASON. Ash ignored it, unlocked the door, and stepped through.

Outside, the air was cold but there was no wind. The sky was an array of pastels above the setting sun. The mountain was orange and gray over a blue city. Beautiful. She turned to tell him, and he caught her hands.

"I love you, Zeta."

She stilled, heart stopped, started. "Ash."

"This is where it started, so because I could pick, because you stopped me from making a mistake, I wanted to tell you that here. Multiverse theory comes up a lot in science fiction, did you know that? I've read a lot of books about all the different ways a minor difference can change everything. But I think for us, we were always supposed to be together. I love you, and it's alright if you're still unsure of me, I'll wait however long you need."

"Ash," she repeated.

"I can move into that apartment above you so I'm close, or just drive back and forth between our apartments if that makes you happy. I'll do—"

She put her hand over his mouth. "Ash, stop talking. I love you too."

He smiled, his face lighting up. "Then, will you marry me? Let me be Future Zeta's problem. Let me be yours forever?"

Butterflies. *Yes.* "I'm not even your girlfriend."

"Then be my fiancée for a while. It doesn't matter, just be with me."

"I'll think about it," Zeta said. *Yes.*

"Ten minutes," he teased.

Epsilon kicked, one of those funny movements where Zeta felt everything shifting. Ash put his hand on her stomach. "Alright?"

"Yeah," Zeta said, "everything's fine. But there is one thing." She bit her lip, frowned.

"What? Tell me."

"You have to meet my friends now."

He laughed, relief washing over his face. "That's all?"

"You shouldn't be so calm. You made me cry."

He kissed her forehead. "And I'll never do that again."

She smiled, leaned against him. "Let's watch the sunset."

"Anything you want, Kitten," he replied.

She watched the sunset and thought about new beginnings.

Epilogue

Zeta looked down at her baby's perfect face. One day out of the womb and eating well. She could hear her phone buzzing, begging to drag her attention away, but all she wanted to do was stare at the little girl pulling milk from her body and wonder at the miracle she had made.

A little over seven pounds with eyes that bordered on gray and dark hair that was straight now but was already showing signs of a curl. A beautiful baby.

The door swung open and Ash walked in, diaper bag over one shoulder, Epsilon already squirming in his arms. At one and a half she didn't really have any words yet, but she was clearly trying to get there. She was dressed for the cool fall day, her mop of dark brown curls pulled back with a hair tie, which, Zeta had to admit, Ash had gotten pretty good with. Lucky, because their second little girl was likely going to have just as much hair.

"I know you haven't seen Mommy in over twenty-four hours,

but be careful," he said, placing her down on the bed. "Say hello to your little sister."

On cue she waved and repeated one of the handful of words that she sort of knew. "Hiiii," she sang. "Et."

"Yes, she's eating. Babies are very hungry," Zeta explained. Just then she finished, came unlatched, and Zeta moved her to pull her gown closed.

Ash reached out for his newest daughter, kissing her head lightly. "Hey there, beautiful."

"How was Epi?" she asked as the toddler spilled into her lap.

"Same as always. I had to pry those two away from each other. I swear she likes my dad more than me."

"That's not true, it's just he keeps candy in his pockets and toddlers are very food motivated," Zeta said, laughing. Her phone buzzed again. Her arm free from the baby, she reached over and unlocked it to look. "Ugh, Jairai, this is not a problem," she said under her breath.

Before she could text back Ash lifted the phone from her hands. "I only let you keep this so you could answer your friends and keep up with your games. You're going to lose phone privileges if I catch you trying to work on your maternity leave again."

"It'll just be a minute." It was her department. She'd finally looked at the offer, and it turned out that Nathanial Cross was much better at business than his son.

Which was fine because his son turned out to be very good at building houses, and Scott, who she met last year at the new, much more family-friendly Christmas party, really wanted to be CEO.

"No," he said sweetly, and bent down, kissing her. "I'm not dealing with clients, you're not dealing with Jairai. And," he said, pulling away and pulling up her hand, "you can take these back."

He slid the wedding and engagement rings back on her finger now that the swelling had gone down from her pregnancy.

"So, Mrs. Cross, ready to try for a boy?" he whispered in her ear.

She laughed, pushed him away playfully. "You're benched for a couple of weeks, Mr. Cross. But we'll see what Future Zeta has to say about it. I think you can convince her. First, we should give this one a name though."

Ash picked up the diaper bag and unzipped it, pulling out a jar filled with folded white sheets of paper.

"We should let Epi pick," Zeta suggested.

"Let's wait until she calms down," he said.

Ash sat on the edge of the bed and Zeta leaned into him, their children between them, sure and relaxed.